Coming Home

A novel

By Priscilla Glenn

ISBN: 1493530682
ISBN-13: 9781493530687

Chapter One

Twelve years.

She had been doing this every year for the past twelve years, but somehow—even after all that time—it still managed to have the same effect on her.

She should have been numb to it by now, or at the very least, prepared for it. But the second Leah Marino turned onto the familiar little side street, her eyes began to sting with the threat of tears.

She took a deep breath, exhaling slowly as she took her foot off the gas pedal and allowed the car to coast unhurriedly down the narrow one-way road.

It always seemed so strange to her that something could be exactly the same and yet completely different all at once.

She'd seen these same houses—packed together like books on a shelf—and their tiny fenced-in yards countless times. She could vividly remember coming down this street in the back of her mother's car, blowing her warm breath against the window and drawing little hearts in the fog that magically appeared there.

But that was years ago. Another lifetime.

The neighborhood seemed to get smaller every year, although she knew that wasn't possible. The cars parked along the street were always different. Some of the houses changed color; some of the gardens were ripped up or the driveways refinished. But at its core, it was the same little world, one that was as comfortingly familiar to her as it was painfully remote.

Leah felt her heart quicken in her chest just before the house appeared on the right, and her shoulders dropped in relief as the unchanged yellow siding came into view, standing out against the whites and blues of the other houses. She was always afraid that one year, she'd drive down to discover the new owners had re-sided the odd-colored exterior, erasing the warm, pale yellow that always reminded her of sunlight on sand.

Her mother once told her that if happiness were a color, it would be yellow.

Leah jumped as the rude squawk of a horn burst into her consciousness, and her eyes flew to the rearview mirror. The large black pickup riding her tail was apparently in no mood to accommodate her sentimental pace, and if she had to guess, she'd say the three cars lined up behind him weren't either.

She sat up straight as something like panic fluttered in her chest. She wasn't ready to leave yet. She'd barely gotten a chance to see it. And she knew if she kept driving, she wouldn't loop around and come back. The spell of this little street would be broken; reality and logic would set in, reminding her that this little yearly indulgence was as childish as it was inconvenient.

The horn blasted again, and this time, the burly man behind the wheel thrust his hand at the windshield, shouting something at her through the glass.

Her eyes scanned the road frantically, trying to find an open space on the cramped little street, but there was nothing. The cars were lined up bumper to bumper along the sidewalk, the only openings being the entryways for those houses that had garages. Not that it mattered. Even if there were an open space, there was no way she could pull off parallel parking on this narrow street, especially not while the kind gentleman behind her cheered her on by blaring his horn and shouting obscenities.

Without thinking, she pulled into the empty space in front of the house's one-car garage. The black pickup sped by with another beep of its horn, this time accompanied by a middle finger pressed up against the passenger window.

"Merry Christmas to you too, sir," Leah said, watching the other cars pick up speed again as they continued down the road.

When the last car had passed, she exhaled, turning to look through the passenger window at the little yellow one-story house. Although she'd been making this trip ever since she could drive, never once had she actually parked the car. It was always a slow crawl down the street, a few quick seconds to take it in, and then back to real life. But now that she was sitting there, so close she could practically reach out and touch it, she was completely overwhelmed by the desire to see it. *Really* see it.

Before she could talk herself out of it, Leah cut the engine and got out of the car, pulling her hands inside the sleeves of her coat as she wrapped her arms around herself to ward off the sharp December wind. She walked around to the passenger side and leaned against the car with a tiny sigh, allowing her eyes to drift over her childhood home.

Up close like this, it looked more modern than she remembered. The shutters—although the same brick color they always were—were brand new. In fact, the windows themselves were new too. The one she remembered to be in the kitchen was now a pretty bay window with a few small pots of daffodils lined up along the sill.

Leah's eyes roved over the fence that led to the side yard. It had definitely been repainted recently, and there were newel posts on either side of it now. Even the short driveway leading into the garage had been repaved.

It was different. Someone was changing it.

She chewed on the corner of her lip, feeling like a bratty child as she tucked her chin into her scarf. What did she expect would happen? It had been fifteen years since she had lived in that house. Did she really think the owners would never make improvements? Never make it their own? She should have been happy that someone was taking good care of it.

The wind picked up again, and she closed her eyes, inhaling slowly through her nose. It still smelled the same—like bike rides and jump rope and hopscotch and barbecues.

And her mother.

That, at least, never changed.

With her eyes still closed, she could see them so clearly, all of them in the side yard: Leah and her brother coloring on the pavement with sidewalk chalk while her mother read a book in a fold-out beach lounger that took up half the yard; her mother showing Leah and her little sister how to tie a jump rope to the end of the fence so they could jump double Dutch even when it was just the two of them; the tiny garden in the corner of the paved yard that her mother used to water with the hose while Leah followed behind with a Fisher Price watering can, giving her enormous, imaginary flowers a summer drink.

"Hello."

"Jesus Christ!" Leah gasped as she whipped her head up, bringing one hand to her heart.

The woman standing before her was tiny, dwarfed in an enormous red coat that hung to her knees. If it hadn't been for the white hair, cropped short around a deeply wrinkled, olive-toned face, Leah might have mistaken her for a child.

She smiled at Leah's reaction, her dark eyes nearly disappearing as her face crinkled further.

"I'm sorry, honey. I didn't mean to scare you."

Leah dropped her hand from her chest with an embarrassed laugh. "No, it's fine. I just didn't realize anyone else was out here."

The woman nodded, her broad, amused smile transitioning into a more demure one. Leah smiled in return, expecting the woman to be on her way, or at the very least, to say something else. But she just stood there, staring at her with expectant eyes, as if Leah were the one who initiated contact with her.

The silence wore on, slowly but surely crossing into awkward territory, and Leah cleared her throat as she began fiddling with her scarf. The woman tilted her head, waiting, and it suddenly occurred to her that perhaps this lady wasn't all there.

"So, um," she said, playing with the frayed edges of her scarf, "are you out for a walk?"

"No, honey. I came out to see you."

"*Me?*" she asked, pointing to herself.

The woman chuckled—a soft, sandpapery sound—before she nodded, and Leah pulled her brow together.

"I'm sorry...do I know you?"

"I was about to ask you the same thing," the woman said, her face crumpling with the amused smile again.

Leah shook her head as if to clear it, trying to place this strange woman.

"No. I mean...not that I can remember," she said after a few seconds, hoping she hadn't just offended someone from her past.

"You've been here before, haven't you?"

Leah looked over the woman's shoulder at the little yellow house. "Not for a long time."

"Just about a year, I'd say."

Her eyes flew back to the woman. "What?"

"You come every Christmas," she said with a smile. "You were here last year."

Leah straightened her posture, saying nothing, and the woman nodded. "It was you. In this car," she said, gesturing to the car behind Leah. "I remember your face. I may look to be past my prime, but I'm still sharp as a tack," she said, pointing to the side of her head with a gloved hand. The bulky black gloves, like the coat, looked far too large to be hers.

When Leah still didn't respond, the woman said, "Last year you stopped in the road. I saw you through the window, and I thought, 'Now what would make such a pretty girl look that way?'"

She swallowed. "What way?"

"Heartbroken."

Leah dropped her eyes as the woman said, "By the time I got my old bones out here to check on you, you were gone." She tilted her head, looking Leah over before she added, "You don't look heartbroken this year. Just...pensive. But I still thought I should check on you."

Leah pressed her lips together, her eyes trained on the ground. She knew she should say something, but she was far too taken off guard to formulate a response.

After a moment, she glanced up at the woman; her smile was unfaltering, but she still had that expectant look in her eyes.

5

"I'm sorry," Leah finally said. "I don't mean to bother you. It's just...I used to live in this house...and I'm running some errands near here...and whenever I'm in the area, I like to stop by and just...remember, I guess. I shouldn't have—"

"Nonsense," the woman said, cutting her off. "Don't you apologize for anything. I like a girl who remembers her roots. Besides, what's Christmastime without a little nostalgia? I think it's wonderful."

The look in the woman's eyes mirrored the unadulterated kindness of her words, and Leah was suddenly consumed with the inapt desire to wrap her arms around this tiny stranger.

Instead, she exhaled the breath she hadn't realized she'd been holding. "Thank you. For understanding," she said, pushing herself off the passenger door. "Anyway, I really need to get going, but it was nice meeting you. Merry Christmas."

She started to walk back around to the driver's side, stopping short when she heard the woman say, "Did you want to see the inside?"

Yes. You have no idea how much.

She took a tiny breath before she said, "No, that's okay. Thank you anyway, though."

"Don't be shy, honey. I just put on some tea. You can come inside, warm up for a bit. Maybe see your old room?"

Leah dropped her head back slightly, blinking up at the sky. She shouldn't do this. For one, it was getting late. She still had errands to run, not to mention the hour drive back home. Plus, despite the fact that this woman seemed harmless enough, there was always the possibility that she was the innocuous decoy, leading an unsuspecting young girl into the house where a demented serial killer waited.

She laughed to herself, shaking her head at the absurdity of that last thought before the woman added softly, "I'd love some company for a while. Just one cup of tea. I know you have to be on your way."

Leah turned to look at her then. She was still smiling, but her happy expression belied the unmistakable sadness that infused her last words. And for some inexplicable reason, she couldn't tolerate the thought of this woman being sad, even for one minute.

"Okay," Leah said, taking a tentative step forward. "But I really can't stay long."

"One cup," the woman promised, her eyes disappearing amid a mass of wrinkles before she turned and shuffled up the short driveway, unlatching the gate that led to the side yard.

Leah followed, stepping into the yard behind her, and without warning, her eyes welled with tears.

It looked so small. How could it be this small? Leah could distinctly remember playing tag with her brother and sister in this yard, the three of them running back and forth until they were gasping for air. Now, she could probably walk across it in four long strides.

She glanced around, her vision blurred from her unshed tears. The yard had been repaved as well. The block of concrete, the one they had imprinted with their handprints and initials, was gone. Her chin quivered slightly as she lifted her eyes, looking at the opposite end of the yard. The tiny garden where her mother had grown her tomato and basil plants had been blocked over with pavers. A barbecue sat above it.

Leah hadn't realized the tears had spilled over until a gust of cold wind amplified the trails of warmth on her cheeks, and she wiped at them hurriedly before glancing up to see the woman standing in the doorway, holding it open with a sympathetic look on her face.

"You're okay, honey," she said softly, and Leah forced a smile as she walked past her and into the house.

It felt like being transported back in time, and she placed her hand on the wall beside her, feeling completely disoriented.

The furniture was all wrong, of course, and the walls were a different color, but the layout was still the same, so that if she stood there long enough, she could see the house as it was when she lived there. Her eyes traveled to the half wall that separated the kitchen from the living room, where two small vases of daffodils sat. She could remember her mother leaning on it with her elbows, peeking out at them with a smile while she fixed dinner.

The sharp whistle of a tea kettle brought her back to the present, and she blinked quickly, dropping her hand from the wall.

"Sit, sit," the woman said, gesturing to the small dining area past the kitchen. "Make yourself comfortable."

Leah walked through the kitchen and over to the table, unzipping her coat and hanging it on the back of one of the chairs.

"Can I help you with anything?" she asked, watching the woman disappear in the nook of the kitchen.

"That's okay, thank you. Just tell me how you take your tea."

"Two sugars, no milk, please."

Leah heard the clinking of glasses and spoons before the woman turned the corner and approached the table with a steaming teacup in each hand. She placed one in front of Leah and patted her hand before she sat across from her, wrapping her frail hands around her own cup. Without her enormous jacket, she looked even tinier, wearing a thin white sweater and gray slacks. Leah's eye was immediately drawn to her neck, where a bulky-looking ring was hanging from a thin gold chain. It looked like a man's class ring.

"I'm sorry, I didn't even introduce myself, did I?"

Leah lifted her eyes from the incongruous piece of jewelry to see the woman extending her hand.

"I'm Catherine."

"Leah," she said, clasping her hand gently.

"Well, Leah, thank you for agreeing to have tea with me."

"Of course. Thank you for inviting me," she replied, lifting the mug and blowing gently on the steaming liquid. She took a careful sip, humming contentedly as the warmth spread down her throat and through her stomach, and Catherine smiled the smile that crinkled her face and made her eyes disappear.

"The house looks wonderful, really," Leah said, looking around. "Especially the outside. You fixed it up beautifully."

"Yes, well, my boy helps me with that," Catherine said softly. She was quiet for a moment as she looked down, and Leah watched her shoulders rise as she took a deep breath, exhaling slowly before lifting her head. "So," she said, taking a sip of her tea, "you're here running errands?"

Leah nodded. "I come down here every year to get some things I need to make Christmas dinner. I live about an hour north, but no one makes homemade pasta like the Italian deli a few blocks over."

Catherine quirked her brow. "Giovanni's?"

"Giovanni's," Leah confirmed with a laugh, and Catherine nodded sagely.

"I can't blame you. I can see driving an hour for the food there."

"It's kind of a Christmas tradition in my family," Leah said with a shrug.

"Traditions are good. They help keep memories alive."

Leah's eyes flashed to Catherine, but she was looking out the window, her expression unreadable as she carefully sipped her tea.

"So," Catherine asked after a minute, bringing her eyes back to Leah, "which room was yours?"

"Um, that one," she said, gesturing to the room off the dining area.

Catherine smiled as she motioned toward the doorway. "Go ahead."

Leah looked at the door before exhaling heavily. Seeing it made her chest ache. Why was she doing this? What was the point? Why did she continue to torture herself, year after year, by coming here?

She placed the cup on the table before she stood and walked the short distance over to the bedroom.

Leah took a few steps inside, trying to reconcile what she was seeing with what she remembered. The walls were grayish blue, no longer the lavender from her childhood. A single full-sized bed was pushed up against the wall where the bunk beds she had shared with her sister had been. She walked over to it and sat down, running her hand over the soft navy blue comforter.

Beside the bed was a wooden table with a small television and another vase of daffodils. As Leah leaned over to smell them, she noticed the far wall; the shelves that had housed all her dolls and stuffed animals were gone. Instead, there were several framed photos. The largest one was a close-up of two little boys, their arms thrown around each other, grinning from ear to ear. They were pointing at each other's mouths, drawing attention to the fact that they were both missing their two front teeth.

Leah smiled, glancing around the room one more time. It was simple, neutral, and no longer hers.

"It's my guest room," Catherine said from the doorway, and Leah jumped up from the bed, rubbing her palms down the sides of her jeans. "My boy stays here from time to time when he—"

They both turned as the front door swung open, banging unceremoniously against the wall.

"Gram?" a voice called. "Do you know some stupid asshole parked in front of your garage? I had to park two blocks over and lug this thing all the way back here."

Catherine glanced at Leah, smiling apologetically before she said, "Language, Daniel."

"Sorry," the voice said. "Just let me get your tree set up and I'll have one of my guys tow it out of here."

Leah's eyes widened in alarm just as Catherine looked at her, waving her hand dismissively in his direction.

He turned the corner then, propping a Christmas tree up against the wall in the living room. Leah could see him through the half wall as he unzipped his jacket with one hand and pulled off his gray wool hat with the other, revealing a mess of inky black hair sticking up in every direction. He placed his keys on top of the wall and ran his hand through his hair, walking through the small kitchen toward the dining area. As he entered the room, he lifted his eyes, stopping short as they made contact with Leah. Against the dark tone of his hair, they were shockingly blue.

"Hi?" he said, his brow furrowed.

"Daniel, this is Leah."

He cast a confused look at Catherine before bringing his eyes back to her.

"I'm the stupid asshole," she said.

She heard Catherine chuckle beside her, and Leah smiled when Daniel had the good graces to look embarrassed.

"Sorry...I..."

"It's okay. Sorry about making you have to walk with that tree," Leah said, motioning toward the living room.

He nodded, still looking sheepish, and Leah couldn't help but find his embarrassed awkwardness somewhat charming. She couldn't decide if she wanted to put him out of his misery or needle him just to keep it going a bit longer.

"Listen," she said, walking over to the chair to grab her coat, "if your tow truck guy is already on his way, could he just tow me over to Giovanni's? That's where I'm headed."

He stared at her for a second before amusement flickered behind his eyes, and the corner of his mouth lifted.

"That's sort of frowned upon," he said, and Leah nodded in feigned disappointment.

"Damn," she said, zipping up her jacket and wrapping her scarf around her neck. "Well, in that case, I better get going. Catherine, it was a pleasure to meet you. Thank you so much for everything."

Catherine shuffled toward her, holding out her arms, and Leah leaned down and gave her a gentle hug. "Anytime, dear. Next year you come right on up to this door and give it a knock, okay?"

"I will," Leah promised, and Catherine gripped her hand and gave it a squeeze.

"You take care, honey."

As Leah made her way toward the door, she nodded a farewell to Daniel, and he returned the gesture; it looked like he wanted to say something, but he remained quiet as he stepped to the side to let her by.

The cold air seemed less offensive as she made her way across the tiny yard, feeling strangely at peace for the first time in a while. Leah unlatched the gate, and as she turned to close it behind her, she let her eyes rove over the yard one last time. This time, she pictured Catherine sitting in a folding chair, drinking a cup of tea while she watched her grandson paint the fence. Leah smiled to herself as she closed the gate and turned toward the street.

She had just reached her driver's side door when she heard his voice.

"Hey, hold up a sec."

Leah looked up to see the screen door swing closed behind Daniel as he jogged toward the gate and unlatched it. "Listen," he said as he approached her car. He shoved his hands in his pockets before clearing his throat. "I just wanted to apologize. For the whole stupid asshole thing."

And there it was again—that endearing self-consciousness.

"It's okay," Leah said. "It *was* a stupid asshole move."

He smiled, revealing a set of dimples. "Yeah. It was."

Leah laughed to herself as she reached into her purse for her keys. "Wow. That was seriously the worst apology ever."

She heard him chuckle, and when she looked up, he was still smiling down at her with those dimples. "Well, damn. Can I try again?"

She shrugged. "Go for it."

Daniel reached forward and opened the driver's side door for her, bowing slightly as he gestured for her to have a seat. "Here you go, milady. My deepest and sincerest apologies for insinuating that you were a stupid asshole." He straightened. "How was that?"

"Better," she said through a laugh as she turned to get into the car. Just before she slid inside, her eye landed on the bay window in the kitchen. She could see Catherine sitting alone at the table, cautiously sipping her tea.

As Leah sat in the driver's seat, she turned to look up at Daniel. "I'm glad she has you," she said sincerely. "Don't ever stop taking care of her."

She watched his dimples fade as his expression fell, and then he nodded.

"It was nice meeting you," Leah said, reaching to close the car door, and he stepped back, shoving his hands in his pockets again.

"You too," he said absently.

She smiled as she pulled the door shut and started the car. Daniel held up his hand as he took another step back, and she returned the gesture as she pulled out onto the street.

She liked the idea of him taking care of her. That kind of thoughtfulness was a trait that jumped out at Leah now, because the absence of it should have been the red flag in her last relationship.

Whatever the reason, she couldn't deny that it was extremely attractive when a guy was as family-oriented as Daniel seemed to be.

And there was something inherently attractive about a guy with manners, too—the way he had apologized for his language, how embarrassed he'd looked at having offended her.

Who was she kidding? There was something attractive about *him.* Period.

The pitch-black hair with the light eyes, the masculine jaw with the boyish dimples. He had the kind of face she wanted to stare at, just to appreciate the way all the pieces complemented each other.

But of course, she hadn't done it. That would have been weird, and completely inappropriate.

For a second, Leah found herself wishing she knew his last name. After all, if he had a Facebook profile, she could examine his picture as long as she wanted without it being weird—

The second the idea crossed her mind, her cheeks flooded with heat, even though no one was privy to the ridiculousness of that last thought but her.

What the hell was she doing?

Since when was she the kind of girl who stalked guys on the internet? Since when was she the kind of girl who pursued guys *at all?* She'd never been the one to initiate a relationship. Besides, she hadn't been involved with a guy in two years, nor did she have any desire to be.

Although, if all it took to turn her into a creeper was a pair of dimples and some manners, maybe there was some subconscious part of her that was tired of being alone.

Leah shook her head at that; she wasn't tired of being alone. She was just tired, and it was making her scatterbrained. She leaned over and turned on the radio, letting the music chase away her thoughts as she pulled up to the intersection.

Giovanni's was about six blocks from her old house; it was an old-fashioned, family-owned Italian deli that hadn't changed since she'd first been there with her parents as a little girl. The red awning out front was faded and worn so that it appeared to be almost pink, and the white block letters that spelled out the store's name were now a murky, grayish color. As Leah pulled onto the deli's block, she was reminded of something else about the place that never changed: there was a line nearly out the door. It was a popular deli on an average day, but during Christmastime it was borderline legendary.

She began her usual routine of circling the block, looking for an open parking space, and on her second pass, amazingly, she noticed a spot had opened up right in front of the door. She cut the wheel sharply, pulling into the spot without using her blinker and glancing around to make sure she hadn't just snagged the spot from someone who had been waiting.

No one.

"Wow," Leah said to herself, cutting the engine and grabbing her purse. In all the years she'd been shopping there, she'd never even gotten a spot on the same block, let alone right out front. "Must be my lucky day."

She stood in line for almost half an hour, tossing items into her handheld basket as she inched up the aisle toward the counter. When she finally reached it, she placed her order, remembering to include the fresh ravioli her brother loved so much he would often eat them raw before she could cook them.

As the girl behind the counter totaled up her order, Leah reached inside her purse to grab her wallet.

And that's when she noticed it.

Her stomach lurched as she shook her wrist. "No," she whispered in a panic, pushing up her sleeve with her other hand. "*Shit!*" she said, rummaging frantically through her purse, hoping it had just slipped off and fallen inside.

"Is something wrong?" the girl behind the counter asked.

"I lost something," Leah said, stepping up to the counter and abruptly dumping the contents of her purse over the top of it. The girl jumped back, a startled expression on her face as Leah sifted through the change, makeup, and receipts scattered across the counter.

She whipped around in a frenzy, her eyes scanning the floor behind her. "Did anyone see a bracelet?" she asked, nudging her way through the line of people behind her. There were a few mumbled *no*'s and *sorry*'s as she scoured the floor near the shelves, looking for any sign of it.

"Miss, I'm sorry, but there's a line," the girl at the counter called.

She continued pushing through the crowd until she had a clear view of the door where she came in. She needed to retrace her steps.

"Miss," the girl called again.

"Yeah, okay," Leah said, her voice detached as she walked backward toward the counter, bumping into people as her eyes continued to comb the floor. By the time she made it back to the front of the line, it was clear that any sympathy from the crowd had now transitioned into annoyance.

She swiped everything on the counter back into her purse and absently paid for her things, turning every few seconds to inspect the floor behind her again.

The woman handed her the box of food, and Leah balanced it precariously in her arms as she rushed out of the deli. It was freezing, but she could already feel a cold sweat breaking out over her back.

She hurried to her car and threw the box inside before turning to examine the sidewalk. The distance between her car and the door to the deli couldn't have been more than five feet, but she already knew that if she had dropped it outside, it would most likely be gone. Someone would have picked it up and taken it, no doubt. Still, she continued her futile search of the sidewalk for another ten minutes.

By the time she got back in her car, she felt like she might actually be sick. Leah arched her back, struggling to remove her jacket in the confines of the driver's seat before shaking it out frantically.

"Please," she said to herself, hoping it would fall out from one of the sleeves.

It didn't.

She contorted her body, checking under the seats, in between the seats, under the pedals, next to the console.

Nothing.

"Shit," she said again, gripping the steering wheel with both hands and letting her head fall back against the seat.

It was gone. She had lost it.

She had lost her mother's bracelet.

Leah's father had given it to her mother on their eighth wedding anniversary, the same day she had given birth to Leah's little sister. Embedded in the white gold of the bracelet were three solitary diamonds. One for each baby she had given him, he had said.

Leah had always loved that bracelet, even before it was hers.

With a pathetic sniffle, she started the car and pulled dejectedly out onto the street. She had combed the deli, scoured the sidewalk, torn apart her purse, shook out her clothing, searched the car. Someone must have taken it. There was nowhere else it could be.

She approached the stoplight at the end of the street, still fighting tears, when suddenly it hit her.

Leah bolted upright in her seat. "Oh my God," she said to herself, slamming on the brake before making an outrageously illegal U-turn in the middle of the intersection. The orchestra of horn blasts only served to amplify her urgency as she sped down the road that would take her back to her old house.

Traffic had started to pick up, making the ride back to the house twice as long as it should have been. By the time she pulled onto her old street, it was already dark. There were still no parking spaces on the road, so she pulled into the empty space in front of Catherine's driveway again, throwing the car in park and not even bothering to turn it off before she jumped out. She ran to the gate and unlatched it, flinging it open as she bolted across the tiny yard.

Leah knocked on the door, standing up on her toes so she could see in the tiny window along the top of the door. After about a minute of silence, she knocked again, this time a bit more forcefully.

Still nothing.

Desperate and having no shame, she walked to the window on the side of the house, cupping her hands around the side of her face and pressing her nose against the glass. The house was completely dark.

"Damn it," she whispered, walking back to her car and plopping inside before she slammed the door closed behind her. She reclined the seat and cranked up the heat, fully intending to wait there until Catherine returned.

Forty-five minutes later, she was starving, she had to go to the bathroom so badly she thought she might cry, and it had begun to snow. The lights were still off in the house, and no one had returned. Was it possible that Catherine had already turned in for the night? If that were the case, she would feel like a complete moron waking the poor woman up and dragging her out of bed for something that might be a lost cause anyway.

Whatever the case was, Leah knew she couldn't stay there any longer.

With a frustrated sigh, she sifted through her purse and pulled out an old receipt and a pen, leaning on the dashboard to scribble a quick note to Catherine.

Catherine,

I think I may have lost my bracelet in your house. It's really important to me, so if you find it, could you please give me a call?

She signed it with her name and her phone number before throwing the pen somewhere on the passenger seat and exiting the car.

Leah walked quickly through the side yard, blinking back the snowflakes that peppered her vision as she opened the screen door and closed the note inside before running back to the car.

Twenty minutes later, she had just merged onto I-95 when a loud bang nearly forced her heart out of her chest. She gripped the wheel firmly, glancing in her side-view mirror; she couldn't see anything that she might have collided with, and it definitely didn't feel like the car took a hit.

Just as her body began to relax back into the seat, the car began to pull awkwardly to the right.

"Oh, you have *got* to be kidding me," Leah groaned, putting her blinker on and fighting her way through the traffic over to the shoulder. She put the car in park and crawled over the console, opening the passenger door and hanging her head outside as snowflakes clung to her hair and eyelashes. Sure enough, the right front tire was completely flat.

She collapsed back into the car, pulling the door closed behind her and covering her face with her hands.

Lucky day, indeed.

Chapter Two

"Christopher, I swear to God, if I see your hand near this plate again, I'm chopping it off and making it the centerpiece."

"Those are some tough words from someone who can't even kill a spider," her brother replied, reaching around her and grabbing another piece of salami off the plate of antipasto Leah was arranging.

She tried to grab his hand, but he was quicker, taking a step back and holding up the stolen piece of meat like Rafiki holding baby Simba in the opening sequence of *The Lion King*.

Leah tried to suppress her smile. "You're a moron. We're eating in like twenty minutes. Stop acting like an animal."

He shoved the salami in his mouth as he leaned toward her, growling rabidly and chewing with his mouth open.

"Oh my God," Leah said with a laugh, pushing him away. "Alexis! Come get your husband out of the kitchen before I kick his ass!"

A minute later, Alexis appeared in the doorway, folding her arms over her swollen belly and trying to look stern. "Christopher, leave her alone."

"Yeah, Christopher, leave her alone," Leah echoed.

"Okay, okay," he said, holding his hands up in surrender before turning to leave. He darted his hand out quickly, swiping a piece of ham on his way out.

Leah rolled her eyes while Alexis sighed. "I swear, when people ask me if this is my first child, I'm always tempted to say no," she said, looking over her shoulder at her husband.

Leah smirked as she drizzled the balsamic vinegar over the salad.

"What can I help you with?" Alexis asked.

"Nothing. Go sit. I'm almost done in here."

"You sure?"

"Yes. Sit. Rest. Your days of sitting and resting are numbered," Leah said with a wink, grabbing the wooden spoon from the counter.

Alexis leaned over and kissed her cheek, discreetly pulling a piece of cheese from the plate between them, and Leah quirked her brow.

"For the baby," Alexis said innocently, popping it in her mouth before she went back out to the living room.

Leah laughed as she brought the salad and the antipasto out to the table and uncorked two bottles of wine. She glanced at her watch before wiping her hands off on her mother's apron and loosening the strings.

"Hey, Sarah?" she called.

"Yeah?"

"Can you come in here for a sec?"

A moment later, her sister's head popped around the corner. "What's up?"

"Can you just watch the sauce for a minute? I'm gonna go upstairs and change."

"Yup," she said, coming into the kitchen and pulling herself up onto the counter, swinging her legs from side to side like a child.

There was only a three-year age difference between them, but Sarah had always seemed so much younger to Leah. Physically, they were complete opposites: Sarah was almost pixie-like, standing at five-foot-one, while Leah towered over her at five-foot-seven. Sarah's hair was long and straight, a warm caramel color that showed hints of red in the sunlight, while Leah's was a chocolate brown, falling just past her shoulders in subtle waves. Their only similarity was their eyes: large and deep green, surrounded by a fringe of thick lashes.

Leah nudged her little sister playfully. "Is Kyle coming later?"

"Yeah, for dessert."

"You know, a guy who comes to spend Christmas with a girl's family after dating her for only two months means business."

"Well, duh. I mean, who wouldn't want to hold on to this?" she said, gesturing at herself.

Leah burst out laughing, throwing the apron at her sister before running upstairs to the bedroom that had been hers as a teenager. Her father had moved them all to Bedford shortly after their mother's car accident. Leah had been about to start seventh grade at the time, her brother about to begin high school, and their father had told them he was moving them for the sake of their education—that the city schools were in bad shape, and he wanted them all to attend a good high school. But even at twelve years old, Leah knew the real reason.

He had a hard time living in that house without her. They all did.

Leah stripped off her "cooking T-shirt"—an old shirt so splattered and stained it looked like a Rorschach test—and pulled a fitted green sweater over her head. She glanced down, tugging the sleeve over her bare wrist. It had been two days since she'd left the note at Catherine's. The optimist in her wanted to believe that maybe her note had blown away in the storm, and that was why Catherine hadn't called. But the realist in her knew that if she hadn't called, she hadn't found it. And if she hadn't found it by now, she wasn't going to.

Leah knew she couldn't hide the lost bracelet forever, but she just wanted to make it through the holiday before she had to come clean and tell her father.

After changing into a pair of skinny jeans, she came back downstairs and turned into the kitchen just in time to see her father sneaking a piece of salami off the serving platter.

"Daddy," she said, and he dropped it quickly, spinning in her direction.

"Princess. You look beautiful."

"Nice try," she said, walking over and sliding the platter out of his reach. "You know you're not supposed to be eating that."

He rolled his eyes. "It's Christmas, Leah. I've been good all year."

"I know, but you have to take it easy with that stuff."

Her father reached over and pinched the tiniest sliver of salami off the plate, nibbling it off the tip of his finger before raising his eyebrows at her. "Happy?"

"Don't be like that," Leah sighed. "I'm just looking out for you."

He walked over to her, wrapping his arm around her shoulder. "I know," he said, kissing the top of her head. "But it's been two years. My blood pressure and cholesterol are both good. You gotta stop treating me like I'm made of glass."

Leah nodded and looked down. It didn't feel like two years since her father's heart attack. It felt like it could have been yesterday. She could remember every horrible detail with perfect clarity, right down to what an awful excuse for a daughter she had been.

"Besides," her father said. "I eat healthy practically every other day of the year."

Leah smiled up at him. "Only because I go on reconnaissance missions through your fridge and cabinets and do your grocery shopping for you."

"I didn't say I was responsible for my healthy eating habits, just that I had them."

The corner of her mouth lifted in a smile just as Christopher's voice boomed through the house. "Not for nothing, but I'm about to eat my fucking arm out here!"

"Watch your mouth!" Leah and her father yelled in unison.

She glanced up at him, rolling her eyes, and he laughed softly, kissing her head again before grabbing one of the serving platters and bringing it to the table.

A few minutes later, they were all seated as Leah poured everyone a glass of wine. As soon as she placed the empty bottle on the table, everyone turned to look at her father, sitting at the head.

He cleared his throat and raised his glass. "Here's to good health, good food, my wonderful children, and my little grandbaby on the way."

"Here, here," Chris said, lifting his wine, and everyone followed, the delicate clinking of glasses echoing around the table.

"We miss you, Dee," her father said just as everyone took a sip.

Over the top of her wine glass, Sarah made eye contact with Leah, smiling sadly, and Leah looked down, focusing on dishing out the food.

As soon as everyone's plate was full, the atmosphere grew light-hearted again; the entire first course was comprised mostly of Sarah informing everyone at the table—as only she could—of all the "crazy shit" she had learned in her most recent psychology class, interspersed here and there with Christopher trying to convince everyone that, boy or girl, he'd be naming his future child Humperdink.

Sarah helped Leah clear the table after dinner, and as they were getting the dessert ready, Kyle arrived. Leah watched her sister's face nearly split in two with the force of her smile, and she released her from any further hostess duties so she could spend time with him.

Leah smiled in approval as Kyle pulled the chair out for her sister and asked her what dessert she'd like, serving her before he took anything for himself. She'd only met him a few times, but he seemed like such a genuine guy. There were so many times she caught herself wanting to tell her sister how much she liked him, but she always stopped herself. The truth was, as convinced as she was that Kyle really cared about Sarah, she couldn't get past the possibility that she might be wrong. It didn't have anything to do with Kyle—there was nothing about him that made her feel unsure. It was just that Leah had been wrong about that sort of thing before.

Devastatingly wrong.

After everything had been cleaned up, Chris and Alexis left, followed by Sarah and Kyle. As her father settled into his recliner with the remote, Leah made her way to the mud room, switching the load of laundry she had started earlier over to the dryer. She came back to the living room and collapsed on the couch, yawning for the fourth time as the day finally started catching up to her.

"Leah, go home and get some sleep."

"I will, as soon as your laundry's done."

He turned in his chair. "I can fold my own laundry, princess."

Leah eyed him doubtfully and he laughed. "It may not be pretty, but it will be folded. Go home and get some rest. You've done enough for today."

She opened her mouth to answer but was cut off by another yawn. Her father lifted his brow at her and she sighed.

"Okay, okay. If you're too tired to fold the entire load, just take out your button-downs and hang them so they don't wrinkle," she said, standing from the couch and stretching.

"What would I ever do without you?" he said sarcastically, but Leah could see in his eyes that there was truth to his words.

She leaned over and kissed his forehead. "Good night, Dad."

"Send me a text when you get home, please."

Leah nodded, dropping her eyes as she remembered how irritated she used to get by his constant request to be notified whenever she arrived somewhere. Sometimes she wished she could go back and slap her younger self. Of course he was uneasy about his loved ones getting in a car and leaving. Of course he had a fear of them never reaching their destination. He had every reason to feel that way.

"I will," she said. "Love you."

"Love you too. Thanks for everything today."

After lethargically gathering her things, Leah walked down the driveway and started the car, pulling out onto the road before it had even warmed up. She had a twenty-five minute drive back to her apartment, and she decided it would be in her best interest not to turn the heat on, hoping the cold would keep her awake. Her eyelids suddenly felt like they weighed a hundred pounds, and all she wanted to do was get home and crawl into her bed.

The muffled sound of her phone ringing inside her purse snapped Leah out of her daze, and she immediately glanced down at the clock on the dashboard.

It was after eleven.

Few things made her more anxious than an unexpected late-night call.

With one hand on the wheel, she leaned over to the passenger seat and began rummaging through her purse. As soon as her hand wrapped around it, she swiped her thumb over the screen and pulled it out of the bag, hoping she made it before the call went to voice mail.

"Hello?"

"Hi. Um…is this Leah?"

Her brow drew together as she pulled the phone away from her ear, squinting at the screen before bringing her eyes back to the road.

"Yes, this is Leah," she said cautiously. "Who is this?"

"It's Danny."

Danny? Who the hell was Danny?

When she didn't say anything, he added, "We met the other day." And then it clicked.

"Oh! At Catherine's house?"

"Yeah. She gave me your number so I could…oh shit. I just realized what time it is. Did I wake you up?"

"No, it's fine. I'm actually driving home right now and trying not to fall asleep at the wheel, so you waking me up is a good thing." She sat up a little straighter, hoping he was calling her with good news.

"Alright, well I just wanted to tell you that I think I found your bracelet."

"*Oh my God!*" Leah gasped. "You're serious? You really found it? Please say you found it. You're not messing with me, are you?"

He laughed lightly. "Well, if I *were* messing with you, I'd feel pretty shitty about it now."

"You're being serious? You have it?"

"A gold bracelet. Kind of looks like it's braided? Three diamonds in the side?"

Leah exhaled heavily as her eyes filled with tears. "Yes," she whispered.

"I have it right here. It was on the floor in the guest room."

"Oh, thank you, thank you, thank you," Leah sighed. "I can't even tell you how relieved I am right now. Will Catherine be around tomorrow? I can come down and get it."

"Well actually, that's what I'm calling about. I'm gonna be in White Plains tomorrow meeting a friend for lunch. Gram said you lived an hour north, so I figured White Plains is probably about halfway for you, right? Do you want to just meet there? I figured it would shorten your drive a little."

"Sure, that works. Where are you having lunch?"

"Uh…The Cheesecake Factory. On Maple Avenue. Do you know where that is?"

"Yep. I've been there a few times."

"Alright, cool. I'll be there around one," he said

"Perfect. Really, Daniel, thank you so much."

"Danny."

"What?"

"You can call me Danny. No one really calls me Daniel."

"Oh, okay. Well, *Danny*, you seriously just made my night."

"Glad I could be of service," he laughed. "So I'll see you tomorrow at one?"

"Tomorrow at one. Thanks again."

"No problem. Good night, Leah."

"Good night."

Leah ended the call, tossing the phone onto the passenger seat before turning on the radio. She cranked it up, singing along while she drummed her fingers along the side of the steering wheel.

She felt like she could run a marathon right now.

It seemed like seconds later that she pulled into the parking space in front of her apartment, and just as she turned the radio down, Leah heard the double beep that signaled an incoming text message. She assumed her father had jumped the gun, thinking she had forgotten to text him.

She was wrong.

Merry Christmas, beautiful. Call me. I miss hearing your voice.

The smile faded from her lips as she read the text. She had removed him from her contact list, so under Sender there was simply a number—but it was a number she knew all too well.

"Unbelievable," she muttered, deleting the message before she tossed the phone back into her purse.

And then she gave it the finger.

She could not believe he was starting up again, and she was even more aggravated that he had managed to ruin her good mood. Did he really think she would want anything to do with him ever again? Did he see her as being that pathetic?

Leah scowled as she got out of the car, realizing that he probably *did*. She had given him every reason to think that, allowing him to manipulate her over and over. Why should he think things would be any different now?

She carefully traversed the icy walkway leading up to her door, balancing her bags and her plastic container full of leftovers. As soon as she was inside, she kicked off her shoes and made a quick stop in the kitchen to put away the food before sending her father a text, letting him know she was home.

Leah stripped down to her underwear and crawled into bed, suddenly too tired to even think about putting on pajamas.

She pulled her comforter up to her chin, and before her mind could rehash the infuriating text, she was fast asleep.

Chapter Three

Danny DeLuca glanced at his watch before shoving his hands back in his pockets.

It was twenty after one.

"Excuse me," someone said as they opened the door to the restaurant, and Danny stepped to the side, allowing the man to pass.

He didn't know what to make of it. She had seemed too excited over the bracelet to be a no-show. Plus, he hadn't pegged her as the kind of girl who would stand someone up anyway.

Not that he even knew anything about her.

He lifted his chin, blowing his breath out in puffs of vapor and watching it dissipate before his eyes. This was a sign. The universe telling him what he already knew. If he had anything resembling a brain in his head, he would walk away right now. Give the bracelet back to Gram and let her handle it.

Danny sighed, pulling his phone out of his pocket.

Ten minutes. He'd give her ten more minutes.

He scrolled through his apps and opened Words With Friends.

"Oh, bull*shit*!" he laughed when he saw Jake's 103-point word. He had built off the *C* in Danny's *laces* to make the word *quixotic*.

The direct message that accompanied Jake's move read simply: *BOOYAH, BITCH!*

Danny smirked as he hit reply: *I'd be impressed if I thought for one second you knew what that word meant, or even how to pronounce it. Dick.*

"Fucking cheater," he laughed, hitting send.

"Hey."

Danny lifted his head to see her standing in front of him, her arms crossed over her chest and her shoulders shrugged against the wind.

He cleared the screen before putting his phone back in his pocket. "I was right about to give up on you," he said, ignoring the quickening of his pulse.

"Sorry. Parking was awful. I forgot about the gift-returners who would be out today," she said, waving her hand in a circle around her head.

He nodded, looking around them. "Ungrateful bastards."

The corner of her mouth lifted in a smile before she said, "You didn't have to wait outside. It's freezing."

Right. He was supposed to be inside. Having lunch.

He shrugged dismissively, scratching the back of his neck. "It's fine."

Leah tucked her chin into her scarf and looked up at him from under her lashes. "You're taller than I remember."

He smiled then. Not just because of how she looked staring up at him that way, but because of her comment. Like they were long-lost friends who had just been reunited.

There was something so damn charismatic about this girl. He'd spent barely five minutes with her that day at Gram's, and yet she had managed to charm him. He liked that she wasn't afraid to call him out on his shit; there was a confidence about her that not a lot of girls had—a toughness—but at the same time, she had been so incredibly compassionate and sweet when it came to Gram.

"So," she said after few seconds of silence, bouncing up on her toes and looking at him expectantly.

"Oh shit. Sorry," he said with a laugh, taking his hands out of his pockets and reaching inside his jacket. He pulled out the tiny sandwich bag with the bracelet inside, holding it out to her, and she unfolded her arms, ripping her gloves off and tucking them under her elbow as she took it from him.

She had the bracelet out in an instant, taking the sandwich bag between her teeth to free her hands as she held her forearm against her stomach, trying to close the clasp around her wrist.

The wind was relentless, blowing the plastic bag and strands of her dark, wavy hair into her face, and every few seconds, she would flick her head to the side, trying to clear her vision while her numb fingers struggled with the tiny clasp.

Danny pressed his lips together, fighting a smile as he watched her blow a raspberry with the bag still between her teeth, trying to get an errant strand out of her eyes. He reached down, taking the plastic between his fingers.

She jolted as her eyes flashed to his, and he quirked his brow, giving the bag a little tug.

Leah released it from between her teeth, and he crumpled the bag and shoved it back in his pocket. "Better?"

She smiled self-consciously. "Yeah, thanks," she said, her eyes dropping back to the task at hand.

When she finally closed the clasp, Leah wrapped her hand around the bracelet, holding it against her skin and closing her eyes. She exhaled heavily as her entire body relaxed, almost as if she had just been relieved of some terrible pain.

She looked so vulnerable standing there like that, and Danny suddenly had the ridiculous urge to pull her against his chest and wrap his arms around her.

"Thank you," she said as she put her gloves back on.

"You're welcome."

"Okay, so," she exhaled, starting to walk backward. "I'll let you get back to your friend."

"Actually…he couldn't make it."

What the hell are you doing?

She stopped short, her shoulders dropping. "Oh. Well, now I feel bad."

"Why do you feel bad?"

"Because you came up here for nothing."

"No I didn't. I came up here to give you back your bracelet."

"You know what I mean," she said with a huff, and Danny smiled.

"Don't worry about it," he said with a wave of his hand. "I work near here. I was gonna stop in and check on some shit anyway."

Yeah. That sounded good.

"Oh. Alright," she said as she started to walk backward again. "Well, thanks again."

With every click of her heel against the pavement as she walked away from him, his unintended resolution became stronger.

And when she turned her back to him, he couldn't stop himself.

"Hey, Leah?"

She stopped, cocking her head over her shoulder.

"Since we're here, did you want to grab lunch?"

Stupid. So fucking stupid.

She turned to face him, but her expression was hesitant. Almost startled.

"Oh. I, um...I don't really...I mean..."

"If you're hungry," he offered. "Since we both made the drive."

She started chewing on the corner of her lip, glancing around as if looking for a way out of the situation.

Leave it alone, asshole.

"So, are you hungry?" he asked, ignoring the voice in his head.

She pressed her lips together as she shrugged slightly. "A little."

He took a step back and opened the door, gesturing for her to enter, and Leah looked at the entrance, still wavering.

"Did you know they have tiramisu cheesecake here?"

She swiped the hair out of her eyes, looking back at him.

"Godiva too," he said. "And Reese's."

Her posture relaxed a bit as the corners of her mouth turned up slightly.

"No dice?" he asked. "How about lemon-raspberry? Caramel apple? Just tell me what's gonna get you in here."

She laughed then, looking down as she shook her head. Danny watched her shoulders rise as she took a deep breath, and then she lifted her head and walked toward him.

"Just so you know, you had me at Godiva," she said, continuing past him into the restaurant.

Danny chuckled as he followed her inside and approached the hostess, and she led them to a small table up against the far window. He leaned over, pulling the chair out for Leah before he walked around to his side.

"Thanks," she said softly, removing her jacket and hanging it on the back of the chair.

As Danny removed his own coat, his eyes instantly dropped to take her in. He felt like such a scumbag, but he couldn't help it. Everything had happened so fast back at Gram's that day, so he hadn't really noticed—although looking at her now, he couldn't understand how he'd overlooked it.

She had one of the most incredible bodies he'd ever seen.

She wore a fitted sweater that reached her hips with some type of stretchy black pants that emphasized the tone of her legs. Slim waist. Phenomenal chest. She was long and lean, with gorgeous, feminine curves in all the right places.

And a pair of knee-high boots.

Jesus.

He forced his eyes back up to her face, realizing what a creep he must have looked like.

Her eyes were on his chest before they flitted up to his face and then away, and he tried to hide his self-satisfied smirk as he sat across from her.

A waitress approached their table before he could say anything, handing them a set of menus and taking their drink order. As soon as she left, Leah opened her menu and looked down, scanning the pages as she chewed on the side of her lip. He could see her body moving slightly as she tapped her foot restlessly under the table.

She was uncomfortable.

Danny would have chalked it up to his insensitive ogling, except he knew she hadn't caught him. Besides, she'd seemed uneasy long before that, from the moment he asked her to join him.

He had no business being there with her. It was an asinine decision, any way he looked at it. But the damage had already been done. So now, he wanted to make the best of it.

Even if it would never go beyond this afternoon.

"So," Danny said, flipping open his menu, and Leah glanced up at him.

"So," she said with a tentative smile.

They looked at each other until Leah started chewing on her lip again, dropping her eyes back to the menu.

"Where were you driving home from?"

"Hmm?"

"Last night. You said you were driving home and trying to stay awake. Where were you coming from?"

"Oh," Leah said, looking up from the menu. "My dad's house."

"Ah," Danny nodded. "Big family gathering for the holiday?"

"Not really," she said. "What about you?"

He shook his head. "Dinner with my sister and her boyfriend-of-the-minute. Stopped by Gram's for a bit. Found your bracelet," he said, nodding toward her wrist. "And then I hung out with my buddy at his job."

Leah made a face. "He had to work on Christmas?"

"He's a bartender. It got busier than they thought it would, so he got called in," Danny said, turning a page of the menu.

"On Christmas night? Where does he bartend?"

"The Rabbit Hole."

"Here in White Plains? That's only a few blocks from here."

Danny lifted his eyes, a slow smile curving his lips. "I know where it is."

She closed her eyes and shook her head quickly as she mumbled, "Right. Duh."

"Have you been there?" he asked, watching the most attractive blush color her cheeks as she refocused on the menu.

She nodded. "A while back."

"That means a lot to you, huh?"

Leah looked up at him questioningly, and he pointed to her wrist, where she was carefully rolling the bracelet between her fingers.

She dropped it like it burned her, looking somewhat embarrassed as she brought her hands under the table and gripped the side of her chair, shifting it slightly.

"It was my mom's," she said, picking up the menu and studying it with renewed intensity.

Danny watched her for a moment before lowering his eyes. There were a hundred reasons he could think of that might have caused her to use the past tense in that last sentence, and none of them were good.

The waitress approached the table with their drinks then, and Leah visibly relaxed, looking like she wanted to jump up and hug her for the interruption.

After they had placed their orders, Danny reached for Leah's menu and handed them both to the waitress.

"By the way," he said. "I never got a chance to thank you."

"For?" she asked, leaning over to sip her iced tea.

"For being so nice to Gram the other day."

Leah smiled the first genuine smile he'd seen since they entered the restaurant. "She's so sweet."

"Yeah, a little too sweet. I don't know what she was thinking, inviting a complete stranger who could have been a lunatic into her house."

Leah raised her eyebrows.

"No offense to you or anything," he added quickly. "It's just that... well, you never know...you know?"

"No, it's okay," she said with a laugh. "I totally understand you being protective of your grandmother."

"She's not my grandmother."

Leah pulled her brow together. "She's not? You call her Gram."

"Yeah, I know," he said, rubbing the back of his neck. Why the hell did he just tell her that? "It's just...I grew up with her grandson. So we're sort of like family."

Please just drop it, he prayed silently.

"Wow," she said.

"Wow? What's wow?"

"I don't know," Leah answered, stirring her drink with her straw. "It's just, I thought it was really nice of you to do all that work around the house for her when I assumed she was family. But, now that I know she's not...I don't know. It's even nicer of you, I guess."

Danny looked down, shredding his napkin with his fingers. "I guess."

Even if he wanted to talk about this, which he didn't, there was no way he could ever explain why he did what he did for Gram. It had nothing to do with being nice. The truth was, he could work in her house every hour of every day for the rest of his life, and it would still never be enough.

"So, you work near here?"

Danny swept the remnants of his napkin into a neat pile before he looked up. She was looking at him with something that could only be described as empathy.

Their first piece of common ground: prohibited topics of conversation.

"Yeah, about fifteen minutes from here."

"What do you do?"

"I own an auto repair shop. D&B Automotive."

"Really?" she asked, squeezing another lemon into her iced tea. "That's interesting."

"You think so?"

"Sure." She shrugged, and Danny smiled.

"No you don't."

"Well, it might not be interesting to *me*," she said through a laugh. "But I'm sure it is to someone who's into cars, which I'm assuming you are."

Danny smirked, resting his elbows on the table. "What do *you* do?"

"I'm a teacher."

"Really? That's interesting."

She sat back against the seat, folding her arms.

"I'm serious!" he said. "That really is interesting to me. I couldn't do it. You must have the patience of a saint."

Leah shrugged. "There are good days and bad days, just like any other job. I'm sure there are days that try your patience at the shop, right?"

"True," he said. "But I'm allowed to curse at the cars."

She laughed before she shook her head at him. She had the prettiest laugh. It made him want to spend the rest of the afternoon finding ways to get her to do it again.

"So, what do you teach?"

"Tenth-grade English."

He scrunched up his face, and Leah rolled her eyes.

"Clearly, your favorite subject."

"Is it anyone's?" he asked, and she scoffed, throwing a sugar packet at him.

"Jerk."

He grinned, picking up the packet and twirling it between his fingers. "Aren't you supposed to be some sort of master of the English language? I would've thought you could come up with a much better word for me than jerk."

"Believe me, I'm just getting warmed up."

Danny burst out laughing as the waitress approached the table with their appetizers. She placed the plates down in front of them, and Danny reached for the pepper, freezing when he saw Leah begin to work away at her salad with a knife and fork.

"What are you doing?"

She glanced up. "Cutting my lettuce."

"Cutting your lettuce," he repeated.

"Mm-hm. I always do."

He put the pepper down, watching her. "May I ask why?"

Leah reached into her salad and held up a piece of lettuce that was the size of his palm. "You can't really *bite* lettuce, so either I can attempt to cram this ridiculous thing into my mouth like a savage, or I can cut it into respectable, human-sized bites."

Danny reached over, taking the piece of lettuce out of her hand. He turned it over a few times as if examining it before he shoved the entire thing in his mouth.

"Totally doable," he mumbled incoherently.

"Mmm. Not to mention extremely attractive," Leah said, and he chewed his mouthful of food, smiling triumphantly.

"You have dimples when you smile."

"Yes, I'm aware," he laughed.

When Leah didn't respond, he said, "So, was there a point to that comment, or were you just stating the obvious?"

She kept her eyes on her salad as she continued to cut. "Just stating the obvious, I guess."

He laughed softly before he leaned on the table with his forearms. "Dimples turn you on."

"*What?*" she scoffed.

"Oh, sorry. I thought we were still stating the obvious."

"Oh my God," she laughed, pointing at him with her fork. "*You* are cocky as hell."

"Nah, not really. I just like it when you blush."

"I'm not blushing," she mumbled, pressing the backs of her fingers against her cheek.

He smiled before he said, "So, what's the deal? Gram said you used to live in her house?"

Leah nodded. "We moved when I was twelve, though. It was so nice of her to let me see the inside. Up until that point, I still kind of felt like that house was mine." She shrugged bashfully. "Silly, huh?"

"Not at all," he said sincerely.

She took a deep breath, seeming to contemplate something before she said, "Like in the side yard. There was this block of concrete that cracked all the way through when my dad dropped his toolbox on it, so he had to remove all the broken pieces and re-pour it. And my sister and brother and I—we all put our hands in it while it was drying." She smiled. "We were pretending we were movie stars. And so my mom came out and caught us, and we totally thought she was going to yell at us." Leah shook her head as she said, "But instead she leaned down and put her hand in it too. And then we all wrote our initials underneath with a popsicle stick, and my mom wrote the date."

Leah looked down at a strand of her hair as she twirled it through her fingers. "Obviously you know it's not there anymore. When I first saw that it was gone, I got really upset, but then I realized I'll always remember that story, even if there's no physical proof of it in that yard. Just like everything else that happened in that house." She released her hair and looked up at him.

It felt like his heart stopped beating.

Say something.

"If you really think about it," she said, "most of the memories you have from when you're small aren't actually yours. They're given to you by other people, either from a picture, or a story, or a video. We're told or shown that it happened to us, and it becomes one of our memories. But that day with the cement?" She shrugged. "That was the first memory that was actually mine."

He blinked at her, nearly choking on the words that were stuck in his throat.

"Anyway," she said with a wave of her hand. "It was just really nice of her to invite me in. It was the highlight of my day. Everything pretty much went to hell after that."

"Right," he said distractedly. "You lost the bracelet."

"Well, that, and then the flat on I-95."

Danny ran his hand through his hair. "That's a pretty shitty place to get a flat," he said, trying to get his bearings. The further they got from the moment, the harder it became for him to say the words.

"Tell me about it. It's even worse in the middle of a snowstorm."

He pulled in a breath between his teeth, shaking his head. "I forgot it snowed that night. What did you end up doing?"

"I called Triple A and waited over an hour for them to get there. I was *starving*. I was so tempted to eat the food I'd just bought for Christmas dinner. And I ended up peeing in a plastic bag."

The second the words left her mouth, she dropped her fork and covered her face with both hands.

Danny's eyes flashed up, his expression incredulous before he burst out laughing.

"*What* did you just say?"

"Oh my God, I'm so sorry. You did *not* need to know that."

He tried to rein in his laugh, but it was useless, and Leah shook her head, her face still hidden behind her hands.

"Okay, *now* I'm blushing," she mumbled. "Why do I have no filter when I'm talking to you?"

"It's okay," Danny said, and she spread her fingers, peeking at him from in between them. "If you want, I can tell you some pissing-in-public stories that will blow yours out of the water."

"No thanks, I'm good," she said with a laugh, dropping her hands from her face and picking up her fork.

"You really should learn how to change a tire, though," Danny said before taking a bite of his spring roll.

She bristled. "I know how to change a flat."

"Oh? Then why didn't you?"

"Just because I *can* doesn't mean I'd want to do it on the side of a snowy highway in the dark during rush hour."

He looked her over, trying to imagine her changing a tire. Those delicate, feminine hands. Her narrow, girlish frame. Could he picture her under a car?

Yeah, he could. And it was hot as hell.

Leah narrowed her eyes at him before her expression straightened, and she nodded. "Ah, okay. I get it. It all makes sense now."

"Get what?"

"You judge people," she said casually, taking a bite of her salad. "You're a judger."

"*What?*" He laughed. "I don't judge people."

"Of course you do. You've done it to me twice now."

"Bullshit! How have I judged you twice?"

"Well, first I was a stupid asshole because of where I parked my car. And now I'm incapable of changing a flat because...what? My nails are done? I'm wearing heels? Or is it simply because I have boobs and a vagina?"

He stared at her, trying to mask his amusement. "I thought we determined that you *were* an asshole because of where you parked your car."

She smiled before regaining control of her expression, trying to look stern.

Danny laughed, taking another bite of his food. "All kidding aside, you have my number from when I called the other night. Program me into your phone. Don't wait for Triple A to dick you around in a situation like that. Me or one of my guys could have been out there in under twenty minutes the other night."

"Thanks, that's nice of you."

"Not a problem," he said, licking the soy sauce off his thumb.

Her eyes dropped to his mouth and then darted back up, her cheeks flushing a light pink as she refocused on her salad.

He wanted to smile victoriously, to puff his chest out like the moronic, testosterone-driven male he was. But instead he focused his attention on his appetizer. Because as much as he *did* enjoy that blush, it was going to be his goddamn undoing.

He took another bite of his spring roll, making a conscious decision not to do anything that would bring it out again.

The waitress came back to the table with their main courses, and the conversation continued to flow effortlessly between them. Leah was the perfect mixture of snarky and sweet, confident and shy. By the end of the meal, Danny felt oddly comfortable with her, like he had known her for years.

Once he had paid the check, despite the objection from Leah, he helped her on with her coat and followed her to the door, holding it open for her as she exited the restaurant.

"Where are you parked?" he asked.

"In the parking garage two blocks down," she said, motioning with her head.

"I'll walk you," he said, grasping at any attempt to prolong the afternoon with her.

He didn't want it to end. But it shouldn't have even started. And he knew that.

"Thanks," she said, wrapping her scarf around her neck, and Danny resisted the impulse to reach for her hand as they started down the block.

By the time they arrived at her car, his chest felt heavy.

She turned to him, bouncing slightly on her toes with a shy smile. "Well, thanks again for lunch. I had fun."

"Me too," he said hollowly.

Her brow pulled together slightly as she tilted her head, but she quickly replaced the expression with another smile. "Okay, so..."

She looked up at him in that way that made him want to hug her. Something momentarily flashed across her eyes, and as soon as he pinpointed what it was, his chest tightened further.

Hope.

She looked hopeful, staring up at him like that.

End this. Now.

"So...get home safe," he said, taking a step back from her.

Her expression dropped at the same time her shoulders did. It was the tiniest change in her appearance; he would've missed it if he hadn't been watching her so closely.

"You too," she said politely before she got in the car and pulled the door closed. He watched as she started it up, rubbing her hands together in front of the vents.

There was no way he could allow himself to see her again. Inviting her to lunch had been a momentary lapse of judgment, but to *consciously* pursue her? That would be completely reckless.

Not to mention selfish.

As Leah carefully backed out of her parking space and continued down the exit ramp of the garage, Danny dropped his head back, covering his face with both hands.

She didn't look back.

Chapter Four

"Do they sell those chicken-cutlet titty boosters in this store?" Leah whipped her head toward her friend, laughing as she pressed her hand over Holly's mouth.

"You do realize this dressing room isn't soundproof, right?"

"Why? Because it's a secret that I'm rocking the chest of a prepubescent boy?" she asked, cupping her small breasts and giving them a squeeze.

"Stop," Leah said, swatting at Holly's hands. "You're proportional."

"And you're delusional," she said. "Turn around, I'll zip you up."

Leah turned, and as Holly zipped up the dress behind her, she felt the form-fitting bodice tighten around her torso. As far as bridesmaids' dresses went, she really had nothing to complain about; it was truly beautiful—a deep rose-colored gown with a strapless sweetheart neckline. The snug bodice transitioned into a soft, sinuous silhouette that flowed delicately to the floor.

"See?" Holly said. "Now *that's* how knockers should look in a dress."

Leah looked over her shoulder at her friend. "You should really think about teaching a class on social etiquette."

Holly winked before turning to examine herself in the mirror.

"Lemme see, lemme see!" Robyn called from outside the dressing room, and Holly leaned over and swung the curtain aside.

Robyn squealed, clapping her hands quickly as she walked in a circle around them. "Perfect! You guys look *hot*." She gave them another once-over before she said, "Awesome. Okay then, get dressed and let's get the hell out of here and get some dinner. And more importantly, some drinks. I'm gonna go get us a table."

She pulled the curtain closed behind her as she walked out, and Leah and Holly smiled at each other. Robyn was—by far—the most composed, unstressed, laid-back bride they had ever known.

One of the many reasons Leah loved her so much.

Leah turned her back to Holly, offering her the zipper. "Okay, do me and I'll do you."

"I don't normally swing that way, but you *do* look hot right now."

Someone cleared her throat loudly in the next fitting room, and Leah fought a laugh, bringing her finger to her lips.

Holly was the first friend she'd made when she moved to Bedford in the seventh grade. On Leah's first day, Holly pulled up a chair next to her in homeroom and asked to see her schedule, scanning it for a minute before she went off on a detailed explanation of where every class was, which teachers were awesome, and which "sucked ass," as she put it. Then she offered to walk Leah to her first class, since they had it together.

They'd been friends ever since.

The summer before ninth grade, they met Robyn—she had just moved to New York from Michigan and ended up working at the same summer camp as Leah and Holly. The three of them were inseparable for the next four years and visited one another every chance they got throughout college. To this day, Leah's father still referred to them as the Three Stooges.

As Leah was putting her clothes back on, her phone buzzed with an e-mail notification. She reached down and grabbed it, opening the message with one hand while she slipped her shoes back on with the other.

It was the delivery confirmation for the flowers she'd sent to Catherine.

She smiled, closing out of the message and tossing her phone back into her purse. Leah had been trying to think of something nice she could do for her ever since their visit, and that morning, she had noticed an advertisement for one of those national online flower distributors on her homepage. The arrangement on the ad was an elaborate display of daffodils in a beautiful embossed vase. She instantly thought of Catherine—how she seemed to have a thing for daffodils—and ordered the arrangement right before she left to meet Robyn and Holly at the boutique.

Once the girls were dressed, they went across the street to the little Mexican restaurant that Robyn loved, only to find her already seated at a table with a pitcher of margaritas and three glasses.

"I would totally propose right now if you weren't already getting married," Leah said as she sat at the table and poured herself a drink.

"Speaking of," Holly said as she took the pitcher Leah handed her, "how's the whole celibacy thing going?"

Robyn groaned, dropping her face into her hands. "I'm *such* an idiot. It sounded like such a good idea, you know? I mean, your wedding night is supposed to be this big, momentous event. What's big and momentous about having sex with someone you've been sleeping with for eight years?"

"So why not just renege?" Holly asked, reaching for a chip and dunking it in the salsa.

"Because we've already made it this far. It's only a couple more weeks. Besides, I'm so hard up at this point that any sex I get will be mind-blowing. Our wedding night is pretty much guaranteed to make me see stars."

Holly lifted her glass. "Well, here's to hoping you don't hump his leg midway through the ceremony."

They all cracked up, earning looks from the other patrons in the restaurant just as the faint sound of Leah's phone pulled her attention from the revelry. She reached into her purse and pulled it out just enough to check the screen.

And then she scowled, sending the call to voice mail before tossing it back into her bag.

"What was that about?" Robyn asked, nodding toward Leah's purse.

"Nothing," she answered dismissively, reaching for the chips. She scooped up a heap of salsa and shoved the whole thing in her mouth, trying to ignore the fact that both girls were staring at her deliberately.

"Leah."

"Ugh, fine," she mumbled around her mouthful of food, reaching for her drink and taking a huge gulp to wash everything down before she said, "He's calling again."

"*Scott?*" both girls said in unison, their voices incredulous, and Leah nodded.

"Fuck *that*," Holly said firmly. "Pick up the goddamn phone and tell him to go to hell."

"When did this start again?" Robyn asked.

"Just before Christmas. So, like two weeks, I guess."

"Have you spoken to him?"

Leah shook her head.

"What a douchebag," Holly huffed, taking a sip of her margarita.

"Whatever. It's not a big deal. I'm just gonna ignore him."

"I just don't get it," Robyn said. "I mean, does he really think you'd take him back?"

Leah grimaced, looking down. This was the last thing she wanted to be talking about. Talking made her remember, and she hated remembering.

She'd been driving home from the hospital the night her father had his heart attack. Leah had cried the entire way, struggling to see through her swollen eyes and the tears that blurred her vision. She had almost lost him—and she knew she could *still* lose him. He was in critical condition, his prognosis uncertain, and she couldn't stop thinking about how much time she had wasted. She was furious at herself. At her obstinate behavior.

And at that moment, she was furious at her boyfriend.

When she had called to tell him what happened to her father, he told her how sorry he was, but when she asked him to come to the hospital with her, he said he couldn't—that his brother was out drinking with some friends, and he'd promised to be available to pick them up at the end of the night.

Scott had never really liked Leah's family—he'd made it very clear in the almost three years they'd been together—so it was typical of him to come up with some excuse as to why he couldn't spend time with them.

But this was different. And he should have recognized that.

He'd told her to keep him updated and that he'd check up on her later, but all she wanted was for him to be there with her. Supporting her.

Leah made an impulse decision, getting off the highway two exits early and heading toward his place instead of her own apartment. She wanted to tell him that he'd let her down.

But more than that, she just wanted to be held.

She wanted him to wrap her in his arms and press his lips into her hair and tell her everything was going to be okay.

That she wasn't a terrible person.

When he didn't answer the door, Leah assumed he'd gone out to pick up his brother, so she used the key hidden in the outdoor sconce to let herself in.

As soon as she opened the door, she knew something was wrong.

She could hear music playing faintly—Dave Matthews Band crooning "Crush." Leah took another step into the apartment, and her eye was immediately drawn to the coffee table, where there was a half-empty bottle of Shiraz.

With two wine glasses next to it.

A horrible, wrenching sensation knotted her stomach as she looked down the hallway toward his bedroom.

And that's when she heard the muffled moan.

She had no idea why she even walked toward the door. She knew what she would find. But it was like some sadistic, unseen force had taken control of her body—her head screamed for her to leave as her legs continued to carry her toward his bedroom.

And then her hand was on the doorknob, turning it gently as she pushed it open.

The smell hit her in the face like a slap—scented candles and alcohol and sex—and she could see his bare back as he held his weight up in his arms, his hips moving steadily between the pedicured feet wrapped securely about his waist.

She stared at the image before her, everything taking on the fuzzy, surreal quality of a dream.

This wasn't real. There was no way this could be happening.

He lifted his head then, whipping it over his shoulder and making eye contact with her. His movements slowed as he looked at her, his expression more confused than remorseful.

From below him, where a mess of red hair was splayed out over the pillow, Leah saw a hand reach up and turn his face, pulling him back down for a kiss.

It was as if the cord that had been tethering her in place suddenly snapped, and she stumbled backward, knocking over the lamp on the table behind her as she turned and ran out the door. She made it as far as the bottom of the stairs outside before she dropped to her knees and vomited.

Leah collapsed on the ground as she continued to gasp for air between coughs and sobs. Despite the fact that she couldn't bear to be there a minute longer, after everything she'd been through that night, she didn't have the strength to move.

He never even came out to find her.

She had no idea how long she sat there on the floor, but eventually Leah pulled herself up and stumbled to her car. She knew there was no way she could drive. She couldn't even see. But she managed to call Robyn, and as soon as she answered, Leah broke into hysterics again, wailing unintelligibly into the phone. Somehow, Robyn was able piece together where she was, and it wasn't long before Holly and Robyn were there, their arms wrapped around her as they kissed her head and rubbed her hair, telling her that everything was going to be okay.

"We don't have to talk about this," Robyn said, pulling her from the memory as she laid her hand over Leah's.

Leah kept her eyes down as she nodded. "Yeah, I'd rather not. I'm just gonna ignore him, and he'll eventually stop, like he always does."

"Yeah, until the next time," Holly said angrily. "Seriously, you should just change your number and end this shit once and for all."

"You know that wouldn't end it, Holly. He knows where I live. He'd still be able to send me things."

The last time he decided he wanted to reconcile, it had been flowers and playlists he'd burned on to CDs for her.

"Hmm," Holly said, pursing her lips. "Well, then how about a taser to his ball sack? Bet *that* would end it."

Robyn snorted as Leah cupped her hand to her mouth, and then all at once the three of them were hysterically laughing.

"Oh my God, your bracelet!" Robyn said suddenly, her eyes wide as she pointed to Leah's wrist.

Leah spun it gently. "Oh yeah. I forgot to tell you guys."

"The old lady found it?" Holly asked.

"No, her grandson did. Well, sort of grandson."

Robyn let out a huge breath. "Ugh, thank God. I kept picturing your dad's face when he found out and it made me want to cry. When did you go back down there to get it?"

"I didn't. Her grandson met me in White Plains."

Robyn and Holly exchanged a look, and Holly put down her glass, folding her hands on the table and looking pointedly at Leah.

She rolled her eyes. "Cut the crap. It wasn't like that. He was just being nice."

"Hmm, a nice guy. Good start. So what's he look like?"

"Um, tall. Black hair. Blue eyes." Leah shrugged.

"Cute?" Robyn asked, her brow lifted.

Leah reached for another chip. "I guess."

Holly narrowed her eyes, pointing at Leah. "Come clean. You want his bod. You think he's sexy."

Leah smirked as she stared at the chip in her hand, turning it over. "He's *kind of* sexy," she conceded softly, and Holly whipped her head toward Robyn, her eyes huge.

"Oh my God, I was only kidding! Leah, that's awesome!"

She shook her head. "It's not a big deal."

"It *is* a big deal," Robyn said, swatting at Leah's arm. "This is the first time in like *forever* that you've even looked at a guy that way!"

"I know. It's unsettling."

"No, sweetie. It's a good thing," Holly insisted. "You can't let that fucktard ruin you. Not all guys are like him."

Leah took a breath and nodded just as Robyn said, "So what happened? You met him in White Plains, and then what? He gave you the bracelet and left?"

"Well, no. We had lunch."

Holly's hand came down on the table, causing the plates and glasses to rattle. "Are you kidding me that you're just telling us this now?"

"You went on a *date*?" Robyn asked.

"No, no," Leah said quickly, wishing she hadn't said anything at all. "We just decided to get something to eat. Spur of the moment. It was more out of convenience than anything else."

"And?"

"And, we talked, and ate, and it was nice."

"So how did you leave it?" Robyn asked, and Leah pulled her brow together.

"Well, I left, and that was it."

"Did you exchange numbers?" Holly asked.

"He already had mine from the note I left when I lost the bracelet, and I have his from when he called to tell me he found it, so..." She trailed off with a shrug.

"Did he ask to see you again?"

Leah shook her head, reaching for her drink.

The girls looked at each other quickly. "That's okay," Robyn said. "I mean, date or not, it was the first time you hung out with a guy alone in almost two years. And you admitted you thought he was attractive. Another huge step. I'm proud of you, girlie."

Leah smiled softly as she picked up her drink. "So," she said deliberately, "are you getting excited about this weekend?"

Holly laughed menacingly, and Robyn shot her a look. "I already told you guys, nothing too crazy."

"Robyn, you're having your bachelorette party on New Year's Eve. How do you think it's not going to get crazy?"

"It can get crazy, but can we just go easy with the penis paraphernalia?"

"Whoa, whoa, whoa," Holly said, holding up her hand. "You're not being serious, are you? If so, I have a *lot* of schlongs to return before Saturday."

Leah choked on the sip she'd just taken, bringing her napkin to her mouth, and Robyn tried not to laugh as she said, "Can we at least come to an agreement that I don't have to *wear* any of them?"

"No promises," Holly said, smiling innocently up at the waiter who had come to take their order.

They spent the rest of the meal discussing last-minute details for Robyn's party. The topic of Danny didn't come up again, and Leah was grateful. She understood why the girls were so excited; she had been turning down every guy who showed interest, every offer to be set up, for the past two years, refusing to even entertain the idea of getting involved with anyone. And despite what Holly had said, it wasn't because she thought all guys were like Scott. She knew that wasn't true. It was just that she didn't have the motivation to try and figure out which ones weren't. And even if she did, it wasn't like she could trust her own judgment anymore. Not when she spent the better part of three years thinking Scott was the best thing that had ever happened to her.

She found it somewhat ironic that overcoming her trust issues was a hundred times harder since the person she couldn't trust was herself.

Besides, they were making the Danny thing out to be a much bigger deal than it was. It wasn't some romantic rendezvous—it was lunch. Plus, he hadn't even asked to see her again, so rehashing it just seemed kind of pointless.

By the time Leah got home, she was so tired and distracted, she almost missed the sound of her phone ringing. As she opened her front door, she pulled it out of her purse and glanced at the screen, tossing the bag down on a chair.

Butterflies flooded her stomach.

Incoming call from Danny.

She had programmed him into her phone—like he'd told her to—just in case she ever had any car trouble and needed help.

At least, that's what she told herself.

Leah closed her eyes and inhaled a deep breath, exhaling slowly before she hit the button to take the call.

"Hello?"

"Hey, it's Danny."

Her smile faltered at the brusqueness of his voice.

"What's up?" she asked. "Is everything okay?"

"Gram just called me. She didn't have your number. Why did you send her daffodils?"

His tone made her stop in her tracks. It was almost...*accusatory*. It didn't make any sense.

"Um," Leah answered, running her hand through her hair, "I just...I mean, I really appreciated what she did for me that day, so I wanted to do something nice for her."

"That's not what I meant," he said. "Why *daffodils*?"

Leah closed her eyes as she rubbed circles over her temple with her fingertips. She couldn't understand what was happening. Was he angry with her? For sending his grandmother flowers?

"I don't know. I saw that she had a bunch of them around her house. I assumed she liked them." Her stomach dropped as she added, "Did I upset her or something?"

Danny exhaled heavily into the phone, and it was several seconds before he spoke again. "No," he said softly. "You didn't upset her. She wanted me to thank you."

"Okay..." Leah said, trailing off.

"Look, I'm at work, though. I gotta go."

She shook her head slightly. "Okay."

"Alright. Bye."

"Bye," she managed.

"Wait, Leah?" he said abruptly.

"Yeah?"

"I didn't...I..." He exhaled again before he said, "I'm sorry."

"Okay," she murmured, wishing she could come up with something else to say besides that stupid word.

"Bye," he said and ended the call.

Leah pulled the phone from her ear and tossed it on the table before she walked through her living room, collapsing on the couch with a huff as she dropped her head back and blinked up at the ceiling.

What the hell just happened?

Chapter Five

"Excuse me," Robyn said, tapping the overweight bearded man on his shoulder. He turned, clearly amused as he looked her up and down. She was wearing a white tank top with the phrase "I'm the Bachelorette" scrawled in pink lettering across the front. On the back was the phrase "Grab my ass before it's too late!" She wore a veil pinned into her blond curls, and much to her dismay, she was wearing a large penis necklace, a red strobe light flashing in its head.

Leah made a mental note to forbid Holly from planning any party of hers for the rest of their lives.

"Clearly, I'm getting married soon," Robyn said to the man, gesturing at herself with her half-empty drink. "And I'm a virgin bride. So I was just wondering if you could give me some pointers, or maybe tell me what to expect?"

Leah bit her lip and looked down; as her shoulders began to shake with the force of her stifled laughter, she turned and walked back toward the table where the rest of the raucous bridal party sat.

"Guys, this is so mean. Let's cut her a break."

"No way," Robyn's sister said. "She did this to me at my bachelorette party. Payback's a bitch." She held up the list she was holding, scanning it intently. It was a bachelorette scavenger hunt of sorts. Robyn had to complete a bunch of tasks before the end of the night, one more humiliating than the next. Her sister took the pen out of her back pocket and removed the cap with her teeth, checking off the box next to number seven: "Pretend you're a virgin and ask a random guy for advice re: the wedding night."

Leah sat down next to Holly, who held up her drink. She smiled, leaning over to clink her Cosmo against it before she drained the rest of it. On top of the shots they had taken earlier, she was slowly but surely making the transition from buzzed to drunk.

Robyn approached the table, her quintessential inebriated smile in place.

"Okay, so Herb," she said, gesturing over her shoulder, "said not to be shy, and that I shouldn't worry if it hurts because it will get better. Oh, and he also said I shouldn't be afraid to experiment with the balls."

The entire table cracked up as Robyn shrugged, drinking the rest of her appletini before she sat down on Leah's lap and rested her head against Leah's.

"Uh oh! The bachelorette needs a drink! I'm on it," said Robyn's old college roommate, and she jumped up and made her way over to the bar.

"Hey," Holly said, leaning over to them. "Do you realize that in twenty minutes, it will be the year you're getting married?"

"Peace out, single life!" Robyn shouted, holding two fingers up and waving them in the face of a man who walked past them.

"Peace out to the idea of her not puking tonight," Holly said to Leah, and they both laughed.

"Alright, girlies," Robyn's cousin sing-songed as she approached the table, "I brought us some goodies!"

Leah looked up to see four young guys standing behind her.

"Excellent!" Robyn's sister said. "We can check off number twelve on the list."

Robyn sighed. "What do I have to do?"

"You have to take a young man over your knee and spank him."

"I'll do it," two of the guys said in unison, and Holly burst out laughing.

Robyn got off Leah's lap and sat on a chair, crooking her finger at one of the guys. "Alright, let's go, naughty boy," she said, and he swiftly laid himself across her lap, beaming like he'd won the lottery.

She spanked him as the girls counted them off, and in the midst of the shenanigans, Leah glanced up to see one of the other guys smiling at her.

"Bobby," he said, holding out his hand.

"Leah," she answered as she reached for it.

"Well, Leah, I know this is going to sound like a line, but you're the most beautiful girl in here tonight."

She smirked. "That *does* sound like a line."

"Well, that's unfortunate, because it's true."

"Thanks," she said softly.

"So, can I get you another drink?"

"Oh. That's okay. I'm good for right now. Thanks."

"Alright. Maybe later," he said with a wink before turning back to his friends.

Leah sat back in her seat to see Holly watching her, her brow lifted.

"No good?" she asked, and Leah shrugged.

"That's okay," Holly said. "I'm still so proud of you for your not-a-date the other day."

Her inhibitions having been completely washed away by her third Cosmo, Leah leaned over to Holly and said, "I think it's *because* of my not-a-date that I'm not impressed by these guys."

"What do you mean?"

"I guess I'm just thinking about Danny," she said, and Holly's eyebrows shot into her hairline.

The truth was, Leah had thought about him a lot that night. It had been four days since that bizarre phone call about the daffodils, and she hadn't heard from him again. Not that she expected to. He'd given her no indication that he would call her after lunch that day, and that last phone call certainly didn't leave her expecting to hear from him again, and yet tonight, she couldn't get him out of her head. It seemed the more alcohol she consumed, the more thoughts of him would invade her mind.

He was the perfect combination of cute, but sexy. Pretty, but rugged. Exuding a gentleness, but at the same time, radiating a raw sex appeal. But she'd met lots of attractive guys in the past few years, and none of them ever occupied her thoughts the way Danny did.

He was such a mystery to her though, and maybe *that* was why she couldn't stop thinking about him. Maybe she was just trying to figure him out.

She could tell he was a good guy—the way he took care of Catherine, the way he was protective of her, proved that. And at lunch, they had gotten along so well. They were comfortable. They made each other laugh. He seemed to enjoy spending the afternoon with her.

And then he left without even the tiniest indication that he wanted to see or talk to her again.

Maybe he has a girlfriend, Leah thought. But then why would he have asked her to lunch in the first place? Unless he really *was* just trying to be a nice guy.

But then there was that weird, angry phone call.

Leah sighed, reaching to take Holly's drink out of her hand before taking a sip. This was exactly the kind of thing she didn't want to deal with. She didn't want to be vulnerable, especially with someone who was so hard to read.

She decided she should just celebrate her partial victory; she had allowed herself to have *some* interest in a guy. That was more than she had been capable of for a long time. It was a small step, but the girls were right: it was a step in the right direction. She didn't have to pursue it for it to be significant. And she wasn't going to pursue Danny.

With that revelation she suddenly felt ten pounds lighter, smiling over at Holly, who was still staring at her with a shocked expression.

"Do you *like* him?" she asked, and Leah waved her off.

"It's not like that. I'm just happy that I'm not completely broken. It makes me think that maybe one day I can have what you guys have," she said, gesturing to her friends.

Holly's face contorted with sadness. "*Of course* you will, Leah. Of course you will." She stood up and wrapped her arm around Leah's shoulder, leaning down to kiss the top of her head. "Now give me back my drink, you bitch."

Leah laughed just as Robyn's sister yelled, "Another round of shots, ladies!"

Stupidly, she agreed.

A few hours later, Leah and Holly were helping put Robyn into her fiancé's car.

"Here. The bartender thought this would be a good idea," Holly said, handing Rich one of the plastic fishbowls the bar used to serve specialty drinks in.

"Gee, thanks," he said, leaning into the passenger seat and handing Robyn the empty bowl. She grinned up at him and slurred something unintelligible.

"Absolutely, babe," Rich said as he buckled her seat belt.

"What did she say?" Leah asked.

Rich closed the passenger door and turned toward them. "I have no fucking idea."

Leah and Holly burst out laughing as Rich pulled up the zipper of his jacket. "How are you girls getting home? Do you need a ride?"

"No, Evan is coming to get us," Holly said.

"Alright, Happy New Year, ladies," he said, giving them warning glances before he leaned over and kissed both their cheeks. "Be good."

Leah and Holly watched them pull away, blowing dramatic kisses until the taillights of Rich's car were no longer visible.

A few minutes later, Holly's boyfriend pulled up to the curb, immediately rolling down the window. "Are you guys insane? Where the hell are your jackets?"

The girls leaned into each other and broke into hysterics as if that were the funniest thing they'd ever heard.

"Fantastic." Evan sighed, getting out of the car and ushering them toward it. "Alright, let's go."

Leah crawled into the back seat, and she and Holly spent the entire ride having disjointed conversations and laughing uncontrollably at anything and everything.

"God, I need to go home," Leah said when she had caught her breath, dropping her head back onto the seat and covering her face.

"We're almost there, Lee," Evan said, glancing in the rearview. "You're not gonna puke, are you?"

"No, I'm not gonna puke, but I might pass out," she mumbled, closing her eyes.

"That's okay," Holly said. "Pass out. We'll carry you."

Evan snorted. "You're not carrying anyone. Maybe *you* should think about passing out for a bit."

Leah tried to stifle a laugh, and Holly held up both hands, flipping them off before she crossed her arms over her chest and rested her head back against the seat.

By the time they pulled into Leah's apartment complex, Holly was snoring lightly, her head lolled to the side, resting on her shoulder.

Evan got out and helped Leah to the door, his hand firmly on her elbow as she wobbled on her heels. He watched until she was safely inside before jogging back down the path to his still-running car and a passed-out Holly.

Leah held on to the wall for balance, sloppily kicking off her heels and tripping over one as she walked down the hall. She still had enough presence of mind to stop in the kitchen and grab herself a bottle of water before she stumbled back toward her bedroom.

She undid the button of her jeans and pulled them down to her knees before she fell back onto the bed, kicking awkwardly to free herself of them. Her arms flopped out to her sides as her eyes fell closed, and then she groaned, remembering she hadn't texted her father.

Leah sat up quickly; the room spun with the sudden movement, and she squeezed her eyes shut and gripped the edge of the bed until the world righted itself. She leaned down, this time much more slowly, and fished through her purse on the floor until she came up with her phone.

As she flopped back onto the bed, the room began to spin again, and she squinted one eye, sending him a text as quickly as she could. With a relieved huff, she flung the phone somewhere on the other side of the bed and scooted down, draping one leg over the side so she could keep her foot on the floor.

Within seconds she passed out.

Leah felt the horrid pounding in her head before she was even fully awake; it felt like an ice pick being slowly tapped into her brain.

"Owwwwww," she moaned, pressing her fingertips into her eyes. It was then she realized that the shrill ringing in her ears was not part of her horrific hangover.

Her phone was ringing.

She turned her head slowly and opened one eye. It was a quarter to seven.

Why would someone be calling her so early?

Leah flipped onto her side, grimacing as the pain in her head intensified with the movement, and she closed her eyes, running her hand over the mattress and feeling around blindly for her phone.

"Make it stop," she moaned just as her hand closed around it, and she tapped her thumb over the screen before dragging it to her ear.

"Yeah?" she rasped.

"Leah, I'm going to focus more on how happy I am to hear your voice, and not on how upset I am with you right now."

She brought her weight up to her elbows, sitting up slightly and wincing as a sharp pain pierced her between the eyes. "Daddy?"

"Why didn't you let me know you got home last night? Of all nights, Leah. New Year's Eve. And you were at a bachelorette party, no less."

She sat up slowly, pressing her palm to her forehead. "I did. I texted you."

"You didn't. I waited."

Leah rubbed the back of her hand over her eyes, her mind racing back over the night. Everything was somewhat fuzzy, but she could have sworn she'd texted him.

"I'm sorry, Dad. I really thought I did." She exhaled heavily. "I...I don't know what to say. You know I always text you when I get home."

"Yeah, I know," he said tiredly. "Alright, go back to sleep. I'm just glad you're home safe."

"Okay. I'm really sorry, Dad. Love you."

"Love you too."

Leah ended the call and dropped her phone on the bed, her brow furrowed. After rubbing her hands over her face, she slid from the bed and padded to the bathroom, the pounding in her head keeping time with her feet against the hardwood floor.

After she'd used the bathroom, she opened her medicine chest and dumped three extra-strength aspirin into her palm, popping them into her mouth as she stumbled back out to the bedroom. Leah drank half the bottle of water before she leaned over and yanked the curtains closed.

And then she flopped facedown on her bed, immediately falling back asleep.

When she woke again, it was one thirty in the afternoon. She felt tired and thirsty and in desperate need of a shower, but that was still significantly better than when she woke the first time.

Leah rolled over and stretched with a groan, exhaling heavily as she let her arms fall back to her sides. The phone call with her father crept into her consciousness, and she pulled her brow together as she turned her head to scan the bed for her cell phone.

She sat up slowly when she spotted it, running her thumb over the screen.

She could have sworn she texted him. She definitely remembered looking for her phone last night for that exact reason. Was it possible she fell asleep before she hit send?

Leah pulled up her sent messages.

And there it was. A text sent at 3:49 a.m. to...

"No," she breathed, her stomach lurching. "Oh, no, no, no."

She had definitely sent the text. But it didn't go to Dad.

It went to Danny.

"Shit," she hissed as she opened the text message, having no recollection of what she'd actually sent.

Jus got home happy newyear I love u.

"*No!*" she wailed, throwing the phone to the other side of the bed as she brought both hands to her face. "Shit, shit, shit!"

Okay, relax, a little voice in her head cajoled. *So this guy has made it clear on two occasions now that he's not interested in you, and you just texted him that you loved him. No big deal.*

"Oh my God," she groaned, grabbing a pillow and pressing it over her face. If she never talked to him again after this, it would be too soon. But her stupid pride wouldn't allow her to move on and forget this little disaster ever happened. She felt the need to explain herself so he didn't think she was some pathetic weirdo.

Leah had no idea why she even cared what he thought of her, but she did.

She sat up quickly, tossing the pillow off the side of the bed as she reached for her phone, staring at the screen for a few seconds before she opened a new text message to Danny.

Sorry about that text last night. I meant to send that to someone else.

She hit send and closed her eyes, dropping back onto the bed as she brought her fingertips to her temples, massaging slow circles. A minute later, the soft double beep of her phone caused her eyes to flip open and her stomach to drop.

It was her text message alert.

Leah held her breath as she opened his reply.

Hold on—you don't love me? I'm in a jewelry store picking out your ring, so if you don't love me, tell me now.

A slow smile spread over her lips. This wasn't angry, standoffish, daffodil Danny. This was Cheesecake Factory Danny.

She hit reply.

Hmm. Well, before I decide, how big is the ring?

Leah placed her phone on her stomach before she stretched her arms over her head, biting her lip to fight the goofy smile she felt forming on her face. The sound of her phone ringing startled her, and she slapped her hand down on her stomach, bringing the phone to eye level as her bottom lip slid out from between her teeth.

He was calling.

She took a breath as she hit the button to take the call, hoping it was still Cheesecake Factory Danny.

"Hello?"

His laughter floated through the phone. "So, I guess size matters to you?"

His voice was playfully suggestive, and she felt her cheeks flush with heat as her stomach fluttered. "Happy New Year, by the way," he said.

"You too."

"I'd ask if you had fun last night, but your sloppy texting kind of answers that question."

Leah laughed, combing through her hair with her fingers. "It really wasn't as sloppy as you're making it out to be. I was trying to text my father. *Dad* and *Danny* are right next to each other in my contacts, and it was almost four in the morning. Cut me some slack."

"Ah, so that text was for your father?"

"Mm-hm," she hummed, wondering if she imagined in the hint of relief in his voice. There was a stretch of silence, and Leah began to chew on her lower lip again.

"So you should probably erase it," she blurted out suddenly.

"Why?"

"I...I don't know. I don't want to, like...get you in trouble or anything."

"Get me in trouble?" he asked. "How would you get me in trouble?"

"I mean, some random girl, texting you that she loves you..." She trailed off.

"I don't have a girlfriend, if that's what you're getting at."

She could hear the amusement in his voice, picture the smirk he was probably wearing.

The one that brought out his dimples.

Heat flooded her cheeks again. He was right; that *had* been what she was getting at, and she couldn't believe she'd gone about it in such a childish way. *Why didn't you just write him a note?* she thought. *Do you have a girlfriend? Circle yes or no.*

Leah heard a muted banging through the phone before Danny called out, "Come in, it's open!"

"Company?" she asked.

"Just a couple of the guys from the shop. We have money on today's game, which means we all have to watch it in the same place so we can humiliate and degrade each other over it."

"Sounds fun," she said with a laugh, reaching over to grab the water bottle off her nightstand. "Well, I'll let you go then."

"Alright. Oh hey, Leah?"

She froze with the bottle at her lips. "Yeah?"

"Maybe you should erase that text from your sent messages. You know. So you don't get in trouble or anything."

She lowered the bottle from her lips as a smile curved her mouth. "I don't have a boyfriend, if that's what you're getting at."

He laughed lightly into the phone. "Talk to you later."

"Bye," she said.

She dropped the phone to the bed and brought the bottle back to her mouth, nibbling on the rim.

He said he'd talk to her later.

She pressed her lips together, fighting the squeal she could feel building in the back of her throat.

Oh, Leah, she thought. *You are so screwed.*

Chapter Six

"Hey, Gram, can you hand me that flashlight?" Danny shifted as the ledge of the cabinet dug into his lower back. He was three seconds away from ripping the goddamn sink out of the wall and throwing it across the room.

"Here you go, love," she said, holding it out for him.

"Thanks," he said absently, placing the wrench on his chest to free his hand for the light.

"I don't know why you won't just let me call a plumber."

"Gram, you're bruising my ego," he said, although he was seriously beginning to wonder the same thing.

She leaned down and swatted his knee. "Oh, stop it with your ego. I know you're *capable* of doing it. I'd just rather you didn't."

"Why?" he grunted as he worked the wrench to loosen a nut.

"Because there are better ways for you to spend your afternoon."

Danny lifted his head slightly, peeking out from under the sink. "You know nothing trumps you," he said with a wink, and she chuckled.

"Stop schmoozing me. Who do you think you're talking to?"

Danny laughed as he positioned the flashlight near his shoulder. As much as he made jokes, what he'd said was the truth; there was nothing that took precedence over her, no matter how much she tried to urge him to feel otherwise, and she knew it.

"Alright, I need a different wrench," he said, sliding out from under the sink and rubbing his lower back. "I'm pretty sure I have the one I need in my car."

"Why don't you take a break?" she said, handing him the glass of iced tea he hadn't even seen her pour. He took it gratefully, leaning his back up against the cabinet and taking a large sip.

"Thanks," he said, wiping the back of his hand over his mouth.

She nodded with a smile, shuffling over to the chair near the table. "So, did you ever get in touch with Leah?"

"What?" he asked, startled.

"For the flowers," she said, taking a seat across from him. "Did you thank her for me?"

"Oh," he said. "Yeah, I did."

"She seems sweet."

Danny took another long sip of his drink. "Yeah," he said, reaching above him to place the glass on the counter near the sink.

"Beautiful too," she said innocently, looking at her pants as she brushed away invisible lint.

"Gram."

"What?" she said.

Danny opened his mouth, only to close it without answering. He shook his head as he pulled himself to his feet. "It doesn't matter."

"Of course it does."

He leaned down, saying nothing as he sifted through the toolbox.

"You deserve to be happy," she said, and he laughed bitterly.

"That's debatable," he said as he straightened, turning to walk toward the door.

"*Daniel,*" she said firmly, and he stopped in his tracks. "Please don't leave while I'm having a conversation with you. It's rude."

He looked down with a nod. "Sorry."

A second later he heard her come up behind him, and then her hand was on his bicep, turning him back around to face her. "You *do* deserve to be happy. That's all I've ever wanted for you."

His teeth came together as he tried to smother the surge of frustration he felt at her words. "Yeah?" he asked tightly. "And what about Leah? Does *she* deserve to be happy?"

"Daniel," she said softly.

"You think getting involved with someone like me would make her happy?" he continued. "You think she'd just overlook everything that comes along with it?"

Gram looked down, twisting the ring on her left hand. "Everyone has baggage, Daniel."

"Gram, *come on*," he said.

When she didn't lift her eyes, his voice softened.

"It wouldn't be fair," he said. "You know it wouldn't."

Her shoulders rose slightly as she took a breath before looking up at him. "You're not dying, love."

He winced as if she'd hit him.

"You still have your whole life ahead of you," she went on. Gram brought her hand to the side of his face as she said, "Don't miss out on the chances you have to make it a wonderful one."

Danny shook his head slightly. "Do you hear what you're saying? So, I'm supposed to just string her along on the off chance that everything goes my way?"

She opened her mouth to respond, but he cut her off. "And what happens when it doesn't go my way, Gram? What happens then?"

She stared up at him, her hand still pressed to his cheek as her eyes filled with tears. "My boy," she said softly. "You can't stop living. You're the one who taught *me* that, remember?"

He looked down, swallowing hard. "You deserve to be happy," she said, using her hand on his face to lift his gaze back to hers. "You deserve to be happy," she repeated, looking him in the eyes. He stared at her as she gave him a watery smile before patting his cheek.

And then she walked past him and into her bedroom, closing the door behind her.

"Fuck," Danny mumbled, rubbing his hands roughly over his face before he walked over to her chair and dropped into it.

The absolute last thing he needed was Gram urging him to call her— because the truth was, he'd been fighting his desire to do just that every day since that goddamn lunch date, and he didn't know how much longer he'd be able to resist that impulse with Gram's prodding battling his common sense.

He couldn't do it. It would be wrong on so many levels to pursue her. Even Gram must have known that. But her hopeless optimism was getting in the way of her judgment; she was still clinging to the idea that everything might work out. Danny understood why; it was the only thing that kept her from falling to pieces. She needed that fantasy in order to get out of bed every morning, and the last thing he'd ever want to do was deprive her of that.

But just because he was allowing her to exist in a fantasy world didn't mean he wasn't strongly rooted in reality.

Gram had said that he still had a future.

But he knew what that future was going to look like, and dragging someone else into it would be repulsively self-serving.

Danny laughed humorlessly, running his hand through his hair.

Maybe he'd gotten caught up in Gram's fantasy world more than he'd realized, because it was ridiculous for him to even be thinking about what the fallout would be for Leah if they got involved. Once she learned the truth about him, she'd go running for the hills anyway. So none of it mattered.

Case closed. End of story.

At least, that *should* have been the end of the story.

But her number was in his phone, taunting him every goddamn day. He knew he should just delete it, but some twisted, masochistic part of him wouldn't allow it.

He had promised himself he wouldn't contact her again after that call about the flowers, but then he'd gone ahead and called her again on New Year's Day, justifying it because *she* had contacted him first; she had texted him, and he was simply responding. After all, just because he wasn't going to pursue her didn't mean he had to be rude.

Maybe that was it.

Maybe that was how he needed to handle her. If she reached out to him, he would respond—he just wouldn't initiate anything himself.

Danny exhaled heavily, running both hands up through his hair as he stood and made his way through the house and out to his car.

He was just going to leave it up to fate.

Danny smirked sardonically at that as he opened the trunk and sifted through his toolbox. Because if there was one thing he could count on, it would be that fate would fuck him over.

Again.

Chapter Seven

"Ugh, what a creeper!" Leah's sister said as she shook her shoulders in an exaggerated shiver. "So he like lurks around your apartment?"

Leah sat on the counter in Sarah's kitchen, running her finger around the rim of her wine glass as her sister opened the oven door to check the lasagna. When they first began their Monday night dinner dates almost two years ago, Leah had declared any and all conversations pertaining to Scott off-limits. Sarah was nothing if not rabidly protective, and in the weeks following their breakup, it was just a little too much for her to handle. Instead, they would spend the evening watching *How I Met Your Mother* and gorging on dessert while vowing to hit the gym the following day as penance.

But as soon as Leah mentioned that Scott had stopped by earlier that day, the door restraining all of Sarah's venom for Scott burst clean off the hinges.

"I don't think he *lurks*," Leah said. "He comes to see if I'll answer the door, and when I don't, he leaves me whatever bullshit peace offering he brought with him."

"And the idiot came today?" she asked, closing the oven door. "Doesn't he realize school started back up for you?"

Leah shrugged. "Who knows. Maybe he intentionally came when I wouldn't be home."

"What did he leave this time?"

"He burned another playlist."

Sarah rolled her eyes as she took a sip of wine. "Yeah, because a good mix tape will make up for the fact that he boned another girl while your father lay dying in the hospital. Oh, oh, and he couldn't be there with you *so* he could nail said whore bag. But no, burn a CD, it's all good."

Leah nodded. "I really appreciate you bringing me back up to speed. I had totally forgotten about everything that happened that night until you just reminded me."

Sarah laughed as she pulled herself up onto the counter beside Leah.

"Honestly, I just don't get it," Leah said. "I mean, he doesn't love me. There's no way he could have done what he did if he loved me, so I don't understand why he's still trying to get me back."

"It has nothing to do with love," Sarah said, reaching for the bottle of wine and refilling her glass. "It's about power. Scott is the kind of guy who needs it to feel whole. It feeds him. He lost the power when *you* were the one who ended that relationship. I don't think it's about wanting *you* back at all, no offense."

"Believe me, none taken," Leah interrupted.

Sarah smirked before she said, "He just wants the power back. *And* if he succeeded in getting you back, he could exert that power in one of two ways. He could try to get control over you again by manipulating you, or he could end the relationship on *his* terms. Either way, he'd have the upper hand. That's all it's about."

Leah stared at the wine in her glass as she swirled it gently. "You know, it's a little freaky to hear all this psychobabble come out of your mouth, especially when it makes sense. Please tell me you don't psychoanalyze me behind my back."

"Never!" Sarah scoffed, taking an imaginary pencil out from behind her ear and pretending to lick the tip before she scribbled furiously on the pad beside her.

Leah laughed as she smacked her sister's leg.

"All kidding aside," Sarah said, "you should get a restraining order or something."

Leah shook her head. She had entertained the idea once before, but the truth was, Scott had never been violent. He wasn't aggressive or threatening. He was a selfish, inconsiderate asshole, sure, and he was a liar, but he would never physically hurt her.

"He hasn't done anything to warrant that. You can't get a restraining order just because someone can't take a hint. I'm sure the police have much more important things to be worrying about besides my persistent jerk of an ex-boyfriend."

"I guess," Sarah said. "It's just so annoying though, because I feel like if he would just leave you alone, you'd be able to move past this whole thing once and for all. I mean, how the hell are you supposed to forget about everything that happened when he keeps showing up every couple of months?"

Leah shrugged, knowing she had a point. Every time Scott decided to pull this stunt, it brought back a mess of awful memories for her, not to mention all of her insecurities.

"And it's pissing me off that it's happening right when you just met this Danny guy. I don't want you to panic and bail on him because Scott's messing with your head again."

"Well, hold on, let's not get ahead of ourselves here. There's really nothing for me to bail on."

Despite the fact that Danny had ended the call on New Year's Day by telling her he'd talk to her later, three days had passed with no word from him. Leah realized that *talk to you later* was a common farewell, and not necessarily meant to be taken literally, but since it was the first time he ended any conversation with her indicating they'd be speaking again, she couldn't help but feel hopeful.

And hopeful was dangerous, because it left her wide open for disappointment.

"But if you like him," Sarah said, "I don't want you to not pursue it because of Scott dredging up all your old baggage."

Leah turned to her sister. "Did you just call me an old bag?"

"I'm being serious," she laughed. "Just promise me that if you like this guy, you'll go for it, no matter what that dumb ass is doing."

Leah nodded, bringing her wine glass to her lips. "I honestly don't know how I feel about him. But if I decide I'm interested…then…I'll try," she said before finishing the rest of her wine.

"*You will?*" Sarah asked excitedly.

She nodded. "*If* I decide I'm interested," she clarified once she had swallowed.

Sarah pumped her fist in the air before she hopped off the counter and grabbed the oven mitt, and Leah took a deep breath, blinking up at the ceiling.

The problem was, she had already decided whether or not she was interested.

And the answer terrified her.

Holly and Robyn—and now Sarah—were so convinced that her lingering issues with Scott were preventing her from pursuing Danny, when in reality Scott's reappearance had nothing to do with her hesitation; what raised a red flag for her was the ridiculously inconsistent behavior she'd seen from Danny since she'd met him almost two weeks ago. He invited her to lunch and seemed to enjoy being with her, only to dismiss her at the end of it. He called her upset and curt over the fact that she'd done something kind for his grandmother, only to be playful and flirty with her on New Year's Day. Then he told her he'd talk to her soon, but he never called.

She couldn't allow herself to be that careless, to get involved—for the first time in two years—with someone who was so unpredictable. She'd be uneasy enough about starting a relationship again without the added uncertainty of never knowing what to expect from him. Someone a bit more consistent, someone who could offer her some semblance of stability, *that's* what she should be looking for. A nice, smooth transition back into the world of dating.

Yet she couldn't seem to get him out of her head.

Yes, he was mercurial. Yes, he was difficult to understand. The trouble was, she found herself *wanting* to understand him. Or at least, to try.

Leah and Sarah ended up eating their lasagna on the couch while flipping through the channels, and just before *How I Met Your Mother* came on, Sarah brought their dirty dishes into the kitchen and came out with a pint of Ben and Jerry's Americone Dream and two spoons, waving them in invitation. They spent the next half hour with the pint wedged in the cushions between them, battling with their spoons for the chocolate-covered waffle-cone chunks.

It was just after ten by the time she left her sister's apartment, and after having slept in for most of Christmas vacation, she was definitely feeling the effects of waking up at five thirty again. Leah yawned heavily as she pulled up to the stoplight at the intersection, flipping aimlessly through the radio stations.

"You suck," she told the console before she turned the radio off.

And then her eye landed on her phone in the cup holder.

She *had* promised her sister she'd try.

Leah dropped her head back on the seat, staring at the roof of the car.

And they *had* ended their last conversation on good terms.

The car behind her beeped as the light turned green, and she sat up and hit the gas.

Come on, Leah. Put on your big girl panties and do it.

Leah glanced back down at her phone. "Oh, what the hell," she murmured to herself as she grabbed it, quickly scrolling through her contacts until she found him.

He answered on the second ring, his voice gravelly. "Leah. Hey."

The rough sound of it caused a fluttering low in her stomach. "Hey. Did I wake you?"

"No, not at all," he answered. "I haven't been to sleep in over twenty-four hours, so it's all good."

"Seriously? Why?"

Danny sighed before he said, "A buddy of mine races cars, and he's entered in this big competition tomorrow. A shitload of money up for grabs. Anyway, he called me last night because he took it out for a spin to test some shit he just put in it, and he hit some black ice and crashed it."

"Oh my God, is he okay?"

"Yeah, he's fine. Just pissed off," he said with a laugh. "Fucked the car up pretty good, and he needed it to be in shape for this thing tomorrow. So me and a few of my guys drove out to him last night. Spent the whole night and all of today working on it."

"Did you get it fixed?"

"Pshh. Did I get it fixed. Of course I got it fixed."

Leah smiled. "Well, I apologize for questioning your automotive prowess. I don't know what I was thinking."

"Me either, but I'm not sure I forgive you," he said through a yawn. "So what's up? Is everything okay?"

"Yeah," she said. "I just wanted to say hi. See how you were."

"Right now, exhausted," he said with a weak chuckle.

"Why aren't you in bed?"

"Trying to get there. I'm driving back from Hempstead and I'm stuck on the Cross Island."

"Traffic?"

"No, glue," he said with a laugh. "Yes, traffic."

"Wise ass," she said, fighting a smile.

"What are you doing up? Don't you have school tomorrow?"

"Yeah," she said, glancing in her rearview before switching lanes. "I just had dinner at my sister's. I'm almost home."

"Oh man. What did you have?"

"Lasagna, why?"

He groaned, and the fluttering in her stomach returned with a vengeance. "God, that sounds amazing. I haven't eaten anything but chips and frozen pizza rolls all day. Tell me what was in it, nice and slow."

"Oh my God!" she laughed. "Knock it off, you sicko!"

Danny laughed into the phone, and the fluttering traveled up through her chest.

Screwed. You are so totally screwed. Beyond screwed.

"So how was your first day back?" he asked.

"Typical. You'd think they'd be reenergized, coming off a week and a half's vacation, but it was like a scene out of *The Walking Dead*."

"Do you watch *The Walking Dead?*"

"No."

"I figured."

"Why do you say that?"

"Because in *The Walking Dead*, they don't sit there zoning out. They tear your fucking limbs off and eat them. Can I assume that's not what happened in your classroom today?"

Leah pulled into her parking space and cut the engine. "You know, you're a little annoying when you're stuck in traffic on no sleep."

Danny burst out laughing as Leah got out of the car and ran to her front door, her head ducked against the wind. "Jesus, it's freezing out here," she said through gritted teeth.

"You're home already?"

"Yeah, just walked through the door."

"Oh. Alright, well, I'll let you get to bed then—"

"No, that's okay," she said a little too quickly. She closed her eyes and took a breath before she continued. "I'm not that tired. Plus, I don't want you falling asleep at the wheel."

While she was fairly confident that he could manage to get himself home in one piece without her, she *wasn't* so sure of when she would get this version of Danny again, if any version.

She wasn't ready to let him go yet.

"Well, I guess it's only fair," he said. "I might as well cash in on what you owe me."

"Oh?" Leah asked, kicking off her shoes and walking back toward her bedroom. "I was unaware I owed you anything."

"The last time you were tired and driving, I kept you awake. So it's only right that you return the favor."

"*Christmas night?*" Leah asked through a laugh. "You kept me awake for like two minutes. Barely that!"

He laughed before he said, "So tell me more about your day. After you fended off the zombie apocalypse, I mean."

"Oh my God, you're getting douchier by the second. Why did I agree to stay on the phone with you again?"

"Don't know, but now you're stuck."

Leah smiled as he added, "Seriously, though. Tell me about your day."

The fact that he would even ask that question lit a pleasant warmth in her chest. "I kind of already did," she said, removing the phone from her ear just enough to pull her shirt over her head. "I taught, and then I went to my sister's for dinner. Nothing exciting."

"What book are you teaching right now?"

Leah lifted her brow as she pulled her pajama top over her head. "Really? You of all people want to talk about English while you're trying not to fall asleep?"

"Try me."

"We're doing *To Kill A Mockingbird.*"

"Ah, good old Boo Radley and Atticus Finch."

"You know it?" she asked, unable to keep the surprise out of her voice.

"I said it wasn't my favorite subject, not that I was illiterate. Me can read."

"Shut up," she laughed.

"It's true. And not just magazines. Actual, real books. With covers. Hard ones."

"Okay," she said through her laughter. "I'm getting off the phone now. You're on your own. Go call one of your friends and have *him* sit through this craziness."

"I would," Danny said, "but I don't think they'd be much help. When I left them a little while ago, they were about to start a game of Asshole."

"Oh my God," Leah said nostalgically. "I haven't played that game in years!"

"I was never a big fan of it. My game of choice was always Flip Cups."

"Ugh," Leah said, climbing into bed. "Chug a beer as fast as you can and then try to turn your cup upside down on a table slick with backwash and vomit while you stifle your own? No thanks."

"Well, it's really a man's game anyway, so…"

"If you mean because it's moronic and requires no thought, then I agree."

Danny burst out laughing as he said, "Jesus Christ! Below the belt, point deducted!"

Leah smiled. "We used to play Never Have I Ever."

"Eh," Danny said. "Truth or Dare was better."

"That's not a drinking game."

"Sure it is," he said. "At least, we played it as one. If you don't want to do the dare, you have to drink."

"Oh, so kind of like Grilled?"

"What the hell is Grilled?" he asked.

"It's like what you described, only more truth than dare. You ask someone a question, and they answer. If they don't want to for whatever reason, they have to drink. People would intentionally ask the most personal and embarrassing questions to try and get you to drink, because by the end of the game, everyone is so drunk, they'll basically answer any question thrown at them. Definitely a quick and dirty way to get to know someone."

There was a beat of silence before he said, "So let's play."

"What, now?" she said with a laugh, lying back on her pillow. "We can't. It wouldn't work."

"Why not?"

"Because if we aren't drinking, there's no penalty for not answering. What would be the motivation to answer?"

"Hmm," he said. "Well, what if we only get one pass? If you can only pass once, you won't be so quick to use it."

"*One pass?*" Leah said uncertainly.

"What's wrong? You got a lot of skeletons?" he said with that maddening cool amusement that instantly had Leah picturing his dimples.

"Two," she said. "Two passes."

He chuckled. "Fine, two passes. You're up first."

"What? Why?"

"This is your game. I'm just a rookie," he said, and Leah sighed.

"Okay…how old are you?"

"Twenty-eight. My turn?"

"Yup," she said, shifting onto her side to turn off her lamp.

"Okay. How old are you?"

"How original," she said, switching the phone to the other ear as she lay back down. "I'm twenty-seven. What's the worst injury you've ever had?"

"Easy," he said. "Broke my leg when I was seven. The bone came through the skin."

"*Ohmygod,*" Leah choked out. "Stop! Ugh!"

"You asked!"

"Yeah, but I had no idea it would be *that* disgusting! Blech! Can you just tell me how the hell you did that? I don't want to know anything else about it."

"Me and my friend were playing superheroes. We thought we could jump off his deck."

"Did your friend get hurt?"

"I went first."

She nodded. "Your friend's a smart boy."

Danny laughed before he said, "Okay, my turn. If you could spend a day with anyone in the world, who would it be?"

Leah's smile fell a little before she cleared her throat. "My mom. My turn," she added quickly. "What's a talent you have that not a lot of people know about?"

He chuckled suggestively, a low rumbling sound, and Leah felt a surge of heat run through her veins. She kicked her covers off as he said, "Hmm, I'm gonna keep it PG for now and go with that I can sing."

"You can sing?" she asked, her eyes widening.

"Yeah."

"Like, 'sing in the shower' sing, or you can actually sing?"

"I can actually sing."

Leah closed her eyes. "Sing now."

"Fuck *that,*" he said with a laugh.

"Please?"

"Not a chance."

"Well, then how do I know you're not bullshitting me?"

"I guess you're just gonna have to trust me," he said, and Leah exhaled heavily.

God, she really, really wanted to hear him sing.

But maybe it was for the best that he wouldn't. Because if his speaking voice was any indication of what his singing voice would be like, it might very well be the thing that pushed her over the edge.

"My turn," he said, pulling her from her thoughts. "What's your biggest fear?"

"My *biggest* fear?" she asked, chewing on her lip.

"No, scratch that," he said. "What's your most embarrassing fear?"

Leah took a strand of her hair in between her fingers and began twirling it. "Okay, um…well, *I* personally don't think this is anything to be embarrassed about, but I don't like the dark."

"You're scared of the dark?" he asked, and she could tell he was smiling.

"I'm not *scared* of the dark. I just don't like it. I don't like not knowing what's around me. It's the same reason I don't really like swimming in the ocean. You have no idea what's lurking a foot below you. Totally freaks me out."

"Oh. Well, that makes sense. I can understand that."

"Really?"

"Sure," he said, and after a beat, he spoke again through barely contained laughter. "So, do you sleep with a night-light then?"

Leah's eyes immediately flew to the small plug-in night-light in the outlet on the far wall. "Such an asshole," she mumbled, and he burst out laughing.

Okay then. Game on.

"Okay, my turn," she said over his guffawing. "How many women have you slept with?"

His laughter morphed into a surprised coughing fit, and Leah smirked.

"Well, shit," he said softly after he'd caught his breath.

"So?" Leah prodded. "How many?"

"Pass."

"Oh come on!"

"Pass."

"You know, you're saying more by using your pass than if you actually answered the question."

"I'm saying nothing," he laughed. "You don't know why I'm passing. How do you know I'm not a virgin? Maybe I don't want to share that with you because I'm embarrassed."

"Oh, you are so full of shit," she said, and she heard him chuckle.

"That question is a death trap. If the number is too high, I'm sleazy. If it's too low, then there's something wrong with me. And since not everyone's standards for what's too high and too low are the same, and I have no idea what yours are, I'm going with pass."

"Fine," she pouted. "Your turn."

"Well, since you brought out the big guns, how old were you when you lost your virginity?"

"Sixteen," she answered. "There, see? I told you that, even though it might cause you to draw certain conclusions about me. And I mean, we already established that you're a judger."

"Oh my God with your judger bullshit." He laughed, and Leah smiled just as she heard him lay on the horn and mumble, "Stupid motherfucker."

"Everything alright over there?"

"We're about to pass the accident, and this fucking moron rode the shoulder all the way up here, and now he's trying to squeeze in. He almost clipped me. Fucking asshole."

Leah sighed. "I'm going to get you a swear jar."

"A swear jar?"

"Yep. Every time you curse, you have to put money in it."

"Okay," he laughed. "And how would that stop me from cursing again?"

"Because once it's full, you have to take all that money and buy me something pretty."

Danny chuckled softly before he said, "Well, there's a flaw in that plan, because buying you something pretty wouldn't exactly be a punishment for me."

Butterflies burst through her stomach as a pleasant tingling prickled its way over her skin.

"Your turn," he said casually.

"Oh…okay," she said, trying to pull her thoughts back together. "Um…what would you say your best quality is?"

"I'm loyal," he answered without missing a beat, and Leah closed her eyes.

He couldn't have answered more perfectly if he tried.

And she was pretty sure he was telling the truth. He knew nothing of her past with Scott, nothing about her hang-ups and fears regarding relationships, so it wasn't as though he was just trying to appeal to that. Plus, she'd seen the proof of it herself, the way he took care of Catherine, who wasn't even his family. Not to mention the fact that he had just spent over twenty-four hours helping out a friend in need.

"My turn," he said, and she could tell by his tone of voice that it wasn't going to bode well for her. "Where's the weirdest place you've had sex?"

"Oh God." She laughed nervously. "Pass, pass, pass."

"*Really*?" He clucked his tongue. "Shame on you."

"Shame on me?"

"Don't you realize you're saying more by using your pass than if you actually told me the place?"

She sighed. "You're so annoying."

"All kidding aside," he said, "my imagination is probably much worse than your reality, so leaving that question up to me to piece together probably isn't the wisest move."

"I'll take my chances."

Danny whistled long and low. "Wow. That bad, huh?"

"Moving on," Leah said with a laugh, nibbling on her thumbnail before she blurted out her next question. "When was the last time you had sex?"

"Damn," he said after a moment. "You give it as good as you get it, huh?"

"You started it," she said, trying to sound playful, but the truth was, it had taken every ounce of courage she had to ask that question. She knew it would tell her a lot, and she wasn't necessarily sure she wanted to know what it would reveal.

"Shit," she heard him say under his breath before he inhaled deeply. "Pass."

Leah felt her stomach drop a little, but she forced a smile, trying to keep it light.

"Wow, really? Are you sure you want to do that? You're out after this."

"Yes, I'm fully aware," he said. "Still pass."

"Okay then, have it your way," she said airily, but the entire time, her mind was racing, wondering what his reason could be for not wanting to answer. Maybe it had been a while for him and he felt embarrassed telling her that. Of course, he had no way of knowing that she hadn't had sex in nearly two years, and that his dry spell was probably a drop in the bucket by comparison.

That is, if this were even about a dry spell.

There was also the distinct possibility that he was currently sleeping with someone, or a few someones, and didn't want her to know that. And unfortunately, of the two options, taking into consideration his personality and his looks, the latter was the more likely scenario.

"Okay, my turn," he said. "Do you have any piercings or tattoos?"

"I have a tattoo," Leah said, still trying to shake off her disappointment.

"Seriously? I never would have thought that. Where?"

"On the back of my neck."

"What is it?" he asked.

"A spiral triskele. Long story," she said, hoping he wouldn't push it further than that.

"Wow. I gotta say though, I love that."

"What, the triskele?"

"No, I have no idea what that is," he said with a laugh. "I mean when a girl has a tattoo in a secret place."

"Oh," she said. "Well, it's not really a secret place."

"I think it is. Unless you wear your hair up all the time, only people close to you would ever get to see it. I feel like the back of a woman's neck is an extremely intimate place."

Seriously, goddamn him.

Why, why, why did he have to refuse to answer her last question and then follow it up with *that?* Almost like he knew how to suck her right back in. Leah started to consider the possibility that he was reading from some type of handbook.

And the title of it might as well have been *How to Reduce Leah to a Besotted, Quivering Pile of Easy.*

"Your turn," he prompted when several seconds had passed and she hadn't said anything.

Leah inhaled deeply and closed her eyes. No more silly questions. She needed to start figuring him out.

"What's the one thing you've done in your life that you regret the most?" she asked.

"Pass."

Her eyes flipped open as the corner of her mouth lifted in a smile. "You can't pass. You don't have any more."

"Yeah, I know," he said curtly, and Leah's stomach dropped for the second time.

She recognized this tone.

"Look, I gotta go," he said. "I just pulled onto my street and I have to find a spot."

"Oh, okay."

"Thanks for keeping me awake, though. I appreciate it. Good night, Leah."

He hung up before she could even respond.

Leah took the phone away from her ear and stared at it for a second before she threw her head back and groaned loudly.

Being with him, talking to him, was the emotional equivalent of bungee jumping. There was the freedom, the adrenaline, the exhilaration of the fall, only to have it come to an abrupt halt, roughly yanking her back in the direction from which she came.

Leah reached up and rubbed her eyes roughly with the heels of her hands.

He could be really sweet sometimes, but he was so goddamn capricious. And he was funny, but his moods were completely unreliable. He *did* have a genuine kindness about him, but he could also be closed off and abrupt, and there was no guarantee as to which version of him she'd be getting.

But far more frustrating to her than any of those things was the fact that even though he'd thrown her for a loop yet again, she was completely captivated by him.

Chapter Eight

D anny had just finished reinstalling the drain plug on the Cadillac's transmission when he felt his phone buzz in his pocket, and he slid the creeper out from under the car, wiping his hand down the side of his coveralls before he pulled it out.

His pulse quickened when he saw her name next to the notification, and he eagerly opened the text.

I'll be at The Rabbit Hole tonight. You should come out if you're not busy.

He stared at her message for a moment before he cleared the screen and slid the phone back in his pocket.

And then he rested his head back on the creeper, throwing his forearm over his eyes.

He wasn't going to go, of course. That would be a horrible idea.

But God, it was so fucking tempting.

She had been so forgiving of the rude way he'd gotten off the phone the last time they had spoken. The second he'd hung up on her that night, he felt like kicking himself. It was such a stupid move; he should have just made something up, some insignificant answer to her question, and it would have been fine. But she had caught him off guard, and instead he panicked and acted like a complete dick.

Again.

And yet the next morning, she sent him a text. Five simple words, but it made his chest feel like hundreds of little bubbles were popping inside.

Have a good day today.

He spent the rest of the day thinking about her, and that night he'd broken his rule and initiated contact with her, sending her a quick text.

Hope you successfully fended off the zombies today. Good night.

She had responded with an LOL and a smiley face, and Danny ended up leaving his phone in the kitchen for the remainder of the night so he wouldn't be tempted to contact her again.

The following day, just before lunch, he'd gotten another text from her.

Hope your day is going well. No cursing at cars today. SWEAR JAR!

He had laughed out lout at that, drawing confused looks from the customers sitting in the waiting area. And that night he'd ignored his self-imposed rule again, sending her a message that wished her a good night and reminded her to turn on her night-light.

They'd been going back and forth like that for the past four days, and he'd managed to convince himself that it was acceptable because it was only texting. It wasn't like they were talking on the phone, or meeting up, or hooking up.

He was still completely fine.

Danny dropped his forearm from his eyes and stared up at the high ceiling of the garage. In his moments of clarity, however, he realized how stupid it was to be doing this with her. Because every text only reinforced how much he liked her. She was sarcastic and quick-witted, but also incredibly sweet and considerate. Not to mention forgiving. On more than one occasion, she seemed to completely overlook the fact that he had fucked up.

And sometimes, for a split second, it made him think that maybe she might forgive him his biggest one; that there was a chance she wouldn't run from him if she knew the truth.

But that line of thinking was idiotic, not to mention dangerous. He shouldn't be entertaining that remote possibility. He shouldn't even be focusing on the things he liked about her; he wasn't doing himself any favors in that regard.

And he absolutely, one hundred percent, should not be looking for excuses to see her again.

Yet even as that thought crossed his mind, he was running through potential reasons to make an appearance at The Rabbit Hole. Technically, he wouldn't be breaking any of his rules if he went; *she* was the one who asked him to go, and he had already determined that if she were to initiate contact, he would follow through.

As if that made him any less culpable.

No. Fuck it. You're not going.

"What's going on over there, deep thinker?"

Danny turned his head to see Jake leaning against the bumper of a car, elbow deep in a bag of Lay's.

"What? Nothing," he said as he sat up and ran his hand through his hair.

"Not nothing," Jake said around a mouthful of chips. "Who was that text from?"

Danny made a face as he stood up and popped the hood of the Cadillac. "What are you, a fucking detective?"

"Was it a chick?" he asked, completely unfazed.

"Go change the spark plugs on the Pontiac out back."

"Did it already," he said, shoving another handful of chips in his mouth. "So what'd this girl say to make you so goddamn pissy?"

Danny ignored him, taking off the transmission's filler cap.

"Did she say your dick was small?"

He laughed before he could stop himself. "You wish, asshole."

"Well, then what the hell did she say?" he asked, balling up the empty bag and making a jump shot for the trash can across the garage, missing by several feet.

"Nothing. She asked me to meet her at The Rabbit Hole," he said, grabbing the bottle of transmission fluid and pouring it through the opening of the funnel.

"*Nice,*" Jake said with a nod, handing Danny a rag. After a few seconds of silence, he said, "Are you gonna go?"

"No."

"Why the fuck not?"

Danny exhaled heavily as he tossed the empty bottle behind him and grabbed the next one, uncapping it. "You know why not."

"No, I don't," Jake said deliberately. "You already know what my opinion of the whole thing is."

Danny poured the second bottle into the transmission, saying nothing.

"I told you, you should be having as much fun as you can right now. Do whatever you gotta do. Go fuck that girl six ways from Sunday."

Danny laughed, trying to keep his hand steady as he glanced up. "I hope you have a daughter one day."

Jake's face dropped. "Dude, fuck you, that's not even funny."

"Go clean that up," he said, motioning to the crumpled bag of chips on the floor, "and then change the brake pads on the blue Mustang."

"On it," Jake said with a salute before he crossed to the other side of the garage, and Danny watched him go, shaking his head as he tossed the empty bottle into the trash and put the filler cap back on.

It wasn't the first time Jake had given him that piece of advice, but in this case, there was one glaring problem.

He didn't want to fuck her six ways from Sunday.

Well, he *did*, but that wasn't all he wanted. Because the day they had lunch together, he didn't want the meal to end, and that night on the phone, he could have talked to her for hours.

With her it would be more than just a fling, more than some hook-up he used to entertain himself while he still could.

"Yo," Tommy said, coming in from the reception area. "Jake said we're hittin' up The Rabbit Hole tonight?"

Danny closed his eyes and dropped his head.

"Did he now?" *Fucking douche.*

"I just texted Damon. He's on tonight, so we should definitely go."

Danny took a deep breath before he opened his eyes and looked up. "Alright. I'm in," he said, vowing to make Jake wash the shop floor every night for the next year.

"Goddamn, this place is ripe tonight," Jake said, taking a sip of his beer as he scanned the crowd below.

The Rabbit Hole was part club, part bar; on the lower level, there was a large dance floor, with the main bar taking up the entire wall on the right. Surrounding the dance floor on all other sides were a few small tables, and above that—on the second level—were the roped-off VIP areas, each one consisting of a large U-shaped white leather couch with a low table in the center. The middle of the second floor was cut out so that each booth looked down on the dance floor and the main bar.

"So which lucky girl is about to turn you down?" Tommy asked from the booth, and Danny laughed.

"This girl can turn me any way she wants," Jake said. "DeLuca, come look at this."

"I've seen girls before," Danny said, his arm draped over the back of the booth.

"Not like this," Jake said, never taking his eyes from the dance floor.

"Humor him," Tommy said, "or we're gonna be listening to his cheesy-ass double entendres for the next two hours."

Danny rubbed his hand over his eyes before he got up with a sigh. "Ten bucks says I can see her plastic parts from here."

Tommy chuckled as he brought his beer to his lips, and Danny walked the few steps over to the balcony.

"Check her out," Jake said. "The blonde in the orange top."

Danny's eye immediately landed on the bright orange halter that ended halfway down the girl's stomach.

And the indecently large breasts that were bursting out the sides of it.

"Wow," Danny said, rubbing the back of his neck. "She seems... classy."

"She's got the sickest tattoo on her lower back. Watch when she turns around."

But Danny was no longer looking at the blonde with the fake chest. His eye was on the dance floor just to the right of the door.

She was here.

Her arms were over her head as she rolled her hips in time to the beat, her body moving in tantalizing waves as she sang the lyrics to the girl dancing beside her.

Holy. Shit.

"Hot, right?" Jake said.

Danny nodded, having no idea what he'd just said yes to. She was wearing dark jeans that hugged her legs all the way down and a flowing white tank top that was missing a strap on one side. The only part of her body that was exposed was that shoulder, and yet she was a hundred times sexier than the girl Jake was frothing at the mouth over.

"Your girl here yet?" Jake asked from beside him.

Danny shook his head slowly, his eyes still on Leah. "No, not yet."

He'd spent the entire day thinking about it, but he still hadn't decided what he was going to do. He never answered her text earlier, so it wasn't like she was expecting him. If he left without seeing her, she'd never even know he had been there.

And as he watched her swaying her hips provocatively to the pulsing beat, he realized that was probably the best plan of action.

Leah scooped her dark hair back into a ponytail with one hand and fanned herself with the other before she gestured to the girl she was with. The girl nodded, grabbing Leah's hand, and they walked off the dance floor together, approaching another girl who was sitting at the bar. She turned to the girls and said something, and Leah threw her head back and laughed, wrapping one arm around her.

"If she stands you up, it's her loss, man," Jake said before he took down the rest of his beer.

"Thanks," Danny said as he smiled weakly, glancing over at him.

Jake clapped him on the back before he said, "I think I need one more beer in me before I talk to orange halter. You want?"

"I'm good," Danny said, leaning his forearms on the railing and clasping his hands in front of him.

"Alright, I'll be back," Jake said, making his way around Danny and heading for the stairs that would bring him down to the main bar.

Danny wet his lips, allowing his eyes to drift over the lower level of the bar, but every few seconds, they would find their way back to her.

The bartender had just brought the girls a round of shots, and the three of them held their glasses up while the smallest one said something that made the others laugh. They all clinked their glasses before taking the shots, and just as they were lining up the empty glasses along the bar, a guy approached them.

"Oh Jesus." Danny laughed, giving him the once-over. Even from all the way up on the balcony, he could see the meticulously gelled blowout and the blatantly fake tan the guy was sporting. Not to mention the button-down shirt he wore open.

With nothing underneath.

He sidled right up to the smallest friend, reaching out to swipe the hair out of her face as he said something to her, and she jerked backward with a look on her face that had Danny flinching for the guy while fighting laughter.

Without answering, she walked around to the other side of Leah, putting some distance between her and her admirer, who was clearly unfazed by the rejection.

Because he went right for friend number two.

Danny watched the guy put his hand on her shoulder, massaging it creepily as he said whatever line he'd been saving up for her. This girl was a little gentler, it seemed; she kept her expression in check as she held up her left hand, pointing at it with her right.

Danny was too far away, but he assumed she was showing him some type of wedding ring.

"Tough break, pal," he said with a laugh, shaking his head.

The guy took a step back, looking like he was going to admit defeat, but then he turned, smiling at Leah as he said something. She smiled politely back before she turned her attention back to the dance floor, and he moved to her side, resting his elbow on the bar as he leaned close to her ear, saying something else.

Danny's smile dropped.

Her expression was smooth as she answered him, never taking her eyes off the dance floor, and the guy smiled, taking the tiniest step closer to her.

And just like that, Danny's decision was made.

Friends. They could be friends. Friends texted each other.

And friends hung out at bars together.

He turned and walked quickly toward the stairway. She seemed to be handling herself just fine, and she had two girlfriends down there with her, but he didn't give a shit. That douchebag had ignited something visceral in him, and he wanted her by his side tonight.

He rounded the corner after passing the bouncer at the bottom of the stairs, scanning the crowd until he spotted her again.

Jersey Shore was still nestled up beside her, using the noise of the bar as an excuse to lean close to her whenever he spoke. She leaned away just enough to be noticeable, but not enough to be rude, forcing a smile and answering briefly before she looked at her friend and widened her eyes.

Just as Danny approached them, he heard the guy say, "Come on, hon. Let me buy you a drink. You're too pretty not to have a drink in your hand."

Without thinking, Danny snaked his arm around Leah's waist, resting his hand on her hip as he pulled her into his side.

"Thanks, but she's all set," he said.

As the guy's eyes met Danny's, his seductive expression faltered.

"Sorry, bro," he said, holding both hands up in a peace offering before he turned and made his way to the other side of the bar.

Danny watched him until he was far enough away that he knew he wouldn't be coming back, and then he looked down at Leah.

"I hope I didn't just blow that for you. Were you planning on taking My Cousin Vinny home?"

She smiled as she turned her body to face him. Danny kept his hand on her so that when she turned, it traveled along her lower back, coming to rest on her opposite hip.

"Take him home?" she said in horror. "No way. I was probably just gonna bang him in the bathroom and then bail."

Danny laughed loudly, and she grinned, her chin lifted slightly as she looked up at him.

Someone cleared her throat loudly, and Danny turned to see the two girls from before staring pointedly at Leah.

Her expression and posture straightened simultaneously. "Oh, sorry. Guys, this is Danny. Danny, this is Robyn and Holly."

Danny took his hand off Leah's hip and reached out, shaking each of theirs. "Nice to meet you," he said. "Did you guys just order drinks?"

"No, not yet," the little one—Holly—said. "We're waiting for the bartender."

Danny stepped forward and held up his hand, and a second later, Damon glanced up at him from behind the bar. Danny made a wide circle over the girls' heads with his finger before pointing back to himself, and Damon gave him the thumbs-up and then pointed up at the second level.

"That's my friend Damon," Danny said to the girls. "You guys are all set."

"All set?" the one named Robyn asked.

"Yeah, you're on the house tonight."

Danny caught the smile that lifted the corner of Holly's mouth as she elbowed Robyn just before he turned back to Leah. "We have a table up there, if you guys want to come up."

He could still see Holly and Robyn in his peripheral vision, although they clearly didn't know that: Robyn was nodding enthusiastically while mouthing an exaggerated "say yes" at Leah, while Holly gave her the OK sign, looking him over as she mouthed the word "hot." He pressed his lips together, trying to keep a straight face as he waited for her reply.

"Um, yeah, sure," she said before turning her attention to the girls, and as soon as Danny followed suit, both girls immediately straightened their expressions. "You guys want to go upstairs?"

"Sure," Holly said nonchalantly. "Danny, this is so nice of you. Thank you."

"No problem," he said. "Follow me."

Danny led the way to the back stairs, nodding at the bouncer who sat on the stool at the bottom.

"What's up, Dan," he said, gesturing for them to pass. As the girls followed him up the stairs, he added, "Have a good night, ladies."

Danny rounded the corner and made his way toward their booth, and as Tommy saw him approaching, he called out, "Danny boy! Where the hell did you just run off to?"

"I saw a friend. Tommy, this is Leah, and that's Holly and Robyn."

"Welcome, ladies," Tommy said, sliding over to make room, and Holly slid in first, followed by Robyn and then Leah.

When Danny slid in behind her, she smiled wryly. "I had no idea you were such a big shot," she said.

"A big shot?" He laughed. "Hardly. I'm just a lowly mechanic who happens to know the head bartender."

"A humble big shot? Those are the most dangerous kind."

Danny smirked and Tommy said, "I think Damon's sending drinks up. Does he know they're up here?"

"Yeah," Danny said just as Jake approached the table with his beer.

"What do we have here?" he asked, eyeing the girls as he slid in the booth next to Tommy.

"DeLuca," Tommy answered, nodding over at him.

"*All three of them?*" he asked, raising his beer in salute. "Impressive."

Danny leaned down, bringing his lips to Leah's ear. "That's Jake. I apologize in advance for him."

She laughed, leaning in conspiratorially as she nodded toward Holly. "Wait until this one gets going. They'll cancel each other out, and then we'll be even."

Danny smiled as one of the waitresses approached them with a tray of six shots, placing one in front of each person at the table.

"Alabama Slammers all around," she said with a wink before she walked away, and Danny's smile fell.

"Who ordered these?" he asked flatly.

Everyone reached for a shot as if he hadn't spoken, and Danny pushed his to the center of the table.

"I'm good, if anyone wants that."

Tommy lowered his shot, looking at Danny over the top of it. "Bro, you have to take it. It's for Bryan."

The words took the air right out of his body. Danny stared at his friend from across the table, concentrating on taking his next breath.

He had no idea what expression he was wearing, but it must have been something truly special because the color instantly drained from Tommy's face before his eyes flitted away.

He could see that Leah was watching him, and he reached across the table, pulling the shot back as his jaw tensed. His knee began bouncing under the table, and all he really wanted to do in that moment was pick up the glass and throw it against the wall.

From across the table, Jake lifted his shot up high, glancing up at the ceiling before he took it, and that gesture pushed Danny over the edge.

He tossed the shot back before placing the empty glass on the table. "Excuse me," he mumbled before he slid out of the booth and walked toward the stairwell.

Danny quickly pushed his way through the crowd on the lower level, yanking the door open and stumbling out into the frigid January air.

As soon as he was outside, he bent at the waist, bringing his hands to his knees as he dropped his head.

"Tommy, what the fuck," he muttered as he straightened, running both hands down his face.

Why the hell would he have done that?

Because he's Bryan's friend too.

Danny dropped his head back, leaving his hands over his mouth as he blinked up at the sky.

Because he's dealing with it his way.

He closed his eyes, shaking his head. He was such a fucking hypocrite. How could he begrudge someone his method of dealing with everything, when both Tommy and Jake had been nothing but accommodating to him?

And his methods weren't always as diplomatic as ordering a round of drinks.

Just let it go.

He rubbed his hands over his face again before he exhaled.

He really needed to push all this shit aside right now, because he had dragged Leah into his night, and the only thing he should be focusing on was having a good time with her.

Let it go. For one night, just let it go.

With a tiny breath to steel his resolve, he turned and opened the door, reentering the bar. By the time he made his way back upstairs, he could see the empty shot glasses had already been cleared. Tommy looked up, catching his eyes as he approached, and Danny gave him a nod. He nodded in return, holding his hand up in understanding just as Leah's head turned in Danny's direction.

"Hey," she said gently, fiddling with one of her earrings as she looked up at him. "Where'd you go?"

Danny rubbed the back of his neck. "Just needed some air for a minute."

She kept her eyes on him for a moment before she nodded. "Yeah, it's definitely hot in here," she said, scooping her hair off her neck with both hands.

He could tell she didn't buy that story for one second.

And yet she smiled up at him as she released her hair, scooting over a few inches to make room for him in the booth again.

He had no idea how she managed to do that—to erase his discomfort with a simple look. And when he sat down beside her, the remaining tension drained from his body as if her presence alone had siphoned it out of him.

"You need a drink, Leah?" Holly asked.

"Um, yeah. I'll take a margarita."

"Danny, what about you?"

"I'm good, thanks," he said.

He watched Holly and Tommy make their way downstairs before he turned to see Leah watching him.

"You're not gonna get anything?"

"I don't drink."

She lifted her brow. "But you just took a shot."

"Well then, I'm already past my quota."

She laughed then, shaking her head. "I'm glad you came out tonight."

If there was any lingering doubt over his decision to approach her, it dissipated with those six words.

"Me too," he said. "So, did Jake behave himself while I was gone?"

"He asked us what we thought of the girl in the orange halter."

Danny chuckled. "And what did you tell him?"

"*I* didn't tell him anything," she said with a laugh. "Holly said, and I quote, 'It's gonna be an expensive evening for you. First, all the drinks you'll have to buy her, and then the next forty years' worth of Valtrex prescriptions.'"

Danny threw his head back and laughed. "Oh my God," he said when he'd gotten himself under control. "I love her already."

"Yeah, well, she's certainly one of a kind," Leah said with a smile as Holly approached the table with her drink.

"Here you go, chick," she said, handing her the margarita. "Danny, are you sure you don't want anything?"

Before he could answer, Leah said, "Yeah, you're really not gonna have a drink with me?" Danny turned in her direction, his brow lifted, and she shrugged. "Just one drink? You already had a shot."

Danny looked back and forth between them. "I feel like I'm on an after-school special."

Leah laughed as she placed her drink on the table, and he turned back to Holly and Tommy. "Alright, I'll take a beer," he said, and Tommy turned to gesture over the railing.

"There," he said, turning back to Leah. "One drink."

"You make me feel like some sort of depraved villain," she said, bringing her margarita to her lips and licking the salt off the rim where she was about to take a sip.

His eye was immediately drawn to her mouth, and he felt a jolt go through his stomach and straight between his legs.

"So, Leah," Tommy said as he slid back into the booth, and Danny took advantage of the respite to try and regain his composure. "How do you know Danny?"

"Well, long story short, I lost a bracelet the last time I was in the city, and he helped me find it."

"Yeah, sounds like Danny," Jake chimed in. "Did he help you before or after he saved a kitten from a tree and assisted an elderly woman across the street?"

Before Danny could respond, Leah leaned over to him. "He's good," she whispered.

"Who's good?" Danny asked, leaning into their private conversation.

"Jake. He's a good wingman. Make sure you tip him well tonight."

Danny scoffed, looking at her in feigned offense. "If Jake's getting anything from me tonight, it's a foot in his ass. And what do you mean *he's good?* You don't think I'm the kitten-saving, granny-assisting type?"

Leah sat back a little, looking him up and down as she pretended to assess him. "Hmm. I guess I can see it. Although you'd probably frighten the kitten and offend the granny with your horrible language."

"No way. Then I'd have to put money in the jar."

A slow smile lit her face as she looked at him. "If you really have a jar started, I'm pretty pumped. I should have my something pretty by this time tomorrow."

"So little faith," he said, and Leah shrugged.

"Old habits die hard," she replied as she brought her drink to her lips.

He watched her lick the rim again before taking a sip, and he swallowed hard. She looked tempting enough tonight; the absolute last thing he needed was to be six inches away from her while she kept licking that glass.

He pulled his eyes away from her mouth and back up to her face; her normally wavy hair was straight and shiny, and she had some shimmery stuff above her eyes that made them look intensely green. And her mouth—that goddamn mouth. She wasn't wearing any of that goopy, shiny shit that so many girls wore, but they were a soft pink color, and so full he wanted to lean over and bite her bottom lip.

"You look really beautiful tonight," he said before he could stop himself, and he saw the surprise register on her face as she paused mid-sip.

She swallowed, clearing her throat before she smiled shyly. "Thank you."

"So Tommy was telling me how you guys all work together," Holly said.

"Oh really?" Robyn asked. "Where do you guys work?"

They spent the next hour talking and laughing over drinks, and Danny was pleasantly surprised by how at ease Leah seemed to be with his friends; she and Tommy had a quick and easy rapport, and whenever Jake said something horrible, she would just roll her eyes or laugh it off.

And on two separate occasions, both Tommy and Jake gave him the signal that meant Leah earned their seal of approval.

Danny had stopped drinking after the beer he'd ordered to appease Leah, but the rest of them continued to order rounds. Jake was regaling the girls with a story about a belligerent customer who had insisted they'd broken his car when they'd worked on it, and when they took a tow truck out to pick it up, it turned out the guy was just out of gas. In his current state, the animation he put into telling the story had Danny cracking up, despite the fact that he'd heard it a million times.

In the middle of Jake's spot-on imitation of the guy, Danny felt something brush over the back of his hand, and he glanced over at Leah. Her brow was pulled together, her eyes trained on his hand as she ran the tip of her index finger along his knuckles.

Right over his scars.

He jerked his hand back instinctively, and she jolted, yanking her own hand back as her eyes flashed up to his. She brought her hands into her lap as she quickly turned her attention back to Jake, looking like a child who had just been caught doing something wrong.

Danny watched her for a second before he looked back down at his hand. A few of them were merely nicks now; little silvery lines against the tanned skin. But the ones across his knuckles were still bright red lines, jagged and angry.

He wet his lips before he looked back at her. Her eyes were downcast as she picked at her fingernail, and he could see a slight blush coloring her cheeks.

But instead of driving him crazy, this time it made him feel sick.

He watched her fingers fiddling awkwardly under the table, and before he could think about what he was doing, he reached over and placed his hand on top of hers, stilling the movement.

She froze, slowly lifting her eyes back to the conversation as her posture straightened.

"DeLuca, what was it the dude said when we told him he had no gas?" Jake asked through his laughter.

Danny chuckled, using his fingers to turn Leah's hand so that it was palm up beneath his. "He said, 'Well, spank my ass and call me Fudgie.'"

Jake fell forward in hysterics as the entire table cracked up, and Danny looked over to see Leah staring at him. He slid his fingers between hers, clasping their hands together, and even through the raucous laughter around them, he heard her tiny intake of breath.

That little hiccup of a sound did more to him than the touch of any woman he'd ever been with.

His eyes met hers as gave her hand a gentle squeeze, and then he turned his attention back to the table.

"Remember, we were gonna have T-shirts made for the shop that said that on the back," Tommy said through his laughter, and Danny nodded with a smile.

That had actually been Bryan's idea.

Leah gently squeezed Danny's hand before she caressed the scars that peppered his skin, and that little movement sent tiny sizzles of electricity up his arm and through his chest. He closed his eyes for a second before he attempted to refocus on the conversation.

It was such a simple, innocent gesture—holding hands—but there was a significance to it that Danny could not overlook, and coupled with the fact that everyone else at the table was completely oblivious to what was going on just beneath it, it seemed that much more intimate.

She shifted her hand and their thumbs met, circling around each other's slowly.

Okay, he was wrong. He had *thought* holding someone's hand was innocent, but this was so goddamn sensual in its simplicity that it made him want to throw her down on the booth and cover her mouth with his.

You need to get the fuck out of here. Now.

His fingers tightened around hers for just a moment before he cleared his throat and slid his hand out of her grasp.

"Alright, I'm gonna head out," he said as he stood, and Leah's expression dropped slightly as she looked up at him.

Give a reason.

"I have to be at the shop early tomorrow."

"On a Saturday?" Jake asked, cocking his head.

Two years. He'd make him clean the shop floor for two years.

"Yeah," he said, running his hand through his hair. "An old friend of mine wants me to do a rebuild for him, and I promised him I'd get it done in good time." He stared at Jake a little longer than he needed to, hoping he got the message, before he turned to the girls.

"It was so nice to meet you guys," he said, and then he looked at Leah. "I'll talk to you soon?"

She smiled, reaching up to fiddle with her earring again as she nodded.

He turned then, because if he had to look at the poorly shielded disappointment on her face for another second, he would slide right back into that booth and spend the rest of the night doing anything she asked of him.

Danny forced his way through the crowd for the second time that night, only this time, instead of feeling desperate to get to the door, he felt a tug in his chest, demanding that he turn back the way he came.

He pushed the door open, ducking his head against the wind as he jammed in his hands in his pockets.

"Such an asshole," he mumbled to himself, shaking his head. He had no idea why the hell he'd done that. Everything was going perfectly. They were having fun. Friends out at a bar. That was his plan for the night.

And then he had to go and put his hands on her.

He laughed bitterly, running his hand over his eyes.

"Danny!"

His head jerked up as he stopped short, looking over his shoulder.

She was standing just outside the bar, bouncing on the balls of her feet as she wrung her hands together in front of her.

He turned, walking back toward her, and she took a tentative step forward before she picked up speed and met him in the middle.

Her eyes were wide, almost panicky, as she approached him.

"What's wrong?" he asked.

She opened her mouth to speak, but then closed it without saying anything.

"Is everything okay?" he asked.

"Yeah, I'm fine," she said. "I just...I didn't say good-bye to you in there. So I just...wanted to say good-bye."

"Okay," he said with the hint of a smile.

"Okay, so," she looked down, spinning her bracelet over her wrist before glancing back up at him. "Good-bye."

The smile he'd been fighting finally broke as he nodded once. "Good-bye."

She stood there, staring up at him, and he knew if he didn't leave, he was going to do something stupid. Danny turned away from her, freezing when he felt her grip his bicep.

He spun to face her just as she took a step toward him, going up on her toes as she brought her mouth to his.

He froze.

She stilled against him, and for a moment, they just stood there, both struggling to get over the shock of what had just happened. But then her lips softened against his as they parted gently, closing over his bottom one.

He still hadn't moved.

He could feel his heart slamming in his chest, preparing his body for action, but it was as if he no longer had control of his body.

Her mouth parted again, and this time she brushed the tip of her tongue along his bottom lip before she closed hers over it.

It felt like something inside his chest snapped.

Danny grabbed her face in his hands, pulling her mouth to his as he kissed her back. She pressed her body against him, and he slid his hand to the back of her head, knotting his fingers in her hair.

Slow down. Too rough.

But he couldn't stop. Her lips were so fucking perfect and he needed this and she was so beautiful and he couldn't stop.

She moaned lightly against his lips, gripping the back of his shirt and tugging him closer as her tongue entered his mouth, and his hand came to her hip, squeezing it firmly as he tried to keep himself grounded.

Fuck. She was going to make him hard right here on the sidewalk.

As if she had heard him, Leah slowed the kiss down, pulling back slightly before bringing their mouths back together, languidly running her tongue over his.

His hand in her hair went slack as it slid down to caress her neck.

She pressed her hips against him as she caught his bottom lip between her teeth, and his other hand slid around to cup her ass, holding her against his body.

And then his eyes flew open as he pushed her away, taking a quick step back.

She gasped as she stumbled backward, staring up at him with wide eyes.

His breath was coming in short bursts, the white puffs of vapor clouding the image of her standing before him.

And then he whirled around, jamming his fists in his pockets as he stormed off down the sidewalk.

Danny ripped the keys from his pocket and hit the button to unlock his door, trying to make his legs move faster. When he finally reached his car, he yanked the door open and slid inside, starting it before he had closed the door behind him.

He didn't even check for traffic before he pulled out onto the street, hitting the gas and causing the tires to squeal slightly as he took off down the road.

Just before he rounded the corner, he made his final stupid move of the night.

He looked up at his rearview mirror.

The last thing he saw before he made the turn was Leah standing on the sidewalk, her fingertips pressed to her lips as she watched him speed away.

Chapter Nine

One week.

It had been one week since she'd kissed Danny outside The Rabbit Hole. One week since she'd totally put herself out there for the first time in years. One week since the fire coursed through her veins and burned in her belly at the feel of his mouth on hers.

And one week since she'd heard from him at all.

He hadn't called. He hadn't texted. But the most frustrating thing of all was, this time Leah knew it was her fault. After all, she had been the one to push boundaries multiple times that night. *She* had been the one to initiate the touching under the table. *She* had been the one to chase him outside after he'd already said good-bye. And *she* had been the one to initiate that kiss.

She wasn't angry at him; it wasn't his fault if he wasn't interested in her that way. In fact, it was something she had sort of suspected all along. But now she'd made it awkward; he probably wouldn't ever call or text her again for fear he'd be sending her the wrong signals.

Robyn and Holly had been so upset on the drive home, alternating between bouts of silence and strings of apologies for pressuring Leah to go out after him that night. She tried over and over to reassure them, telling them it just meant Danny wasn't into her, and it was probably better she found that out sooner rather than later. This seemed to placate them, and Leah found it somewhat amusing that *she* was the one doing the consoling when she had just made a complete fool of herself in front of a guy she really liked.

At least it provided her with a much needed distraction.

Leah placed her cup of tea on the coffee table before she fell back onto the couch with a sigh, stretching her arms above her head. Her phone buzzed with Holly's ring tone, and she leaned over, swiping it off the coffee table before bringing it to her ear.

"What's up?"

"Hello my love. Are you showered and ready?"

"Showered and ready for…?"

"It's Friday night. Let's go out."

Leah yawned, rubbing the back of her hand over her eyes. "Not tonight."

"Please, Leah? It's the last weekend before Robyn's wedding, and then she'll be gone for two weeks on her honeymoon."

"Okay, so go out with Robyn. We can hang out whenever."

There was a stretch of silence on the other end before Holly exhaled. "Don't go backward, Leah. I don't want you sitting home and moping over him. It's not worth it."

"I'm not moping," Leah said.

She wasn't moping or pouting or fuming or brooding. She wasn't… anything.

"Leah."

"I swear, I'm not moping," she said with a laugh. "I'm just tired. We can hang out tomorrow, okay?"

"Okay," she sighed in acquiescence. "Call me if you change your mind."

"I will."

"Alright. Peace out, baby."

Leah laughed. "Peace out," she said with an eye roll before she ended the call.

After a minute she sat up, grabbing her mug and turning off the television before she made her way down the hall, shutting off the lights as she went. Leah grabbed the book she had just started before she padded into the bathroom and ran herself a bubble bath.

"Exactly. What. I. Needed," she breathed as she submerged herself under the steaming water, placing her book on the edge of the tub as she rested her head back and closed her eyes.

She read until the water chilled, and then she pulled herself lethargically from the bath and drained the tub, throwing on a pair of flannel pajamas and crawling into bed.

The next thing she knew, her eyes flipped open as a shrill sound echoed in her ears. In her disoriented state, she reached for her alarm clock, swatting to turn it off.

She hit the button, but the sound continued.

Leah lifted her head as she slowly gained coherency, realizing it would be Saturday; her alarm wouldn't be set. When it finally registered that her phone was ringing, she bolted upright. The room was pitch dark, and she turned to look at the clock on her nightstand.

One fifty-seven in the morning.

Leah leaned over, sliding her hand along the top of her nightstand and cringing when she heard the clink and subsequent splash that meant she had just knocked over her glass of water.

"*Shit*," she hissed, reaching to turn on the light. By the time she got it on and spotted her phone, it had already gone to voice mail.

She brought the phone to her face, squinting against the offensive light to see who had called.

One missed call from Danny.

Her hand flew to her mouth as she sat there, cursing herself for taking so long to get to the phone. Why was he calling her? And at two in the morning, no less. Should she call him back? Text him? Maybe he was leaving a voice mail?

As she sat there staring at the phone and contemplating her next move, it started ringing again. Her stomach flipped as she saw the words flashing on the screen.

Incoming call from Danny.

She tapped the screen before bringing it to her ear.

"Hello?" she said softly.

"Leah," he said, sighing heavily into the phone. "God, I don't even know what to say."

She pulled her brow together as she sat up further, running her hand through her hair. His voice sounded strange.

"Danny? What's going on? Is everything okay?"

"No. I want it to be okay, but I don't know what to do anymore. And I'm sorry I kissed you, but I'm not sorry, you know? I just…I wish you knew. God, I wish you already knew, because I don't wanna have to say it."

"Wish I knew what?" she asked. "Danny, what are you talking about?"

He sighed softly. "You have no idea how much I want to see you right now, but he took my keys, and this is bullshit because I'm fucking fine."

Leah closed her eyes as she pinched the bridge of her nose. Because she realized then why his voice sounded so odd, why he'd called her at two in the morning.

He was completely wasted.

She sighed heavily before switching the phone to her other ear. "Who took your keys?"

"Joe."

"Who's Joe?"

"Bartender," he said. "But I'm fine. He knows I'm fine! Goddamn it, I just want to go home."

Behind his drunken slur, there was an unmistakable desperation in his voice.

Something was wrong.

Plus, hadn't he just told her last weekend that he didn't drink? And here he was, absolutely hammered.

"Where are Tommy and Jake?"

"Not here."

Leah's eyes widened. "*They left you alone like this?*"

"I just don't know what to do anymore. About anything," he said dejectedly, his words running together. "All I wanna do is go home."

"Where are you?" she asked, swinging her legs over the side of the bed.

"Outside."

She huffed heavily, rolling her eyes. "Outside where?"

He didn't respond, but she could hear a rustling sound, like he was walking quickly.

"Danny, you have to tell me where you are."

"McGillicuddy's."

"Okay, where is that?"

"Valhalla," he said, and the despondency was gone from his voice, leaving him sounding oddly detached.

Leah dropped her head back, blinking up at the ceiling before she sighed heavily. "Alright, you need to go inside, okay? I'm coming to get you, but I don't want you to go anywhere else." She slid off the bed and pulled a pair of yoga pants and a sweatshirt out of her drawer.

"Leah?"

"Yeah?" she said, stepping out of her pajama bottoms.

"I don't deserve this. I just really need you to know that, okay?"

She froze with one leg in her yoga pants. What the hell was he talking about? His keys being taken? Her coming out to pick him up? Or something else entirely?

Either way, his words were dripping with misery again, and she quickly pulled her pants on as she held the phone with her shoulder.

"I'm leaving right now. Just go back in the bar, alright? Don't go anywhere."

"Yeah, alright," he said distractedly before ending the call, and Leah tossed her phone on the bed as she pulled off her pajama top and threw on the sweatshirt. She combed through her hair with her fingers as she sat on the end of her bed, doing a Google Map search of McGillicuddy's in Valhalla. The directions said the trip would take twenty minutes, but at this time of night, with no traffic, she could probably make there in ten.

Ignoring the little voice in her head that told her she was crazy for doing this, she scooped up her keys and purse and walked out of her bedroom.

If nothing else, Danny had become a friend of hers, and she would do this for any one of her friends, she told herself as she locked up the apartment and made her way down to the car.

Besides, there was something in his voice, something in the fraught way he spoke that caused a knot in her stomach. He needed help, and he had called *her*. It didn't matter what had happened between them last weekend. After all, what kind of a person would put her own ego before helping someone in need?

Leah made it to the bar in just under fifteen minutes, pulling up to the curb right out front. She didn't really know the area and wasn't thrilled about walking around alone this time of night, so she hoped getting him to leave would be quick and painless.

She exited the car and pulled her hands into her sleeves, wrapping her arms around herself as she approached the bar.

Behind the impressive oak door, McGillicuddy's was nothing but a dive bar; a few random patrons sat scattered about rickety wooden tables, and Leah's heart rate kicked up a notch as she scanned the area, not seeing him.

Just as she was about to take out her phone and try to call him, she spotted him at the far end of the bar by himself. His head was down, his elbows resting on the bar as he spun a half-empty drink in his hand, and Leah frowned.

Why would they have served him again? The bartender took his keys, but gave him another drink?

Leah walked briskly toward the back of the bar, glaring at the bartender as she passed. When Danny heard her approaching, he lifted his head. "Leah?"

She put her hands on her hips. "Danny."

He blinked at her, stunned. "You're here?"

Jesus, does he not even remember calling?

"Yes, I'm here. Come on. You're going home," she said, taking the drink from his hand and placing it on the bar. She realized a beat too late that perhaps it wasn't the best idea; she had no idea what kind of drunk he was, whether he would get angry or belligerent if she took his drink away.

But instead he slunk out of the chair, sliding his arms around her waist and pulling her against him. She brought her hands up to his biceps to brace herself, and he buried his face in her hair as he inhaled deeply. "You're here," he said again, and this time it sounded like a prayer.

Leah stood frozen for a moment before she closed her eyes.

He's drunk. He has no idea what he's doing. He doesn't even remember calling you. Just get him home.

"Okay, come on," she said, using her hands on his biceps to push him away gently. He held her firmly for another second before he relented, releasing his hold on her and taking a step backward. Leah slid her hand down his arm before timidly wrapping her hand around his wrist to keep him next to her while she leaned over the bar.

"Excuse me?" she said, and the bartender looked up. "Can I have his keys?"

The bartender shook his head, his expression never changing as he went back to drying glasses and stacking them. "I don't have his keys."

"Okay, well is Joe still working?"

The bartender chuckled as he slung the rag over his shoulder. "Sweetheart, either you've had a little too much to drink, or you're at the wrong bar. There's no Joe that works here."

Leah stared blankly at him before she turned to Danny. "Where's Joe? Where's the guy who has your keys?"

He dropped his head, resting his forehead on her shoulder as he fisted the side of her sweatshirt. "The other bar," he mumbled, and Leah closed her eyes, sighing heavily.

At least now she knew why he'd been served. This wasn't the place that had cut him off. The only good news was that she knew he hadn't driven to McGillicuddy's, so the other bar had to be within drunken walking distance.

"Excuse me?" Leah said, leaning over the bar again, and the guy glanced up, a condescending expression on his face. "Is there another bar near here?"

"Across the street," he said, as he turned to lift a bin of glasses from the floor.

"Thanks," she said before she turned her attention back to Danny, sliding her fingers under his chin and lifting his head. He opened his eyes, smiling softly as he focused on her face.

"Come on. I need you to walk with me," she said, wrapping her arm around his waist. She had no idea how she was going to hold him if he couldn't walk, but as she took a step, thankfully he followed.

"Get home safe," the bartender said as they passed, and she held her hand up behind her in acknowledgement. As they exited the bar, Leah's eyes scanned the opposite street until she located a tiny pub called The Alley.

"There?" she asked, and Danny shrugged.

"Sure."

Leah shook her head. "No, I'm not asking if you *want* to go there... ugh, just forget it. Let's go," she said, pulling him across the street.

As they entered the bar, the guy standing behind the tap turned to look at them. "You here for his keys?" he asked, and Leah nodded.

"Yeah, sorry about this," she said.

"Don't you apologize," Danny murmured into her hair. "You have nothing to be sorry for." He pressed his lips to the crown of her head, and Leah squeezed her eyes shut, trying to ignore the fluttering in her stomach that the intimate gesture invoked.

He's drunk. He's drunk. He's completely oblivious and drunk.

The bartender fished under the bar and came up with Danny's keys, handing them to Leah.

"Thanks for looking out for him," she said as she turned them toward the exit, and the guy nodded, giving her a flimsy salute.

Once they were back out on the street, Danny began leaning a bit more of his weight on her, and she wrapped both arms around his waist, trying to steady him. "Just a little farther, okay? My car is right there."

"Where's my car?" he asked, and Leah shook her head.

"You're not driving tonight. Please don't argue, okay? I have your keys. You can come back and get your car tomorrow."

He leaned down, pressing his lips to the top of her head again. "I would never tell you no," he said into her hair. "But you already know that, don't you?"

She gritted her teeth together, trying to focus on getting them across the street. Right foot, left foot. Right foot, left foot. Not his breath in her hair, or his hands on her body, or those words on his lips. Right foot, left foot.

She managed to help him into the passenger side, and as she walked around the back of the car, she saw him fall forward, burying his face in his hands as he rested on the dashboard. She stopped short, biting her lower lip as she looked in the back seat for a plastic bag, or a container of some type.

She hadn't even thought about the possibility of him getting sick.

Leah rubbed her hand over her forehead before she slid into the driver's seat and closed the door, and she placed her hand on his lower back, rubbing soothing circles.

"Do you feel sick?"

He shook his head.

"If you need me to pull over, just tell me, okay?"

He nodded.

She took a breath as she dropped her hand from his back. "Alright," she said as she exhaled. "Where do you live?"

"In my apartment," he mumbled into the dashboard.

"That's helpful, Danny," she sighed, looking around the car. She noticed the outline of his wallet through the back pocket of his pants, and Leah bit her lip before she reached over and slid her hand into his pocket, removing the wallet.

"Leah," he groaned. "What are you doing to me?"

"I need your ID so I can get your address. Just shush, okay?"

She quickly typed his address into her phone's GPS before folding his wallet and dropping it into her cup holder, and just as she pulled out onto the street, he fell back against the seat, his hands falling limply into his lap.

"A year. Can you believe it? How could it be a year?"

"What's a year?" she asked softly.

He dragged his hands down his face before he exhaled heavily. *"What the fuck was I thinking?"* he yelled, causing Leah to jump, and she glanced over at him, blinking quickly.

"I wasn't thinking, you know? I just...I wasn't. But what was I supposed to do?" he said, his voice softening significantly. "What was I supposed to do?"

He covered his face with his hands as he rested his forehead on the dash again, and then he slammed his fist down on top of it. "What was I supposed to do?" he asked again, and Leah's stomach twisted.

She had not the slightest idea what he was talking about, but there was so much pain in his voice that she felt like she might cry.

She knew what that kind of suffering felt like.

Leah took a tiny breath as she reached over and resumed rubbing circles on the small of his back.

"And then you," he mumbled against the dashboard.

She held her breath, waiting for him to continue, but he never did. He didn't speak again for the remainder of the drive, and Leah kept her hand on his back, trying to soothe him. It wasn't until she pulled up to the curb in front of his building that she realized she might have a huge problem on her hands. If he had passed out, based on how drunk he was, there'd be no waking him up. If that were the case, she had no idea how she would get him out of the car and up the stairs.

Leah cut the engine, looking over at him. She watched his back expand and contract with every breath, but he still hadn't moved.

"Danny?" she said softly, and to her surprise, he turned his head to look at her. He blinked a few times, his eyes bleary and unfocused as he tried to sit up.

"Hey, it's okay," she said as she leaned over and ran her hand through his hair, and he closed his eyes. "You're home. Let's get upstairs, okay?"

He nodded wearily, and she exited the car and came around to his side, helping him out onto the sidewalk. He was leaning most of his weight on her as they walked into the lobby, and as they stood waiting for the elevator, Leah's legs began to tremble with the task.

You're almost there. Hang in there.

Danny rested his chin on the top of her head as he ran his hand over the back of her hair. "You're so good, Leah," he sighed.

She smiled softly as the doors dinged open, and she managed to get them both inside before the doors closed, leaning them up against the wall. He rested his head on top of hers again, and she could see in the reflection of the doors that his eyes were closed.

She could tell he was close to passing out, and Leah glanced at the numbers lighting up above their heads, willing them to go faster.

As soon as the doors opened, she stood up, pulling him to a standing position as she rubbed her hand up and down his side. "Come on, Danny. Almost there, okay?"

By now she was using all her strength just to keep him steady as they stumbled down the hallway toward his door. She had his keys in her hand, and she opened the door quickly before tossing them somewhere on the floor. She needed both arms to help him now, and every muscle in her body strained with the effort.

Leah glanced around the small space quickly, noticing two doorways off the living room. Assuming that his bedroom had to be one of them, she began walking them in that direction.

"Come on. A few more steps," she said, her voice strained as they tripped and staggered across the living room, and when she turned them into the first doorway and saw his bed, she thought she might cry with relief.

Leah gave him a gentle shove and he lurched forward before falling back onto the mattress with a groan, his eyes already closed.

"Holy shit," she said to herself, rolling her neck as she leaned up against the wall to catch her breath.

She stared at him, his chest rising and falling with his arms splayed out at his sides, and that's when she noticed what he was wearing: a dark blue button-down, black slacks, and a belt. She glanced down at the black dress shoes still on his feet and sighed, walking the few steps over to the bed before kneeling down.

Leah undid his laces and removed his shoes, placing them up against the far wall so he wouldn't trip over them if he got out of bed for any reason tonight.

Okay, that was the easy part.

She stood at the foot of his bed, her hands on her hips as she looked him over.

It would be like seeing him in a bathing suit. It's not a big deal.

With a deep breath to strengthen her resolve, she climbed up onto the bed and sat on her heels at his side. Just as she brought her fingers to the buckle on his belt, she felt his hand slide up her thigh, coming to rest more than halfway up.

Her breath caught in her throat.

"I lied to you," he said hoarsely, his eyes still closed.

"About what?" she whispered, her fingers still frozen on his belt buckle.

He laughed lightly, but his face contorted in disgust. "So many things."

She didn't want to be affected by him anymore, but she felt her heart drop at his words.

He lied to her?

Leah shook her head quickly. It didn't matter. None of it mattered. He didn't want her, and they weren't anything to each other. She was just going to make sure he was comfortable, and then she was going to get the hell out of there.

With renewed purpose, she undid the belt buckle, followed by the button on his slacks. Leah gripped the zipper with the ends of her nails, trying to avoid any contact as she slid it down. His hand rode a bit further up her thigh, his thumb beginning to make soft, sensuous passes over the thin material of her pants, and as Leah moved from the bed, his hand slipped from her leg and slapped down onto the mattress. She stood beside him and leaned over, hooking her fingers in the waistband of his pants.

"I lied to you about lunch," he mumbled.

Before she could even decide if she would play into this or not, he went on. "I wasn't meeting a friend."

Leah pursed her lips as her stomach churned. She didn't want to hear the rest. Instead, she gripped the top of his pants and yanked somewhat forcefully. They jerked over his hips, and she immediately pressed her lips into a hard line as she closed her eyes.

Boxer briefs. Tight, gray boxer briefs.

She exhaled slowly and opened her eyes, tugging his pants the rest of the way down and removing the belt before she folded them and draped them over a nearby chair. She came back to the bed and climbed on, dutifully keeping her eyes above his waist as she started undoing the buttons of his shirt.

His hands came up and grasped hers, stilling her movements as his eyes fluttered partially open.

"I wasn't meeting a friend. I wasn't meeting anyone. I lied because I wanted to see you."

The breath left her body in a soft rush. She had not been expecting *that.*

"Oh," she managed softly, but her voice was so quiet, she doubted he heard her.

He rubbed his thumbs over the backs of her hands as his eyes fell closed again. "It was stupid, you know? I didn't even know you," he mumbled groggily. "But I kept thinking about you. I saw you at Gram's, and I kept thinking about you, and I didn't even fucking know you."

Leah gently slid her hands out of his grasp as she tried to refocus on undoing his buttons, but she could feel her heartbeat kick up in her chest.

"I had no right to ask you out," he said with a slight shake of his head. "So I bullshitted you. I bullshitted myself, and I pretended we were just meeting so you could get your bracelet. And then I saw you, and I didn't want you to leave."

He was ranting, the words spilling from his mouth like an avalanche, and part of her wanted to stop him. She didn't want to hear this. Because if what he was saying was true, why did he leave her the way he did last weekend? Why had he spent the past week pretending she didn't exist?

His hand slid up her thigh again, and Leah ignored it, focusing all her attention on undoing the buttons.

"So I made you have lunch with me," he muttered. "And you know what? I was kind of hoping I'd hate you. It would have been so much easier if you were a bitch, or an idiot, or someone who annoyed the shit out of me. 'Cause then I could have just put this shit to bed."

His hand left her thigh as he brought it up to his face, rubbing his eyes roughly before he let it fall back to the bed with a slap.

"But of course you weren't any of those things," he said with another humorless laugh. "You were smart, and sweet...and fucking beautiful," he added, clasping both of her hands in his again.

She slipped them out of his grasp. "Danny, don't."

He smiled softly. "I figured we could just be friends, you know?" His voice was low and throaty as he added, "No harm in that, right?" He shook his head as he pressed the heels of his hands into his eyes before running them up through his hair. His eyes flew open, but they were bleary and unfocused. "But every time I talk to you, I like you more and more, and every time I see you....it's so fucking hard, Leah."

She sat there, unmoving, her fingers poised over one of the buttons as she tried to make sense of his words.

"*And that kiss,*" he said, covering his face with both hands as he groaned. "My God, that fucking kiss."

Her heart was thundering in her chest now; there were a million questions she wanted to ask, but she couldn't formulate them into words.

"And I can't see you," he said firmly, dropping his hands to the bed as he shook his head. "I can't. It's not fair to you. Shit, it's not even fair to me."

Why? Why isn't it fair?

But the words wouldn't come.

"I just wish…God, I wish…" He trailed off as what could only be described as agony clouded his expression, and Leah felt a lump form in her throat.

"Shh," she said, leaning over to run her hand through his hair, and his eyes fell closed. "Just close your eyes. You're okay. You'll feel better when you wake up."

She sat there for a minute, gently running her hand through his hair until his brow smoothed out and his body relaxed.

Her mind was reeling; none of what he'd said made any sense, and yet she knew he had just given her a huge piece of the puzzle that was him. She just needed to sit down and piece it together.

But not now. Right now, she just wanted to go home.

Leah brought her hands back to his shirt, undoing the remaining buttons before gently sliding it off his body and draping it over the chair with his pants. He was wearing a fitted white V-neck shirt underneath the button-down, and she left it on, figuring that was about as comfortable as he was going to get.

Water. Get him some water.

She made her way through the living room and over to the tiny kitchen, opening his fridge and grabbing a bottle of water. As she walked back to his room, she stopped in the bathroom and grabbed the small wastebasket.

He was sitting up when she entered, his face contorted in sadness as he stared without seeing at the wall in front of him.

"Hey," Leah said softly as she sat on the bed beside him.

He didn't move.

"Hey," she said again, bringing her hand to his face and turning him toward her. It took his eyes a second to focus on her, and when they did, he smiled sadly. He reached up and took the end of her hair between his fingertips.

"You're gonna leave," he whispered.

His words made her chest feel heavy, and Leah closed her eyes, needing a break from the intensity of the night. She had no idea why she was responding so viscerally to his suffering, but in that moment, all she wanted to do was take it away for him.

"No, I won't," she said softly. "I'll stay here if you want me to."

Danny shook his head as his eyes dropped to watch his fingers twirling a strand of her hair. "You're gonna leave and never look back."

She pulled her brow together, waiting for him to go on, but he simply sat there, running his fingers through the ends of her hair.

Leah brought her hand back to the side of his face, and he lifted his gaze. "I'm gonna stay tonight. I'll be in the next room if you need me. There's a pail on the side of the bed," she said, leaning over and dragging it closer. "And here," she added, uncapping the bottle of water and holding it out for him.

He looked down at the bottle and then back up at her, his expression softening.

"It might help a little. For tomorrow," she said with a shrug.

Danny stared at her for a second before reaching for the bottle, taking three long gulps before wiping the back of his hand across his mouth.

"Okay, you need to lie down now," she said, taking the bottle from his hand, and just as she was about to stand from the bed, he brought both of his hands to the sides of her face, his fingers sliding behind her ears as his thumbs caressed her cheeks.

Leah froze, lifting her eyes to his, and for the first time that night, they seemed completely at peace.

"My sweet girl," he whispered, and then his lips were on hers.

Compared to the explosiveness of their last kiss, this was a slow burn; Danny kissed her reverently, the gentle brushing of his lips igniting every nerve ending in her body before he pulled away slightly, turning his head faintly from side to side as he ghosted his lips over hers.

And then he lay back onto the mattress, his hands slipping from her face as he threw his forearm over his eyes.

Leah brought both hands to the bed as she closed her eyes, exhaling a long, quivering breath.

Holy. Shit.

She had no idea how long she sat there trying to pull herself back together, but eventually she stood, grabbing the comforter at the foot of the bed and pulling it up over him.

He didn't move, and Leah exhaled in relief; he was finally asleep.

She walked around to the other side of the bed and pulled the trash can a bit closer to him as she placed his bottle of water on the bedside table.

"Good night, Danny," she whispered before she made her way out to the living room.

She stood in the middle of the room, contemplating her options. Driving home at nearly four in the morning wasn't really something she was looking forward to. Plus, she *had* told him she would stay the night.

Although chances were, he wasn't going to remember that.

Leah's eyes moved from the front door to the couch, where a large afghan was draped over the back of the cushions.

"Oh, screw it," she mumbled, walking to his front door and locking it before she picked up his keys from the floor and placed them on the little table in the entryway. She went back to the living room and kicked off her shoes as she grabbed one of the throw pillows and propped it against the arm of the couch.

It was more comfortable than she thought it would be, and she reached up and grabbed the afghan, flipping onto her side as she curled herself into it.

Her body was completely exhausted, but her mind was on overdrive. She wanted so badly to make sense of everything that had just happened. She wanted to know what had caused him to drink so heavily. She wanted to know why he was trying so hard to stay away from her if he was attracted to her. She wanted to analyze his words, his actions, until she could rid herself of the confusion and apprehension coursing through her body.

She wanted to think about all of that, but the only thing her mind would focus on was that kiss, and the look in his eyes as he called her his sweet girl.

And so eventually she stopped trying to think of anything else and surrendered, replaying that moment over and over, letting it lull her to sleep.

Leah opened her eyes to the unnerving, disoriented feeling of waking up in a strange place. As soon as she remembered where she was and why, she bolted upright on the couch, swiping the hair from her eyes as she looked around.

The clock on the cable box said eleven forty-six.

"Jesus," she mumbled, rubbing her eyes before she stood from the couch and threw the afghan over the back of it again. After placing the throw pillow back where it belonged, she sat on the arm of the couch, chewing on her bottom lip as details of the night came flooding back to her.

Danny, completely wasted and clearly upset in her car. Danny's lips in her hair. *I lied to you. About so many things.* His hands clasping hers as he told her he couldn't be with her. That it wouldn't be fair to either of them. *My sweet girl.* That soft, chaste kiss that once again left her reeling.

Leah ran her hands down her face as she exhaled, and then she stood from the couch and padded over to the doorway of his bedroom. She leaned against the doorframe, folding her arms over her chest as she looked at him.

He was lying on his stomach with his head turned away from her, his arms up at his sides and his hands shoved under the pillow. Leah noticed that the bottle of water on the nightstand was empty, and she tiptoed over to the pail, cringing as she peeked inside.

All clear.

Her shoulders dropped in relief, and she watched the rise and fall of his back for another minute before she left his bedroom.

Leah went to the bathroom and splashed cold water on her face, using some toothpaste on her finger to brush her teeth as best she could.

When she was through, she walked back out to the living room and stood in the center of it.

She didn't know what she should do.

She didn't want to just leave without talking to him about everything, but she knew he needed sleep right now. She couldn't hang around his apartment all day waiting for him to wake up, and even if she could, trying to have a serious conversation with someone who was hung over was just a bad idea, plain and simple.

But she did need to talk to him. She needed to make sense of everything once and for all, because as much as he'd told her last night, so much was still left unsaid. If anything, Leah felt more confused than she was before he confessed his feelings to her.

Go home. Call him tomorrow, after he's had some time to recover.

With a plan in place, Leah felt a little better as she stepped into her shoes and scanned the apartment once more. She knew he would be hurting when he woke up, whenever that was, so she tried to anticipate anything he might need. She went to the fridge and got another bottle of water, quietly placing it on his nightstand as she grabbed the empty one.

As Leah tossed the bottle in the trash, her eye landed on his coffee maker, and she decided she would set up a pot of coffee for him before she left.

She opened a few cabinets, finding the coffee on the third try, and just as she brought it to the counter and popped off the lid, she gasped.

Realization washed over her, bringing a rush of nausea with it as the puzzle pieces clicked into place.

How could she not have seen it earlier?

"I had no right to ask you out."

"I can't see you. It's not fair to you."

"I lied to you."

And then, something he had said to her a while back:

"I don't have a girlfriend, if that's what you're getting at."

Leah stood there unmoving, the lid of the coffee still in her hand.

It was so *obvious.*

How close had she come to being the other woman? There was some girl out there who was with Danny, who maybe even loved him, completely oblivious to their phone calls, their texting, their kisses.

Oh my God, I kissed him. I kissed another girl's boyfriend.

Her heart started racing, and she felt as if she might be sick. This was all hitting far too close to home for her, and she knew she needed to get out of there.

Immediately.

With trembling hands Leah snapped the lid back on the coffee and turned, gasping loudly as the can slipped from her fingers and crashed at her feet. The top popped off, spraying coffee grounds across the floor.

Danny stood in the doorway, his arms stretched above his head as he gripped the frame. The way his arms were lifted caused his T-shirt to ride up, revealing the faint trail of hair that disappeared beneath the waistband of the flannel pajama bottoms he had put on. His hair was a rumpled mess, and his eyes were squinted against the light.

He looked at her, the corner of his mouth lifting in a smile as he brought one of his hands down and touched his finger to his nose.

"Not it for cleaning that up," he said, his voice husky with sleep.

"Do you have a girlfriend?"

Confusion instantly marred the playful look on his face, and he took his finger off his nose and slid his hand up into his hair. She didn't plan on blurting it out that way, but she couldn't stand this any longer.

"No," he said. "I already told you I didn't."

"You also told me you lied to me."

Danny's eyes fell closed as he shook his head gently, and then he dropped his head back, covering his face with both hands. "Fuck," he said, his voice muffled behind them. He slid them down his face before he met her eyes again. "What did I tell you last night?"

"Do. You. Have. A. Girlfriend?" she asked, her voice livid. "Yes or no?"

"No. I swear to you, Leah. No, I don't."

She stared at him and he stared right back, never breaking eye contact. He seemed completely sincere, which ironically only made things worse, because now she was more confused than ever.

"What did you lie to me about, then?" she asked.

"Nothing."

She laughed bitterly, shaking her head. "I can't do this. I can't play these games." She walked toward him and twisted her body, squeezing between him and the doorframe before she stormed into the living room and grabbed her purse. She turned and came to an abrupt halt, nearly walking right into his chest. Danny reached out and steadied her, gently grasping the tops of her arms.

"Leah, please," he said, and she shook her head, refusing to make eye contact.

"I can't take lying, Danny. It's the *one thing* I can't take." She went to step around him, and his grip on her arms tightened.

"Please. Can you just let me explain?"

Leah closed her eyes, exhaling softly. Part of her just wanted to distance herself from the whole situation as soon as possible, but the other part of her desperately wanted to hear what he had to say. If she left now, she knew a piece of her would always wonder if she'd made the right decision, and in a way, she was almost more afraid of that than of being vulnerable with him.

She opened her eyes, keeping them trained on the floor, but she nodded slightly, and Danny exhaled as she felt his grip on her arms loosen.

She turned her back on him, walking over to the couch and taking a seat, and he sat on the coffee table in front of her, leaning forward and resting his elbows on his knees. He dropped his head and took a deep breath before he lifted his eyes back to hers.

"First of all, thank you for taking care of me last night. I'm sorry you had to deal with me like that."

"Don't apologize for that. I didn't mind taking care of you. That's not why I'm upset."

He nodded gently as he wet his lips. "I just...I want to make this better, but I don't even know what I said to you last night."

She sat up a bit straighter, running both hands through her hair. This was it. She was going to put it all on the line, and hope he would do the same in return.

"Look," she said. "I don't want to play games with you. You're always so back and forth, and I don't like that I never know what to expect from you."

He pulled his brow together before dropping his eyes to the floor, and Leah chewed on the corner of her lip, summoning the courage to say the rest.

"I mean, can we just be real with each other? I like you. I really do. And if you don't or you can't feel the same way, for whatever reason, then just tell me."

He lifted his eyes back to hers, a defeated expression on his face. "I *do* like you, Leah. A lot. That's the problem."

"Why is that a problem?"

Danny looked down again, shaking his head slightly. She waited for him to speak for nearly a minute before she broke the silence, trying her luck with a different question.

"What did you lie to me about?"

He sat up, gripping the edge of the coffee table. "I never lied to you. Everything I've told you about myself is true. It's just...there are things I haven't told you."

"Lies of omission, then."

Danny looked up to the ceiling, inhaling deeply. "It's not lying. It's just...not sharing everything." His eyes met hers as he said, "You've done it too."

"What are you talking about? What haven't I told you?"

Danny shrugged. "Lots of things, I'm sure. What happened to your mom, for instance."

Leah pursed her lips as his point hit home. There were things he didn't know about her either. Things she chose not to share. How could she condemn him for something she herself had done?

"Okay," she said, kicking her shoes off before sitting cross-legged on the couch. Leah pulled the throw pillow onto her lap as she said, "She died in a car accident. Some guy was driving drunk and came over the divider. Hit her head on."

Danny closed his eyes and shook his head slightly. "I'm sorry," he said softly. "Recently?"

"About fifteen years ago."

The room fell silent, and Leah kept her eyes on the throw pillow as she picked at a fraying thread. After a few seconds, she saw him lean forward, and she looked up to see him resting his elbows on his knees, his hands clasped in front of his mouth.

"Does it get easier?" he asked.

The second the words left his mouth, something passed between them, and she smiled sadly. "In some ways yes, and in others, not even remotely."

He nodded, his eyes dropping to watch her fingers play with the loose thread on the pillow.

"Who did you lose?"

He swallowed hard, and it was a moment before he said, "My best friend."

"Bryan?" she asked, and his eyes flashed to hers as he straightened abruptly.

"How did you know that?"

She shrugged. "It was just a guess. The round of shots at the bar. Tommy said they were for Bryan, and you seemed to get upset."

Danny took a breath, his shoulders relaxing before he nodded. "Yeah. Bryan."

The room fell silent again, and Danny scooted forward, finding a frayed string on the other side of the pillow and mimicking Leah's actions.

"How long ago?" she asked, pretty sure she already knew the answer.

"Yesterday was a year."

Leah nodded. They both knew he didn't need to say anything else, and it was a moment before he spoke the words that were like a slap to her face. "He was Catherine's grandson."

Her head snapped up, and unexpectedly, her eyes filled with tears. She had no idea why that affected her the way it did, but the idea of that woman burying her grandson absolutely crushed her. An image of Catherine flashed in her mind: the oversized jacket, the big bulky gloves, the man's ring hanging from a chain on her neck.

Was it possible those things were Bryan's?

She closed her eyes, forcing a tear to spill over, and before she could react, she felt the pad of his thumb brush under her eye, sweeping it away.

Leah opened her eyes and looked at him; he had the most tender expression on his face, and she suddenly realized how backward it was, that *he* was comforting *her* over the death of his friend. She reached up and took his hand, sandwiching it between both of hers as she brought them to rest on the pillow in her lap.

"What happened to him?" she asked, running her thumbs over the back of his hand.

Danny wet his lips and looked down. "Head injury."

That was incredibly vague, but Leah knew enough not to push the issue. Instead, she kept running her thumbs over the rough, damaged skin of his knuckles.

"That's why I got so freaked over the flowers," he said, and her thumbs stopped abruptly as she looked up.

"Why did that make you so mad?"

He shook his head with a sigh. "I wasn't mad. It's just...she keeps those things all over the house because when we were little, Bryan used to pick them from other people's gardens and bring them home to her." He laughed lightly. "She kept telling him that it was stealing and that it wasn't a nice thing to do, but he could never understand how bringing his grandmother flowers was a bad thing. And she always put them in water. Always. Even after lecturing him about stealing, she'd put them up in a vase. Every fucking time."

He looked down, a smile on his face as he shook his head at the memory. "When you sent them, it just freaked me out. I didn't know how you knew to get those for her. I didn't even think about the possibility that you'd seen them in her house." He lifted his eyes to her face. "I'm sorry about that, by the way. That was so shitty of me."

She shook her head. "It's fine."

It was quiet as they sat there, his hand in both of hers.

"Losing Bryan," she finally said, and he looked up at her. "That's not the reason you keep pulling away from me."

He pulled his hand from hers and Leah straightened, instantly lamenting the loss. Danny gripped the edge of the table and closed his eyes. "I don't know how to explain this to you."

"Just say it. Whatever it is, just say it."

He sat completely still for a moment before he pushed off the table with a huff, walking around to the other side. He stood there, blinking up at the ceiling with his hands clasped on top of his head. "Fuck...I just..." He let his hands fall, shaking his head before he looked back at her.

It hurt to watch the struggle on his face. She could see that he wanted to tell her, but fear, or embarrassment, or both, were stopping the words in his throat, and she had no idea how to make it easier for him.

Tell him something. Something about you. Something you're not proud of.

"You want to hear something awful?" Leah said gently, and Danny stopped pacing as he looked at her. "About two years ago, my father had a heart attack."

She twirled the loose thread around the tip of her finger until she felt it ache with the cut-off circulation.

Tell him. Tell him something you're ashamed of, so he knows it's okay.

Leah exhaled. "Before that night I hadn't spoken to him for a year."

She stared at the throw pillow on her lap until it was a mass of jumbled colors before her eyes, and she felt the couch dip under his weight as he sat beside her.

"Why?" he asked softly, reaching over and pulling the thread until it unraveled from her finger.

She curled and uncurled her aching finger as she shook her head sadly. "You have to understand something, Danny. After my mom died,

I did my best to take on her role. I mean, there I was—twelve years old—cooking dinners and doing laundry, making sure my little sister took her bath, reminding my father of doctor's appointments."

She turned her head to see that he was watching her intently. "Nobody asked me to do it. I wanted to. I wanted our family to be normal again, and a normal family needs a mother."

Leah looked back down, playing with the same thread on the pillow. "Everyone relied on me, you know? My dad was so frazzled for a while after, and he couldn't do it all on his own. So I stepped up. I was basically a really young mother. Or a really old teenager, however you want to look at it," she said with a tiny laugh, and then she lifted her head, looking at him. "But I never felt like I was losing anything, you know? I had good friends. I played sports. I never felt like I'd given anything up. I loved my family. I *wanted* to take care of them."

Danny reached over, swiping a stray hair away from her face, and instinctively she leaned into his touch.

"Everything was fine until I went away to college. I mean, you would think I would have been good at being independent, right? But I was miserable. I felt *so* guilty being away from them that I couldn't enjoy any of it.

"So after the first semester, I came home and enrolled in a local college. My father didn't ask any questions; he just welcomed me back with open arms, and everything went back to the way it was before."

Danny was watching her carefully as she spoke, but she could see in his face that he was confused; that he didn't understand how any of this fit in with her being estranged from her father.

Here we go.

Leah inhaled deeply. "The year after I graduated, I met Scott. He was funny and sweet and handsome and just…perfect," she said, her voice trailing off as she shook her head. It was so hard to say those words, to view him in that light now. "He was so good to me. And it was nice to be the one being taken care of for once. I didn't realize how badly I'd needed that."

She stopped as her chin began trembling, and she pressed her lips together.

"Hey," Danny said softly, running his hand over the back of her hair. "You don't have to do this."

Leah turned so that she was fully facing him on the couch. "I want to," she said.

He looked down before he nodded, and then he took one of her hands, interlocking their fingers before resting it on the pillow between them.

She gave it a gentle squeeze before she said, "About six months after Scott and I began dating, he started getting upset over the amount of time I spent with my family. In a twisted way, part of me thought it was really sweet that he wanted that much of my time, that he didn't want to share me with anyone," she said, shaking her head. "God, I sound so stupid when I say that out loud."

"You don't," Danny said. "You're allowed to make mistakes, Leah."

She smiled sadly. "It went far beyond a mistake. Because the more time I spent with him, the more I started looking at things differently. He would plant these little seeds in my mind—it was so gradual, so smooth, I didn't see it. He would talk about how much it upset him that I lost my childhood—how it wasn't my fault my mother died, and that I shouldn't have had to pay for it. How it wasn't the job of a teenager to take care of a family."

Leah could feel her embarrassment growing, but she forced herself to keep her eyes on him as she said, "He told me that my father shouldn't have let it happen, that he watched me grow up too fast and didn't do anything to stop it. He said he shouldn't have allowed me to come home from college either—that if he truly wanted what was best for me, he would have done everything in his power to make sure I got to experience life. He said my family took advantage of my kindness. And after a while, I believed him." She shook her head. "And I was so thankful that I found someone who cared about me *that* much. Someone who was looking out for me, and not the other way around."

Danny leaned over and ran the backs of his fingers across her cheek, wiping away the tear she hadn't realized had fallen. Leah reached up, swiping at her cheeks quickly before she exhaled.

"My family didn't like him. They said he wasn't good for me, and of course Scott said that was because he was revealing truths they didn't want to acknowledge. He said they were mad because he opened my eyes to what was really going on. Everything he said made sense, you know?"

Danny nodded; he was trying to keep his expression smooth, but she could see something brewing just below the surface.

Leah bit her lip as she looked down at their hands clasped on the pillow. "So, I distanced myself from them. I would argue with them over stupid things. I'd get mad when my father called to check in with me. I refused to call and check in with him. It was disgusting. Most people go through their rebellious stage when they're fifteen or sixteen, and there I was, a grown woman, acting like a child."

Another tear slipped over her lash line, but she was quicker this time, swiping at it before it had a chance to fall.

"So one night my father and I got in a huge fight over Scott, and I told him I wasn't going to let him control my life anymore. I left, and that was that. I wouldn't answer his calls or his texts. I wouldn't go see him. Almost a whole year went by, and I refused every attempt he made at reconciling with me. My whole life was centered around Scott, the one person I thought really cared about me and wanted what was best for me. And he had me all to himself, just the way he wanted."

She turned to Danny, her cheeks heating with embarrassment. "The night of my father's heart attack was the first time I'd seen him in months. And when I saw him in that hospital bed, with all the wires and machines, all I wanted to do was apologize to him." She shook her head. "But he was unconscious. They didn't even know if he would make it."

Leah shrugged as she said, "After I left the hospital that night, I went to Scott's apartment and found him in bed with another girl."

Danny's head whipped up, and the initial shock on his face transitioned into sympathy before settling on anger.

She nodded slowly. "So there it is. I threw my family away for a controlling, manipulative liar. If my father had died that night, he would have died thinking I resented him, after everything he'd done to try to hold my family together, after how hard he worked to take care of us all."

He stared at her, his eyes swimming with pain and something else Leah couldn't quite place.

She used the end of her sleeve to wipe her nose. "I'm pretty awful, huh?"

Danny didn't say a word. Instead he unclasped their hands and wrapped his arm around her, pulling her against his chest. She stilled for only a second before she relaxed against him, her face buried in the crook of his neck. He brought his lips to the top of her head, leaving them pressed there as he gently played with the ends of her hair.

Leah closed her eyes and exhaled. She would relive that story again and again if it ended with being in his arms, because the way he was holding her made her feel like she was someone worthy of forgiveness.

It was some time before Danny finally spoke, and when he did, she could feel the gentle vibrations in his chest.

"Leah?"

"Hmm?" she said, her eyes still closed.

"The guy who killed your mother. Do you hate him?"

Leah's eyes opened as she sat up, looking at him. It seemed like such a strange thing to ask, but his expression was smooth as he waited for her answer.

"Um...I don't know. I mean, I never really think about him. He died on impact."

He looked down and nodded. "Do you think he got what he deserved?"

Leah chewed on the inside of her lip. Did she think he got what was coming to him when he lost his life? She looked up sheepishly as she asked, "Would it make me a terrible person if I said yes?"

Danny looked down before closing his eyes. "No. It wouldn't."

She sat there staring at him, trying to comprehend what he was really asking her. His questions seemed completely irrelevant to their discussion, and yet she knew there must have been some connection she was missing.

"I *will* tell you, Leah," Danny said after a long silence. When he finally looked back up at her, his expression was a mix of sincerity and fear. "I have to tell you, because I don't want to stop spending time with you." He rubbed his hands over his eyes as he said, "It's just...I don't even know what I'm up against right now. I need just a little more time."

"Okay," she said softly, and his eyes met hers.

"Really?"

She nodded. "You can take whatever time you need. I just can't be lied to. I don't ever want to be lied to."

"I won't ever lie to you, I promise you that."

She smiled softly. "That's all I ask."

They sat there for a moment, looking at each other, and then Danny closed his eyes as he brought his fingertips to his temples, massaging slow circles.

"You're feeling it, huh?" Leah asked.

"I think I'm gonna be feeling this shit for days," he said, wincing slightly as he continued to rub.

She laughed as she stood from the couch, and his eyes flew open. "Where are you going?"

"You need aspirin," she said. "Bathroom?"

He nodded, closing his eyes again. "Medicine chest above the sink. On the bottom shelf."

Leah got him the aspirin and stopped in his bedroom to get him the bottle of water she'd left there earlier before returning to the couch and handing them both to him. After he had swallowed the pills and about half the bottle of water, he looked over at her.

"Thanks. I'm still not cleaning up those coffee grounds."

She laughed and he smiled up at her, revealing the dimples that made her chest flutter. Danny grabbed the pillow and positioned it behind his head as he lay back onto the couch.

And then he lifted his arm, inviting her into the space beside him.

She probably should have shown some hesitation, just to maintain some semblance of dignity, but instead she immediately crawled over to him, laying her head on his chest. He exhaled contentedly as his hand came to the back of her hair, lazily running his fingers through it, and Leah closed her eyes.

It felt so perfect to be lying with him this way, like they had done it a million times before. And she knew she would crave it now, like an addiction that weakened her until it was fed.

Leah sighed softly as she curled her fingers into his shirt, and she felt him kiss the top of her head as he continued playing with her hair.

She didn't have all her answers yet, but she would. And it was enough to know that for now—to believe that whatever he had to tell her wouldn't be significant enough to change what was happening between them.

Because she didn't want to have to walk away from him now.

Chapter Ten

"How's that working out for you?"

Danny kept the wad of food tucked in the side of his cheek as he glanced over to where Leah was leaning against his counter, her arms crossed over her chest, fighting a smile.

He brought his fist to his mouth. "S'good," he mumbled.

Leah chuckled as she pushed off the counter and reached above the refrigerator for the bread, and Danny slid his plate away with a sigh. "Alright. You can say it."

Her smile broadened as she turned and took the dish from him. "Say what? I told you so?" she asked, dumping the contents in the trash. "I would never."

He brought his fist back to his mouth and closed his eyes, and she laughed again, giving him a gentle nudge. "Go lie down. Give me five minutes to work my magic," she said, coming back to the counter and pulling a slice of bread from the bag.

Danny stood quickly and walked toward his bedroom, thankful to get away from the smell of his attempted breakfast. It had been a tried and true hangover cure that he and Bryan accidentally discovered when they were teenagers after drinking themselves sick off a bottle of rum they'd found in the back of Gram's cabinet. The following morning, Bryan made them each a bacon, egg, and cheese Hot Pocket, figuring if they could get themselves to vomit, they would feel better. Instead, they were miraculously cured after eating them. It was a trick they'd used for years after that.

Danny crawled into his bed and dropped onto his stomach with a huff. He knew it wasn't going to work, even before he pulled one out of the freezer and Leah looked at him like he'd lost his mind. He'd barely even touched alcohol in the past twelve months, and it had been *years* since he'd been as drunk as he was last night, so he knew it was going to take more than a Hot Pocket to get him straight again. But he was really hoping it might work. And not just because he felt like shit.

He just wanted that memory to be real.

Bryan was disappearing. Every day he slipped a little further away. He was there in pictures and in stories, but he wasn't *real* anymore.

Danny just wanted something tangible. Something that would prove Bryan had actually existed.

He rolled over and flung his forearm over his eyes as another wave of nausea swept over him. He could hear her in the kitchen, the clinking of silverware and the opening and closing of cabinets as she busied herself, and he wished for the hundredth time that he hadn't consumed his body weight in liquor last night, because he wanted to be enjoying this.

Leah, in his apartment. In his kitchen, making him breakfast like it was the most natural thing in the world.

She told him he could have whatever time he needed to get his thoughts together, but Danny knew she wasn't going to wait forever. He also knew that as soon as he explained everything to her, whatever this was would be over. His window of time with her was closing, and he wanted to soak up every second of it before she walked away for good.

And when she left him, he was going to feel it. There was no doubt about that now. In the past few hours, she had managed to slip through the last of his defenses and stake her claim on a piece of his heart. Not because she had helped him get home last night, or because she granted him the extra time he needed to explain himself. Not even because she had stayed to help nurse his hangover.

No, what had completely won him over was the way she tried to absolve him of whatever sin he'd committed by offering up her own transgressions. She laid her shame down at his feet without a second thought—for the sole purpose of easing his suffering.

It had been a long time since he'd seen that level of bravery and selflessness in anyone.

And just like that, his world shifted. It had been such a quiet moment of transformation, nothing like the earth-shattering explosions that had changed the course of his life over the past year, but in its tranquility, it was just as powerful. With that one altruistic move, she had managed to become the measure of what a person should be in his eyes, the standard any woman would have to meet if she had even the slightest chance of winning his heart.

Danny heard her coming down the hall, and he sat up slightly, resting his weight on his elbows as she turned the corner into his bedroom with a plate in one hand and a mug in the other.

"You can quit playing sick now," she said. "I already cleaned up the coffee."

He smiled as he sat up further and reached for the plate she offered him. "Jesus. How about a little sympathy? I'm dying over here."

"Oh, you poor baby," she crooned as she sat on the edge of his bed, tucking her leg beneath her and resting the mug on her knee. She had twisted her hair up into some kind of messy knot that managed to be both adorable and sexy at the same time; it made him want to toss the plate over the side of the bed and pull her down to the mattress so he could cover her body with his.

Instead, he took a breath and sat up fully, balancing the plate on his thigh as he looked down at what she'd made for him.

"What the hell did you put on this toast?"

"My magic cure."

Danny lifted his eyes. "It looks like cat puke."

Leah laughed as she pulled her other leg up onto the bed to face him fully. "It's mashed banana with a little bit of butter. The salt in the butter will help you retain water, and the bananas have potassium and electrolytes, which you really need right now. Think of it as a sports drink, only without all the sugar that messes with your stomach. Plus, solid food is always a little easier to keep down anyway."

Danny quirked his brow as she held out the mug. "And this is hot water with lemon juice. Ideally, there should be honey in here too, but you didn't have any." He took the mug from her as she said, "The lemon will help settle your stomach. Plus, it'll give you a little boost of vitamin C."

"Wow," he said with a nod before he looked up at her. "So, are you a raging alcoholic?"

Leah huffed as she grabbed a pillow and propped it up against his headboard. "I should've let you suffer through the Hot Pocket, you ingrate."

Danny laughed as she sat back against the pillow and pulled her knees into her chest. "I have an older brother who used to party a lot when we were in high school," she said. "It was sort of my job on weekend mornings to make him presentable before my father saw him and kicked his ass."

"But how did you know *this* stuff would work?" he asked before lifting the mug and taking a careful sip, the hot liquid instantly soothing him.

"I didn't," she said with a shrug. "It was a lot of trial and error. There were quite a few nasty concoctions before I found this, so you should thank your lucky stars you're getting me as a seasoned veteran."

Danny smiled as he moved to sit back against the headboard beside her, taking a bite of the toast and chewing slowly. "It's not bad," he said. "Shouldn't be too rough when it comes back up."

Leah shook her head as she grabbed the remote from his nightstand and turned the TV on. "When you're finished, I'll accept your apology in the form of jewelry or designer shoes," she said, and he laughed around his mouthful of food.

"Hey!" he complained as she flipped right past ESPN.

"Sorry, but it's not gonna happen."

Danny lifted his brow. "Isn't this my television?"

"Yes, but I got the remote first. That was always the rule in my house. Besides, you don't have to pretend you only watch sports. There are no other guys around. Judgment-free zone over here," she said, gesturing around herself as she continued to channel surf.

"Hmm. That's actually kind of a relief," he said, turning back to the TV. "So...porn then?"

She scoffed, waving her hand at him dismissively just as he leaned over to put his plate between them, and the sharp crack of the remote hitting him square in the forehead was immediately followed by Leah's panicked gasp.

"*Oh my God,*" she said quickly as she spun toward him, placing her hand over Danny's where it was pressed between his eyes. "Oh my God, are you okay?"

"No porn. Duly noted," he winced, and she pulled his hand away and replaced it with her own as she rubbed his forehead.

"I am so sorry," she said through laughter.

"Well, you *sound* devastated."

She laughed harder then, and his smile finally broke before he started laughing with her.

Leah ran her fingers over the red mark between his eyes before she reached down and handed him the remote. "You win. We can watch whatever you want. Porn. Sports. And I'll pretend to love every minute."

Danny took the remote as he said, "I get assaulted in my own home and my only compensation is control of the television?"

"Well, what would you prefer?"

He kept his eyes on the TV as he started flipping through the channels, but a smirk lifted the corner of his mouth.

"Right." Leah laughed as she sat back against the headboard. "Because in your current condition, I'm sure you would rock my world."

Danny reached for his toast. "Believe me, if given the opportunity to rock your world, there isn't a hangover in existence that would prevent me from getting the job done thoroughly," he said before taking a bite.

He placed the toast back on the plate and glanced over at her; she was staring at the screen, tugging gently on her bottom lip as her cheeks flushed a delicate pink.

"Well, your confidence is still intact, I see," she mumbled, and he smiled.

It had nothing to do with confidence; it was just that he could picture what it would be like to have her, and he knew without a doubt that once his hands were on her body, everything else in the world would fall away. His hangover, his reservations, his past.

His future.

And as for being thorough? That hadn't been bragging. That had been a promise.

"Stop!" Leah said suddenly, stilling his hand on the remote, and Danny looked up to see three overweight men in white coats standing in front of a tray of cupcakes.

"This?" he asked. "What the hell is this?"

"You're kidding, right? Tell me you've never seen *Cake Boss.*"

"What the fuck is *Cake Boss?*"

"Swear jar," she said, taking the remote from him and turning up the volume. "It's a reality show about a bakery in Hoboken."

Danny pulled his brow together as he took another bite of toast, his eyes pinned on the screen. "So you just watch these dudes bake for an hour?"

"First of all, they don't bake. They *create,*" she said, and Danny brought the back of his hand to his mouth to stifle his laughter. "Second of all," she continued, "it's not just about them baking. You get customers' back stories, you get a look at the lives of the guys who own the shop. Plus, the cakes they make are insane. I want to go there so bad."

Danny grinned at her adulation as he brought the mug to his mouth. "So, why don't you?"

"I will one day, when I have the time. It's not like a normal bakery. It's famous. People wait in line for hours just to get inside."

"Huh," Danny said, finishing his toast. "I wonder if people wait that long because they want to be on TV or if the shit they make is *that* good."

"The shit is *that* good," she said confidently, and Danny chuckled.

"What if you go and it isn't? Are you ready for that level of disappointment?"

Leah rested her head back on the pillow as she turned to look at him. "I don't mind a little disappointment now and then. It just means you've got high standards. I'd rather shoot high and be disappointed sometimes than just live in the middle with the illusion of being satisfied."

Danny's smile fell as he continued looking at her. It wasn't the first time she'd done that: said something endearingly comical, only to follow it up with something so profound, it made him feel like the world had momentarily stopped while he absorbed her words.

She reached up then, placing her hand on his cheek as she ran her thumb over his forehead. "You've got a welt now," she said softly.

He swallowed as a current of warmth trickled down his body, like a string of dominos that had been set off by the touch of her fingers.

Her eyes dropped to his mouth for just a moment before they flitted back up, and her hand slipped from his face as she sat up quickly. "Do you want more toast?" she asked, grabbing the empty plate between them and sliding off the bed.

"No, thank you," he managed, and she nodded before she turned and headed out of his room.

Danny fell back onto the bed, blinking up at the ceiling as he exhaled the breath he hadn't realized he'd been holding.

Jesus Christ, he wanted to kiss her again.

When they'd kissed outside The Rabbit Hole—a memory that still made his pulse spike whenever he thought of it—Leah had been drunk. And he was almost positive he had kissed her last night, but of course, *he* had been drunk.

He wanted to kiss her when they were both sober.

But he couldn't take liberties like that, not while he still harbored secrets. Right now she needed to be the one calling the shots. She needed to set the tone, dictate the pace. He couldn't risk screwing up right now. Not when he knew how badly he'd be screwing things up in the future.

Danny closed his eyes and exhaled heavily, clasping both hands behind his head before he opened them.

"Holy fuck," he said just as Leah entered his room, and she turned her head, following his line of sight. As soon as her eyes fell on the screen, she smiled.

"Told you," she said, coming back to the bed. "Amazing, right?"

"That's a *cake?*" he said, and she nodded.

"Yup. And every part of that is edible."

"No fucking way," he said, staring in amazement at the life-sized roulette table, complete with a functioning wheel. "You can eat the numbers? And the chips?"

"They're fondant," she said, moving to lie down beside him. "It's like a malleable frosting. You can make it any color you want, sculpt with it." She rolled onto her side, facing him with a sigh. "I should have been a baker."

He smiled as he turned toward her, lying on his side as he mirrored her position, and his eye was immediately drawn to the delicate silhouette of her profile—her neck curving into her shoulder, her waist tapering into the swell of her hip.

It was one of the most sensual things he'd ever seen.

Danny brought his eyes back to her face, and she smiled softly. "Do you feel better?"

"I do," he said. "I can't believe I do, but I do."

Leah lifted her brow. "You doubted me?"

"For the first and last time," he said, and a slow smile curved her lips.

"That was a very diplomatic answer."

"Thank you. I'm exceptional at taking my foot out of my mouth."

She laughed softly before dropping her eyes, and he watched her expression straighten as she bit her lip. Then she moved, pressing him onto the mattress as she rested her head on his chest.

"Is this okay?" she whispered, draping her arm over his stomach, and Danny closed his eyes as he brought his hand to her back.

"Yes," he said, trailing his fingertips from her waist to the nape of her neck.

"I know we did this earlier, but we weren't in your bed then, and I don't want to...I just want to..."

She trailed off, and Danny nodded against the crown of her head before he whispered, "I know. Just this."

Leah exhaled softly. "It just...it feels nice."

"It does," he said gently, pulling her into his side, and the channel changed suddenly as she rolled over the remote.

"*Show me sand the floor.*"

Leah gasped just as Danny pumped his fist in the air.

"Alright, *Cake Boss* is impressive, but it's no match for *The Karate Kid*. We're leaving this on," he said.

"Totally," she said emphatically as she tossed the remote behind her before snuggling closer. "This is one of the greatest movies of all time."

Danny shifted slightly, looking down at her. "Are you being sarcastic right now?"

"Not at all," Leah said, playing with the hem of his shirt as she kept her eyes on the TV. "When they did the remake of this with Jackie Chan, I took it personally."

Danny laughed as he rested his head back down on the pillow. "Jacket on, jacket off!"

"*What?*"

"That's how they did it in the new one. Put your jacket on, take your jacket off. That's how he learns to fight."

"Oh my God, I hate it even more now," Leah said against his chest, and he smiled, running his thumb over the sliver of exposed skin on her lower back.

They watched in captivated silence as Daniel-san realized all the chores he'd been forced to do had taught him how to defend himself, and as he stared at Mr. Miyagi in awe, Danny nodded.

"There it is. Mind. Blown."

"Right?" Leah said. "The first time I saw that scene, I'm not gonna lie, it gave me a little bit of a crush on him."

"Yeah, well, it was good to be Ralph Macchio in the eighties."

"I was talking about Mr. Miyagi."

Danny burst out laughing before he pulled her a little closer.

She fit so perfectly. And not just physically, although he couldn't deny that when she was beside him this way, it felt like she was just a natural extension of his body, as if they were two halves of the same whole.

But it was more the way she fit into his life. In a perfect world, he could see this being his existence. Spending lazy weekends cuddling with her on the couch, watching TV and cracking jokes. Wasting hours talking about things that were ridiculous and significant and sometimes both at once.

It was so easy to forget the ugliness of his reality when she was with him.

They spent the next hour watching the rest of the movie, and with absolutely no effort at all, she managed to claim another piece of his heart. The way she fiddled with the hem of his shirt without even realizing she was doing it. The way her hair smelled like spring with a little bit of coconut mixed in. The way the sound of her laugh made him laugh, even when he didn't think anything was funny.

And by the time the credits rolled, he couldn't resist anymore.

Danny used the tips of his fingers to brush the hair away from her forehead before he trailed them down over her cheek, and she lifted her eyes, looking up at him. He moved in slowly, and he heard her breath catch just as the end of his nose touched hers.

And then he stopped.

Her terms. It needs to be on her terms.

"Leah," he said, his voice barely above a whisper.

He watched her throat bob before she murmured, "What?"

Danny lifted his chin so that their mouths were only centimeters apart before he whispered, "Can I?"

For a moment the world seemed to stop.

And then she nodded.

His mouth was on hers before she'd even finished, and she instantly leaned into him, surrendering her mouth as she allowed him to control the kiss.

He concentrated on keeping his lips gentle, parting them slightly and brushing them over hers, and she followed his lead, kissing him back with cautious reverence that made it feel like tiny flints were igniting in his veins.

It was too chaste to be dangerous, but far too sensual to be innocent.

He pulled away as soon as he felt his control slipping, and she immediately rested her head back on the pillow, exhaling shakily before she pressed the heels of her hands into her eyes. "You're good at that."

Danny smiled, blinking up at the ceiling. "I think *we're* good at that."

She ran her hands up into her hair and let out a puff of breath. "I think it's time to take you back to your car."

Danny nodded, raking his teeth over his bottom lip. "I think you're right."

They both lay there, unmoving, until Leah said, "Ten more minutes of cuddles. That's it. And then we go."

His lip slid out from between his teeth as he smiled. "As you wish," he said, and she whipped her head toward him.

"Did you just quote *The Princess Bride?*"

"I did."

She stared at him for a second before she curled back into his side. "Fine. Twenty minutes," she said as she rested her head on his chest, twisting the hem of his shirt between her fingers.

Danny smiled into her hair. "Twenty minutes," he repeated, knowing that if she asked him right now, he'd give her every single minute he had left.

Chapter Eleven

"Wow," Robyn said as she fell back against Leah's couch. "No shit," Holly added.

"I know."

"I'm excited," Robyn beamed, and Holly sighed.

"I'm nervous."

"Well, I'm both," Leah said, "so I guess that works."

Holly nibbled on the side of her thumbnail. "Slow, Leah. You need to go very, very slow."

"She knows that," Robyn said. "Don't be condescending."

"I'm not being condescending, I'm being cautious. I mean, he openly admitted he's harboring some huge secret. That's already starting off behind the eight ball, don't you think?"

"Okay, but at least he told her about it, even if he's not ready to talk about it yet. If he were some kind of shady bastard, he wouldn't have said anything."

"Guys, stop," Leah interrupted. "Holly, I hear what you're saying, and I'm gonna go slow with him. It's just..." She shook her head. "I wish I could explain it without sounding like an idiot, but there's something about him. He's genuine. I can feel it in my bones."

It was quiet for a beat before Holly said, "You also thought Scott was genuine."

"*Holly!*" Robyn barked, and Leah dropped her eyes as Holly covered her face with both hands.

"I'm sorry, Leah. I just meant that—"

"No, it's okay," Leah said, her eyes still trained on her lap. "You're right. I know you're right. But this time...everything just *feels* different. I can't explain it."

And she couldn't explain it. All she knew was that she felt oddly connected to Danny. There was something about him that spoke to a long-forgotten part of her—that awakened something dormant in her soul and made her *want* things again.

Ever since that first day at the Cheesecake Factory, something had changed for her. It was as if letting her guard down with him had somehow shaken her foundation, and every layer of resistance and detachment she'd built up for the past two years had crumbled in on itself. And instead of panicking—instead of scrambling to pick up the pieces and rebuild—she found herself wanting to kick the debris away and breathe in everything around her.

Every conversation, every interaction with him, freed her a little more.

It was there even in the little things, like the way her body reacted to the timbre of his voice, or the simplest of his touches. The way seeing him in pain caused a lump in her throat, like she was the one hurting. Her connection to him felt mature, as if it was something that had existed long before she had felt it or acknowledged it.

What happened between them that morning only reinforced it; she had confessed her biggest disgrace, her most humiliating regret, only to have him wrap her in his arms without even flinching at her offense. Like he had known all along and had already forgiven her.

She could try to explain it to Holly and Robyn, but Leah knew they wouldn't understand. Hell, *she* didn't even really understand. But that didn't make it any less real for her.

Holly moved from her spot on the floor, crawling over to where Leah sat on the couch before she rested her head in her lap. "I'm sorry. You know me and my big mouth love you and are just looking out for you."

Leah smiled, running her hand over the back of Holly's hair. "I know. And I will go slow. I promise."

Holly lifted her head, smiling at Leah before she hopped to her feet. "Okay, should we put the movie in now? Ryan Gosling is shirtless in this, so like seriously, what the fuck are we waiting for?"

Leah and Robyn laughed as Holly walked over to the DVD player with the movie. She'd brought it over, along with some takeout from the girls' favorite sushi restaurant, in honor of their last girls' night before Robyn got married. But as soon as they'd walked into Leah's apartment, the relentless third-degree interrogation took precedence over the food and entertainment. She'd known them too long, and they could see all over her face that something had changed for her. Within ten minutes of their arrival, Leah had told them everything, beginning with Danny's drunken phone call and ending with her bringing him to his car earlier that afternoon.

"Oh, here," Robyn said, reaching into her bag and pulling out a small stack of envelopes before tossing them to Leah. "We got your mail on the way in."

"Thanks," Leah said, quickly sifting through the stack as Robyn started taking the containers of sushi out of the bag. There were two bills and a magazine subscription renewal.

And one other.

Leah laughed humorlessly as soon as she saw it.

"What?" Holly asked, coming back to the couch with the remote.

"Well, he's certainly goal oriented," Leah said as she tossed the envelope onto the coffee table before her. "You gotta give him that."

"Oh my God, is that from Scott?" Robyn asked.

Leah nodded.

"What is it?"

"Don't care," Leah said as she took one of the containers from the table and popped off the lid.

"I do," Holly said, swiping it from the table and tearing the envelope open.

"Is it a love letter?" Robyn asked. "Do a dramatic reading!"

Leah laughed as Holly shook her head. "Not a love letter. Too heavy," she said, reaching her hand in and pulling out a stack of pictures. She plopped down between Leah and Robyn on the couch as she started flipping through them.

The first one was of Leah and Scott at the beach the summer they first met. She was sitting in between his legs on their towel, leaning back against his chest and smiling as he kissed her cheek. The next one was the two of them at the baseball field where Scott played with his team from work. It was a candid shot, neither of them looking at the camera; Leah stood with her arms around his waist, her eyes closed and her cheek pressed against his chest. Scott had his arms wrapped around her shoulders with his chin resting on the top of her head. The next picture was of the two of them lying in Scott's bed, their heads together as Leah held the camera away from them and snapped the shot. They were both wearing lazy, contented smiles, and Leah closed her eyes momentarily to ward off the memory. They had spent that entire day in bed, making love over and over, only getting up to use the bathroom or get a drink.

It went on and on. Various pictures of them hugging, kissing, laughing, smiling. Just when Leah thought she couldn't take any more, the onslaught of images finally ended.

And then came the index card.

I know you remember how this used to be. Look at us, Leah. You were happy with me. One mistake isn't enough to change that, and you know it. You were upset. You had a right to be. But you made your point, and I've certainly served my sentence. Let's stop wasting time. We're better together, and you know that too. You still love me, beautiful. As much as I still love you.

Holly shook her head in disbelief as Robyn bit her lip, glancing nervously at Leah.

A few seconds of pregnant silence passed before Leah said, "Guys, I'm not gonna do what you all think I'm gonna do, which is, you know...*flip out!*" she yelled, waving her arms maniacally in the air.

Holly and Robyn instantly laughed at her *Jerry McGuire* reference, and Leah grabbed the stack of pictures from Holly's hand before she stood.

"What are you gonna do with those?"

"Purge," she said as she walked toward the kitchen.

Leah turned the corner and approached the garbage can, stepping on the pedal to lift the lid. Just as she was about to toss the pictures in, she stopped, sifting through them one more time.

She *had* been so happy in all of them.

But so much had happened since then that it felt like she was looking at a different girl. And truth be told, Leah felt bad for her. She felt bad that the rug was right about to be pulled out from underneath her, and this girl didn't have the slightest idea.

Leah flipped until she was once again looking at the index card.

I know you remember how this used to be.

But she couldn't. It was like when she was a little girl, and she'd watched a show that explained how magicians made rabbits and other things appear in hats. After that she could never watch a magic show again, not after she'd seen them for what they really were. A ruse. A sham.

A lie.

And that was exactly what this felt like. Looking at these images felt like watching a magic trick that had already been exposed. It left her feeling disappointed, and more importantly, unimpressed.

With a flick of her wrist, she tossed the photos into the trash can, letting the lid close on that era of her life once and for all.

"Jesus Christ. So is this typical, or is Robyn one of those dictator brides?"

Leah laughed, rolling onto her side to turn off the light before scooting further under her covers. "It's pretty typical," she said, switching the phone to her other ear. "You've never been in a bridal party?"

"Once," Danny said. "For my cousin, when I was like twelve. But I definitely don't remember it being a three-day affair."

"Well, it's typical for *girls*, I should say."

"Of course. You guys always have to make shit more complicated," he said, and Leah smiled.

She'd spent the past few months being excited over Robyn's wedding, but tonight, for the first time, she wished it wasn't going to occupy her entire weekend.

She had spoken with Danny on the phone every night that week, and this time when he called, he asked if she wanted to hang out that weekend. Leah explained to him that she'd be spending Friday getting massages, manicures, pedicures, and facials with the bridal party, followed by the rehearsal dinner. Saturday was the wedding, which of course would occupy her entire day, and then Sunday, the entire bridal party, along with Robyn and Rich's families, would be attending a celebratory brunch at the hotel.

"Alright, maybe next weekend, then," he said. "I have something I want to show you."

"Well, I'm getting back late Sunday afternoon. We could do something Sunday night if you want. I don't have work on Monday."

"You don't?"

"Martin Luther King Day," she said.

"Ah, that's right."

"Can you do a Sunday night? I don't know what your hours look like on Monday."

"I make my own hours. One of the perks of being the boss."

Leah shook her head. "You think you're so cool."

Danny chuckled. "Let's do Sunday night then. Text me when you get back."

"Okay," she said through a yawn.

"Alright, I'll talk to you then. Have fun this weekend."

"Thanks," she said, her eyes falling closed. "Good night."

"Good night sweet girl," he said before ending the call.

Leah's eyes flipped open before she smiled, reaching over to place her phone on her nightstand. It was the first time he'd called her that since his drunken rant the weekend before, but it sent the same thrill through her.

With a tiny sigh, she curled into her comforter and closed her eyes.

She fell asleep imaging those words falling from his lips before he pressed them to hers.

As cliché as it was to say a bride looked like a princess on her wedding day, that was the only way Leah could think of to describe Robyn. She couldn't remember a time her friend looked more beautiful. And it wasn't just her fairy-tale gown, or her elegant up-do, or her delicate makeup. It was because she was so unbelievably happy. Her smile didn't leave her face the entire day, and every time Leah saw Robyn and Rich look at each other, it felt like she was intruding on a private moment. They were in their own little world, so wrapped up in each other, so conspicuously in love. It was extremely humbling to be around.

Leah said good-bye to Holly and Robyn on Sunday afternoon, wishing Robyn a wonderful honeymoon and telling Holly she'd talk to her later that week. She hadn't told her about her plans with Danny that night for fear of getting a lecture about not taking things slow enough.

Before Leah left the hotel, she texted Danny, and he asked her to meet him at his apartment around seven. He also told her that she shouldn't eat anything because he'd have dinner ready for them, a notion that left her apprehensively intrigued.

She spent the afternoon running errands before she showered and headed down to his place, and as soon as she neared his building, a series of flutters started low in her stomach. She had thought of Danny so many times that weekend, wondering what it would have been like if he had come to the wedding with her. Picturing him in a suit, his black hair in sexy disarray, smiling his adorable smile. Laughing with her, holding her hand as she introduced him to people.

Kissing her softly as they danced.

Leah parked at the end of his block, and the fluttering in her stomach doubled as she rode the elevator to his floor.

When the doors finally opened, she approached his apartment and closed her eyes, taking a deep breath before she opened them and knocked. There was a muffled rustling sound, followed by the muted thud of footsteps.

A few seconds later, the door swung open, and the fluttering moved up into her chest. His dark hair was tousled to perfection, and he had a hint of a five-o'clock shadow defining his jawline. He was wearing a pair of worn jeans with a gray zip-up hoodie over a white T-shirt.

And her favorite dimpled smile.

"Hey," he said, leaning over to kiss her cheek before he stepped to the side to let her in, and she was immediately greeted with the smell of Chinese food.

Leah hummed as she walked past him into the apartment. "Good call. That smells amazing."

"You got here before I could take it out of the containers and put it in pots and pans on the stove."

Leah laughed as he took her coat and hung it by the door. "Right, because I totally would have believed that."

"Hey, I can cook," he said in feigned offense as he walked over to the table and pulled a chair out for her.

"I know," she said as she sat. "I was there for the Hot Pocket."

Danny laughed, shaking his head. "Why did I ask you to hang out again?"

"No clue. Maybe you're a masochist."

Danny pushed her chair in before he walked around to the other side of the table. "Sometimes I think so," he said, but his voice was strangely devoid of humor.

Leah glanced up at him, but by the time he sat across from her, his dimples were back on display.

"So how was the wedding?" he asked as he started opening containers. He looked up at her, his smile still intact.

Maybe she'd imagined it.

"It was really fun," Leah said, reaching for the bottle of water in front of her. "Robyn looked amazing. Everything went smoothly."

"It went smoothly? What's to mess up? Both people say 'I do,'" Danny said, holding out a pack of chopsticks and a fork for Leah to choose from.

She grabbed the fork. "Girl stuff again. But there's a lot of behind-the-scenes stuff that can get messy if it's not well planned. Or if the bride is a bitch." She smiled. "Thankfully, neither was the case this weekend."

Danny placed two opened cartons of food in front of Leah before he started opening the others. "Do those bitch brides actually exist? I thought that shit was just for TV."

"They exist," Leah said, looking inside the containers. One was filled with sesame chicken, and the other contained pot stickers.

Leah's mouth dropped. "How did you know to order this?"

"What?" he asked, his eyes trained on the chopsticks he was unwrapping.

"Sesame chicken and pot stickers? What made you order this?"

"Because it's your favorite," he said simply as he reached into his container with his chopsticks and pulled out a piece of broccoli.

"How did you know that?"

He popped the broccoli in his mouth. "You told me," he said around his food.

"I did?"

He laughed softly. "Yeah. It was Tuesday night. Or maybe Wednesday. One of the nights I spoke to you this week."

"Huh," Leah said. "I don't remember that." She reached into the container and pulled out a pot sticker.

"I pay attention."

Leah glanced up, and he winked at her before he grabbed his water bottle and twisted off the cap. She watched him take a long sip, suddenly overwhelmed with the desire to swat the bottle away from his lips and replace it with her mouth.

"What?" he asked as he put the bottle down and picked up his chopsticks.

"Nothing," Leah said. "Just...watching you show off."

"Show off?"

She nodded to his chopsticks, and he laughed.

"I'm not showing off. This is how you're supposed to eat this stuff."

She shrugged, spearing a piece of chicken with her fork and bringing it to her mouth, and he smiled, putting his container down and leaning across the table.

"Here," he said, taking the fork from her hand and replacing it with the chopsticks. He manipulated her fingers around the sticks, his brow furrowed in concentration, and Leah kept her eyes trained on his face.

Maybe it was the fact that she had anticipated being with him all weekend, but right now, everything about him—his touch, his laugh, his voice—was driving her crazy.

"There," he said, pulling his hand away. "Try it now."

Leah strained to keep her fingers in the position he'd placed them in as she brought them down to her food, unsteadily gripping a piece of chicken between them. She raised it carefully from the container, grinning with pride as she glanced up at Danny, but the sticks shifted in her hand. She tried to pinch them together quickly, but they slipped and snapped together, sending the chicken flying across the table into Danny's chest before it bounced into his lap.

She pressed her lips together, staring at him, and he looked down at his lap and then back up at her before they both started laughing. Danny grabbed the piece of chicken and popped it into his mouth before he reached across the table and took the chopsticks.

"Okay, you're cut off," he said, handing her back the fork.

Leah smirked as she took it from him, spearing a piece of chicken just as the double beep of her phone alerted her to an incoming text. She reached down with one hand and pulled the phone out of her purse, swiping her thumb over the screen to read the message.

She laughed softly before replying.

"What's so funny?"

"My dad," Leah said, finishing her reply before she pushed the phone away. "He just asked me how old my brother was when he stopped sleeping with his stuffed dinosaur, which could only mean my brother is at his house right now and they're having a heated discussion over this very topic. I'm sure I'm being called in as a referee."

Danny smiled. "How old was he?"

"Fourteen. My brother's gonna say I'm full of shit, but that boy was fourteen." She watched as Danny lifted his chopsticks and grabbed some lo mein; with a quick roll of his wrist and a twist of his fingers, he had the long noodles twirled into a neat roll on the end of the sticks. He glanced up at her and brushed his shoulder off haughtily before bringing it to his mouth, and Leah rolled her eyes, causing him to chuckle.

Her phone beeped twice and she leaned over. "My brother," she said before tapping the screen. Leah smiled as she held the phone up, turning it around for Danny to see.

YOU ARE SO FULL OF SHIT!

Danny laughed as she placed the phone back on the table. "Told you," she said.

"Your family seems cool."

"They're the best," she said, taking a bite of a pot sticker. "You gotta have a thick skin to roll with us."

"I believe it," he said with a laugh.

"What about you?" Leah asked, taking a sip of her water.

"What do you mean?"

"What's your family like?"

He laughed humorlessly. "Not like yours."

Leah twisted the cap back onto her water. "You don't get along?"

"We get along, I guess." He shrugged. "We're just not that close."

"Do you have a big family?"

"Just me, my mom, and my sister."

"What about your dad?" she said.

"I don't know my dad."

Leah watched him for a second before she dropped her eyes. "Did he pass away?" she asked, sifting through the chicken with her fork.

"No, he left before I was born."

"Oh." After a few seconds of silence, she said, "I'm sorry."

He shook his head. "It's fine. I mean, I'm not fucked up from it or anything. I guess I could have been, but I had a family. It just wasn't my real one."

"Your mom wasn't around either?"

Danny exhaled, running his hand through his hair. "No, not really."

Leah bit her lip before she said, "We don't have to talk about this."

"I don't mind," he said. "I mean, if you don't mind hearing this shit."

She shook her head. "I want to know about you. Even the shitty stuff."

He smiled sadly, his eyes dropping for a second before he said, "Here's the thing about my mom. She did her best, but life dealt her one crappy hand after the other. She got pregnant with my sister when she was eighteen. Supposedly *that* guy had the decency to hang around for a year after she was born before he took off."

Danny looked up as he said, "I'm sure it sucked. I mean, I can't imagine being left with a baby that young. And I guess at that age, the only way she could think of to fix it was to find a replacement for him. She went looking for a guy who could take care of them. And she thought she found him."

"Your father?"

Danny nodded. "I still don't know if she got pregnant to try and keep him or if it was an accident, but either way, he obviously wasn't into it."

Leah frowned, and he said, "So she ended up a single mom to two kids from two different guys who wanted nothing to do with her." Danny reached over and spun the bottle of water on the table. "She had to work two jobs just to pay the bills, and when she wasn't working, she was out trying to find the next man who would take care of our family. So we never really saw her. I mean, the two jobs thing couldn't be helped, but I just wish she had realized we didn't need the man. We would have been fine without a father as long as we had a mother."

Leah pressed her lips together as Danny shrugged. "Who knows. Maybe the man was more for her than it was for us anyway. God knows she must have needed the validation."

"That's really sad," Leah said softly, and he nodded.

"I know. So I don't resent her. But I was left by myself most of the time because of it."

"What about your sister?"

"My sister was older than me. She stayed away from the house most of the time because she could. And as soon as she became a teenager, I was lucky if I saw her twice a week." Danny's hand moved from the bottle of water to the cardboard container in front of him, fiddling with the lid as he said, "I don't blame her either. I mean, I got out of there as soon as I could too."

Leah nodded, and he said, "Things got better when I was in second grade. That's when I met Bryan, and after that I spent pretty much all my time with him. He lived with his grandmother a few blocks over."

"Catherine," Leah said, and Danny nodded.

"Yeah. His mom had him young too. Younger than my mother was. So Gram was the one who raised him so his mom could finish school."

Leah dropped her eyes and swallowed. So, Catherine didn't lose a grandson.

She lost a son.

"I'd come home from school and go to Bryan's house instead of my own. And Gram would feed us, help us with our homework, tell us to wash our faces. You know, normal mom shit."

"She calls you her boy," Leah said, and Danny smiled.

"She called us both that." He looked down, poking at his food with the end of his chopsticks. "That's how I got into cars, you know. Bryan's grandfather was amazing with them. He was always messing with something in his car, even when it wasn't broken. It drove Gram crazy," he said with a laugh.

Leah smiled, and he said, "When we were older, we used to wait for him to get home from work so we could watch him mess around with the car. Eventually, he started letting us work on it too."

He picked up his drink, taking a quick sip before he said, "When he died, Gram put away his life insurance policy. She always said she was saving it for a rainy day. But when Bryan and I decided to open our shop, she ended up giving us that money and then some so we could make it happen. Pretty much cleaned out her bank account for us."

"Wow," Leah said softly, trying to fathom how much she loved these two boys. "So it was Bryan's shop too?"

Danny nodded. "D&B Automotive."

"Danny and Bryan," Leah said.

"Danny and Bryan," he repeated. "He always complained that he should get a higher cut of the profits since I got to have my initial first." He smiled at her before he said, "I still cut the profits fifty-fifty. I give Bryan's share to Gram. She wouldn't take it at first, so I used to just hide bits and pieces of it around the house, thinking I was slick. She was on to me, though."

Leah smiled sadly. "You take such good care of her."

"She deserves it," Danny said. "I would do more if I could."

Leah nodded, and it was quiet for a minute as the two of them fiddled with the food in front of them. Suddenly Danny cleared his throat as he shifted in his seat, and she knew this conversation was over.

"So," he said, taking another bite of food. "Is your brother older or younger?"

"Older," she said. "He's twenty-nine."

Danny nodded. "Does he make your boyfriends run the gauntlet now?"

"What do you mean?" Leah asked, dipping a pot sticker in soy sauce.

"After what that piece of shit did to you. Has he been tough on all your boyfriends since then?"

"Oh," Leah said, averting her eyes.

"You don't have to tell me. I was just wondering. I'd grill the shit out of my sister's boyfriends if it were me, and we're not half as close as you guys seem to be."

"No, it's not that I don't want to," she said, twisting the fork between her fingers. "It's just that...I don't have an answer."

Danny furrowed his brow, and Leah took a small breath before she said, "I haven't had a boyfriend since Scott."

"None?" he asked, unable to hide his surprise.

Leah felt warmth in her cheeks, and the knowledge that she was blushing only caused her to blush more deeply.

"Don't be embarrassed," he said gently. "I'm just surprised. No one's approached you in two years?"

"No, I was approached. I just..." She trailed off with a shrug.

"Didn't trust anyone?"

"I didn't trust myself. I spent years thinking Scott was this amazing person. I would have sworn to it. I turned my back on people because of it. And it just messed with my head that I had been so wrong. After that I just didn't trust my own judgment anymore." She shrugged. "Besides, my dad needed to be taken care of for a while after that, and I just threw myself into that because..."

"Because it was like your penance."

It wasn't a question, and she didn't answer. She didn't need to.

"So you haven't dated anyone in two years?" he asked.

She shook her head.

"What about..." He trailed off, running his hand through his hair. "Have you *been* with anyone since Scott?"

She shook her head again, and she saw him fall back against his chair with his brow raised. "Whoa," he said so softly, she couldn't even be sure he'd said it.

She needed to change the subject.

"So what did you want to show me?"

He smiled softly, seeing right through what she was doing, but he played along.

"Do you want to see it now?"

"Sure," she said, and he nodded, pushing his chair back from the table before he stood. He motioned with his head for her to follow him as he made his way toward the door.

"Are we leaving?" she asked.

"No, it's in the building, it's just not up here," he said, grabbing his keys off the small table in the entryway. He held the door open and allowed her to step outside before he closed the door behind them and locked it.

They walked to the elevator in silence, and every few seconds he would glance over at her. He seemed nervous, although Leah was aware that she might just be projecting her own anxiety on to him.

As they stepped inside the elevator, Danny pushed the button for the basement.

"The basement?" she asked.

"It's in storage," he said simply as he looked up to watch the lighted numbers go out one by one as they descended the floors.

With one final ding, the doors opened, and Danny stepped off the elevator, turning back when Leah didn't follow.

She stood there, wide-eyed and completely immobilized.

"What's wrong?" he asked, and she shook her head slightly. He stared at her until understanding washed over his face, followed by a slow smile, and then he reached down and clasped her hand, intertwining their fingers.

"Come on," he said. "I know my way around down here."

He stepped out of the elevator, pulling Leah behind him into the darkness of the basement. It was a long corridor, nearly pitch black except for two exit signs at each end of the hallway, which only served to cast an eerie red light in each direction.

Leah inhaled a deep breath, and he gave her hand a gentle squeeze.

"You're fine," he said through a tiny laugh just before a loud metallic banging gave way to a creepy humming noise. Leah yelped, tugging on his hand so that he stumbled back into her.

"It's just the heat kicking on," he said with a laugh. "We're almost there."

After a few more steps Danny stopped walking, and Leah could hear the jingling of his keys as her eyes began adjusting to the darkness. She could just make out the outline of a door before them, and then she heard it swing open as Danny took a step inside and reached above him, pulling a string that illuminated a tiny dim light in the room.

It was a small space, about the size of a walk-in closet, filled with boxes and crates and plastic bins. Danny walked farther into the room and Leah followed, still gripping his hand.

"Can I have my hand back for a sec?" he said through a barely contained smile. "I need to move some stuff." Leah nodded before she released him, crossing her arms over her chest as her eyes combed the tiny space.

"Can we hurry? I really don't like it down here."

He laughed as he turned from her, lifting a box off one of the piles before moving it to the other side. Leah watched him move two more boxes before he stepped back, wiping his hands down the sides of his jeans.

"Okay," he said, turning to her as he held out his hand, and she took it as he pulled her gently toward him.

He placed his hands on her shoulders and moved her so that she was standing in front of him. Leah's eyes scanned the area before them. At first all she could see was a few crates full of books and what looked like old car magazines.

And then she saw it.

She gasped loudly as both hands flew to her mouth, and she felt his hands slide down from her shoulders and rub the tops of her arms.

"I hope this was worth the trek down here," he whispered.

She turned her head to look up at him, her eyes wide with shock and her hands still clamped over her mouth. He smiled gently before urging her forward, and she turned back around and dropped to her knees, her hands falling from her mouth as she ran them over the rough concrete.

She dragged them over the jagged *LM* that had been etched in the stone. She used her fingertip to trace the *CM* and *SM* next to it.

And then she reached the *DM*.

She didn't trace it. Instead, she just pressed the pads of her fingers into the grooves, as if she could somehow embed the initials into her skin. Leah carefully slid her hand up until it sank into the indentation of her mother's handprint.

It was a perfect fit now.

A soft sob fell from her lips, and she was suddenly aware of his hand on her back, rubbing gently as he crouched behind her.

"I repaved that yard last fall because some of the blocks sank in, and there were raised edges all over the place. I was afraid Gram was gonna trip over one." He continued rubbing up and down her back, his voice a soothing murmur as he said, "I spent the entire day breaking up the concrete in the yard, but I couldn't do it to this one. The little handprints, with the big one..."

He trailed off, and Leah felt him run his hand over the back of her hair. "It just hit a nerve with me. So I got a crowbar, and I pried it up. I didn't know what to do with it, but I just couldn't junk it. I ended up burying it under some stuff in Gram's basement. She never even knew I did it."

Leah hiccupped on another sob, and he ran his hand down her hair again. "When you told me about this at The Cheesecake Factory, I wanted to tell you. I really did. But I wasn't sure it was still there, or if it was still in one piece, and I just wanted to make sure before I got your hopes up. I went down to Gram's and brought it up here while you were at the wedding this weekend."

Leah stared at her hand resting in the imprint of her mother's, and she said the only thing she could think of to say, even though it didn't come close to expressing what she was feeling.

"Thank you," she whispered as two more tears rolled over her cheeks.

"You're welcome," he said, his voice soft, and then she felt him press his lips to her temple before he stood. "I'll bring this up to you whenever you want it."

Leah sat there for another few minutes, letting her fingers meander over every dip, every bump, every line. Danny stood behind her, allowing her the silence and time she needed.

Finally she stood, turning to look at him for the first time, and his eyes met hers as he ran the backs of his fingers over her cheek, wiping away the remnants of her tears.

"Are you ready to go back upstairs?"

She nodded, and he held his hand out for her to take. "It's gonna be really dark out there again because your eyes are used to the light. Just hold my hand. We'll walk quick, okay?"

She nodded again, and he clasped her hand before he reached above them and pulled the string, submerging them in darkness. They walked the few steps out into the hall, and Leah stood behind him, holding his hand in both of hers as he locked the storage unit before they made their way back toward the elevator.

They rode the entire way back up to Danny's floor in silence, but the air between them seemed to sizzle and crackle with electricity. She kept sneaking fleeting glances at him, wondering if he could feel it—the current in the air that made every hair on her body stand on end. By the time the doors opened, her heart was racing, and she was struggling to keep her breathing even.

They walked to his door in silence, and she stood behind him as he fumbled awkwardly with his keys. She heard him inhale slowly, and she reached forward, bringing her hands to the sides of his waist as she pressed her lips to the back of his shoulder.

His head fell forward as the breath left him in a rush, and his hand tightened around his keys for a moment before he lifted his head and opened the door.

Danny tossed the keys onto the entryway table as he walked briskly into his apartment, and Leah took a step inside and closed the door softly behind her, leaning back against it with her eyes trained on him. He was standing a few feet ahead of her, his back to her and his head down.

"Danny," she said gently, and his shoulders rose with a slow breath before he lifted his head, turning to face her.

They stood there, motionless, both staring at the other.

And then he moved.

With three long strides, he was suddenly in front of her, grabbing her face as he crashed his mouth to hers.

Leah's hands slid up under his arms, gripping the backs of his shoulders and pulling him against her as her heart thundered in her chest.

It was like their first kiss all over again; the second his lips touched hers, a thousand butterflies exploded in her stomach, sending searing tingles down her spine and across her skin.

His hands left her face as he wrapped his arms around her waist, hoisting her up and causing their lips to break contact, and Leah wrapped her legs around his hips as he buried his face against the side of her neck.

"Leah," he said roughly, pressing her back against the door before kissing the skin just below her ear, and she tilted her head to the side, giving him better access.

Her breathing quickly grew labored as he lavished her throat with attention, kissing up the column of her neck and over her chin until their mouths met again. She slid her hands up into his hair and curled them into fists. He rewarded her with a throaty moan against her mouth, and then his hands were clutching the backs of her thighs as he spun abruptly and began stumbling through his apartment.

She continued to kiss him, panting and sighing into his mouth as his fingertips dug into the flesh of her thighs. Her shoulder hit something and it crashed to the floor, but he kept his pace, staggering blindly through the living room until finally they turned into his bedroom.

Leah assumed he was taking them to the bed until her back hit the wall with a thud, and all at once she could feel how hard he was—the incredible, firm pressure between her legs.

She ripped her mouth from his and gasped, and he groaned deep in his throat.

"We have to stop," he said, kissing down the side of her neck and over her collarbone, interspersing his kisses with little nips that lit her skin on fire and set off a steady throbbing low in her belly. Her hips moved of their own volition, rolling against his, seeking friction.

"Leah, we have to stop," he panted, but he pressed his hips back into hers, eliciting a low moan from her lips.

"Oh God," she breathed, tightening her legs around his hips before bringing her mouth back to his.

He kissed her hard, gripping her waist before lifting her slightly, and Leah unwrapped her legs from his body before sliding down the wall. Danny kept his hands firmly on her sides as she slipped down the front of his body, causing her shirt to lift slightly. He seemed to hesitate for just a second before she felt his fingers curl under the hem, and in one swift movement, he pulled it up and over her head.

"Goddamn it," he said hoarsely as he brought his hands back to her body, cupping her breasts as he leaned down and kissed along the lacy edge of her bra, and Leah slipped her hands up under his shirt, lightly raking her nails down his stomach. He hissed in pleasure before claiming her mouth again, his kisses shifting from passionate to desperate.

Leah reached forward, hooking her fingers in the front of his jeans and giving him a firm tug, bringing his hips flush with hers again. She could feel how badly he wanted her, and the knowledge alone made her entire body ache.

"We can't," he murmured against her mouth, placing his hand on her bare stomach and pushing her back slightly, and Leah gripped his wrist and slid his hand down the flat plane of her abdomen until his fingertips dipped under the waist of her jeans.

"Shit," he breathed, and she felt the muscles in his forearm flex in protest for just a moment before he plunged his hand down, sliding beneath her panties. He touched her gently, and that single cautious stroke sent bolts of electricity rocketing up through her body. She sucked in a sharp breath as she threw her head back, slamming it against the wall. Under any other circumstance, she knew it would have hurt, but the only thing she could feel was the pressure of his touch right where she needed it, slowly working her into a frenzy.

She moaned softly, writhing against his hand, and he dropped his head to her shoulder. "Jesus Christ," he rasped out. "Leah, please."

He began to remove his hand from her pants, and she grabbed the sides of his face, pulling his mouth back to hers and kissing him with every ounce of want he had awakened and revived and kindled inside of her. Never before had she been so aware of the thin line between pleasure and pain. Every touch, every kiss, felt so incredibly good, and yet her desire for him was agonizing.

"Danny," she breathed against his mouth. "We don't have to stop. I want you."

She felt his body tense, and then he pulled away from her abruptly, taking two quick steps backward before he sat on the edge of his bed and ran both hands down his face. "I can't, Leah."

"Please," she said, her chest heaving with her labored breath. She realized she should have been embarrassed at her behavior, at the fact that she was begging, but she was too wild with desire to care. She wanted him. She wanted to touch every inch of him. She wanted to hear his sighs and his moans and her name on his lips. She wanted to make him feel that good.

He dropped his hands from his face, gripping the edge of the bed on either side of him, but he wouldn't look at her. She took the tiniest step toward him, and a muscle in the side of his jaw flexed before he said, "I think you should go."

She froze, unsure if she had heard him correctly. Several seconds passed, but he still wouldn't look at her. He sat there with his eyes trained on the floor and that muscle in the side of his jaw flexing over and over.

"You want me to leave?" she asked, her breath still unsteady, and he closed his eyes.

"Yes. I'm sorry."

Leah continued to stare at him, and as the intensity of the moment dissipated and her desire slowly ebbed, she realized how exposed she was—physically and emotionally. She crossed her arms over her uncovered breasts, turning to scan the floor for her shirt, and as soon as she found it, she bent and scooped it up, holding it over her chest as she walked swiftly from the room.

Once outside, she pulled her shirt over her head as she passed through the dining room, grabbing her purse from the floor and her cell phone from the table. Just as she walked out the front door, she heard a sharp bang that sounded like Danny had hit something.

Leah bypassed the elevator and went directly to the stairwell, refusing to chance the possibility that he would come out while she was still waiting for it to arrive.

Her body was responding to what he had asked, carrying her down the steps, bringing her out to her car, starting it up and putting it in drive; she was going through the physical motions of leaving, but her mind felt like it was on a time delay. It was such an abrupt and jarring shift to go from swimming in desire that potent to drowning in rejection, and her thoughts were still scrambling to catch up. And she knew that when it happened, when she finally began to process what had just transpired between them, she would want to be as far away from this place as possible.

Leah cranked the radio, trying to put some noise in her head. She just wanted a little more time before she was forced to think. With the unnecessarily loud music eradicating any possibility of it, she focused only on the curve of the road, the white and yellow lines rushing toward her windshield, the taillights of other cars, and she sank into the comforting numbness of it all.

When she pulled into her parking space and cut the engine, somehow the sudden silence seemed even louder than the music it had replaced, and she sat there staring out of the windshield, trying for a few more minutes to keep her thoughts at bay.

The double beep of her phone snapped her out of her daze, and she reached into her purse apathetically, pulling it out and glancing at the screen.

One new message from Danny.

I'm so sorry Leah. That wasn't about u, it was about me.

A breathy laugh fell from her lips as she tossed the phone back into her purse. He'd had almost an hour, and the best he could come up with was the "it's not you, it's me" routine?

She shook her head as she exited the car, and a rush of cold air hit her in the face, pulling her from her fog and forcing her to feel. And then it all hit her at once.

Confusion. Rejection. Embarrassment. Resignation.

As she entered her apartment and walked straight back to her bedroom, she was certain of two things: she had feelings for Danny, and his issues went far deeper than she initially thought.

In another time, in another life, she may have been able to tough this out with him, to ride out the storm and let him figure himself out while she sat on the sidelines, rolling with the punches and taking a few hits every now and then. But Leah knew she didn't have it in her to do that now. She promised herself that she would never let a guy screw her around again, and while she knew Danny and Scott weren't even close to being cut from the same cloth, the bottom line was, he obviously wasn't ready for what she wanted.

The back and forth, the push and pull, the mixed signals—she had thought they were past all that after their conversation last weekend, but apparently that wasn't the case. And she valued herself too much to be treated that way, even if she knew it wasn't coming from some-place malicious. She wouldn't allow herself to settle for something less than what she wanted, or to wait around hoping for something she might never get.

Life was too short, and she'd already wasted so much time.

Holly had been right; she had gone too fast with Danny. There were things he needed to figure out, broken pieces of his life he need-ed to fix. And she needed to walk away and allow him to do it. It would be best for both of them at this point. And maybe when he figured ev-erything out, when he could give her one hundred percent of himself, they could try again.

Leah kicked off her shoes and pulled the blanket up over herself, not even bothering to change out of her clothes.

She knew what it felt like to care about him, what it felt like to want him so badly it erased all rational thought from her mind.

And as she closed her eyes, she began dreading what it would feel like to miss him.

Chapter Twelve

He couldn't believe he was doing this.

Danny closed his eyes and shook his head as he grabbed the pen, scribbling down Leah's address before he closed the lid on his laptop.

It was bad enough to look up a girl's address online, but to do it so he could show up at her place uninvited? It didn't get much creepier than that.

He ran both hands down his face as he exhaled, because in the past twenty-four hours, he'd managed to be both a tease and an asshole, so creep wasn't really that far of a stretch.

He had texted her twice last night after his initial apology, once asking her to let him know she made it home okay, and the other a few hours later, asking if he could call her in the morning so they could talk. She hadn't answered either one, and he'd gotten the worst sleep of his life because of it.

He just wanted to explain what had happened the night before. Even if she decided she never wanted to speak to him again, she still deserved an explanation.

He'd already had plans to go in to work late that morning, but now he was debating going in at all. It wasn't just the fact that he was exhausted—he could work through that. It was because he was completely miserable, and he didn't feel like dealing with Jake or Tommy or anyone else who would try to get to the bottom of what was up with him.

Instead, he spent the morning lying on his couch, running through all the ways he could have handled things differently last night. He'd heard the saying hindsight was twenty-twenty, but that wasn't accurate.

Hindsight was a stupid motherfucking asshole.

At around ten o'clock, his phone went off with a text message, and despite the hours he spent warning himself not to get his hopes up, he couldn't help but feel defeated when he read her words. She told him she wasn't mad at him, but she just needed some space—that it would be best for both of them if they took a break for a while.

As much as it killed him to do it, at first he complied. He didn't text her back, figuring that after disrespecting her the night before, the least he could do was respect her wishes now. After all, she didn't say it was *over*; she just said she wanted some distance for a while.

But the problem was, he didn't know if he had a while to give her.

Which ironically brought him full circle, because that was exactly why he shouldn't have started anything with her in the first place. It was as if the universe was sending him a reminder: *Hey, asshole, you should have left her alone to begin with, but since you apparently have no self-control, I'm making the decision for you.*

About an hour later, he finally decided to get up and go to work; he needed a distraction, and working in the garage was something that always succeeded in clearing his head.

But when Danny got to his front door, he noticed her jacket, still hanging where he had draped it the night before, and he stopped with his hand on the knob.

Did she realize she'd left it there? She hadn't mentioned it in her text. But then again, her text wasn't exactly conversational. Should he message her and tell her he had it? Or would she think he was just making a pathetic attempt at trying to speak to her? Although, how could it be a pathetic attempt if the jacket really *was* at his place?

Danny closed his eyes and pinched the bridge of his nose.

He couldn't do this—this overanalyzing every fucking thing until his head was spinning. And he definitely couldn't look at that jacket every time he walked in and out of his apartment for the next few weeks.

And just like that, his decision was made. There was an easy solution to both of those problems.

He was going to go to her. He would give her back the coat, and he would tell her everything. Not just why he did what he did last night.

Everything.

He was going to lay all his cards out on the table and deal with the consequences, and if her desire for a temporary break turned permanent, well then, wasn't that what he had been expecting from the beginning? There was no point in prolonging the inevitable anymore.

So he looked up her address. And then he sat on his couch, staring at the floor with the piece of paper in his hand and a lump of foreboding in his stomach.

He'd never had to tell anyone what he was about to tell her. The people who were important to him already knew, and those who weren't read about it or heard about it second or third or fourth hand. But he'd never had to say the words—and he knew that somehow, saying them to *her* was going to make it a thousand times harder.

He pushed off the couch and walked toward the front door, grabbing her coat and his keys before he made his way downstairs. After programming her address into his GPS, he turned the radio off and started driving.

Danny spent the first half of the drive practicing what he was going to say, playing with the words to try and soften their effect, but it was a senseless exercise; any way he said it, it was horrible. In fact, the more he heard it out loud, the more awful it became until finally he cranked the radio and drove the rest of the way listening to some insipid pop music countdown.

By the time he was walking up the small pathway to her front door, his anxiety had transitioned into a sense of urgency; he just wanted to get it over with and deal with the end result, whatever it might be.

Danny took a small breath before he knocked on her door. It was a minute before he heard the sound of someone approaching from the other side, and then there was silence. He knew she must be looking through the peephole to see who was outside, but he couldn't bring himself to lift his eyes.

The silence wore on, and for a second he thought she wouldn't open the door. But then he heard the deadbolt slide back before she pulled the door open slightly, and he raised his eyes to hers.

Her expression was smooth as she looked at him.

Guarded.

"What are you doing here?" she asked softly.

Danny wet his lips before he held up her jacket, and she glanced down at it before bringing her eyes back to him.

"Thanks," she said, reaching to take it from him, and he handed it over before shoving both hands in his pockets.

"I'm ready to tell you everything, Leah."

The tiniest flicker of surprise flashed across her face before she composed her expression again, folding her jacket over her arm.

"I know I don't deserve it," he said, "but just hear me out. After that, if you want nothing to do with me, I promise I won't ever bother you again."

She stood there in silence, her eyes searching his face, and then she bit her lip before she stepped to the side, granting him access to her apartment.

He walked past her and into her living room, the nerves temporarily winning out over his resolve, and he reached up and rubbed the back of his neck as he heard her close the door behind him.

"How did you know where I lived?"

Danny jammed his hands in his pockets again. "I looked you up," he said as he turned to face her. "I'm sorry. You weren't answering my texts, and to be honest, I thought if I asked, you would've told me not to come, and I had to come. I can't do this anymore. The partial truths and the bullshit and the secrets."

She sighed softly, laying her coat over a nearby chair before she motioned for him to sit down. Danny lowered himself onto the edge of her couch, leaning forward to rest his elbows on his knees as he dropped his head.

A few seconds later, he heard her come into the room, and he looked up as she curled into the chaise lounger next to him, her eyes on the hem of her sweatshirt as she twisted it between her fingers.

He took a deep breath before he shifted to face her, and her fingers stilled as she glanced up at him.

"Last night," Danny started, and her eyes instantly dropped. "I'm really sorry about the way I handled that."

Her eyes were still pinned on her sweatshirt, but Danny could see her cheeks flooding with color.

"It wasn't that I didn't want you. I did. I wanted you so fucking bad. I still do."

Leah's eyes flashed up, her expression taken aback, and he felt his shoulders soften.

"Did you really think it was because I didn't want you?"

She shrugged. "What else was I supposed to think?"

He exhaled heavily before dragging both hands down his face. "God, I'm an asshole," he mumbled. "You have to understand something, Leah. You had just told me you hadn't dated anyone, hadn't *been* with anyone in two years, and then you wanted *me*. It didn't matter how bad I wanted you. I couldn't do it. Not before you knew the truth. You were making a decision without having all the information. I didn't want you to regret being with me, and there's a good chance that after you hear what I'm about to tell you, you would have. And I refuse to be another reason for you to doubt yourself."

Danny leaned back against the couch, running both hands up through his hair as he said, "I'm sorry I asked you to leave the way I did, but Jesus Christ, Leah, I only have so much self-control. I was trying so hard to do the right thing, but the way you were looking at me... and the way you were kissing me...and then hearing you say *please*." He closed his eyes and exhaled, the memory causing his stomach to flip in a way that had nothing to do with nerves. "I didn't know how much longer I could hold out with you right in front of me. I was hanging on by a fucking thread as it was," he said, rubbing his hand over his eyes.

He heard her shift slightly, and he turned his head to look at her.

"Just tell me," she said softly.

Danny nodded as he sat up slowly, turning toward her. "You asked me once why I kept pulling away from you. Why I said it was a problem that I had feelings for you." He took a steadying breath. "It's because there's a good chance I'll be leaving soon."

"Where are you going?"

Fuck. Just say it.

He swallowed around the knot in his throat as his eyes met hers. "Prison."

She sat completely still for a few seconds before she closed her eyes and pressed her fingertips into her temples. She looked more confused than upset, although Danny knew that was about to change.

"What did you do?" she said weakly.

Danny knotted his fingers together as he said, "I didn't plan on it, Leah, and I didn't mean to do it."

She dropped her hands as she opened her eyes. "What did you do?" she repeated more firmly.

He took a deep breath before he said, "Bryan isn't dead."

Her eyes flew to his; there was fury behind them, and he held up his hand quickly. "I didn't lie, Leah. He's alive because machines do everything for him. Pump his heart, make him breathe, give him food. His body is alive, but he's gone. He's been gone for a year. There's no brain activity. There's nothing left. It's just that Gram can't let him go, because she's still hoping. But he's gone."

Leah stared at him, her eyes softening slightly before she shook her head. "What does that have to do with you going to prison?"

Danny leaned forward, rubbing the heels of his hands into his eyes. It physically hurt to say these words. He had known it would be hard, but he hadn't expected physical pain. It felt like his chest was caving in.

"The night it happened, I was with him. We were hanging out at this bar in Manhattan, and Bryan kept ordering round after round of Alabama Slammers." He smiled sadly before he said, "That was his shot. He'd always start the night off with one, but that night he just kept going. And I went right along with him.

"At some point during the night, these three guys came up to us. We had no clue who they were, but apparently they knew this girl that Bryan used to mess around with. So the one guy started with Bryan, talking about how he was gonna make Bryan sorry for fucking his girl. The bartender was quick, though. The whole thing got broken up

184

before it could come to blows, and the guys were asked to leave because they were the ones who instigated the whole thing."

Danny rubbed his hand over his forehead before he said, "So they left, and we went about our business. We didn't even think twice about it. Typical drunk assholes at a bar. We'd seen it a million times. Hell, we'd *been* them a few times. Nothing out of the ordinary, you know?"

She nodded gently, and he said, "By the time the bar was closing, we were both pretty fucked up, and I went to the bathroom—" He stopped suddenly, his jaw flexing in rapid succession as he rode out the sharp pain in his chest.

Danny cleared his throat. "I went to the bathroom, and when I came out, it was just chaos. And I knew. I just fucking knew. Some people were moving toward it, and some were trying to move away, but after a few steps, I could see them over the tops of people's heads— the same guys from earlier. I don't know how they got back in. They must've known a bouncer or something, because it didn't make any sense why no one was trying to break it up this time." Danny shook his head. "And if I hadn't gone to the bathroom, or if we hadn't been so fucking drunk..." His jaw tightened again as he felt rage and regret start to trickle through his veins, and it was a moment before he could speak again.

He glanced up at Leah; she was staring at him with equal parts sympathy and dread, like she knew where this story was going. And even though he knew that she didn't, he grabbed on to the small thread of compassion she'd thrown him and pulled himself through the rest of the story.

"He couldn't hold his own," he said hoarsely. "Bryan was wasted, and there were three of them. And I had to get through that goddamn crowd." He closed his eyes and sighed. "I could see everything, but I couldn't get there fast enough. Bryan got hit and went down, and one of the guys kicked him hard in the side of the head. Right in his temple."

He saw Leah press her fist to her mouth as she shook her head slightly.

"And I lost it," he said. "I charged the guy, and we went over a table and through the front window of the bar." He looked down and flexed his hand, watching his scars expand and contract with the movement. "I don't remember a lot after that. I remember hitting the ground outside. And the broken glass. And the blood all over my hands. I had no idea where it was coming from."

He looked up at her; her fist was still pressed against her lips, but her eyes were welled with tears. "And the next thing I knew, I was being thrown over the hood of a cop car and cuffed. They were reading me my rights, telling me to remain silent, and I just kept shouting at them to go help Bryan."

Danny pressed the heels of his hands into his eyes again as they began to sting, and he took a slow breath before continuing. "They took me to a station and put me in a cell, and no one would tell me what happened. No one would tell me." He shook his head slowly. "A few hours later, they came in and said I had made bail. I walked out to the vestibule, and Gram was there."

He dropped his head back against the couch and closed his eyes. "And she just crumpled in my arms and started wailing. And then I knew."

Danny heard her move beside him, and before he could open his eyes, she was crawling onto his lap, wrapping her arms around him as she buried her face into his neck.

He snaked his arms around her waist and pulled her against his body. Even though he knew the worst was yet to come, she felt so good in his arms that he couldn't stop himself. He needed this right now. He needed *her*.

He heard a tiny muffled sob, and Danny closed his eyes as he pressed his lips against her shoulder. He wished the story ended there. He wished he deserved the sympathy she was showing him right now. Danny tightened his arms and held her closer, wanting to soak up every last second of what he was surely about to lose.

"I don't understand," she mumbled into the crook of his neck. "So now this guy is pressing charges against you? How can he do that? Why isn't *he* in trouble for what he did to Bryan?"

Leah, please don't hate me.

"He's not the one pressing charges," he whispered against her shoulder.

She sat up and looked at him, her brow pulled together and her face streaked with tears. She looked so troubled and so saddened and so beautiful that he would have rather torn his arm off than say his next words.

He reached up and brushed at the tear stains on her face. "When we went through the window, an artery in his neck was severed. They took him to the hospital that night, but they couldn't stop the bleeding in time."

Her brow smoothed out, but she shook her head. "What…what do you mean?"

Danny looked up at her, wiping the other cheek with the pad of this thumb.

"Did he…?" She trailed off, and Danny nodded.

Something like panic overtook her expression as she said, "So you're…?"

"I'm being charged with manslaughter."

Leah stared down at him, and he watched the rapid rise and fall of her chest as her breathing grew ragged, that same panicked look on her face.

He looked at her dark hair falling over her shoulders, those beautiful, expressive eyes, her delicate nose, the lips that could steal his breath and make him feel alive at the same time. He wanted to memorize everything about her while he still could.

And then, without warning, she threw herself forward, wrapping her arms around him so tightly, he could feel her muscles trembling with the effort.

His heart stopped in his chest before it picked up double time.

Every time he had envisioned this moment, it always ended with some variation of her leaving, some version of her being horrified, afraid, disgusted.

But never once had he imagined *this.*

"Leah." He sighed as he cradled her in his arms, and another sob broke from her lips, stifled by the front of his shirt.

"But you didn't mean to do it," she said through her tears. "It was an accident. Just tell them it was an accident."

Danny closed his eyes as he rubbed his hand up and down her back. She was *defending* him. And in a way, it was almost more painful than it would have been if she told him to go to hell.

"It doesn't work that way, sweet girl," he whispered.

She nodded against his chest before she sniffled. "So there's no way? There's no way this will be okay?"

Danny slid his hand up under her hair, massaging her neck gently. "The best I can hope for is that the judge will take into consideration what happened with Bryan, that I have no priors…and maybe he'll be understanding of the situation."

"The judge? What about the jury?"

"It's not going to trial," he said. "I'm copping a plea. It's better that way."

"How?" she asked, wiping her nose with her sleeve as she sat up to look at him.

"It should lessen the sentence," he said softly.

It was quiet for several seconds before she whispered, "How long?"

He ran his fingers through the back of her hair. "A couple of years, probably."

She closed her eyes as her chin trembled violently, and he used his hand behind her neck to pull her back down to him.

"I'm so sorry, Leah," he whispered as she buried her face in his shirt.

"Don't apologize," she said, her voice breaking before she sniffled and hiccupped against his chest, and he held her, running his hands over her back, her arms, her hair, anywhere he could reach.

After several minutes she spoke again, her voice softly breaking the silence. "How much more time do you have?"

"I don't know. A lot of stuff got held up in the beginning because of everything with Bryan and his involvement in all this. It's all paper pushing at this point. The court date for my sentencing hasn't been set, but my lawyer says it will be sometime this year."

She nodded against him.

"And I'll understand, Leah. I swear to you, I'll understand."

"Understand what?" she whispered.

"If this changes how you feel about me."

She sat up, looking down at him, and he stared back up at her. "I'll understand," he promised.

And he would. He wouldn't hate her for walking away. He wouldn't even hate her if she thought he was a monster, because the truth was, he'd never felt like more of a monster than he did in this moment, watching her hurt for him.

She stared at him until her eyes welled with tears again.

"This is a lot to take in," she said as they spilled over her lower lashes.

"I know," he whispered, wiping them away with his thumbs.

"I just...I need to think. There's so much..." She trailed off and shook her head, and he nodded.

"I know. It's okay."

She looked down at him, and he smiled at her, hoping she couldn't see the sadness behind it.

Leah brought her hand to his cheek, and he leaned into her touch.

"I just...I want you to know that no matter what happens, I *know* you, Danny," she said. "I know who you really are."

He stared up at her, and the vice-like pain in his chest began to soften for the first time since he had entered her apartment. There was nothing she could have said in that moment more perfect than the words she'd just spoken.

Because no matter what she decided after this, even if she chose to walk away and never look back, in a way, she had just absolved him.

She had looked straight through all the horror and the ugliness, and she still saw *him*.

And when she laid her head back down on his chest, he rested his cheek against her hair and closed his eyes, wondering if there would ever be a man on this planet who was worthy of her.

Chapter Thirteen

L eah sat at her desk, spinning a paper clip between her fingers. She just wanted this day to be over.

Every Tuesday she ran the After-School Help program, or ASH, as the students called it. From two to four thirty, students could come to receive extra help in whatever classes they were struggling with, although most often it was overrun with athletes just looking for a quiet place to do their homework before practice began.

By the time the bell rang after Leah's last class, it had already felt like the longest day she'd ever experienced, so the two and a half hours she still had to endure before she could go home seemed insurmountable.

She thought work would provide her with a much needed distraction, but no matter what she did, she couldn't focus on anything except what had happened the day before. She could see everything so vividly—the scene he described, his face as he told her—and she'd spent most of the day on the verge of tears because of it.

The images of Bryan trying to defend himself against three guys—the vicious kick to the head—were burnt into her consciousness, and she hadn't even been there. She couldn't imagine what it must be like for Danny.

She knew if it were her, she would never get over it—watching something that disturbing happen to her best friend.

But Bryan had been more like Danny's brother.

For a split second, she imagined what it would feel like to watch Christopher suffer that way, and the thought alone was enough to incapacitate her.

And when it wasn't those images torturing her, it was the memory of that look on his face as he explained everything to her; even worse than the guilt and sadness in his eyes was the defeat, as if he were waiting for her to condemn him, or dismiss him, or recoil from him.

It was absolutely heartbreaking.

He had told her he'd understand if her feelings for him changed, but the truth was, it only reinforced them. Because when he spoke, all she could hear was how he had tried to defend his brother—how he had attempted to protect someone he loved, and he had failed.

He was a good person who made an impulse decision with disastrous results, and Leah just couldn't get past the unfairness of it all—that Bryan was gone over something so senseless, that Danny would be paying such a heavy price for something that was clearly an accident.

That she was about to lose another person she cared about.

He was the first person she had allowed past her defenses in years, and he was going away. How many times could that happen to one person? How many times would she be forced to endure it?

She didn't know if she could survive it again.

It made her want to grab two handfuls of her hair and scream, because all she wanted to do was wrap her arms around him and protect him from what was coming his way. But if she did that, who would protect her?

She already cared about him so much, and it frightened her to think of how much she might feel for him if she continued down this path. Could she withstand that? Letting herself fall for him completely and then losing him? For *years*?

She couldn't imagine cutting him out of her life, but at the same time, it would be incredibly foolish and careless to keep going like this. There was no right answer, and thinking of it made her feel disoriented and irritable and completely exhausted.

By the time ASH ended, Leah felt weak, like she might be coming down with the sickness she'd been lying about all day whenever people asked her what was wrong with her. She got in her car, desperate to get home and crawl into bed, but as soon as she started it up, she heard Holly's ring tone playing from somewhere inside her purse.

Leah threw the car into reverse before she pulled the phone from her bag.

"What's up?" she said, holding the phone between her shoulder and her ear as she craned her neck to back out of the space.

"*Ughhh!* I'm about to lose it. Are you done with that extra-help thing?"

"Yeah, I'm on my way home right now. What's wrong?"

"I need your help. Can you come to Evan's apartment?"

"Right now?" Leah asked.

"Right now."

"Why? Is everything okay?"

"Yeah, I'm fine, I'm just under a time crunch and I really need your help. Please? I'll explain when you get here."

Leah's shoulders dropped in defeat as she exhaled softly. This day was never going to end.

"Alright. I'll be there in like fifteen minutes."

"Oh thank God," Holly said as she exhaled. "Okay, see you then."

Leah ended the call and tossed her phone into her bag. She pulled off the road and made a U-turn, hoping Holly would be a better distraction than work had been.

About twenty minutes later, Leah walked up to Evan's front door, stopping as she heard a muted thud followed by Holly's chorus of "goddamn stupid-ass motherfucking piece of shit!"

Leah smiled her first genuine smile of the day before she knocked softly.

"Holly?"

"Come in!" she called, and Leah opened the door and froze.

Holly was sitting in the middle of Evan's living room, surrounded by pieces of black lacquered wood, a bunch of crumpled papers, several panes of glass, a sea of screws and bolts, and multiple screwdrivers. She looked up, her expression pathetic as she blew her bangs out of her eyes with a huff.

"Hey," she said weakly.

"What the hell is all this?" Leah asked, and Holly dropped her face into her hands and whimpered.

"Evan's anniversary present."

"You got him debris?" she asked, dropping her purse on the dining room table before she tiptoed through the living room, trying not to step on anything.

"Our three-year anniversary is tomorrow, and he's been wanting this entertainment center forever, but since we're trying to save up to buy a place, he won't spend the money on himself, so I wanted to surprise him, and I bought it, but I didn't realize I'd have to put it together, and he's gonna be home in like two hours, and I'm so totally fucked," she ranted, swatting at one of the crumpled pieces of paper and sending it flying across the room.

"Okay, relax," Leah said with a laugh as she sat down next to her. "We're two college-educated women; we should be able to put this thing together in a couple of hours. I mean, there are instructions, right? We'll just follow them. How hard can it be?"

Holly looked at her incredulously as she gestured to the disaster on the floor in front of them, and Leah smiled. "Alright, go in the kitchen. Take a break. Get us something to snack on and let me reorganize everything in here."

"Okay," Holly said as she stood, stretching her arms over her head before she hopped over the mess in front of her and made her way to the kitchen.

Leah started by flattening out all the crumpled pieces of paper and figuring out which ones were the instructions, and then she organized all the planks, screws, bolts, and panes of glass in the order in which they'd be needing them. By the time Holly came back with chips and salsa and a beer for each of them, she had worked out a fairly straightforward system. She explained it to Holly, and for the first ten minutes or so, the only words spoken between them were either asking for parts or reading instructions.

Holly was working on securing one of the shelves to the backboard while Leah attached the hinges to the glass doors, when suddenly—without even fully deciding to do it—Leah spoke.

"Danny told me his secret."

"Really?" Holly said, sifting through the pile of screws. "When?"

"Yesterday," she said, this time with a bit of trepidation as she realized she'd just opened the door to a conversation she wasn't exactly sure she wanted to have.

"Well, that didn't take long," Holly said, awkwardly twisting the screwdriver with both hands. "So...what is it?"

Leah chewed on the inside of her lip as she finished securing the hinge. She had never been as conflicted over something as she was about this—in fact, as the day wore on, the warnings were getting louder while the pull she felt toward him intensified. And as uneasy as she was to discuss this with Holly—or with anyone for that matter—maybe doing so would help her start to make sense of what she was feeling.

"Okay, well, remember how I told you his friend died a year ago?"

"Yeah," she said, shaking out her hand before she continued twisting the screwdriver.

"Well, turns out he's been on life support this whole time. Danny says he's gone. No brain activity or anything. But his family is still hoping for him to turn around."

Holly grimaced. "Ugh, that's so sad. Did he finally tell you how it happened?"

"Yeah," she said, her stomach turning. "He, um...it was a bar fight."

Holly's hand stopped twisting as she glanced up. "A *bar fight?*"

Leah nodded.

"So like, he was killed?"

"Technically, yeah."

"Oh my God. That's horrible."

"I know," Leah replied softly, looking back down as she started working on the next hinge.

Holly sat there unmoving for a second before she shook her head, turning her attention back to the screwdriver. "As awful as that is, I don't understand why he was so afraid to tell you that."

Here we go.

"Well, that's not the secret. I mean, that's part of it, but...that wasn't the part he was nervous to tell me."

"Okay..." Holly trailed off, leaving the floor open for her to continue.

Leah cleared her throat softly before she said, "Danny was there the night it happened. He got involved. Went after the guy who did it."

"That's not surprising," Holly said.

"Well, he's probably looking at jail time now," she said, her hands working furiously on the task before her. She could see Holly out of the corner of her eye, her brow pulled together as she shook her head.

"Why the hell would *he* go to jail? Why wouldn't they put away the animal who assaulted his friend?"

Leah smiled sadly; Holly was mirroring her exact line of thinking from yesterday.

She took a small breath to steady herself. "Because he's dead."

Holly finally looked up. "Wait...who's dead? The guy who beat up his friend?"

Leah nodded.

Holly stared at her for what seemed like forever before understanding finally swept over her face, followed immediately by horror.

"It wasn't intentional," Leah said quickly, suddenly feeling extremely protective over him. "He was just trying to get him away from Bryan, but they went through a window, and the glass ended up cutting the guy's neck. Danny doesn't even fully remember what happened. It was an accident."

Holly wet her lips before she looked down.

"He's a good person, Holly. Probably one of the best people I know."

Holly kept her eyes on her lap, rolling the screwdriver between her fingers. After a minute of silence, she said, "So, what did you tell him?"

"I told him I needed to think."

She nodded slowly. "Do you know how long he'd be going away for?"

"He's not sure. It's manslaughter, not murder, but still...probably a couple of years."

Holly winced before she picked up another screw and began working it into the shelf. "Shit, Leah. I mean, how can you...is there even anything to think about?"

"Of course there's something to think about!" Leah snapped. "I care about him, Holly. He was only protecting his friend. You even said yourself it was understandable. It was a freak accident. It doesn't change who he is, and it doesn't change how I feel about him!"

Holly kept her head down as she said, "I'm not questioning his character, Leah. I get that he's a good guy. That's not what my issue is here."

Leah exhaled, running the back of her hand over her eyes. "I know. I don't mean to snap at you. I'm just so confused. I don't know if I can walk away from him. He doesn't deserve that."

"Okay, but you have to stop putting other people's needs before your own."

"But he *is* what I need," she said, freezing as soon as the words left her mouth. She hadn't realized how true that was until she had said it out loud.

"Leah," Holly said softly.

"I don't know what to do. I'm not sure I can do it again."

"Do what again?"

"Lose someone," she said, and Holly's shoulders dropped as her expression softened. "I mean, I lost my mom. I lost Scott...or at least, I lost the person I thought Scott was." She shook her head. "But both of those situations were out of my control, you know? I didn't see them coming, so I had no choice but to deal with the aftermath. And I just keep thinking that here, I have a choice. I know what the future holds, and I can walk away this time. I can save myself the heartache."

Holly sighed softly before she dropped her eyes and picked up the screwdriver, and Leah went back to securing the hinge. For a few minutes, they worked on the entertainment center in silence, the air heavy with unspoken words.

"This thing with you and Danny," Holly finally said, "I think your paths crossed for a reason. Maybe it was meant to be fleeting. Maybe you were just supposed to help each other move on from certain things in your past. Or maybe you're supposed to be together forever."

She looked up at Leah as she said, "I wish I could help you, but I don't know what the right choice is, Leah. The only person who can figure that out is you. And you're capable of doing it. I know you don't think you are, but you need to stop doubting yourself. What happened with Scott wasn't your fault. He was an opportunist. That doesn't make you incompetent; it makes *him* an asshole."

The corner of Leah's mouth lifted in a smile as Holly said, "So you take some time to think about it, and you figure out what's going to make you happiest, and then you do it."

Leah kept her eyes on the floor as she nodded.

"And you know that whatever you choose, I'll support you. No matter what happens."

Leah smiled as she lifted her eyes. "I know. And thank you."

"Of course," Holly said. "You're my girl, and I love you."

"I know that too."

Holly smiled before she looked down and tightened the last screw, and then she held up the board with the shelf she had just attached. She grinned triumphantly just as one side of the shelf disconnected, the plank of wood slipping until it was hanging awkwardly by one screw.

Leah pressed her lips together, fighting the laugh she felt bubbling up in her throat, and Holly closed her eyes before she took a deep breath, putting the board back on the floor.

"The things we put ourselves through for love," she sighed as she picked up the screwdriver, and Leah nodded, wondering if it was really the entertainment center she was referring to.

Leah turned the corner and popped her head into the main office, saying good night to the secretaries before she made her way out to the parking lot. As soon as she was sheltered in the refuge of her car, she dropped her head back on the seat and exhaled heavily.

It had been over a week since Danny came to her apartment and told her everything, and with the exception of two "good night" texts, she hadn't spoken to him at all. She missed him more than she was prepared to deal with, but she knew it would be unfair to continue calling him if she hadn't yet figured out what she wanted.

But she thought of him all the time.

Work was the only thing that provided her with a reprieve; she'd gotten much better at putting on a happy face during the day, but as soon as she left school, her mind and her body began functioning as separate entities. Her body would be occupied with driving, or cooking, or cleaning, or getting ready for bed, operating entirely on autopilot as her mind surrendered to the thoughts of Danny she'd avoided all day.

She would imagine what it would feel like to be with him, reveling in the way he made her feel, the way he made her laugh, the way he touched her, the way they seemed to connect on every level, and she'd find herself swaying toward that decision. And then she'd imagine standing in a courtroom, watching Danny being led away through a set of doors she wasn't allowed beyond, and her throat would instantly close up as she found herself retreating.

Leah opened her eyes and stared at her reflection in the rearview mirror. She didn't want to go home, because she knew what was waiting there for her—another night of restless sleep after an endless battle of logic and emotion.

She sat up and started the car, pulling out onto the road and going in the opposite direction of her apartment.

She had no idea how much she would tell him, or if she would tell him anything at all, but at that moment, she just wanted to be with her father.

Leah stopped at a grocery store first, picking up a few things so she could make dinner. As soon as she pulled into his driveway, she saw the curtains in the living room pull back before they fell closed again, and seconds later he was outside in his bare feet, helping her carry in the bags.

"Daddy! There's snow on the ground!" she scolded. "Go back inside, I got it."

He ignored her, meeting her halfway down the driveway and kissing the top of her head as he took the bags out of her hands.

"Is everything okay?" he asked.

"Yeah, everything's fine. I just felt like coming for a visit."

He stared at her for a second, and Leah could tell by his expression that he didn't buy it, but he smiled before turning to walk back up the driveway toward the house.

"So," he said as he put the bags on the counter in the kitchen, "do you need my help in here?"

Leah smirked. "You look like a racer on the block right now."

"What is that supposed to mean?" he laughed.

"Go," she said through a chuckle as she began unpacking the bags. "I know the game is on. I'll call you when it's ready."

"You sure?"

"I'm sure. I don't know how I'll ever manage to put a meal together without your culinary expertise, but I'll try."

He laughed to himself as he turned to walk out of the kitchen. "Just like your mother with that smart mouth," he said, and Leah smiled.

She focused all her attention on preparing dinner; she breaded the chicken, she washed and steamed the vegetables, she mixed the lemon herb sauce she used to season them, and because it was her father's favorite, she made a package of Stove Top stuffing.

"Dad?" she called, removing two plates from the cabinet.

"Yeah?"

"Do you want to eat in there?"

"No, the Lakers are playing like shit. I can't watch this while I'm eating."

Leah laughed as she loaded two plates with food and brought them to the table before she grabbed two bottles of beer from the fridge.

"Alright, it's ready," she called as she popped the caps off the bottles and brought them to the table.

"This smells great, princess. Thank you." He walked past her and took his seat at the table, and she smiled before picking up her silverware.

"So what's going on with you, Leah?"

She stilled with the knife and fork in her hand before she forced a smile and resumed cutting her chicken.

"What do you mean?"

"If you don't want to talk about it, that's fine, but something's up," he said, pointing at her with his fork. "You think I don't know my own daughter?"

She kept her eyes on her plate as she continued to cut, but she sighed softly. On some subconscious level, she realized this was why she had come. If anyone would give it to her straight, it would be her father. But she couldn't bring herself to disclose everything. He hadn't even met Danny, and she didn't want the first thing he learned about him to be the fact that he was facing jail time. Her father was a fair and honest man, but he was still a father, and he'd never want that for her.

"I met somebody," she said, her eyes on her plate.

"I had a feeling," he said, and she looked up to see his eyes on her as he took a sip of his beer.

"Why do you say that?"

He shrugged. "You've been different."

"Different how?"

He placed his beer back on the table. "It's subtle. But lately, when you smile, it reaches your eyes again. I haven't seen that in a long time."

She looked away from him, trying to swallow the lump in her throat brought on by his words.

"You've been guarded for a long time now, so if someone finally got through to you, he must be pretty special."

She nodded, still looking down. "He is."

When her father didn't respond, she glanced up at him. He was watching her intently as he said, "So what's the problem?"

"It's just...it's not gonna be easy," she said, taking a small bite of her chicken and chewing slowly.

Her dad chuckled. "Anyone who says a relationship should be easy has never been in one." The corner of Leah's mouth lifted as he added, "So what makes you think this one will be so hard?"

Leah twisted the fork between her fingers. "He's probably going to be leaving soon."

"For good?"

"No, not for good. But for a while probably."

"Ah," her father said, taking another sip of beer. "And you're worried about having a long-distance relationship?"

She smiled softly. "Something like that."

"People do it all the time, Leah."

"I know people do it. I just don't know if *I* can do it. You know that I've had a really hard time opening up since Scott." Her father scowled at the mention of his name as Leah said, "And when I think about allowing myself to get attached to this guy, and then having him leave..." She trailed off, shaking her head. "I don't know if I'm strong enough for that. It'll be too hard."

He didn't respond, and for the next few minutes, they ate in silence. Leah kept stealing quick glances at her father, but his expression was even as he continued eating.

"Your mother had a terrible pregnancy with Christopher," he said suddenly, and Leah pulled her brow together as she looked up at him.

"I mean really awful," he said. "For the first five months, she was sick all day. And I mean *all day*. I thought it was called morning sickness because it happened in the morning. What the hell did I know," he added with a chuckle. "I made the mistake of mentioning that to her one time. I never said it again."

Leah smiled, and he said, "About halfway through the pregnancy, she started keeping food down, but that's when the heartburn started. Everything she ate would give her heartburn. A glass of water would cause the woman to belch fire."

Leah laughed, picking at the label on her beer.

"And then about six weeks before Chris was due, she started having contractions, so her doctor put her on bed rest. She was only allowed to be on her feet for ten minutes a day. I brought her every magazine, every book, every movie I could think of to try and keep her occupied, but the poor thing was just crawling out of her skin." He smiled softly and looked down. "And then came the labor. Thirty-seven hours. And these were the days before they were so ready to stick that thing in your back. That...that...epicenter."

"Epidural," Leah corrected with a laugh.

He waved his hand in the air. "Whatever that thing is called. They weren't so willing to give those things out. So your mom did it natural." He shook his head. "Thirty-seven hours. I'll never forget it. To this day I don't know how she did it."

Her father smiled before he dropped his eyes, and Leah reached across the table, giving his hand a squeeze.

"And then when Christopher was around nine months old, she said she wanted to have another one. I couldn't believe it. I figured after everything she'd gone through, we wouldn't be having any more children. I mean, I was thrilled she wanted more. I just couldn't believe she did."

He looked up at Leah. "So I asked her, 'Dee, are you sure you wanna go through all that again?' And you know what she said to me?"

"What?"

He looked her in the eyes. "She said the reward more than made up for the suffering."

Leah swallowed hard as she felt the sting of tears pricking her eyes, and he placed his hand on hers. "So if something seems too hard, princess, before you throw in the towel, you should always ask yourself, 'Will the reward be worth the suffering?'"

He gave her hand a quick squeeze before he picked up his fork and resumed eating.

Leah sat there, unmoving, allowing the weight of her father's words to sink in. After what seemed like forever, she glanced up to see him watching her, and a slow smile curved her lips.

"Whenever I get to meet this guy, you have to remind me to thank him."

"For what?" she asked.

He gestured toward her with his beer bottle. "For giving me back that smile."

Leah lay in her bed, holding her cell phone against her stomach as she stared up at the ceiling. The more defined her plans became, the faster her heart pounded in her chest. She had thought about it the whole way home from her father's house; after spending the week isolated from Danny, she knew she still wanted him in her life; she just wasn't sure in what capacity. Could she begin a relationship with him, knowing what was at stake? Or would it make more sense to remain his friend?

Would she even be able to draw the line at friendship, if that's what she decided?

The only way she was going to figure that out would be to spend time with him.

She didn't trust herself alone with him. Not yet. Not with the unresolved sexual tension still raging between them every time they were in the same room together. But this weekend would be the perfect chance to see him again—and to let the people who mattered to her get acquainted with him.

Before she had even made the conscious decision to do so, she was scrolling through her contacts. Her thumb hovered over the call button for just a second, and then she closed her eyes and tapped it before bringing the phone to her ear.

He answered after the first ring.

"Hello?"

Butterflies fluttered through her stomach at the familiar sound of his voice, and she smiled. "Hi."

"Leah," he said softly. He cleared his throat before he said, "How are you?"

"I'm doing okay. You?"

"Not too bad."

A pregnant silence filled the space between them, and Leah chewed on her bottom lip as she twirled the ends of her hair between her fingers. "So, I wanted to ask you something."

"What is it?"

She released her lip before she said, "Do you want to have dinner this weekend?"

When he didn't respond right away, she said, "Robyn gets back from her honeymoon tomorrow, so me and Holly and her boyfriend are going over there Saturday night as sort of a 'welcome home' thing."

It took him a few seconds to respond, and when he finally spoke, he seemed taken aback. "And you want me to go with you?"

"Yeah. If you want to. It'll be pretty laid-back. You know, just hanging out. If you have plans or something, it's okay—"

"No, I don't have plans," he said. "I, um...I can go. It sounds fun."

"Great," she said, her pulse kicking up a notch in anticipation. "Do you want to meet at my place around six?"

"Yeah, that works."

"Okay. So I'll see you Saturday then."

"Okay," he said, still sounding caught off guard.

"Alright," she said, coiling her hair around her finger. "And... Danny?"

"Yeah?"

Leah closed her eyes. "I also called to tell you...that I miss you."

He exhaled into the phone, and this time when he spoke, his words were flooded with relief and something else she couldn't quite place.

"I miss you too, Leah."

Chapter Fourteen

"So when can we hang out with her again?"

Danny shook his head as he opened his soda. "Could you do me a solid and swallow your food before you talk?"

"Why?" Jake mumbled around his meatball sub. "You can understand me."

"Yeah, because that was my issue. Not the fact that I'm getting sprayed with fucking shrapnel from your mouth."

Jake smirked. "Don't change the subject. When can we chill with her again?"

"I think you're getting way ahead of yourself," Danny said, taking a bite of his pizza.

"How am I getting ahead of myself? She knows what's up and she's still around. You hung out with her twice in the past two weeks."

Danny chewed slowly before taking a sip of his soda. Jake was right, of course; Leah hadn't disappeared from his life, and he *had* seen her two times since he'd told her everything.

The first time, when they had hung out at her friends' apartment, things started off awkwardly between them; on the drive over to Robyn's, there were a lot of uncomfortable silences and forced small talk. It was as if they didn't know how to behave in this 'in-between' phase that had them fighting all their instincts and inclinations toward each other.

As soon as they'd gotten there, though, things improved almost instantly. Robyn and Holly were just as amiable and welcoming as they had been that first night at The Rabbit Hole, and the guys were both down-to-earth, working-class guys who were easy to talk to.

Danny had no idea if any of her friends knew his deal, but if they did, either they didn't care, or they were phenomenal at faking tolerance. Regardless, as soon as Leah was around them, she loosened up. Maybe she was waiting for their approval. Maybe she just needed to be in the presence of a support system. But either way, her interactions with Danny became more natural and relaxed until they were talking and laughing like nothing had ever caused a rift in what had started between them.

After dinner Robyn brought out the game Catch Phrase, and they spent the rest of the night laughing their asses off as they tried to get one another to guess the clues. It was the most fun he'd had in a long time.

When they drove back to her place that night, he walked her to her door before he was about to head back to his car.

And that's when she kissed him.

A quick peck on the mouth, but it was enough to have him feeling like he could run the whole way back to his apartment.

The second time they'd hung out, Leah had gone with her sister-in-law to some sort of prenatal appointment about ten minutes away from his shop. She'd texted him and asked if he wanted to grab lunch on his break, and Danny met her at the diner down the block. That time there was no awkwardness whatsoever; they talked effortlessly throughout the meal, and when they'd said good-bye, she hugged him and told him to call her later.

The idea that she still wanted to spend time with him, that she continued to treat him the way she had before she found out he had ended someone's life, it all seemed too good to be true—and despite the fact that he had accused Jake of getting ahead of himself, the truth was, Danny was afraid *he* might be the one guilty of it.

He took another bite of pizza. "Just because she didn't give me my walking papers doesn't mean she wants to be with me."

"It means she still wants to be around you."

Danny shook his head. "I'm not gonna push her. I don't know what she wants. This has gotta be on her terms, alright? Just leave it alone."

He needed to keep reminding himself of that. Because the more he thought about their situation, the more hopeful he became, and he couldn't afford to be on a different page than she was.

"Invite her out for your birthday."

Danny laughed in disbelief. "Did you not hear a single word I just said?"

"No, I heard you," Jake said around another mouthful of food. "I just think you're being a fucking tool."

Danny stopped chewing as he stifled a smile. "Since when is it acceptable to call your boss a fucking tool to his face?"

"Come on, man," Jake said. "I see what this is about. You don't want to get your hopes up in case she's not offering you what you want from her. But the bottom line is, this girl likes being around you. Maybe she wants to be your friend, maybe she wants to be more. I get the whole 'give her space' thing, but if you play this too cool, you're gonna fuck it up. You don't wanna look indifferent. You think she's gonna stick around in *any* capacity if she thinks you don't give a shit either way?"

Danny stared at his friend. Maybe it was because Jake spent so much of his time saying things that were intentionally provocative or offensive, but on those rare occasions when he came from a place of sincerity, his words seemed that much more profound.

"Invite her out for your birthday," Jake suggested again. "Friends go out for each other's birthdays. You're not making any assumptions or declarations by including her. Me and Tommy aren't even bringing chicks, so it's not like there's gonna be a couples vibe or anything. You like this girl. You like being around her. Stop wasting time you don't have."

Danny ran his hand through his hair as Jake's words echoed in his ears, bouncing around his skull and burrowing into his consciousness until they were beating in his blood.

You like being around her. Stop wasting time you don't have.

He hadn't seen what he was doing as wasting time, but Jake did have a point. His days were numbered, and he wanted to spend as many of them with her as he could, friends or otherwise.

Stop wasting time you don't have.

Danny twisted the cap back on his drink. "I'll think about it," he said. "Can we shut the fuck up about this now?"

Jake gave him a flimsy salute before he shoved the rest of his sandwich in his mouth.

"By the way," he garbled around his mouthful. "I'm not bringing a girl, but I might still try to get a blow job in the bathroom. Leah doesn't need to know that, though."

And just like that, Jake was back.

Danny burst out laughing before he threw a wad of tin foil at him, and Jake shrugged, wiping his hands on his pants before he stood and made his way back out to the garage.

Danny shook his head as he turned back toward the table, and then he reached in his pocket and pulled out his phone, staring at the screen for just a moment before he opened a new text window and clicked on her name.

You free this weekend? We're hitting up Dave and Buster's for my birthday.

He hit send and exhaled, putting the phone on the table before he picked up his pizza.

A minute later his phone vibrated with her response, and he stopped chewing as he swiped the screen with the side of his finger.

Happy birthday! And definitely. Call me later.

He smiled, clearing the screen before sliding the phone back in his pocket.

No more wasting time you don't have.

"I'm not going in that thing," Leah said as she took a sip of her beer, and Jake scoffed.

"Oh come on. It's a game!"

"Yes, it's a game. A 4D game where you lock yourself in a confined space and not only see and hear but also *feel* the monsters attacking you if you don't kill them fast enough. No thanks."

"What are you, eight?" Jake said. "It's not real."

"Then *you* go in!" Leah said through a laugh.

Jake smirked, resting his elbows on the table as he leaned across it toward Leah. "Care to make this interesting?"

She put her beer down and mirrored his position, leaning toward him. "Always."

Danny grinned as he brought his drink to his lips, his arm resting on the back of the booth behind her.

"Okay," Jake said, sitting up and looking around the table. "Okay, so..."

"He's got nothing," Tommy said with a laugh, and Danny chuckled as Leah sat back against the booth, turning her head to look up at him. He looked down at her, a smile curving his lips, and she shifted in her seat, closing the small distance between them so that their bodies were touching from shoulder to knee.

His arm came down from the back of the booth, wrapping around her shoulders, and she brought her hand to his knee under the table.

From the second he had picked her up that night, he could tell something was different. Not only was the awkwardness between them gone, but any hesitation, any sense of restriction, had completely vanished as well. On the ride down, she had reached over the console and held his hand. And several times throughout dinner, she had found an excuse to touch him. A playful slap here, a shoulder rub there, and now her hand on his leg.

On the surface Danny was completely calm and collected, but underneath, his adrenaline was racing with every touch, with what it could mean, with the awareness that each one heated his veins and made his heart beat faster and his breathing grow shallow.

"Got it!" Jake finally said, grinning triumphantly. He reached across the table to the remnants of their appetizers and pulled two buffalo bites off the plate. He put one in front of Leah, and the other in front of himself before grabbing the hot sauce from the side of the table and shaking an excessive amount on each one.

"Dude, those are fucking Firehouse wings," Tommy said. "What are you doing?"

"Upping the ante," he said before he reached into Tommy's plate of nachos, pulling two jalepeno peppers out of the cheese and placing them on the top of each piece of chicken, like a cherry on top of a sundae.

"Is he gonna make me eat that?" Leah said in Danny's ear, and he leaned down to her, reveling in the scent of her hair.

"You don't have to do anything you don't want to do. Tell him to fuck off."

"Swear jar," she said, and Danny grinned as she sat up to face Jake. "Alright, what are we doing?"

"We each eat this. Whole thing. One bite. Whoever drinks first, loses. And if you lose, your ass goes in Dark Escape."

Danny watched as Leah pursed her lips, weighing her options.

"So, we're not allowed to drink anything," she clarified, and Jake smiled.

"Not unless you want to lose."

Her shoulders rose as she took a deep breath, and then she exhaled in a rush. "Okay, let's do it."

"*Seriously?*" Jake asked.

"Yeah," she answered with a smile. "Why? Were you all talk just now?"

Danny smirked as he and Tommy made eye contact across the booth.

"Nope," he said a beat too late, picking up the horrifically enhanced buffalo bite, and Leah did the same, holding it out to him.

"Cheers," she said, tapping hers to Jake's, and then they both popped them into their mouths.

For the first few seconds, they chewed in silence, but then it started.

Jake's face turned beet red as he began to chew faster in an attempt to get it over with, and Leah pressed her fingertips to her lips, blinking rapidly as her eyes began to tear.

Danny brought his hand to the back of her neck, rubbing gently as he leaned toward her ear. "You can drink. I won't let him make you go in there."

She shook her head. "I'm good," she managed hoarsely, and then she closed her eyes and swallowed hard.

Across the table, Jake was banging his fist against the side of the booth, his eyes clamped shut as he tried to force himself to swallow.

"*Woo!*" Leah exhaled, her eyes watering heavily as she reached for the spoon in front of her, and then she leaned across the table, dragging it along the mound of sour cream on the top of Tommy's nachos.

Danny watched her bring the spoon to her lips, licking the excess sour cream off the sides before she put the spoon in her mouth, sucking on it like she was eating a lollipop. She slowly pulled it from her lips, turning the spoon around and dragging her tongue up the back of it to remove every last drop before she placed it back on the table.

Holy. Fuck.

He glanced across the table to see if the others had been watching her—if they were reacting to what she had just done—but Jake had both fists clamped in front of his eyes, breathing like he was about to give birth, and Tommy had his head thrown back against the booth, laughing hysterically.

He turned back to see Leah staring up at him. Her face was flushed and her eyes were still glassy, but she certainly wasn't feeling Jake's pain.

"What?" she asked softly, and Danny stared at her, saying nothing. "Why are you looking at me like that?"

He opened his mouth but closed it before he could formulate a response, and the corner of her mouth lifted.

"Are you kidding me?" she said through her smile.

"What?"

"Did that just turn you on?"

"What? No! No...I didn't...I was just..."

Her smile grew more pronounced, and Danny dropped his head, exhaling a breathy laugh.

"Really? *Hot sauce?*"

"No," he said softly. "That thing you just did with the spoon."

Leah smirked. "Ah," she said with a nod. "Well, that was one of the most awful things I've ever experienced, so I'm glad to hear it at least *looked* sexy."

He laughed, lifting his eyes to hers, and she smiled, reaching up and running her thumb over his cheek.

"*He's out!*" Tommy yelled. "*Done!*"

Leah and Danny whipped their heads in Tommy's direction to see Jake with his head thrown back, chugging a glass of water so quickly that two streams were running out of the corners of his mouth and down his chin.

"No, no!" Leah laughed. "Not water!"

"Fuck," Jake said as he slammed the glass down on the table with tears pouring down his face. "What are you, superhuman? I'm on fucking fire!" he wailed, reaching for Leah's water.

She grabbed his wrist, stopping him. "Not water," she said through her laughter. "Here." She grabbed his spoon and scooped up a heap of sour cream, handing it to him.

Danny watched Jake shove it in his mouth with a groan, and suddenly spoons and sour cream became a lot less erotic.

"Fuck," he mumbled around the spoon. "Fuck, that's better." He pulled it out of his mouth and took another scoop of it before shoveling it back in.

After one more spoonful, Jake wiped his eyes on his sleeve and looked at Leah. "How did you know that would work?"

"You're never supposed to use water if you eat something spicy. Capsaicin is the chemical that burns in spicy foods, and the only thing that disengages it is the chemical casein. You can find it in most dairy products, like milk, or yogurt. Or sour cream," she said with a smile. "But there's nothing in water. It just spreads the oils around your mouth and makes it worse."

The entire table stared at her.

"Are you some kind of evil genius?" Jake asked, and Danny laughed before looking down at Leah. He loved that she was smart—in fact, it was one of the things that turned him on the most about her—but when she used that intelligence to shut Jake down?

It was one of the sexiest things he'd ever seen.

"So that's what you did? You ate sour cream right after?" Jake asked, and Leah shrugged.

"You said no drinking. You didn't say anything about sour cream."

Tommy burst out laughing before he said, "Holy shit, she *is* an evil genius! I fucking love this girl!"

Leah laughed, resting her head on Danny's shoulder, and he put his arm around her again.

Me too, he thought, rubbing his hand up and down her arm as she played with the hem of his shirt.

As Danny turned into Leah's apartment complex, she gave his hand a gentle squeeze. "Thanks for inviting me out tonight. I had a lot of fun."

He smiled. "It wouldn't have been half as fun without you there, so thank *you*. Hearing Jake scream like a girl inside that game was the best birthday present anyone could have ever given me."

Leah covered her mouth, laughing at the memory. After Jake lost the bet, the four of them walked over to Dark Escape 4D so Jake could pay up, and the shrieks and squeals coming out of the booth had all three of them leaning on one another for support while they cracked up. Her stomach muscles still felt sore from it.

In fact, she couldn't remember the last time she laughed as much as she did tonight. She and Danny had played a game of Nothing But Net, where they went head-to-head with each other to see who could make the most baskets before the clock ran out, and they spent more time trying to distract each other from shooting than they did trying to make their own baskets.

Then there was the Skee-Ball incident; Leah had tried to show Danny how to flick his wrist so he could get the high score every time, and he ended up accidentally flinging the ball into the lane two down from them and scaring the hell out of the teenager playing there.

And when the four of them played Dance Dance Revolution against one another, Leah thought she might pee her pants from laughing so hard.

She loved his friends. And she loved spending time with him. She loved flirting with him and touching him and talking to him and being with him.

She loved the way he rubbed the back of her neck whenever he thought she was uneasy. She loved how he smiled at her when he didn't think she could see him.

And she loved that, despite the palpable sexual tension between them, he had been a perfect gentleman all night.

Danny pulled the car into an empty space in front of her apartment, and before he could say anything, Leah turned to him.

"Do you want to come in for a little while?"

He turned to look at her. "Um...yeah. Okay."

"Okay," she said before undoing her seat belt, and Danny cut the engine as she exited the car.

They walked up the path to her door in silence, and once they were inside, Leah took his coat, hanging it beside hers in the closet. She closed her eyes, taking a small, steadying breath before she righted her expression and turned to face him. He was standing by the door, his hands shoved in his pockets.

"So," he said, rolling up on the balls of his feet.

"So."

His eyes met hers, and the way he was looking at her made her want to pin him up against the door.

Instead, she cleared her throat and said, "I have something for you."

"You do?"

She nodded. "Don't get excited though. It's not a big deal. Actually, it's kind of silly."

They stared at each other for a few seconds, and Leah felt her stomach flutter as a slow smile curved his lips.

"So...can I have it?" he asked through a laugh.

"It's in the kitchen," she replied, turning in that direction.

"Did you get me a Slap Chop?"

"*What?*" she laughed. "Why would you guess *that?*"

"I don't know. You said it was in the kitchen and it was silly."

"Okay, let's get one thing straight. The Slap Chop is not silly. It's a stroke of genius," she said as they turned into the kitchen.

"A guy chopping a handful of almonds while telling the audience, 'Wait until you see my nuts' is a stroke of genius?"

She turned toward him, fighting a laugh. "You watch too much TV."

"Said the girl who owns the Slap Chop."

She laughed then, taking the plate off the counter before she turned and held it out to him.

"It's no roulette table with a functioning wheel, but I tried."

The smile on his face dropped. "You *made* this?"

"Mm-hm," Leah said, placing it on the counter in front of him. "Well, not the cars, obviously."

She looked up at him, but he was staring down at the cake in awe. It was a typical square cake, but the entire bottom half was made to look like a road with two cars driving across it. On the top half of the cake was a sign that matched the shape and typography of the sign for Danny's shop, where the words *Happy Birthday Danny* were written.

"It's all fondant. The road, the sign. So you can eat everything. I tried to make the cars out of fondant, but they looked like mutant insects, so I cheated and used toys."

He spun the plate slowly, looking at it from all sides, and then he looked up at her. "I can't believe you did this."

She shrugged. "It wasn't a big deal. It was fun."

"And time-consuming. And incredibly thoughtful."

She smiled up at him, and he shook his head before looking back down at the plate. "I can't remember the last time I had a birthday cake."

"Are you serious?"

"Yeah, I mean, once you pass ten, it kind of loses its grandeur, don't you think?"

"No way! What about making your birthday wish, then?"

He shrugged, and she shook her head in disbelief.

"Well, let it be known that on *my* birthday, this girl needs her cake and her birthday wish. No exceptions."

He smiled. "When's your birthday?"

"May third."

"Noted," he said. "Wait, do I have to make one myself?"

"Tell you what," she said. "You can buy one and tell me you made it, and I'll pretend to believe it."

He laughed before he put his arm around her and pulled her into his side. "Thank you. I love it," he said against the top of her head before he kissed her there. The flutters in her belly scattered up through her chest, and she closed her eyes, resting her hand on his stomach.

"This kitchen is incredible, by the way."

"I know," she said, her head still resting on his shoulder. "It was the thing that sold me on getting this apartment. That, and the bathroom."

"What's so special about the bathroom?"

Leah smiled. "Do you want a tour?"

He unwrapped his arm from around her and gestured grandly. "After you."

Leah walked out of the kitchen with Danny behind her, and she nodded to the right. "Living room, but you saw that last time you were here." She turned and walked a few steps to the left and said, "The formal dining room."

Danny smiled at the little nook off the kitchen area that was just large enough to fit a small table and four chairs.

"Spare bedroom," she said, waving her arm like a *Price Is Right* girl at the doorway to their left. Danny popped his head in for a second before he nodded his approval, and Leah smiled.

"Brace yourself," she said, reaching her hand into the next room and turning on the lights.

Danny moved to stand in the doorway beside her, his eyes combing the room. "Holy shit," he said. "That's the biggest tub I've ever seen."

"Right? It's a spa tub. Isn't it gorgeous?"

"If a tub could be gorgeous, I guess this one would be. I'm more concerned with that shower, though. Why are there forty-seven showerheads in it?"

Leah laughed. "The guy who lived here before me worked for Kohler. He designed bathrooms for a living."

Danny nodded, his eyes roving the room, and Leah huffed as she crossed her arms over her chest. "You're supposed to be making a bigger deal than this."

"*Oh my God!*" he said, rubbing his eyes before widening them. "Is this real? I have to be hallucinating. This is the most incredible thing I've ever seen in my life! I'm ruined for all other bathrooms now!"

She stared up at him, completely expressionless, and when she saw the first signs of his dimples, she pushed his chest before stepping back out into the hall.

"You suck," she said, and he laughed, switching off the light in the bathroom.

He stepped back into the hall with her, and she pointed to the last doorway. "And that's my room."

Danny walked over to the door, turning on the light before he took a few steps into the room, and Leah stood behind him, trying to imagine seeing it for the first time like he was.

The walls were a warm terra-cotta color, the floor cherry hardwood. Her bed was up against the wall to the right, covered in a puffy cream-colored comforter and several oversized throw pillows. Up against the wall to the left was her dresser with her stereo and a few pictures on top. A flat-screen TV hung on the wall above it.

The far wall was made up entirely of floor-to-ceiling shelves; along the top, there were vases of flowers and a few scented candles. The shelves on the bottom were full of books. And the ones in the center consisted of row after row of Leah's CDs.

Danny looked over his shoulder at her. "Can I?" he asked, gesturing to the shelves, and she nodded.

Leah leaned up against the doorframe, folding her arms as she watched him approach the wall. He crouched down, checking out the neatly lined-up books on the bottom.

After a minute he straightened, looking over the shelves with her music. "I don't think I know anyone who still has CDs," he said with his back to her as he pulled one of them out, glancing at the cover before sliding it back in its place.

"I love my CDs. All that music is on my computer and my iPod. I just..."

Danny glanced back over his shoulder. "You're just a packrat?" he said with a smirk.

"The politically correct term would be *sentimental*," she said, and she heard him laugh softly. "But yeah...I guess I can be a packrat. But only with things that mean something."

"All these mean something?" he asked, ducking his head to look at the second row.

"In some way, yeah. It might be a song that means something, or in some cases it's the whole album that reminds me of a certain time in my life. In others, it's just the memory of buying the CD itself—who I was with, or what was happening when I bought it." She shrugged, even though he wasn't looking at her.

Danny nodded absently, taking a step to the right and leaning in as he read the album titles, and Leah pushed off the doorframe and walked into the room, her eyes on him as she sat on the edge of her bed.

She felt slightly unnerved, almost as if she were watching him read her diary. She had always believed the type of music a person listened to was a fairly accurate portrayal of who they were, and she couldn't help but wonder what he was surmising about her as he studied the shelves.

Danny slowly ran his finger along the cases; there was something almost sensual about the way he did it, and out of nowhere, she imagined him repeating the movement, this time along the skin of her inner thigh, and she swallowed hard.

Danny's finger stopped abruptly, and then he pulled one of the cases out and turned around, holding it up for her.

"Really?" he asked.

N'SYNC: No Strings Attached.

She folded her arms as she looked up at him. "I didn't buy them all yesterday."

"I don't care when you bought it," he said with a laugh. "There's no excuse for this."

"I Thought She Knew."

"You thought *who* knew?"

"No." Leah laughed. "That's the name of the song that landed that one a spot on the shelf. 'I Thought She Knew.' It's an a cappella song. Really pretty lyrics."

Danny looked down at the CD case, turning it over to read the back.

"Plus, hot guys sing it, so."

He glanced up with a smirk before he shook his head. "They're not objects, Leah. They're real men with feelings and debatable talents."

She pressed her lips together, fighting a smile as he turned to slide the case back on the shelf, and then he reached up and pulled another one down.

"If you're gonna make fun of every CD I have up there, I'm kicking you out of this room."

He laughed to himself before he turned to face her, the case sandwiched between his two hands.

"Which one do you have?" she asked, craning her neck to see, and he turned his body, shielding it from her as he shook his head.

"You'll see in a second," he said, walking the few steps over to her stereo and hitting the button to turn it on. Leah watched as he placed the CD into the machine, and then he skipped forward a few tracks before hitting play.

The opening chords to Ray LaMontagne's "Hold You In My Arms" filled the room, and Leah immediately closed her eyes. When she opened them a few seconds later, he was leaned up against the wall, watching her.

"I love this song."

"Me too," he said, pushing off the wall as he walked toward her. "I guess your taste in music isn't so shitty after all."

She laughed lightly, looking up at him as he came to stand in front of her.

"Dance with me," he said, extending his hand.

"Dance with you?"

He nodded. "It's my birthday, so you really can't say no."

"Hey now. Your birthday's over."

Danny glanced down at his watch. "Not for another two hours."

She laughed as she gave him her hand, and he pulled her up to face him. For a second they just stood there, looking at each other, and then their smiles slowly faded as the atmosphere shifted. Leah dropped her eyes, the sudden intensity of the moment catching her off guard.

Danny gently raised their joined hands, and her heart began thumping erratically as she felt his other arm snake around her waist, his open palm resting on her lower back.

She took a tentative step toward him, their bodies almost flush as she slid her left hand up his arm and over the top of his shoulder, coming to rest just below the nape of his neck.

He started to sway them ever so slightly, and Leah smiled at the absurdity and the charm of them dancing in the middle of her bedroom.

"You're much better at this than I expected," she said. "Dance Dance Revolution was not your friend tonight."

"Oh, I threw that battle," he said dismissively. "I didn't want to deal with Jake and Tommy being totally emasculated by my performance. Plus, every woman in the place would have swarmed me after that, and it would have been really awkward for everyone."

She pressed her lips together, but the smile broke through anyway, and he flashed his dimples before he turned them around and dipped her.

Leah dropped her head back and laughed, and Danny slowly pulled her back up, looking down at her as he used their joined hands to brush the hair away from her face.

And then he leaned in, his cheek brushing against hers as he sang the next words softly in her ear.

When you kissed my lips, with my mouth so full of questions,
It's my worried mind that you quiet.
Place your hands on my face, close my eyes and say
That love is a poor man's food. Don't prophesize.

In those first few seconds, it felt like her heart had stopped, but by the time the verse ended, it was pounding so wildly she was sure he could feel it against his chest; Danny lifted his head and she pulled back, her lips slightly parted as she stared up at him.

The sexy, throaty timbre of his voice still resonated in the room; it poured through her body, warming her veins and making her feel heavy and sedated, like drinking wine in front of the fireplace while a snowstorm raged outside.

It was sex and salvation and desire and serenity, stirring something primal and innately feminine in her.

Leah's breathing became shallow as she continued to stare up at him, and he kept his eyes on hers, still swaying them gently to the music. It felt like a current was running just below the surface of her skin, making her hypersensitive to everything around her: his hand on her back, the soft sound of his breathing, the scent of his skin.

And that voice.

She wanted to hear it again. She wanted to fall asleep listening to it every night. She wanted him to wake her up with it every morning.

Leah took a step forward, closing the tiny distance between them and pressing her body against his, and he dropped his head slightly and exhaled. The warm rush of his breath danced over the side of her neck, causing goose bumps to prickle over her skin, and Leah turned her head slightly, breathing him in as they moved to the music.

She had wanted this for so long—to feel his body up against hers again. She'd imagined it so many times, but those daydreams were pitiful echoes of the reality.

All at once she realized she was trembling, and Leah tightened her arm around his back, trying to steady herself against him. She knew what she wanted, why she had asked him to come in, and now that he was right in front of her, she could feel the apprehension beginning to swirl with the growing desire in her belly.

Danny's hand moved on her back, his fingertips teasing the sliver of exposed skin above the waist of her jeans.

"You're shaking," he whispered, slipping his hand up the back of her shirt and tracing soothing circles on her overheated skin. Leah's eyes fell closed as she dropped her forehead to his shoulder. With every pass of his fingers, a tingling sensation rippled over her skin, making her feel almost dizzy.

She had never in her entire life physically responded to someone the way she did to Danny, and it was as terrifying to her as it was thrilling.

Leah gripped the back of his shirt, her forehead still pressed to his shoulder, and the solid steadiness of his body made her trembling that much more obvious.

Danny lowered his chin so that the only thing separating his lips from her ear was the delicate veil of her hair. "Are you okay?" he asked softly, and she nodded against him, not trusting her voice.

He flattened his hand against her lower back, pressing her closer to him, and that was all it took for her mind to completely surrender to her body.

Leah turned her head slightly, nuzzling his neck before she placed a soft kiss just under his jaw, and their swaying came to a halt as he froze. She stilled instantly, her lips unmoving on his neck.

Danny took a deep breath before he gently removed his hand from hers, and Leah's stomach dropped.

And then he wrapped his arm around her waist with the other and pulled her against him, so that any measure of space between them was completely forsaken. She exhaled against his skin as he started swaying them again, his movements fluid and carnal and intoxicating and perfect.

Her free hand came up to cup the back of his neck, and when she resumed kissing his jaw, he tilted his head up slightly, his fingertips digging into her lower back. Emboldened by his reaction, she trailed her kisses upward, pressing her mouth just below his ear before lightly grazing her teeth over his skin.

He made a tiny sound in the back of his throat, and she kissed him there before trailing her fingers down the back of his neck.

"Danny?" she whispered, and he pulled back just enough to look down at her. She wet her lips before tentatively lifting her eyes to his. "Will you kiss me?"

His eyes fell closed, and Leah saw his throat bob as he swallowed. And then his hold on her loosened as his hands came to her sides, slowly trailing up the length of her body and over her shoulders. His fingertips ghosted along the sides of her neck, making her shiver.

He used his thumbs under her jaw to tilt her face up before he ran them over her cheeks.

And then he nodded, slowly closing the distance between them.

He kissed her carefully, his lips gentle, and Leah tried to keep hers pliant as she responded, but it was like trying to stop a cresting wave from breaking. She could feel the swell of it rising with every touch of his lips, building and building until finally she tightened her hold around his neck and deepened the kiss with a sigh.

He moaned quietly into her mouth, and every tingle, every delicious sizzle of electricity that had been dancing over her skin collected at once, melting together until it felt like her entire body was humming.

Within seconds, their kisses had grown feverish and their breathing labored, the soft rasping sound of it blending with the music in the background. She had never known what it was to lose control until she'd met him; she'd felt it the night he'd given her the block of concrete, and she knew she was already there again, in that place where the only thing that mattered was what her body wanted, where she needed to be touched and how, where she wanted to touch him.

There was nothing else but that. No thought, no reason, no consequences. Nothing existed except his mouth on hers and his hands on her body and the crushing desire for more, more, more.

She reluctantly broke their kiss, and Danny grunted softly as her lips left his. He watched her ease up onto the bed behind them, crawling backward until she was kneeling in the center of it. Leah crossed her arms in front of her body and gripped the hem of her sweater, pulling it up over her head before tossing it to the floor, and Danny's eyes finally left hers as they dropped to take her in.

His chest rose and fell quickly as his eyes raked over her body, and it was as if she could actually feel them trailing over her skin.

And then he leaned forward, placing his hands on the foot of the bed as he began crawling toward her.

She felt her legs go weak, and she dropped from her kneeling position to sit on her calves just as his lips met hers again. He applied gentle pressure, pushing her backward until she fell onto the pile of pillows behind her.

Danny held his weight in his arms as he kissed her, nudging her legs apart with his hips before lowering his body onto hers.

She gasped as she felt his pressure between her thighs, and when he gently pushed his hips into her, she moaned into his mouth.

"That sound," he said hoarsely between kisses. "Do you have any idea what that sound does to me?"

His mouth moved seamlessly down her throat, and when she felt the heat of his kisses on the swell of her breast, she arched up slightly, tangling her fingers in his hair.

His hands slid between her body and the mattress, and she felt him take the clasp of her bra between his fingers.

"Can I?" he whispered against her skin, and she nodded fervently, arching up higher.

The clasp popped open, and Danny pulled the garment from her body before dropping it over the side of the bed. And then his mouth was back on her, this time without the barrier of clothing between them, and her hips thrust upward of their own accord as she sucked in a sharp breath.

His hands came to her hips, pinning them to the bed as he kissed his way back up her neck, stopping just before their lips touched.

"Easy," he whispered, planting a soft kiss on her mouth, and then he was gone again, trailing his mouth down the center of her body.

Leah closed her eyes and reached above her, grasping the headboard as she tried to keep herself still. Instead of focusing on what she wanted to happen, she started concentrating on what was happening right now. With her eyes closed, she didn't know where he would touch her next—whether it would be with his lips, his tongue, or his hands—and the anticipation only amplified whatever he was doing, so that the tiniest graze of his finger set her on fire.

She felt him remove her jeans, but she kept her eyes closed, holding her breath as she waited for his next move.

"Leah," he said softly, and she opened her eyes and looked at him.

He was kneeling at the foot of the bed with her jeans in his hand, and he dropped them on the floor as his eyes traveled up the length of her body, laid out for him like an offering. He shook his head slightly before he lifted his eyes to hers.

"You are so beautiful," he whispered.

She released the headboard and sat up, taking his face in her hands as she kissed him, and he wrapped his arms around her. She could feel the rough material of his shirt against her breasts, and she reached down and tugged the hem.

"I want to feel your skin on mine," she said against his mouth, and he nodded before he broke the kiss, reaching behind his head and pulling his shirt off. Leah brought her hands to his chest, tracing the contours with her fingertips before trailing them down over his stomach.

He remained perfectly still, his eyes closed and his breathing shallow as she touched him. His body was strong, lean and muscled, and she kissed along the top of his chest before she lay back onto the mattress and pulled him with her.

"You feel good like this," she whispered, running her hands over his back as the skin of his chest brushed against hers with every movement.

He slowly brought his mouth back to hers, his kisses once again careful and measured. It seemed like every single one was designed to tease and torment her, and after several minutes of his gorgeous torture, she was squirming beneath him.

Leah whimpered pathetically against his mouth, and she felt it curve into a smile.

"Relax, sweet girl," he said, his lips grazing hers as he spoke. "I'm gonna make you feel good this time, I promise."

He lowered his head and kissed her, and then she felt his hand trail down her stomach before it slipped below the front of her panties.

Her hands flew back up to the headboard as she tried to regain the control she had managed before, but it was just like the last time he'd touched her that way; it was like he'd known her body for years. He knew exactly what to do and how to do it, and within two minutes of him touching her, she was panting heavily, her hips lifting off the bed as she neared her release.

Suddenly his hand stilled, and Leah's eyes flashed open as she lifted her head.

"Why are you stopping?" she breathed, and he smiled before he leaned over and kissed her neck.

"Not yet," he murmured against her skin.

"Danny," she started, and then he covered her mouth with his. She wanted to protest. Hell, she wanted to *plead*. But when he kissed her that way, the only thing she could bring herself to do was kiss him back.

After a minute he lifted his head, watching her reaction as he began moving his hand again, and she bit her lip to stifle the sound building in her throat as she turned away from him. She hadn't known it would be like that—that she could pick right up where she left off that easily. Leah squeezed her eyes shut as her legs began to quiver, and this time as she started to gasp, he removed his hand from her body completely.

She slapped her hands down on the mattress and threw her head back. "Oh, son of a bitch!" she cried, and he laughed softly, kissing along her jawline.

"Swear jar," he said, nuzzling beneath her ear.

She slid both hands up into her hair as she tried to catch her breath. "You're making me crazy," she panted.

"I know," he said, licking the spot beneath her ear. "You have no idea how sexy you are right now."

"Danny," she breathed, bringing her hands to his face and forcing him to look at her. "Please don't make me wait anymore."

He leaned down so that their noses touched as he reached between them and slid her underwear over her hips, and she shimmied out of them before kicking them away.

And when his hand slid down her stomach again, she gripped his wrist, stopping him.

He froze, lifting his head to look at her.

"That's not what I meant," she said softly.

Danny pulled his brow together, and she released his wrist, lowering her eyes as she reached between them, fumbling with the button of his jeans before she popped it open. As she slid his zipper down, she raised her eyes back to his, and understanding swept over his face.

"Leah," he said huskily. "Are you sure?"

She nodded. "Yes," she whispered. She was sure about this. She was sure about him. She was sure about *them*. There wasn't a doubt in her mind anymore where she belonged.

"I want you," she said, running the backs of her fingers over his stomach. "And I don't just mean tonight. I want *us*, Danny."

He closed the small distance between them, pressing her back into the pillows as he kissed her deeply, and Leah gripped the waistband of his jeans and boxers and slid them down over his hips.

Danny removed them the rest of the way, grabbing his wallet out of the pocket before he tossed them on the floor behind him. Leah watched him remove a condom and open the wrapper, and all at once, her stomach twisted with anxiety.

She closed her eyes and concentrated on taking slow, deep breaths.

"Leah," he said gently, placing his hands on her thighs, and she opened her eyes.

She could see the concern on his face, and she reached out for him; he came down to her immediately, resting his weight on his elbows as he cradled her face.

"I'm okay," she said with a tiny smile. "I'm just a little nervous."

"What are you nervous about?" he asked, playing with the hair by her temple, and she closed her eyes.

It had been so long for her, and she just wanted it to be good for him. The way he made her feel tonight was so far beyond anything she'd ever experienced. She wanted to make him feel that way too.

"It's just that...it's been a while," she said, her eyes trained on his shoulder.

"Hey," he said gently, and she lifted her eyes to his. "You're in control here. However you want this to go, whatever you need, just tell me."

She smiled softly. Of course he was thinking of her.

"I'm not nervous about *me*," she said, watching her fingers draw patterns on his shoulder. "I just...I want to make you feel good."

She glanced up just in time to see his dimples slowly appear. "Leah," he said through a laugh. He circled his fingers around her wrist and guided her hand down between them until she was touching him.

Oh God.

"You feel that?" he asked softly. "That's how you make me feel. And we haven't even started yet."

She made a tiny sound as she closed her hand around him and guided him to her body, and he exhaled in a rush, dropping his forehead to hers.

And then he was pressing into her.

She reached up and clutched the back of his shoulders, and as soon as his hips were flush with hers, her entire body erupted in goose bumps.

"Fuck," he said under his breath, and Leah saw the muscle in the side of his jaw flex before he tentatively moved against her. She arched her head back as a shiver ran through her body, and she felt his hands slide between her and the mattress, holding her hips against his own as he rocked into her again.

"Goddamn, you feel so good," he breathed.

She wanted to answer. She wanted him to know what he was doing to her, but his rhythm had effectively stolen any and all words from her mouth. Instead she wrapped her arms around him, groaning and sighing into his shoulder as every one of his movements pushed her closer to the brink she'd been teetering on all night.

After being on the verge twice before, it didn't take long for her to feel the tightening in her belly, the incredible tension he was building inside her, and she clutched at his back as his name fell from her lips.

Danny crashed his mouth to hers, saying something against her lips that she couldn't understand; she was too lost in what was happening to her body. It was as if a rubber band had been stretched impossibly beyond its capacity, and she was waiting for it to snap at any second. And just when she thought it would, it somehow stretched even further.

Danny shifted the position of his hips, and Leah gasped loudly as her hands flew back to the headboard above her. Whatever he was doing now caused the beautiful pressure in her belly to spread down into her thighs and up through her chest. Everything inside her felt wound tight and ready to shatter, and she didn't know how much more of the build-up she could take; it was already more intense than any orgasm she'd ever had.

"Oh God...please," she panted, tightening her grip on the headboard.

"Come on, baby," he whispered, reaching down to hold her hips, and then moved against her as he tilted them up.

Leah arched off the bed as the rubber band finally snapped, sending concentrated shock waves of pleasure crashing through her body. She knew she must have cried out, but she couldn't see or hear anything at all; all of her awareness was focused on the torturous ache being washed away by the indescribable feeling pulsing through her veins.

He kept moving against her, dragging out every last second until she felt like her bones had disconnected, rendering her completely useless. And just as she felt herself starting to come down, Danny did something with his hand that drove her right back up, unexpectedly sending her over the edge a second time.

This time she heard herself cry out, but it was lost in the beautiful sounds that were spilling from Danny's lips as he buried his face in her hair.

His movements slowed until he collapsed on top of her, snaking his arms between her and the mattress and pulling her against his body. Leah uncurled her hands from the headboard and wrapped her arms around him, burying her face in the crook of his neck and inhaling his heady scent. She could feel him placing soft, feather-light kisses along the top of her shoulder, and for a few minutes they laid that way, trying to get control of their breathing.

"Holy shit," Leah finally said, her voice thick and lazy, and Danny hummed languidly in response. She closed her eyes. "That CD just earned a permanent spot up on the shelf."

He laughed against her shoulder before he slowly rolled off her, his hand finding hers on the mattress.

Danny twined their fingers together. "That was..." He shook his head, running his other hand over his eyes. "I don't even have words for what that was."

"I didn't even know that *existed*," she said, and he chuckled as he leaned over, his lips hovering over hers.

"I don't think it did before us," he whispered. He placed a soft kiss on her lips. "Be right back," he said before kissing her again, slowly at first, and then more deeply so that her already enervated body melted back onto the mattress. By the time he sat up and swung his legs over the side of the bed, she was once again struggling to catch her breath.

Danny stood and made his way to the bathroom, and she sat up slowly, stretching her arms overhead as she found her muscles again.

Water. She needed water.

She pushed herself off the bed and grabbed Danny's balled-up shirt from the floor, pulling it over her head as she made her way to the kitchen. She opened the fridge and grabbed a bottle of water, taking down half of it in a matter of seconds.

Leah leaned against the counter with her hip, slowly screwing the cap back on, and that's when her eyes landed on it.

She smiled, placing the bottle on the counter as she opened the drawer in front of her and pulled out two forks. After she had removed a candle from the box on the counter and lit it in the center of the cake, Leah grabbed the forks and bumped the drawer closed with her hip before she made her way back to the bedroom.

Danny was lying in her bed, the sheet riding low on his hips and both hands clasped behind his head, causing his biceps to bulge.

He was sex incarnate lying there like that, and Leah was tempted to toss the cake over her shoulder and crawl on top of him.

Danny laughed when he saw what she was holding, and he sat up as she placed the cake on the bed before climbing on behind it.

"You have to make a wish this year," Leah said.

He smiled at her before he closed his eyes and scrunched up his face, making a big show of pondering what he should wish for. And then his expression straightened, and with his eyes still closed, he blew out the candle.

When he opened them and looked at her, his gaze was adoring, and she leaned forward and kissed him softly before she handed him a fork.

Danny lay on his side, propping his head up on his hand, and Leah mirrored his position, facing him with the cake resting on the bed between them.

They ate until they couldn't take another bite, and Leah moved what was left of the cake to her dresser before she came back to the bed.

"You look good in my shirt," he said, grabbing her waist and pulling her on top of him. He held her hands to the bed on either side of his body, and when she looked down at him, he quirked his brow suggestively.

She smiled, leaning down until their lips were almost touching. "What are you, insatiable?"

Danny laughed softly; his warm breath smelled like cake, and Leah wet her lips before closing the tiny space between them and pressing her mouth to his.

An hour later, she was lying on her side with Danny's arm around her waist and his chest pressed against her back. As she skirted the border between consciousness and sleep, Leah felt him sweep her hair over her shoulder, and then his mouth was on the back of her neck.

She tilted her head forward, an involuntary reaction that gave him better access, but she couldn't manage much more than that.

"Mmm," she hummed sleepily. "If you wanna go again, just try not to wake me while you're doing it."

He laughed against the back of her neck before removing his lips from her skin. The air felt cool now compared to the heat of his mouth, and when he trailed the tip of his finger down the back of her neck, she shivered.

His arm slid over her waist again as he pulled her against him, and Leah snuggled back into his chest with a sigh.

"What does it mean?" he asked softly.

"Hmm?" she hummed, her eyes still closed.

"This," he said, trailing the tip of his finger over her neck again. Right over her tattoo.

"Oh," she murmured, her voice soft with sleep. "It means a couple of things."

"Tell me," he said, his breath fluttering her hair.

Leah trailed her fingertips up and down his forearm. "In Celtic, the spiral triskele is the symbol for mother. That's actually the first reason I was drawn to it."

He kissed the back of her shoulder as she said, "But the triskele itself is usually a symbol for the progression of life...how it's constantly changing, but it always brings us to another beginning," she mumbled sleepily. "Always a new start. And I love the idea of that."

Danny pressed his lips over the tattoo again. "Me too," he said softly.

Leah brought his hand up to her mouth, kissing his palm before she intertwined their fingers. She felt so safe, so comfortable, so content wrapped in his arms, with the heat of his skin on hers and the gentle thudding of his heart against her back. As exhausted as she was, she found herself fighting sleep just so she could enjoy it a little longer.

And in that moment, she realized what the intense feeling was that flooded through her every time Danny put his arms around her. It was the same feeling she would get as a little girl when her family would pull into their driveway after spending a week on vacation. It was the same feeling she got when she crawled back into her own bed for the first time after moving back in with her father during college. And it was the same feeling she got every Christmas when she pulled onto that little street in the Bronx and stopped in front of Catherine's house.

Her eyes stung with tears behind her closed lids, and she smiled softly, knowing for sure that she had made the right decision.

Because for her, being in Danny's arms felt like coming home.

Chapter Fifteen

Leah stood at the side of the bed, clad only in a T-shirt and a pair of underwear as she ran a brush through her wet hair.

She smiled to herself, looking down at him.

His lashes were fanned out beneath his eyes, the stubble rough and dark on his jaw. One of his arms was hanging over the side of the bed, his other hand resting low on his stomach.

The sheet was barely covering him, and Leah gave herself a minute to admire his body before she turned to head back to the bathroom.

Two arms wrapped around her waist, and she yelped as he pulled her down onto the bed and started tickling her ribs. Leah squealed as she flipped over, attempting to grab his wrists.

Finally, after much effort, she was able to get hold of them, pinning them to the bed above his head as she straddled his stomach.

"Asshole," she laughed between labored breaths, and he smiled up at her.

"I'd be nice if I were you. You do realize you're only pinning me right now because I'm feeling charitable."

"Oh really?" she asked, leaning all of her body weight into her arms as she held him down on the bed. "Try it."

With no effort at all, he raised his arms, and Leah locked her elbows, trying to keep him pinned. He lifted her entire body off him, holding her there for a few seconds while she struggled to push his arms back to the bed.

Danny chuckled as he lowered his arms to the mattress above his head, allowing her to pin him once again, and she shook her head as she relinquished her hold on him. "You know, pretending to be asleep is kind of a creepy move," she said as she lay down on his chest.

"Is it as creepy as watching someone sleep?"

"Touché," she said, and he laughed, arching his back as he extended his arms.

"I need coffee," he said, his voice strained as he stretched, and then his body relaxed as he brought his hands behind his head.

Leah leaned down so that their noses were touching. "I'm on it. There are towels for you in the bathroom," she said, kissing him quickly before hopping off the bed and heading out to the kitchen.

As Leah started a pot of coffee, she heard the water turn on in the shower.

"I feel like I'm about to step into a car wash," he called from the bathroom, and she laughed as she opened the fridge.

"You're gonna love it!" she called back, grabbing all the things she'd need to make omelets. She grated some cheddar cheese and used her Slap Chop to cut up some tomatoes, peppers, and onions, and then she cracked four eggs into a mixing bowl. Just as she was about to start whisking them, she heard the sound of keys in her door and she froze.

The only people who had keys to her apartment were her sister, Holly, and Robyn, and she couldn't imagine what either one of them would be doing coming to her place right now.

The front door opened and then closed, followed by the sound of soft footsteps. Finally her sister came into view, walking past the kitchen on her way to Leah's bedroom.

"Sarah?"

She jumped, whipping her head in Leah's direction. "Oh, hey," she said, turning into the kitchen. "You're up."

"Yes, I'm up," she laughed. "Why are you sneaking into my apartment when you think I'm sleeping?"

"Because Kyle is coming to dinner at Daddy's tonight and I was gonna steal your blue cashmere sweater to wear," she said, reaching over and grabbing a pepper from the chopping board. As she popped it in her mouth, she did a double take at the bowl in front of her, eyeing the four eggs about to be whisked. "Jesus, Leah. Hungry?"

She opened her mouth, fumbling for a response, and before she could come up with something, she heard his voice.

"Alright, that actually *did* ruin me for all other bathrooms—" His words cut off abruptly as he turned into the kitchen, finding Sarah in there with her. He was clad in only a towel slung low around his hips, the little droplets of water from his shower still clinging to his chest and shoulders. His hand came to the towel, securing it as he cleared his throat.

"Hi," he said awkwardly.

Sarah grinned from ear to ear. "Hi," she said, immediately turning to look at Leah.

"Sarah, this is Danny," she said, looking at him and attempting to apologize with her eyes. "Danny, this is my sister."

He smiled softly before turning his attention to Sarah. "It's nice to meet you, Sarah," he said, extending his hand to her.

"You too," she said, shaking his hand as her smile grew more pronounced.

"Okay, well, I'm just gonna go get dressed," he said, holding up his hand in both a farewell and an apology before he turned and walked back down the hall.

Sarah slowly turned back to Leah, her grin threatening to split her face in two. Leah heard the sound of her bedroom door closing, and Sarah folded her arms and shook her head.

"Well, well, well," she said.

Leah picked up the whisk and began vigorously whipping the eggs.

"So," Sarah said. "Are you guys dating? Because obviously, you're fucking."

The whisk slipped from her hand, splashing egg all over the counter.

"Jesus, Sarah," she said with a nervous laugh, picking the whisk back up.

"Well? Are you together or just banging? Because goddamn, there'd be no shame in that game," she said, leaning back out of the doorway and craning her neck to see if she could get another glimpse of him.

"There is seriously something wrong with you," Leah said with a laugh. She went back to whisking the eggs, and when there was no response from Sarah, she lifted her eyes to see her sister staring at her, a tiny smile on her lips.

"Well?"

Leah sighed. "It's very, very new."

"But you're together." She said it as a statement.

Leah nodded.

She grinned again, coming around the counter and giving Leah a huge hug. "Yay," she squeaked in her ear, and Leah smiled.

Sarah let her go and leaned against the counter, grabbing another pepper. "Did Daddy and Chris meet him yet?"

"Not yet."

She nodded, popping the pepper in her mouth. "He should probably wear clothes for that."

Leah laughed again, shaking her head as she dumped the veggies and cheese into the eggs. "So, Kyle's coming to dinner tonight?" she asked, turning the tables on her.

"Yeah. I never thought I'd be one of those annoying girls who says this, but...I think he's the one."

Leah raised her eyebrows. "Really?"

She nodded. "Anytime I think of the future, whether it's next week or next year, I can't picture anything without him there. That's never happened to me before."

Leah glanced at Sarah as she poured the egg mixture into the pan on the stove. "Ohhh, someone's got it *bad*," Leah sing-songed.

"Shut up."

"All jokes aside, that's awesome, Sarah. I'm happy for you guys."

"Ditto," she said, and they smiled at each other.

Just then they heard the bedroom door open, and they both immediately straightened as if they'd just been caught doing something wrong. They realized the absurdity of their actions at the same time, disintegrating into laughter just as Danny turned the corner into the kitchen. He was wearing his clothes from the night before, and his hair—as usual—was in sexy disarray, the messy wet tendrils sticking out in every direction.

He ran his hand through it, smirking at them as they continued to giggle like little girls.

"I'm not even gonna ask," he said as he walked over to where Leah stood by the stove and reached for the coffee pot. "Sarah, do you want some coffee?"

"No, thank you. I can't stay. I just came here to get a sweater from Leah."

"Funny, I don't remember saying you could have it," Leah responded, poking the spatula under the edge of the cooking omelet.

"That's probably because I didn't ask."

She heard Danny chuckle as he poured some coffee into a mug, and she shook her head. "It's in my closet, on the right side."

"Sweet," she said, turning and walking down the hall toward the bedroom.

Leah turned to Danny, her expression apologetic. "I am so, so sorry. I didn't know she was coming."

He smiled as he leaned up against the counter, bringing the mug to his lips. "No worries," he said before taking a sip. "It could have been worse. At least I wore the towel out here. I was undecided there for a minute."

"Well, that would have been eventful."

He laughed as he came up behind her, wrapping his arm around her waist and resting his chin on her shoulder. "What are you making?"

"Omelets," she said, and she felt him turn his face, nuzzling her still-damp hair.

"Mmm," he hummed, and she smiled, knowing it had nothing to do with the food.

"Can you push the toast down?" she said, lifting the edge of the omelet with the spatula. "This is almost ready."

"Yep," he said, kissing the side of her neck quickly before he turned toward the toaster.

Sarah turned back into the kitchen holding Leah's sweater. "So Danny, are you coming to dinner at my dad's house tonight?"

Leah whipped her head toward her sister, her eyes wide, and then she glanced quickly at Danny; his hand was frozen on the tab of the toaster. "Um," he said, pushing it down slowly, "I didn't have plans to."

"Come," Sarah said. "My boyfriend will be there, and my brother and his wife. It will be fun."

He turned toward her, smiling easily. "Thanks for the invite. Maybe I'll swing by."

"Great," she said with a nod. "Okay, I'm out of here. See you guys later." She winked at Leah before she turned from the kitchen, and then the front door opened and closed. Leah kept her eyes on the omelet, poking at it with the spatula.

For a minute, neither one of them spoke.

"I don't have to go, you know," Danny finally said. Leah turned to see him leaned up against the counter, watching her. "I don't want you to be uncomfortable."

"That's not it at all," she said as she removed the pan from the stove, slicing the omelet in half with the edge of the spatula before dishing it out onto plates. "I would love for you to come. It's just...I don't want you to feel obligated just because she asked. She'll understand."

"I don't feel obligated."

Leah looked over at him. "You really want to come meet my family?"

"I'd love to meet your family," he said as if it should have been obvious.

They looked at each other for a few seconds, and Leah smiled as little butterflies flitted through her stomach.

"Well, this will make my dad happy at least. He wants to meet you." Danny raised his brow. "He knows about me?"

"Of course."

It was quiet for a beat before Danny spoke softly. "Everything?"

Leah froze, her hand wrapped around two forks in the utensil drawer. She took a small breath before she looked up to see him watching her intently.

"No," she said, dropping her eyes, and she could see him look down as he nodded slowly. "It's not that I'm...you know I don't...it's just...he doesn't know you yet. I didn't want that to be the first thing he learned about you."

"I totally understand. I appreciate it, actually."

Leah heard the tiniest hint of sadness behind his words, and she put down the forks and walked over to where he was leaning against the counter. She wrapped her arms around his neck, and Danny's hands came to her waist, gently rubbing up and down her sides.

"I'm not ashamed of you," she said, and he nodded, looking her in the eyes.

"I know."

She went up on her toes and pressed her lips to his, holding them there until the loud growling of her stomach interrupted the moment. She felt his lips curve into a smile against hers, and she pulled back.

"I'm hungry," she said.

"I can see that." He laughed, brushing the hair away from her face.

Leah turned and grabbed their plates, and Danny grabbed his coffee and hers, following her out to the table.

They sat down and immediately dug into the food, and Danny shook his head as he chewed. "You're spoiling the shit out of me with this," he said, nodding toward his plate.

"You could make this, you know. It's not hard."

"You're overestimating my culinary abilities."

"You put cars back together!" she laughed. "I'm pretty sure you could make an omelet."

He grinned, taking another bite. "So what time should I pick you up tonight?"

"Pick me up?"

"Well, yeah. I have to go home first. I'm not gonna meet your dad in my walk-of-shame clothes."

"No, I know you have to go home," she said with a laugh, "but you'd have to pass my dad's house to come up here to get me."

"So?"

"So you'll be driving an extra twenty minutes to turn back around and do another twenty back down."

"Okay."

"Okay, so that's a ridiculous waste of time and gas. You don't have to do that."

Danny put his fork down on the table and leaned toward her. "Leah?"

"Yeah?"

"What time should I pick you up tonight?"

She stared at him for a second before she conceded with a sigh. "Five thirty."

Danny smiled, taking his elbows off the table as he picked up his fork. "There. Now, was that so hard?"

As Leah and Danny walked up her father's driveway, she bit the corner of her lip, glancing over at him. She couldn't understand how he could be so calm; her stomach rolled incessantly the entire drive to her father's, and now that they were nearing his front door, she felt like she might be sick.

Danny noticed her looking at him, and he gave her a tiny smile, squeezing her hand as they walked up the steps. They stopped in front of the door, and Leah looked up at him.

"Last chance to back out," she said, and he smiled.

"I'm all in," he said, placing a reassuring hand on the small of her back, and she took a deep breath before she turned and opened the front door.

The sounds of talking and laughing instantly greeted them, immediately followed by the smell of Sarah's lasagna.

Here we go, she thought just as her brother's voice boomed through the house.

"Oh, you've got to be fucking kidding me! Somebody paid this ref off!"

She flinched and shook her head, looking up at Danny.

"Does he have a swear jar?" he asked.

Before she could answer, Sarah and Alexis came out of the kitchen.

"Hey guys!" Sarah said excitedly, taking the bottle of wine out of Leah's hands. "Danny, I'm so glad you decided to come." She went up on her toes and kissed his cheek, and he smiled his dimpled smile at her.

"Here, let me take that," she said, reaching for the dessert box with the Giovanni's logo scrawled across the top. "Whatever's in here needs to be hidden before my brother sees it."

She turned and walked back toward the kitchen, and Alexis stepped forward, holding out her hand. "Hi, Danny. I'm Alexis, Chris's wife."

Danny took her hand and leaned down, planting a kiss on her cheek. "Nice to meet you," he said, and she blushed slightly.

Leah removed her coat and Danny followed suit. As Leah reached for it, Alexis intercepted it. "No, let me take those. You guys go inside. Danny, the boys are all drinking beer. Do you want one? Or a glass of wine?"

"A beer would be great, thanks," he said, handing her his coat. Alexis smiled with a nod, turning toward Leah to take her coat. She made eye contact with her, raising one eyebrow before she continued toward the hall closet.

Leah turned to Danny, looking up at him as she took a breath. "Ready?"

He nodded. "If you are."

She forced a smile and turned to walk toward the family room. Goddamn him, he was still the epitome of calm and collected. Meanwhile, her pulse was rushing in her ears as they approached the room.

As they reached the doorway, three heads turned to look at them simultaneously. Her father was sitting in his usual place in the recliner, and her brother was laid out across the couch, one hand behind his head. Kyle was on the love seat, one arm draped across the back and the other holding a bottle of beer on his knee.

"Hey, look who's here!" Chris said, swinging his legs over the couch as he sat up, and her father shifted in his chair, gripping the sides as he pushed himself up to stand.

He walked toward them, glancing at Danny before he brought his eyes to Leah. "Princess," he said, reaching out to give her a hug. He ran his hand up and down her back as he whispered, "Relax," in her ear.

She nodded, taking a deep breath before he released her.

Chris and Danny were already shaking hands; her brother looked amiable enough, but Leah knew him well enough to see that he was assessing Danny as he looked at him.

"Danny, this is my dad."

Danny smiled, extending his hand. "Nice to meet you, Mr. Marino."

Leah watched her father carefully as he reached forward and clasped Danny's hand, and she exhaled in relief when she saw that Danny was meeting her father's gaze. For as long as she could remember, her father had always said that he never trusted the intentions of a man who couldn't look him in the eye when they shook hands.

"Good to meet you, Danny."

"Here you go," Alexis said from behind them, and Leah turned to see her handing Danny a beer.

"Where's mine?" Chris said, and Alexis shrugged.

"My guess would be in the fridge."

Danny pressed his lips together and looked down, only allowing himself to laugh when everyone else did.

Her father turned and walked back to the recliner. "Have a seat, Danny."

He took a few steps into the room, and Leah was about to follow just as Alexis said, "Hey, Leah? Sarah said she needs you in the kitchen."

She glanced at Alexis before she turned to Danny, biting her lip.

"Beat it, mother hen," Chris said casually, and she shot him a dirty look before turning her eyes to Danny.

246

"*You okay in here?*" she mouthed, and he nodded encouragingly.

"He'll be fine," Alexis said softly, wrapping her arm around Leah and guiding her to the kitchen.

As soon as they entered, Sarah handed her a glass of wine.

"Thanks," she said, taking a long sip as she leaned up against the counter.

Alexis held up her hands. "Okay, I'm just gonna say it. Gor... geous," she said, making it sound like two separate words.

"You should see him shirtless," Sarah said, smirking at Leah over her wine glass before taking a sip.

"No way," Alexis said as she fanned herself. "I couldn't handle it. Pregnancy hormones are a force to be reckoned with."

"I hate both of you," Leah said, blushing crimson, and the girls laughed.

The three of them continued working on dinner, and at one point, Christopher came into the kitchen to get another round of beers. As he turned from the fridge, he made eye contact with Leah, and she raised her brow at him. He smiled softly before he winked, and then he made his way back out to the family room.

At that small token of approval, Leah felt some of the tension leave her shoulders, and she smiled to herself as she chopped up the vegetables for the salad.

A little while later, Alexis and Leah were dishing out the lasagna while Sarah called the boys in for dinner. Kyle came through the kitchen first, kissing Sarah's temple before he continued through to the dining room.

The sound of laughing caught her attention, and Leah turned as Chris and Danny entered the kitchen together. Chris smirked at her, tousling her hair roughly as he passed, and she swatted at him, jerking out of his reach. Before she could fix it, Danny came over to her, running his hands through her hair and detangling it.

"Hi," she said.

"Hi," he said, tucking her hair behind her ear.

"Are you having fun?"

"I am. They're great. And you look much better," he said, wrapping his arms around her waist.

She brought her arms up, interlocking her fingers behind his neck. "I look better?"

"Yeah. You don't look like you're about to shit yourself anymore."

She unlocked her hands from behind his neck and pushed him, and he laughed, pulling her into a hug. Leah rested her cheek against his chest and closed her eyes.

"Was I that obvious?" she mumbled.

"Just a little," he said against the top of her head, kissing her there before letting her go.

Her father walked into the kitchen then, clapping Danny on the back as he passed. "Brees better come through next week."

"It'll happen," Danny said, and Leah looked up at him, her brow furrowed.

"What was that about?"

"We got a bet going on next week's game. Me and your dad against Kyle and your brother."

"Okay, but what does that have to do with the weather?"

"*What?*" he said through a laugh. "What are you talking about?"

"My dad just said a breeze better come through next week."

Danny stared at her for several seconds before he burst out laughing. "Oh my God," he said, taking her face in his hands. "Do you have any idea how adorable you are?"

He leaned down and planted a soft kiss on her lips before he turned into the dining room, and she heard his laughter start back up again.

She shook her head, still confused as she finished cutting up the last of the garlic bread, and then she brought the tray into the dining room. As soon as she sat, she heard Chris chuckle softly before clearing his throat.

"So, Leah," he said, "Do you want to get in on this wind bet? I'm gonna see if I can find my anemometer."

The boys disintegrated into laughter, her father included, and the girls were looking at her with equal parts sympathy and amusement.

She turned to Danny, who was trying to get control of his laughter as he looked at her apologetically.

Chris laughed. "Drew Brees is the quarterback for the New Orleans Saints, you asshole. Brees. B-R-E-E-S. Aren't you supposed to be an English teacher?"

She looked at Danny. "You ratted me out?"

"I had to," he said, trying not to smile. "Your dad asked me what was so funny."

She pursed her lips and nodded slowly. "Okay, I see how it is," she said, picking up her fork and turning to her brother. "And Chris, for your information, *Brees* and *breeze* would be considered homophones—words that sound the same but are spelled differently and have different meanings. They're easy to confuse if you don't see them written down, in case you were interested."

He paused for a second, looking up at the ceiling thoughtfully before he brought his eyes back to hers. "Yeah, I'm not interested at all, actually."

The table broke into laughter again, and this time Leah joined them, shaking her head. Danny clasped her hand under the table, bringing it up to his mouth and giving it a quick kiss before he released it.

Dinner couldn't have gone more perfectly if Leah had scripted it herself. Both Danny and Kyle were newcomers to the Marino Sunday dinner, but it felt as if they'd always been part of the tradition. The boys talked cars for a little while once they found out what Danny did for a living, and even though most of what they were saying went right over Leah's head, she found herself listening intently to the conversation. Danny sounded so intelligent, so ardent, so confident, that she could have listened to him for hours, even if none of it made sense to her.

After dinner the girls brought dessert out to the table, and everyone sat around, sipping coffee and talking casually. At one point Kyle was telling a story, and Leah looked at Danny to find his gaze focused on the other side of the table. He looked almost wistful, and Leah followed his line of sight to where Chris and Alexis were sitting; they were looking at Kyle as he spoke, but Chris's hand was on Alexis's belly, rubbing it gently as he listened to Kyle's story.

She reached under the table and took his hand, and Danny blinked quickly, snapping out of whatever spell he was under as he looked down at her. She gave his hand a tiny squeeze, and he smiled before he returned it.

Just as everyone was finishing up, Leah excused herself to the laundry room to sort her father's laundry, and by the time she got back to the kitchen, only Sarah and Kyle were left. Sarah was putting the leftovers in plastic containers, and Kyle was loading the dishwasher.

Leah walked toward the family room and popped her head in. Chris and Alexis were sitting on the couch together, watching TV.

"Where are Daddy and Danny?" she asked.

"Outside," Chris answered.

"What are they doing out there?"

Chris shrugged, his eyes on the television. "Don't worry. Dad wouldn't do anything out there. Too many witnesses."

Leah rolled her eyes, walking to the window and pulling the curtains aside. The outside light was on, faintly illuminating the driveway, and it took her a second to find them. As soon as she did, her eyes stung with the threat of tears.

They stood at the top of the driveway behind the pickup Danny had borrowed from Jake. Danny was off to the side, his hands in his pockets and his head down. The truck bed was open, and Leah's father leaned on it with both hands, staring tenderly at what lay inside.

After a minute he stood, turning to Danny, and Leah watched as Danny raised his head. They were too far away for her to see their expressions, or even if their mouths were moving, but they stood there for a moment, facing each other. And then her father walked toward him, putting his hand on Danny's shoulder.

Leah stepped back and let the curtain fall closed, suddenly feeling as though she were eavesdropping. A wave of emotion crashed over her, and all at once, she wanted to laugh, or burst into tears, or both.

Sarah and Kyle joined them in the living room, and Leah curled up in her father's recliner, attempting to watch TV with everyone else. About ten minutes later, she heard the garage door being opened, and she knew Danny and her father were carrying the slab of concrete into the house.

Eventually she heard the sounds of them coming up the basement stairs, and as the door opened, Leah turned to see her father standing at the top. His eyes met hers, and then he walked over to where she was sitting, bringing his hand to her cheek as he stared down at her. She smiled up at him, and his lips curved into a gentle smile in return before he dropped his eyes and took a tiny, quivering breath. He walked out of the room then, and she knew he must have needed a few minutes to himself.

Leah turned her attention back to the basement steps; Danny was leaning against the doorframe, his hands in his pockets and his eyes on her. Before she had even made the conscious decision to do it, she was out of the chair and crossing the room to him. He pushed off the wall as she approached, and Leah immediately wrapped her arms around his waist, hiding her face in his chest as she inhaled the scent that was quickly becoming vital to her. He brought his hand to her hair, holding her against his chest as he pressed his lips to the crown of her head.

And that was the moment she knew she had fallen in love with Danny DeLuca.

Chapter Sixteen

Leah had just finished curling her hair when she heard her phone beep with an incoming text, and she leaned over and swiped the screen.

We're running a little late. Are you guys on your way?

Leah picked up the phone and texted her sister back.

Not yet. Danny should be here any minute. We'll meet you guys there.

A minute later, Sarah's response came through.

K. Get a table if u guys get there first.

Leah put her phone down on the sink before she checked her makeup in the mirror. She and Danny were meeting Sarah and Kyle at one of their old hangout spots to celebrate the promotion Kyle had just gotten at work.

She walked out of the bathroom and back to her bedroom to grab her purple platform heels, or as Robyn called them, her "happy shoes." She *felt* happy. It was such a simple concept, but it had eluded her for so long that she was constantly aware of its presence in everything she did. Everything felt new, like she was looking at the world through a different pair of eyes, rediscovering and suddenly appreciating things that the old Leah had overlooked.

The two weeks since Danny's birthday had been the best two weeks of her life—an incredible blur of laughing and talking and cuddling, of smiles and shared secrets and making love.

She never imagined, even in her most sanguine teenage dreams, that being in love could ever feel like this.

Leah heard a knock on her door, and she stuck her head out of the bedroom. "Come in!" she called. "I'll be out in a sec!"

She heard the front door open and close as she pulled her shoes out of the closet and stepped into them, and then she walked over to the full-length mirror, taking one last look at herself before she made her way out to the living room, her heels clicking against the hardwood floor.

"So guess what?" she said, stopping short when she saw him in the dining room. He was sitting with his elbows on the table and his hands clasped in front of his mouth. As soon as he saw her, he lowered his hands and smiled, but she could see that it was forced.

That there was a struggle behind his eyes.

"What's wrong?" she asked.

He inhaled slowly, and Leah watched his throat convulse as he swallowed. "My lawyer called today."

Her stomach lurched, and she a felt a cold prickle down her spine. "What did he say?"

Danny wet his lips before he looked up at her. "We have a sentencing date."

It felt like her throat was closing. She tried to take a breath, but it was as if her lungs were full of glue. "When?" she managed, her voice barely audible.

"May second."

Leah stood there for a minute, trying to process what he had just said.

May second. The day before her birthday.

She crossed the room to him, and he sat up as she approached, allowing her to crawl into his lap. Danny dropped his head to her shoulder, and she curled her arms around him, trying to keep her breathing even.

She couldn't react right now. She couldn't fall apart. She needed to keep it together.

But what was the point of being strong? What difference would it make? If she cried or if she didn't, if she screamed or if she remained stoic, if she bargained or denied or accepted or fought, none of it would change anything. None of it would prevent what was about to happen.

May second. Less than two months away.

They sat there in silence, their arms around each other as Leah's thoughts ran rampant. One minute her mind was racing with what this meant for them, what it meant for *him*, and the next it was eerily devoid of anything whatsoever.

"What do we do now?" she whispered, her voice not sounding like her own.

She hadn't felt so utterly helpless since her mother died.

Danny took a breath before he lifted his head, looking up at her as he took one of her curls between his fingers. "We go meet Sarah and Kyle at the bar, and we celebrate his promotion."

"What?" Leah asked, her brow furrowed. "Danny, no."

"We made plans, Leah."

"Who cares?" she said desperately.

"I do!" he said, and then he closed his eyes, taking a breath as he reined himself in. "I do," he said again, this time more calmly. "We can't let this dictate the next two months. What are we gonna do, Leah? Sit here and mope? Wallow in it? I'm not gonna let this take any more time from me than it has to."

Leah wet her lips and nodded. "Okay," she said, dropping her eyes. "Okay. You're right."

Danny used his fingertips under her chin to lift her eyes back to his. "I don't want this to influence everything we do now. It can't be like that."

She nodded again.

"I mean, I know it's gonna be…" He trailed off, shaking his head. "We have to at least try."

His eyes were imploring as he looked up at her, and she knew that if he needed to maintain a sense of normalcy, she would do it, no matter how difficult it was going to be. And in a way, she understood. He had no control over what was coming his way in two months, but he *could* control everything up until that point.

And maybe that's how she needed to deal with it too.

"Okay," she said softly, pressing her lips to his. "Okay."

"Okay," he whispered, brushing the hair away from her face.

She smiled down at him, trying to keep the sadness out of it, and he twisted one of her curls around his finger.

"It looks nice like this," he murmured, watching the silken strand slip through his fingertips.

She brought her hand to his face, running her thumb over his cheek.

"Are you ready to go, or do you need another minute?" he asked.

"I'm ready," she whispered.

He nodded, looking up at her. "Me and you tonight. Nothing else, okay?"

"Nothing else," she repeated softly.

"Okay," he said, lifting his chin and pressing his lips to hers, and she concentrated on the feel of his mouth. The way he tasted.

And nothing else.

Nothing else.

Paddy's was a local bar that had been a favorite of Leah's in the years right after she graduated college. There was a fun, younger crowd vibe, but without all the chaos that most college bars boasted. She hadn't been there in a long time, but as soon as she and Danny walked through the doors, it felt like she'd never left.

Everything was the same, from the layout of the tables to the pictures on the walls to the music that was playing. It was comforting, and familiar, and exactly what she needed at that moment.

"Sarah says they're like ten minutes away," Leah said to Danny as she put her phone back in her purse. "Do you want to go grab us a table and I'll get us drinks?"

"Yeah."

"See the jukebox back there?" Leah said, and Danny lifted his chin, looking over the crowd. "There's a little nook on the other side of it. The tables back there are usually open."

"Alright," he said, leaning down to kiss her temple before he turned and walked through the crowd.

Leah made her way to the bar, resting her elbows on top of it as she glanced around the familiar space.

"What can I get you, hon?"

She looked up just in time to see the bartender's face light up with recognition.

"Leah! Sweetheart! How are ya?"

"I'm good, Sammy. You?"

"Oh you know, same old, same old," he said, leaning on the bar in front of her. "God, it's been a while. You look good, kiddo!"

Leah smiled. Sammy was the sweetest old man she'd ever met; he had been the bartender at Paddy's for as long as she'd been going there, and he seemed to remember every face, every name, every story that crossed his path.

"Thank you. You're looking pretty good yourself."

"Bah," he said, standing up and waving his hand at her. "Quit makin' an old man blush."

Leah laughed, and he smiled. "So what can I get ya?"

"Can I get a pitcher? Whatever you have on special is fine."

"You got it, sweetheart."

Just as Sammy turned away from her, Leah felt two arms wrap around her waist, and she leaned back into his embrace.

"No open tables?" she asked, turning her head to look up at him.

And then her heart stopped.

"Hey beautiful," he said, rubbing his thumbs over her stomach through the fabric of her shirt.

After a stunned second she turned in his arms, using her hand on his chest to push him away. He took a step back, relinquishing his hold on her, but he smiled.

"You look incredible," he said, and she shook her head.

"Scott, don't—"

"We need to talk," he said, his face growing serious.

"I don't have anything to say to you."

"Fine. Don't talk then. Just listen."

"I don't want to do this now," she said, stepping to the side in an attempt to walk around him, but he picked up on it immediately, stepping forward and putting his hands on the bar on either side of her.

"You won't do it anywhere else," he said smoothly. "I've tried."

She looked down at his arms, caging her in, and then she lifted her eyes to his, her expression steely.

"Just let me say this. She meant nothing to me, Leah," he said, and she scoffed before rolling her eyes. "I mean, we worked together, and she was constantly flirting with me, and I just…I was under a lot of stress, and she was always there, right in front of me. I mean, shit, a man can only take so much temptation. I had to get it out of my system. But it didn't mean anything. *She* didn't mean anything."

As Scott spoke, she stared over his shoulder, her expression disinterested as she searched the bar for any sign of her sister and Kyle.

"I know you're mad because I didn't come out after you, but I knew you needed some time to calm down—"

Leah whipped her head toward him, her expression incredulous as a tiny laugh escaped her lips. "So, what? You figured you'd just finish fucking her while I cooled off?" She laughed outright then, shaking her head. "You know, for all the time you've had to plan this speech, you'd think it would be a little less pathetic." She pushed his arm off the bar and took a step past him.

Scott stepped back and to the side in one swift movement, blocking her path. "I know you're still upset—"

"Actually, I'm not. I'm over this whole thing. Which is why I want to be left alone," she said, stepping to the other side.

This time he reached out and grabbed her wrist, pulling her back in front of him.

"Take your hand off me," she said, her voice low but firm.

She was not in the place to deal with this tonight; she had already been teetering on her breaking point before they'd even walked through the doors of the bar. She had nothing left for him.

He leaned in and cupped her face in his hand. "I can't let you go. That's what I'm trying to tell you. I still want you, Leah. I still want us."

She leaned back and his hand slipped from her face, but he tightened his hold on her wrist so that she couldn't walk away.

"Scott, knock it off. You're hurting me."

"You don't think *I'm* hurting?"

Leah closed her eyes and shook her head. She needed to change her approach. She needed to stop antagonizing him. If she had any hope of putting some distance between them, she was going to have to placate him.

"Look," she said. "I don't want to make a scene. Let's not do this here. We can talk, but just not here, okay?"

His eyes searched hers before she felt his hand go slack on her wrist. "Okay," he said. "Where, then?"

Leah slipped her wrist out of his hand, and before she could answer, she felt someone grip her other hand and pull her away. She glanced up just as Danny drew her against his side, his eyes trained on Scott.

"Is everything okay over here?" he asked, his eyes appraising her quickly before settling back on Scott.

"Hey, buddy, no one needs you to play the hero. We know each other, okay? This is none of your business."

Scott reached for Leah's arm, and Danny used his hold on her to pull her partially behind him, shifting his body in front of her.

"She *is* my business," he said, his voice disconcertingly calm. "And if you put your hands on her again, we're gonna have a problem."

Scott looked at Danny, the corner of his mouth lifting in a smile, and Leah's heart began thudding in her chest. She didn't like the look on Scott's face, and at that moment, she didn't care how much she hated him, or that he didn't deserve a chance to explain himself. Her only priority became separating the two of them.

Leah tugged gently on Danny's hand. "We do know each other," she said, and Danny looked down at her, his jaw relaxing slightly. "Please, just let me handle this."

"Yeah, let her handle this."

"*Scott*," Leah barked, and Danny's eyes widened before they flew back to him. As soon as Danny realized who he was, the muscle in the side of his jaw flickered, and Leah immediately brought her hand to his face, pulling his attention back to her. He looked down again, but this time his expression didn't soften.

"I'll take care of this, okay? And then we'll leave. We'll go somewhere else."

Danny stared down at her, hesitating as his eyes searched hers. She knew he must have seen the panic there—that he attributed it to her being uncomfortable about talking to Scott, when in reality she was afraid of what would happen if she *didn't* talk to him.

Leah forced a smile. "I'm fine. I'll be okay. Let me handle it."

Danny dropped his eyes, his jaw still flexing as he inhaled. "I'll be right over there, okay?"

She nodded as she leaned in and kissed him quickly, and as Danny straightened, his eyes turned to Scott. He held his gaze for just a moment before he turned and walked the few feet to the end of the bar.

"So, I guess that's your man?" Scott said, his brow quirked in amusement. "He's a little overprotective, don't you think?"

"Scott, listen to me," Leah said gently, trying to appeal to the kindness she remembered in him, because even though she knew those three years were based on lies, she needed to believe there was something good in him somewhere, some part of him that might still care enough about her to do the right thing. "This is over, okay? Whatever your reasoning was for doing what you did, it's never gonna be okay with me."

He shook his head slightly. "You're not looking past your anger. You're not remembering what this was like," he said, trailing the back of his finger down her arm.

She moved it out of his reach. "You don't get it. It's not about me being angry. It's about me knowing that I don't want to be with you."

A flash of hurt registered behind his eyes at her words, but it was gone before she could react to it. "Is it because of this asshole?" he asked, nodding over her shoulder.

Leah glanced over to see Danny leaned up against the bar, his arms folded over his chest as he watched them.

"We were over long before this," she said, "but if you really want to know, then yes. I don't want anyone but him."

Scott stared at her for a moment, his eyes searching hers. "Kiss me," he said suddenly.

"*What?*"

"Kiss me," he repeated. "If you can honestly tell me you feel nothing after kissing me, then I'll let this go."

"I don't need to kiss you to know that I feel nothing."

His mouth lifted in a faint smile. "See? You're scared," he said. "You're scared because you remember what it was like. How I made you feel. What I could do to your body. You remember. And you know that if you kiss me, you won't be able to deny it," he said, bringing his hand back to her face.

Leah took a step back, and out of the corner of her eye, she saw Danny unfold his arms as he straightened.

Her heart leapt into her throat, and she knew she needed to end this immediately.

She reached up and removed his hand from her face. "Okay, that's enough. Stop calling me, stop texting me, and stop sending me things. If you really care about me the way you say you do, then you'll respect what I want. And it's not you."

And then everything seemed to happen at once.

She turned away from Scott and started walking toward Danny, but his eyes were focused behind her. He moved toward them suddenly, fury washing over his face just as Leah felt a hand grip the top of her arm and spin her around. Before she could get her bearings, Scott grabbed the back of her head and pulled her toward him, crashing his mouth to hers.

Her hands flew to his chest, pushing against him, but he had one arm wrapped tightly around her waist and his other hand clutching the back of her head, holding her mouth securely against his. Leah whimpered, and he took it as a sign of encouragement, forcing his tongue into her mouth.

And then his mouth was gone as she was yanked backward.

Her eyes focused just in time to see Scott with his arm cocked back, ready to swing at Danny.

"No!" she yelled. "*Don't!*"

Scott swung, connecting with Danny's chin. His head jerked back slightly with the force of the hit, and then he lunged forward, grabbing Scott by the throat.

"Danny!" she screamed. "Stop it!"

She hurtled forward, attempting to grab his arm, but he pulled it easily from her grasp as he swung at Scott, hitting him square in the mouth. She went to grab him again, but she was jerked back suddenly.

Instantly, a group of men converged on them, blocking them from her sight. Someone's arm was wrapped firmly around her waist, but she didn't fight against whoever it was. Instead she stood there, looking on with panic as the group of men undulated with the struggle before they finally broke apart.

Two of the men, who she could now see were bouncers, dragged a still-shouting Scott toward the back exit, his mouth covered in blood.

She turned just in time to see Danny's back as he stormed through the front door of the bar and out onto the street, someone following closely behind him.

Leah attempted to follow him, but the arm around her waist pulled her back. "Are you out of your mind trying to get between those two?"

She turned around, finally acknowledging the person holding her, and she tried to remove the arm from around her waist as she made a move for the door again.

Sarah tightened her grip. "Hey," she said calmly. "Let him cool off. He's with Kyle. He'll be fine. Just give him a minute."

Leah turned to look at her sister, her shoulders sagging in acquiescence as she fell back on the barstool behind her.

Her eyes instantly welled with tears.

"What are you crying about?" Sarah said. "He's not hurt."

Leah turned her head and stared at the door as her chin began to quiver.

"It was just a few punches, Leah," she said with a tiny laugh. "It's not the end of the world."

"I can't believe this," Leah mumbled, shaking her head.

"Oh, please don't tell me you're mad at him. You know Scott deserved that. In fact, he's had that coming for a long time."

She glanced at Sarah. Of course she didn't understand. How could she?

"I'm just a little shaken up," Leah said, and Sarah reached over and rubbed her shoulder.

"Alright, well, you can relax now. Kyle will come back and get us when he calms down. Here," she said, handing her a beer. "Drink."

Leah took a careful sip, struggling to swallow it.

"If you want the truth," Sarah said, "I kind of wish they had let that go a few minutes longer. Scott could have used the lesson in humility."

Leah sat there, staring at her beer as her stomach churned. Of course Sarah thought her reaction seemed excessive. She didn't know that this was more than just some bar fight. She didn't know what this could have meant for him.

Leah replayed the scene in her mind, recognizing all the places she should have handled the situation differently. She could have asked Sammy for help as soon as Scott wouldn't let her leave. He would have tossed Scott out in a second if he was making her uncomfortable. She should have done everything in her power to diffuse the situation before Danny felt like he had to get involved.

Leah looked down and shook her head, because if she were being honest with herself, she should have handled the situation long before that. She should have dealt with him as soon as he started contacting her after their breakup, instead of taking the easy way out and ignoring him all this time. So in truth, she had brought this all on herself.

And consequently, she had brought this down on Danny.

The image of Danny swinging at Scott flashed in her mind, and her eyes welled with tears again. How could she have been so careless? She had put him in a situation where he felt like he needed to take action.

She had left him no choice.

And what would have happened if he'd gotten arrested tonight protecting her? How would that have looked to the judge trying to determine if he was a violent criminal?

Leah swiped under her eyes as she willed her heartbeat to return to normal, but it was in vain. Every second that passed caused the knot in her stomach to grow tighter. Where was he? What if Kyle wasn't able to calm him down? What if Scott went after him again outside?

She took another sip of beer, and the taste made her feel like she was going to be sick. Leah pressed her fingers to her mouth and closed her eyes.

She felt Sarah nudge her with her elbow, and when Leah opened her eyes, Sarah nodded toward the front of the bar. Kyle stood in the doorway, gesturing for Leah to come outside, and she pushed off the stool so quickly that it crashed back against the bar as she made her way through the crowd.

As soon as she stepped outside, she looked around frantically. "Where is he?"

"He's in the car. He's okay now, but I'm thinking you guys should probably call it a night."

She nodded quickly. "Okay. Thank you," she said. "I'm sorry about your night—"

"Don't worry about it," Kyle said, cutting her off as he put his hand on her back. "You okay?"

Leah forced a tiny smile and nodded, and then she turned and kissed Sarah on the cheek, telling her she'd call her tomorrow.

As Sarah and Kyle went back into the bar, Leah turned and walked briskly through the parking lot toward Danny's car. As she got closer, she slowed, nearly stopping; she could see the outline of him sitting in the driver's seat, his hands gripping the wheel and his head down.

She pulled the door open and slid into the seat, closing it softly behind her, waiting for him to say something. To do something.

Nearly a minute passed, but he remained in the same position, unmoving and silent.

If he was angry with her, he had every right to be. She had been irresponsible, and because of it, he had to risk everything to defend her.

Leah kept her eyes trained on the dashboard as she chewed the inside of her lip. She wanted so desperately to talk to him, but she also knew that timing was everything. If he hadn't fully cooled off yet, she didn't want to say or do anything that would aggravate the situation.

After a minute she saw Danny close his eyes and shake his head ever so slightly. He dropped his hand from the wheel—the first real movement he'd made since Leah sat beside him—and he brought it to the ignition, starting the car.

The entire drive home was spent in silence. Danny kept his eyes on the road and both hands on the wheel, and although she stole several fleeting glances at him, he did not look at her once.

As they pulled into the empty space in front of Leah's apartment, her eyes began to sting with the threat of tears. She wanted him to say something—anything—and when he didn't, she dropped her eyes, nodding softly before she turned and exited the car.

As soon as she was outside, the tears she'd been fighting all night finally spilled over, and she picked up the pace, desperate to get inside the refuge of her apartment.

Leah pushed through the door and walked straight to the kitchen table, dropping her purse before she splayed her hands over the wood and bowed her head. And then she heard the front door close softly behind her, and her breath caught in her throat as she lifted her head.

She hadn't expected him to follow.

Leah kept her back to him as she tried to pull herself together. There were a million things she wanted to say, but she didn't know where to start, or where to draw the line for that matter. All she knew was that she wanted to make this better. The last thing she wanted to do was fight with him.

"I'm so sorry, Leah," he said suddenly, his hoarse whisper cutting through the stillness.

She turned around to see him standing in front of the door, his head down as he played with the keys in his hand.

"What are you sorry for?" she asked, her voice barely audible. "This is all my fault."

His hand instantly stilled as he lifted his eyes to hers. "Your fault?" he asked. "You think this is *your* fault?"

She nodded her head imperceptibly, her eyes trained on him.

Danny dropped his eyes, his jaw muscle flexing rapidly.

"How is it your fault that he's a disrespectful prick?" he asked, lifting his eyes to hers. "How is it your fault that he tried to intimidate you?"

Leah opened her mouth to answer, but Danny cut her off. "And how is it your fault that I was fucking stupid enough to let him get a second chance at it?" he said, his voice rising in anger. "How is it your fault that I left you alone with him, even after I saw him corner you, after I saw him *grab* you? I left you alone with him, for what? So he could put his hands on you *again*? His fucking *mouth* on you?"

He turned quickly, whipping his car keys across the room; they crashed up against the front door with a clatter, and Leah jumped, pressing her lips together.

"How is it your fault that I fucked up? I fucked up, Leah! I keep fucking up! And you paid for it! Just like Bryan paid for it! Just like Gram's paying for it, and Jake, and Tommy and everyone I give a shit about in this world is paying for it!"

He was yelling now, and Leah stood there, her eyes pooling with tears. Because they weren't talking about Scott anymore.

And all at once, she realized what had happened tonight was so much bigger than him.

On some level Danny had been a powder keg for the last year of his life. That phone call today was the strike of a match.

And Scott had tossed it in.

Danny cursed under his breath, dropping his head back and covering his face. "It's not your fault," he said from behind his hands. "You didn't deserve what happened tonight. I shouldn't have left you with him. I fucked up."

"You were just doing what I asked," she said, her voice trembling, and Danny's hands fell from his face at the sound of it. "I put you in a position where you felt like you had to protect me. And that was so stupid of me, because I don't want you to leave me for any longer than you have to—"

Her words cut off suddenly as she burst into tears, and she cupped her hand over her mouth.

Saying those words out loud had completely demolished her, because it wasn't hypothetical anymore. It wasn't something that might happen someday. That phone call made it real. The date was set. It was so close.

He was in front of her immediately, pulling her into his arms, and she covered her face with her hands as she sobbed into his chest.

"Please don't cry," he crooned softly, running his hand over the back of her hair. "I'm so sorry for yelling like that. I'm not mad at you. You know I'm not mad at you."

Leah's breath hitched as another sob fell from her lips, stifled by his shirt.

Danny pulled back and ducked down, bringing his eyes to her level as he removed her hands from her face and replaced them with his own. "Don't cry, sweet girl," he said, pressing his lips to her forehead. "I'm so sorry. For all of it. I just...I can't stand the idea of anyone hurting you. It makes me crazy."

His voice was dejected, cracked into a million pieces, and she hiccupped repeatedly, trying to calm down. Danny brushed his thumbs under her eyes, pressing his forehead to hers. "And I know that I'm the one hurting you now, and I don't know how to fix it, and it's killing me. Because I love you, Leah," he said, brushing his lips over hers.

Everything stopped.

Her tears. Her breathing. Her heart.

Danny pulled back slightly, his hands still on her face as he met her eyes. "I love you," he repeated softly.

Her heart came back alive in her chest, pumping wildly, every beat sending those magnificent words coursing through her body, repairing her from the inside out. And for that one moment, all the guilt and anxiety and fear and frustration vanished. The only thing that existed for her was the immeasurable connection she felt to him, fortified by his words—the intense satisfaction of knowing that the person she loved with her entire being loved her in return.

"I love you too," she whispered, her breath hitching as the tears slipped over her lashes.

He closed his eyes and exhaled, and for a moment, his face relaxed, and everything was gone for him too.

Leah lifted her chin, closing the distance between their mouths, and Danny released her face, wrapping his arms tightly around her waist.

"So much," she whispered in between kisses, and Leah felt his lips curve into a smile against hers.

She brought her arms up around his neck, and he tightened his hold on her, lifting her off the floor. Leah wrapped her legs around his hips, and he walked them back to her bedroom, their lips never breaking contact.

As soon as her back hit the bed, she arched up, pulling her sweater over her head, and when she tossed it across the room, she could see that Danny was already undoing the buckle of his belt. She sat up quickly, taking over the task so that he could remove his shirt, and once it was off, he slipped his fingers under the cups of her bra and pulled it up over her head, completely bypassing the clasp.

There was urgency in their movements, earnestness in their kisses, fueled by the phone call, the fight, their declarations. Within two minutes of entering the bedroom, their bodies were already joined, and they clung to each other, clutching and clawing and gasping and still needing more. It was like they couldn't get close enough, and the desperation left them zealous and feral.

The unrelenting movement of Danny's hips gradually pushed her across the bed so that by the time it was over, her head was hanging off the other side, and his hand was on the opposite wall, bracing them.

The intensity of it left them both gasping and shaking, and they held each other, kissing and whispering until their hearts finally slowed and their breathing evened out.

Eventually, Danny moved them to a more comfortable position, and Leah lay with her head on his chest and her leg thrown over his thigh as he gently pulled her hair through his fingers.

"I have a favor to ask you," he said softly.

"Anything."

Danny inhaled deeply. "I have to go to Brooklyn next week to meet with my lawyer, and I'm bringing Gram. He needs to interview her, but the thing is, he's gotta go over some shit with me too, and I don't want her in the room for that. She doesn't need to know the specifics of things," he said, running a hand over his eyes.

"Why does he want to talk to her?"

"He's already spoken to her a few times, but they're finalizing everything now. He's trying to establish the relationship I had with Bryan. If the judge recognizes that this was about family, and not some college bar brawl, he might be more understanding."

"So he wants to talk to her about your childhood?"

"Yeah. Our childhood, right up through when it happened."

"Oh," she said softly.

"The thing is, I'm not sure how long this meeting with me is gonna take now that..." He exhaled. "Now that the wheels are in motion. And I don't want to leave her alone in the lobby while I'm in there. She gets really emotional every time we have to do this, and I just—"

"I'll take care of her," Leah promised softly. "We'll go get a cup of tea somewhere. Have some girl time."

"It's on a weekday, though."

"So I'll take the day off."

Danny brought his lips to the crown of her head. "Thank you," he said before kissing her there. "And I just want you to know that...I won't do that again," he added softly.

"Do what again?" she asked, trailing her fingertips over his waist, and she felt his stomach muscles twitch in response.

"I won't lose it like that again. Tonight was..." He shook his head. "It's out of my system."

Leah lifted her head, resting her chin on his chest as she looked at him. "No, it's not," she said softly. "And you can't expect it to be."

Danny blinked up at the ceiling.

"I know what you meant before," she said, laying her head back down on his chest as she played with his fingers. "That you don't want to live the next two months under a cloud of dread. And I agree. We should try to enjoy as much of it as we can. But there will be days when we can't ignore it. And that's okay, Danny. It's okay to need a time-out." She pressed her lips to his chest. "Tonight was just one of those nights."

Danny slid his hands under her arms and pulled her up the front of his body so that she was lying on top of him. He reached up, scooping her hair back into a ponytail and holding it there with one hand as he brought the other to her face.

"You are incredible," he said tenderly, running his thumb over her lips, and she kissed the pad of it. "You are beautiful, and smart, and thoughtful, and perfect, and I don't deserve you."

"Well, that's too bad, because you're stuck with me," she said, and he smiled up at her, using his hand in her hair to pull her mouth down to his.

The sound of her phone beeping with a text message interrupted the silence, and Leah lifted her head, breaking their kiss.

"That's probably Sarah checking up on us," she said, leaning over the side of the bed and swiping her phone from the nightstand. She lay back down on him, and he kept his hands on her waist as she opened the text.

And then she gasped loudly, shooting straight up in bed, and Danny bolted upright beside her.

"What is it? What happened?"

"Alexis is in labor!" she squealed, dropping the phone and clapping her hands quickly like a child.

Danny exhaled in a rush, running his hand down his face. "Jesus, you just scared the shit out of me."

"Sorry," she said, throwing herself forward and knocking him back onto the bed. She held her weight in her arms as she grinned down at him, and he laughed lightly, looking up at her.

"I'm gonna be an aunt!" she squeaked.

"You're gonna be an aunt," he repeated, tucking her hair behind her ear.

She sighed, lying down on his chest, and his hand came to her hair again, lazily running his fingers through it.

They lay there quietly for a while, and Leah listened to the rhythmic beating of Danny's heart, letting it lull her into a state of serenity. Eventually the rise and fall of his chest evened out and became regular, and Leah assumed he had fallen asleep until his voice broke the silence.

"Do you ever think about having kids?"

Leah nuzzled his chest, relishing the gentle vibrations that rumbled through it as he spoke. "I do," she said.

It was quiet for a beat before he said, "I remember being young, like twelve years old, and thinking about what a good dad I would be. I think it was because my dad was such a worthless bastard. Like, in a way, I wanted to prove to myself that I could do what he couldn't."

Leah lifted her head, resting her chin on his chest. "You'll be an amazing dad," she said gently.

He glanced down at her and smiled sadly. "I hope so. It's just...I'm twenty-nine years old. And I'm about to lose some time. Maybe a lot. And I know men can have children whenever, but...women can't."

Suddenly, Leah remembered the night he met her family—the way he had looked at Christopher as he rubbed Alexis's belly.

Leah lowered her head, pressing her lips against his chest as she spoke. "Even if it were five years," she whispered hoarsely, "you'd be thirty-four. I'd be thirty-three. Women can still have children safely at thirty-three."

The second the words left her mouth, she froze. Leah felt his chest stop moving, and she closed her eyes, turning away from him as she rested her cheek on his chest.

She couldn't believe she had just said that.

They had only just said "I love you" for the first time, and already she was deducing that she would be the mother of his children.

"I didn't mean…I wasn't assuming…I was just trying to show you…" She fumbled over her words, eventually letting them trail off.

They both lay there, saying nothing, and although his hand still rested on her head, his fingers had stopped playing with her hair.

After what seemed like an interminable silence, Danny spoke, the low timbre of his voice penetrating the stillness.

"Leah?"

"Hmm?"

He trailed his hand over the side of her face, taking her chin in his hand and lifting it as he turned her toward him.

"I want them to be just like you."

She stared at him, a slow smile spreading over her lips, and he lifted his head, bringing their mouths together.

And she wrapped her arms around him as they kissed, figuratively and literally embracing her future.

Chapter Seventeen

L eah and Danny sat on the couch outside his lawyer's office. Danny was resting his elbows on his knees, looking down at his hands as he wrung them together, and Leah sat next to him with her hand on the small of his back, rubbing her thumb back and forth. They didn't speak, and she knew he probably preferred it that way. Each time she looked at his profile, she could see that his brow was pulled together, or his jaw was clenched. He looked so vulnerable, and she wished there was something she could do to make what he was feeling go away.

As much as the three of them tried to keep the conversation light on the ride to Brooklyn, there was an obvious undertone of anxiety. The last time Leah had seen Catherine, her smiles had been warm, inviting, genuine. This time they were strained and contrived.

Throughout the ride Danny contributed to the conversation, his voice sounding easy and fluid, but his body betrayed him. He sat up straight, his shoulders rigid and his hands tight on the wheel. Leah knew he could sense Catherine's apprehension and grief, and it was slowly eating away at him.

When they arrived at the office, Danny's lawyer—a man named Eric Warden—took Catherine inside immediately. As soon as the door closed behind them, Danny's carefully cultivated façade melted away, and all of the stress and guilt Leah knew he'd been feeling all morning came rushing to the surface. And so they sat on the sofa in silence. She knew no words were capable of taking those feelings away, but she hoped her presence at least dulled them a little.

Catherine was in Eric's office for a little under an hour. When she came out, she held several crumpled tissues in her hand. Her eyes were glassy and bloodshot, and she looked completely drained.

Leah watched an intense pain flicker behind Danny's eyes before the façade was back in place, and he smiled, walking over to give her a hug.

When he let her go, Eric stepped back into his office and turned to Danny. "Ready?" he asked, and Danny nodded before he looked at Leah.

She walked over to them, putting her hand on Catherine's shoulder. "Catherine, do you want to go have a cup of tea? I noticed a diner down the street when we got here."

Danny nodded. "That's a good idea, Gram. It'll be more comfortable than waiting out here. I'll meet you guys over there when I'm done."

She smiled unsteadily. "That sounds lovely, sweetheart."

Leah turned to Danny, giving him a hug as she brought her lips to his ear. "She'll be fine, I promise. Go do what you have to do."

"Thank you," he said before he pressed his lips to her forehead, and then he turned and walked into the office. Eric smiled and gave them a small nod before he shut the door.

"Ready?" Leah asked, and Catherine nodded weakly.

They walked the block and a half down to the diner in relative silence. The interview with Eric had taken a lot out of her, and the last thing Leah wanted was to make her feel obligated to keep up some mindless small talk. So, she was going to follow her lead; if Catherine preferred to sit in reflective silence rather than talk, then that's what they would do.

Once they were seated, they each ordered a cup of tea and a muffin, and as the waitress left their table, Catherine removed her coat.

"Funny, isn't it?" she asked in her soft, raspy voice. "You and I having tea together again?"

Leah smiled. "I bet you didn't think you'd be seeing me before next Christmas."

"Actually, I had a feeling I'd be seeing you again." She smiled genuinely for the first time that day as she said, "Old Italian ladies all have a sixth sense. We know everything."

Leah laughed as the waitress approached the table with their tea and muffins, and it was quiet for a minute as they both fixed their tea.

"You know," Catherine said, dunking her tea bag in the steaming mug, "when you left my house that day, Daniel took me out to dinner, and every few minutes, he'd find a way to turn the conversation back to you. 'So, who was that?' 'Why did you invite her inside?' 'How long did she stay?' 'What were you talking about?' I think he was trying to be casual." She looked down with a smirk as she removed the tea bag, shaking her head. "Men are so transparent," she chuckled softly, placing the used tea bag on the tiny saucer.

Catherine wrapped her frail hands around the warm mug. "I'll admit that a little part of me wished I'd had some way to contact you. And then, wouldn't you know it, we came home and found your note." She smiled to herself. "And that's when I knew I could relax, because there were higher powers on the job."

She looked up at Leah with a tiny laugh. "The night he found your bracelet, he had this little glint in his eye. Like Christmas morning. Even better than finding it was finding his excuse to call."

Leah's stomach fluttered at the realization that he'd been interested in her, even back then.

"I do believe everything happens for a reason," Catherine said, running her finger along the rim of her mug. "I've always believed that. I only had one child. My daughter. There were some complications during delivery, and I wasn't able to have any more."

"I'm sorry," Leah said, and Catherine smiled sadly.

"Thank you. You know, I was okay with it, really. The only thing that made me sad was that I wasn't able to provide my Louie with a son. He never said it, but I knew he wanted one." She took a deep breath. "But God has a plan for everyone, and he works in mysterious ways. My daughter...she made some poor choices in her life. But those choices gave me Bryan."

Catherine smiled, her eyes focused on her mug as if she were seeing something different than what was in front of her. "It wasn't the way it should have gone, and it wasn't the way I planned it, but it was wonderful all the same, raising that little boy." She nodded slowly, and then her shoulders bounced with a quiet laugh. "And then along came Daniel. When I met him, he was six years old."

She brought her delicate hand up to her chest, pressing it over her heart. "He was one of the kindest little things I'd ever met. He had a warmth in his heart, even back then."

Leah looked down and smiled, imagining a six-year-old Danny—a sweet little boy with big blue eyes and messy black hair.

"What a pair they were," Catherine said with a chuckle. "They certainly kept me on my toes. Such good boys. Thick as thieves. They would do anything for each other..." She trailed off, and her eyes welled with tears.

Leah reached across the table, placing her hand over Catherine's, and for a minute they sat that way, neither of them speaking.

Eventually, Catherine grabbed her napkin with her free hand and dabbed at her eyes, taking a steadying breath.

"My sweet Daniel," she said, more to herself than to Leah. "I wish they'd understand that losing Bryan has been punishment enough for him."

There were no words to say. Leah knew what she was feeling. The sadness. The anger. The frustration. The overwhelming desire to convince the people who held Danny's future in their hands what an amazing person he was, despite what he had done. And because she knew the feeling, she knew there was nothing anyone could say to alleviate it.

"You're good for him, you know," Catherine said.

Leah raised her eyes.

"And I know he's my boy, and I'm a bit biased, but he's good for you too, isn't he?"

Leah nodded, her eyes beginning to sting, and Catherine reached over and patted her hand.

"He'll take good care of you, sweetheart."

The waitress approached the table then, asking how everything was and if they needed anything else. Once she left, Catherine changed the subject, asking her questions about her job, what made her want to be a teacher, what her favorite things to teach were.

A little while later, Leah got a text from Danny asking if they were still at the diner. She told him they were, and a few minutes later, he came through the door looking completely exhausted and ready to go home. Catherine insisted that he sit down and eat something since he hadn't eaten anything all day, but he refused.

The drive home was once again quiet; Danny's posture was rigid, but he managed to keep his face smooth the entire way back to Catherine's. As soon as they'd dropped her off, though, he gave up the charade, and the tension began rolling off him in waves.

Leah sat quietly beside him, her hand clasping his on the console, drawing lazy, soothing patterns on the back of his hand with her thumb.

When they were a few minutes away from her apartment, Danny's stomach growled loudly.

"You really haven't eaten anything all day?" she asked.

He shrugged. "I haven't been hungry all day. I could probably eat now, though."

"Do you want me to make you something when we get back?"

"No, that's okay. I'll just grab a quick snack."

"Okay," she said, scooting over to rest her head on his shoulder.

Once they were back in Leah's apartment, she headed to the bedroom to change as Danny went to the kitchen to find something to eat, and on her way back out of her room, an idea finally dawned on her.

All day long she'd been trying to come up with something that would make him feel better, and there was one thing that always helped her relax when she was stressed or upset. She knew the kind of worry Danny was dealing with far surpassed anything she'd experienced, but she hoped it still might take the edge off for him.

Leah turned into the bathroom and sat on the edge of her tub, leaning over to turn the faucet on. After adjusting the water to the right temperature, she plugged the drain and allowed the tub to fill, and then she turned and reached into the cabinet under the sink, pulling out the lavender orchid-scented bath gel.

Leah squeezed a generous amount of it under the running faucet, and almost instantly, the frothy bubbles appeared, slowly increasing in volume as they crept across the surface of the water. The scent of the gel permeated the air, increasing in potency as it mixed with the hot water.

As the tub continued to fill, she went back to the cabinet and grabbed some tea candles, lining them up along the back ledge of the tub up against the wall. By the time she was finished lighting them, the tub had filled completely, the glistening bubbles nearly spilling over the sides. She turned off the faucet and set the plush bath mat down on the floor before she dimmed the lights and surveyed the scene. And then she smiled to herself as she turned and headed out to the kitchen.

He was leaned up against the counter, an open bottle of water in one hand and a half-eaten granola bar in the other. When he heard her come into the room, he looked up and smiled weakly.

"You doing okay?" she asked softly, and he nodded.

"Just tired," he said, taking the last bite of the granola bar.

"I know something that might make you feel better."

"What's that?" he asked after he had swallowed.

"It's a surprise," she said, taking the bottle of water out of his hand and placing it on the counter. "Come with me."

She grabbed his hand and pulled him toward her, and when he stepped away from the counter, she came behind him and went up on her toes, cupping her hands over his eyes.

"What are you doing?" he laughed.

"Bringing you to your surprise," she said, guiding him out of the kitchen. His shoulder banged the doorframe as they exited, and she flinched. "Whoops. Sorry."

Leah steered him slowly down the hall and turned him into the bathroom, stopping as she came around to his side. "Ready?" she asked, looking up at him.

"I think so," he said with a tiny laugh.

She removed her hands from his eyes and they fluttered open; after a stunned second, he pulled his brow together.

"You want me to take a bubble bath?"

She nodded. "I'll never understand why guys don't do this for themselves."

His expression was skeptical as he looked back at the tub, overflowing with bubbles and surrounded by candles, and Leah rolled her eyes, pushing him gently toward the tub. "I'm telling you, it's awesome. You'll love it."

He crossed his arms. "It even *smells* girly in here."

"It's aromatherapy bath gel. You'll appreciate it more when you're soaking."

Danny eyed the teeming bubbles, looking totally unconvinced.

"Oh my God," she said. "Would you quit being such a baby and just get in?"

His lips curved into a small smile. "You know what would make this seem a little less effeminate?"

Leah threw her hands up in defeat. "I don't know. A cigar and a dirty magazine?"

He burst out laughing. "That's not a bad idea," he said. "But no, I was thinking it might not be so bad if you got in there with me."

She put her hands on her hips, shaking her head before she turned to leave the room.

"Where are you going?"

Leah looked over her shoulder. "To get another towel."

Danny smiled before he reached behind his head and pulled his shirt off.

By the time Leah came back to the bathroom, he was already submerged in the frothy bubbles with his head resting on the bath pillow and his eyes closed. She smirked as she stripped off her clothes and grabbed a clip, pinning her hair up in a messy twist as she approached the tub.

As she eased herself into the water, Danny sat up, taking hold of her waist and turning her so that she was sitting between his legs with her back up against his chest. Leah rested back against him, letting her head fall onto his shoulder with a sigh.

"Mmm," she hummed as the heat of the water began to permeate her muscles. "Nice, right?"

"It's okay," he said, and she laughed. Danny's hands trailed up her arms and over her shoulders, and he gripped them gently, pressing his thumbs into the back of her neck as he began rubbing soothing circles.

Her head fell forward as he continued his ministrations, using a bit more pressure as he worked his way down her shoulders, and Leah groaned softly as he worked out a muscle knot on the right side. "I should be doing this for you. This is supposed to be about helping *you* relax."

"Making you feel good helps me relax," he said, bringing his arms under the water and wrapping them around her waist. He pulled her flush against his chest, kissing the side of her head. "Thank you. I really did need this tonight," he said into her hair.

Leah trailed her fingertips over his leg under the water. "Do you want to talk about it?"

"Not really."

Leah nodded, and for a minute they just sat there, her head on his shoulder and his arms around her waist.

"Was there something you wanted to know?" he asked.

"No, not if you don't want to talk about it."

Danny shifted his head, looking down at her. "No, it's okay. Ask me. You have a right to know what's going on."

Leah chewed on her lip before she said, "Okay, well, I just wanted to know if you knew what the worst-case scenario was."

"You mean what's the most time I could get?"

Leah nodded.

"Ten years."

She closed her eyes, thankful she was facing away from him, because she knew the piercing pain in her chest would be written all over her face. "Is that probable?" she asked weakly.

"My lawyer doesn't think so," he said, rubbing his thumbs over the skin of her stomach. "One of the main reasons we copped a plea was to avoid that. Plus, he's building his entire case around the fact that I'm a respectable person with good standing in the community, that I was blatantly provoked. The more evidence he has to support that, the more likely the sentence will be mitigated."

"Okay…so what does he think you'll get?"

"His guess is two to four."

She should have been happy, or at the very least, relieved. Two to four was so much better than ten. Yet a lump still formed in her throat, and she swallowed repeatedly, trying to clear it before she had to speak again.

"What's gonna happen to the shop?" she asked hoarsely.

Danny removed his hand from her stomach, bringing it above the water and trailing his fingers through the bubbles. "I've been training Jake for the past six months. He's gonna take it over."

She lifted her brow. "You're giving it to him?"

"For a while, yeah. He'll run it while I'm gone, and when I get out, I'll take it back from him. He's been talking about opening up his own shop in Queens for a while now, so this will be a good experience for him. Plus, the money he'll make as co-owner will set him up pretty nicely for what he wants to do."

"Co-owner?"

"I arranged it so he'll still be giving Bryan's share to Gram."

Leah closed her eyes; she didn't think it was possible to love him more than she already did, but she was wrong.

It grew quiet again as Danny scooped up handfuls of bubbles, spreading them down Leah's arms, along the tops of her shoulders, over her collarbone.

"Was there anything else you wanted to know?" he asked.

When she didn't respond right away, he said, "Ask me, Leah."

She took a tiny breath. "What about your apartment?"

"My lease is up this summer. I'm gonna have to sort through all my stuff. I'll store some of it at Gram's, and some of it will go to the guys, and I guess some shit I'm just gonna have to get rid of. And then when this is all over, I'll find a new place."

Leah nodded as Danny shifted, sinking a little further into the water and taking her with him.

"Are you afraid?" she asked softly.

He took a deep breath, his chest rising dramatically beneath her.

"Yes. But probably not for the reasons you're thinking."

Leah turned her head slightly, looking up at him.

"I'm not afraid of being in prison," he said. "I'm afraid about what will be happening out here while I'm gone."

"What do you mean?"

Danny looked down, shaking his head. "For one, I don't like that Gram will be alone. Jake's going to make sure she's taken care of financially, but—"

"I'll take care of her."

He smiled sadly, kissing her head. "You've been taking care of people your whole life, sweet girl. You don't need someone else to look after."

Leah sat up, turning toward him as she shook her head. "It's not a burden, Danny," she stated simply. "It's a given. I love you, and you love her. So of course I'm going to make sure she's okay."

Danny stared at her for a moment, the adoration clear in his eyes before he closed them. He dropped his head back on the edge of the tub, exhaling before he said, "It's not just Gram I worry about. I'm afraid of leaving you too."

"Don't be. You don't have to worry about me. I can take care of myself."

He opened his eyes. "I know you can. You're one of the strongest people I know, and I really hate that life keeps making you have to prove it."

Leah swallowed, dropping her eyes to the heap of frothy bubbles between them.

"You've been through enough, Leah. You shouldn't have to suffer through anything else. And the idea that you'll be suffering because of me…" He closed his eyes and shook his head. "It makes me fucking sick to my stomach."

"Danny," she said softly, her eyes still downcast.

"And what if that asshole starts back up again?" he asked, his voice hardening slightly.

Leah shook her head before he was even done with his question. "No. That's over. I'm not going to take the easy way out anymore. Honestly, after what happened at Paddy's, I really don't think he'll be coming around again, but if he does, I'll do whatever's necessary. I'll tell my brother. I'll call the cops if I have to."

Danny looked down with a nod, but she could see in his face that he wasn't appeased. There was something he wasn't saying.

"If you think I'm strong enough to handle this, then what are you afraid of?"

He wet his lips before he lifted his eyes to hers. "I'm afraid you're gonna resent me."

Leah's back straightened. "Well, you have no reason to be afraid of that, because it won't happen."

"Leah," he said gently, "there's not a question in my mind that what we have is real. I don't doubt it for a second. But your life is going to be put on hold. Years of your life, wasted. For me. Because of me. And I just…I don't want you to have any regrets."

She opened her mouth to speak, but he shook his head. "Just know that I wouldn't blame you if it became too much. If it became too long, and you needed to move on. I wouldn't hate you if it happened. I'd rather you take care of your needs than resent me. You deserve to be happy, with or without me."

He held her eyes for a few more seconds, making sure his words were received, and Leah shook her head slightly, looking down as she trailed her fingertips through the suds.

"When I was a junior in college, I was working on this project with a girl from one of my classes. I remember sitting in the library with her one day, and she was going on and on about how much she hated her father's girlfriend, and it hit me all of a sudden that in all the years since my mother had been gone, my father hadn't been out on a single date. Not one."

Danny glanced up at her, his brow slightly furrowed as he tried to figure out the relevance of what she was saying.

"I couldn't believe I'd never realized that before, but after that I couldn't stop thinking about it. By that point it had been almost ten years, and I just kept thinking about how lonely he must have been. And then I started feeling really guilty, because the only reason I could come up with for why he wasn't dating was because of us—because of me and Chris and Sarah. I figured he didn't want to upset us, or to make us think he was trying to replace her. I mean, that had to be it, right? Because why else would somebody *choose* to be alone?"

Leah saw the sadness flicker behind Danny's eyes as she said, "I really hated the thought that he was depriving himself of being happy because of us. And I wanted him to know that he deserved to have a life too. That if he moved on, it would be okay, and we would understand. I just wanted him to have a chance at being happy again."

Leah scooped up a handful of bubbles and leaned forward, spreading them over the strong planes of Danny's chest.

"So one day, I told him." She smiled, shaking her head. "He listened to me go on and on, justifying actions he hadn't even taken yet. And when I finally finished, he smiled at me and thanked me for my concern. And then he told me it wasn't necessary. He said he hadn't been on a date because there was no reason to go on one."

Leah looked up at Danny. "He said that if he was lonely, it wasn't because he needed to be with *someone*. It was because he needed to be with *her*. And if he couldn't have that, he didn't want anything else."

Danny's eyes softened as he looked at her, and she smiled.

"You know, I don't think I ever fully understood what he meant until just now. It won't be a man I'll be needing when you're gone. It won't even be companionship. It will be *you*."

The way Danny was looking at her caused a faint tingling over her skin, and she found his hand under the water, twining their fingers together.

"And I'm lucky, Danny. Really, I am. Because my dad...all he wants is her. And he'll never have that. But you," she said, placing her hand over his heart, "you're coming back to me. I know it's not forever. So I can wait."

Danny's eyes fell closed, his throat bobbing as he swallowed. When he opened them, he shook his head slightly.

"Do you have any idea how perfect you are?" he whispered.

Leah dropped her eyes. "I'm far from perfect."

She felt his fingers under her chin, lifting her gaze back to his.

"You're perfect for *me*," he amended.

And when he leaned forward and brought his mouth to hers, there wasn't a doubt in her mind it was true.

Chapter Eighteen

"Here, have a little more," Gram said, leaning over to put another slab of corned beef on Danny's plate, and he shook his head, using his hand to deflect it as he chewed.

"Nuh-uh," he said around his mouthful of food. "I'm tapping out."

"Oh, come on now," she said, swatting his hand away before dropping the piece of meat on his plate. "I've seen you eat more than this."

"Gram, I'm seriously gonna puke," he said, sitting back and holding both hands over his stomach.

"It's a holiday, Daniel. You're supposed to stuff yourself with good food on a holiday."

Danny laughed, tossing his napkin onto the table. "I've never met a Sicilian woman so enamored with Saint Patrick's Day. Aren't you supposed to be wandering around the house mumbling something about 'those damn Irish'?"

"Oh hush," she said, taking her seat on the other side of the table. "Besides, it's a holiday that involves cooking large amounts of food. That's good enough for me."

"You know, you're only supposed to cook large amounts of food when you have a large amount of people who are going to eat it. *This*," he said, gesturing to the spread on the table, "was a bit of an overshoot for two people, don't you think?"

Gram shrugged. "I don't know how to cook for only two people."

Danny burst out laughing as he stood, grabbing his plate and hers. "This is true. I should be morbidly obese by now."

Gram chuckled as he rinsed off their plates before putting them in the dishwasher, and then he did the same with the pans on the stove before he grabbed a few plastic containers and brought them back to the table so Gram could start packing up the leftovers.

"Here," he said, handing one to Gram before he started to fill the other. "Do you want to save the cabbage, or will that go bad?"

"Daniel, we need to talk about something."

"About what?" he said, piling the slices of corned beef into the container.

Gram placed her empty tupperware on the table. "Can you sit down first?"

Danny froze with his hand on the platter before he lifted his eyes to hers. "Are you okay?"

"I'm fine," she stated simply.

He stood there for a few seconds, studying her expression, trying to assess her honesty.

She gestured to his chair. "Sit, please."

Danny slid the fork back onto the platter before he walked back to his chair and sat down, shifting it so that he was facing her fully. He had only seen her look this way a handful of times, but they were all associated with bad memories.

It wasn't anger or sadness that filled her eyes. Instead, it looked more like resignation. Or resolution.

Or both.

She smiled gently as she turned to face him.

"I've been doing a lot of thinking, and…it's time," she said.

"Time for what?"

Gram reached across the table and laid her open hand in front of Danny; instinctively, he brought his hand up from his lap and took it in his own.

She gave it a gentle squeeze before she said, "It's time to let Bryan go."

Her words had the effect of a battering ram to his stomach; first the stealing of his breath, followed by the immediate onset of panic, and then finally the staggering pain.

They were so unanticipated that Danny couldn't even open his mouth to attempt a response. In some twisted way, there had always been comfort in the fact that Gram hadn't given up. Danny knew Bryan wasn't coming back, but the fact that she still believed…it made it seem like perhaps—in some far-off, remote world—there was the tiniest possibility it could happen.

He didn't want her to give up. He needed her to believe, even when he couldn't.

"It's been long enough, Daniel. He's tired. I know he's so tired."

Danny's stomach was churning, and he swallowed repeatedly, trying to keep his dinner down.

No. Don't give up on him.

"There's a thin line between being hopeful and being selfish, and I think I crossed it a long time ago. I just hope he'll forgive me for making him stay so long."

"Gram," Danny choked out, but his voice sounded strange, like it was coming from some place far away and not his own mouth. "Doctors aren't always right. Maybe—"

She shook her head. "I know my Bryan. He would have come back to us if he could have. He would have fought and fought and fought. But he's tired, love. It's time for him to rest."

Danny removed his hand from hers and ran it up through his hair before shaking his head. "We don't have to decide this now."

"Yes, we do," she said softly.

"*Why?*" Danny snapped, slamming his hand down on the table.

Gram didn't even flinch. Instead, her shoulders softened as her eyes met his. "Because I want you to be able to say your good-byes... before you go."

The chair screeched abruptly as he stood from the table and walked through the kitchen. With a quick jerk of his arm, he swiped his keys off the half wall and strode out the front door, slamming it closed behind him.

Danny sat in the back seat of Leah's car, staring at the buildings as they blurred past the window. Every so often he'd glance at the rearview mirror, watching the reflection of her eyes until they flicked up and found his. Whenever it happened, he'd feel his pulse slow in his veins, the nauseous swell in his stomach temporarily subside. Every time. As if she were somehow siphoning all of his anxiety, all of his suffering, with merely a look.

He looked over to where Gram sat in the passenger seat, her eyes trained on her purse, which sat primly in her lap. She'd been quiet all morning, lost in some faraway place, so that Danny found himself having to say something two or three times before she heard him.

After Danny had stormed out on her that night, he drove around aimlessly for two hours before he eventually ended up at Leah's apartment. Gram had said she was doing it because she wanted Danny to have a chance to say good-bye.

But all Danny heard was that she was giving up on Bryan because of *him*.

It took Leah hours to convince him otherwise. But she was patient, and she was gentle. She let him rant. She let him yell. She let him pace. And she let him fall apart.

And then she lay with him until three o'clock in the morning, despite having to get up for work the next day, talking him off the ledge and helping him understand what it was really about.

Helping him see that Gram was right.

She offered to drive them to the hospital when it happened, knowing how difficult it would be for either one of them to make the drive back.

He never would have asked her to do something like that—to subject her to something as morbid as saying good-bye to someone who had spent the last year of his life in the ICU. She'd had enough of hospitals and good-byes. But he was selfish enough in that moment to accept the offer. And as they pulled into the parking lot of the hospital and he caught her eyes in the mirror again, he forgave himself for the decision.

Because there was no way he would have been able to do this without her.

They walked up to the building in silence, Leah a step behind Gram and Danny as he traversed the corridors with ease, bringing them to the elevators that would take them up to the ICU. He'd done this so many times, his body could complete the task without the help of his mind.

But this time it felt foreign.

Every sound was amplified. The clicking of shoes on the linoleum. The squeak of wheels as machinery and beds were moved from place to place. The chatter of people. The delicate beeping that meant someone was surviving.

He wanted to plug his ears.

Gram had gone to the hospital earlier that week to complete all the paperwork, which meant the second the elevator doors opened, there was nothing left to do but go through with it.

There was no time to buy. No excuses to use. No reason to delay.

It felt like the walls of the elevator were closing in, and Danny reached out and put his hand on the wall to his left, pushing his weight into it, trying to keep it at bay.

He felt a hand on his back then, the feminine fingers splayed out as she applied gentle pressure, and he closed his eyes, concentrating on the feel of it until his arm finally went slack and fell from the wall. A few seconds later, the doors dinged open, and she kept her hand on his back, grounding him as they approached the nurses' station.

When the woman behind the front desk saw them approaching, she stood and smiled gently at Gram.

"Mrs. Giordano. If you'll have a seat right over there, I'll have Dr. Racine paged for you."

Gram nodded but didn't move; she seemed frozen in place, and in that moment, something in Danny's chest shifted slightly, just enough to remind him that he wasn't the only one suffering.

"Come on, Gram," he said softly, wrapping his arm around her and walking them over to the seating area. He felt Leah's hand slip from his back, and a jolt of panic went through him, but he concentrated instead on the feel of Gram beneath his arm, thin and frail and trembling.

You're not the only one. Don't leave her alone in this.

They sat in two of the chairs, and Leah stood a few feet away, her arms folded over her chest and her eyes scanning the area. He could see she was trying to hold it together, and he felt the shift in his chest again.

He needed to be present now. He needed to shoulder this. For both of them. Because he'd be damned if he had to watch the women he loved take on any more of his burden.

A woman approached them then, dressed in lavender scrubs. She had one of those friendly faces that made Danny feel like he'd met her a thousand times, even though he'd never seen her before today.

"Hello. My name's Amanda. I'll be with Dr. Racine today."

"Hello," Danny managed softly.

"I know this isn't easy," she said. Her voice was like aloe on a sunburn, and for a moment, Danny found himself wondering if that was something they taught in nursing school. "Anything you need from us, please let us know. We'd like to support you in any way we can."

Danny wet his lips as he looked down. "Thank you."

"I just wanted to take a minute to walk you through the process so you know what to expect once we go inside. Is it okay if we do that now?"

Danny nodded, rubbing his hand up and down Gram's arm. She was completely stoic, resting her head on his shoulder as she stared straight ahead.

"Okay. When you're ready, the doctor will remove his breathing tube, and then I'll turn off his epinephrine drip. After that, his blood pressure will drop, and his breathing will begin to taper off."

He closed his eyes, biting the inside of his bottom lip until he tasted blood.

"We'll be monitoring his vitals back at the nurses' station. You can stay with him as long as you like."

Danny cleared his throat before he lifted his eyes. "Will it hurt?" he managed.

"No. If Dr. Racine thinks it will take a while for him to pass, he'll order some medication to make him comfortable. He won't feel any pain."

Although Gram's mask-like expression hadn't changed, Danny tightened his arm around her as he ran his hand over his eyes.

"What do you mean by a while? How long will it take?"

"We won't know what we're looking at until we see how his vitals respond without assistance. It could be a few minutes, or a few hours. In some cases, it could be a few days."

Danny saw Leah close her eyes before turning away.

I can't. I can't do this. I can't.

"Do you have any other questions?" the nurse asked gently, placing her hand on Danny's shoulder.

He kept his eyes trained on the floor as he shook his head.

"If you do, or if you need anything else, please don't hesitate to ask us."

"Thanks," Danny said hoarsely, looking down at Gram. Her glassy eyes were still fixed on some far-off point.

"Let us know when you're ready," she said before she stood, placing her hand on top of Gram's before she continued on to the nurses' station.

"Gram," Danny said, and she blinked a few times before turning her head to look up at him. "Do you understand everything the nurse just said?"

After a few seconds, she nodded.

"Okay," he said, rubbing his hand over her arm. "Okay...you let me know when you're ready."

Gram took a deep breath before she said, "I need to use the powder room."

"Alright," he said, moving to help her up, and when he took a step with her, she shook her head.

"I'd like to go alone."

Danny gradually released his hold on her, making sure she was steady on her feet. "Are you sure?"

She nodded, giving his hand a squeeze before she let go and started down the hall, and he kept his eyes on her until she turned the corner and was out of sight.

Danny lowered himself into the chair behind him, dropping his forehead to his clasped hands. And then Leah was standing in front of him, resting her hand on the back of his head.

Without lifting his head, he reached forward, wrapping his arms around her hips and pulling her to stand in between his legs before he buried his face in her abdomen.

"This is…" he whispered.

"I know," she murmured, running her fingers through his hair before she leaned down and pressed her lips to his head, leaving them there as she added, "But he'll never be gone, Danny. Because you still love him. And he'll always exist through you because of that. They leave, baby, but they're never gone."

She straightened, and he lifted his head, resting his chin on her stomach as he stared up at her. She smiled a watery smile as she ran her fingers through his hair again. "You're doing the right thing," she whispered.

He nodded before pressing his face into her stomach again, and she stood there, caressing his hair until Gram returned from the bathroom.

"I'm ready," she said softly, and Leah stepped back, allowing him to stand.

"Alright," he said, running his hand over his eyes. "Let me just…I'll…"

"I'll go get them," Leah interjected. "Stay here with her."

He exhaled as Leah turned toward the nurses' station, thankful for her offer; he didn't think he'd be able to speak to anyone right now. He wasn't even sure how he was still standing.

Gram came over and took his hand, holding it gently as they stood waiting for Leah to return.

A few minutes later, Dr. Racine turned the corner with the nurse named Amanda from earlier. He approached them and held out his hand, shaking Danny's as he said something Danny didn't hear. Instead, his eyes were on Leah where she stood a few feet away, her watery eyes pinned on him.

"*I love you*," she mouthed.

"If you'll follow me," Dr. Racine said, pulling his attention from Leah, and Danny blinked quickly before he nodded.

The doctor and nurse walked a few steps ahead as he and Gram followed them into Bryan's room.

This was usually the part where Danny could exhale; no matter how many times he walked through the ICU, it always unsettled him. Solemn faces. Voices barely above hushed whispers. No flowers. No balloons. Everything sterile. Angular. Cold. Machines beeping in a repetitive chorus of hope, or trilling in warning. Faces worn from vigils that had lasted days or weeks, or worse, the faces streaked with the tears of a vigil that had ended.

But then he'd get inside Bryan's room, the door would close behind him, and he'd exhale. He'd pull up a chair and sit next to the bed, and he'd talk to his best friend as if they were sitting on the wall outside the shop having lunch. He'd tell him about his life, about work, about the guys. He'd tell him about the weather, about movies he'd seen. And most recently, he'd tell him about Leah.

It was a little piece of normal inside a cyclone of sorrow.

But today, as the door closed behind him, he didn't exhale. He didn't pull up a chair. He didn't smile or talk or share.

He didn't move at all.

Gram released his hand as Amanda guided her to the other side of the room, pulling up a chair for her to sit by Bryan's bedside. Danny was still rooted to the floor as the doctor looked over the readouts on Bryan's machines and the nurse helped Gram get comfortable in her chair. She said something to her that Danny couldn't hear, and then Gram pressed her lips together before she nodded.

"Okay," Amanda said, placing her hand on Gram's shoulder before she turned to Dr. Racine, looking at him meaningfully.

Danny watched as he approached the side of the bed and took hold of the tube in Bryan's mouth. When he stepped back a few seconds later, there was a small plastic cylinder still attached to Bryan's lip by some medical tape, but the long, serpentine tube—the one Danny knew was sending life-giving oxygen into his lungs—was gone.

His eyes were drawn to Amanda on other side of the bed as she reached up and clicked a switch on the machine above Bryan's head.

The drip. The thing that kept his blood pumping through his body. Gone.

Something like panic fluttered in his chest, making it hard to breathe, and his eyes flew to Gram; she was sitting in the chair on the opposite side of the bed, smiling softly as she stroked her hand up and down Bryan's arm.

He thought he'd made his peace with this. He'd known for a year now that Bryan wasn't coming back. *She* was the one who had hoped. She was the one who had believed, against all odds, that one morning he would open his eyes. Danny had always known it was a pipe dream. He'd said his good-byes long before this.

So then why was this so hard?

Gram looked so calm—peaceful, even—and he felt like he was about to lose it. Like he wanted to pound his fists against the nearest object and scream until his throat was raw and bloody and his body collapsed in on itself.

The doctor slid a chair up to Bryan's bedside opposite Gram, nodding at Danny before he walked to the other side of the room to consult with the nurse.

Danny walked the few steps over to the chair and sank down into it, pressing his hands into the tops of his thighs to try and stop them from trembling.

He stared at Bryan's face, trying to make him appear. Trying to animate it. Trying to remember his mannerisms. His facial expressions. His laugh.

When Danny wasn't with him, it was always so hard to do. He could conjure images, but the details were hazy, like looking at a picture on the bottom of a pool.

But with Bryan in front of him, everything was suddenly sharp. His impassive face provided the blank canvas for Danny to recreate image after image of his friend—happy, sad, confused, angry, amused—all crystal clear and perfect. Whenever he'd leave after a visit, Danny would always promise himself that this time, he wouldn't forget. He'd replay the images in his mind like a slideshow as he drove home, trying to commit their clarity to permanent memory. But it was like trying to hold water in his fist.

He failed every time.

Bryan's face was thinner than Danny's memories, something he'd gradually grown accustomed to, but today his jaw was covered in a light five-o'clock shadow. Gram and the nurses had spent the last year keeping up a steady system of shaving him, cutting his hair, his fingernails.

Preserving him.

But no one had shaved him today.

Dr. Racine approached Gram's side of the bed, placing his hand on her shoulder. "It won't be too much longer now," he said gently.

Danny straightened as his stomach jolted, sending bile up into the back of his throat.

No. NO.

His heart started racing, urging him to do something. Ask them to perform CPR. Beg them to hook the tube back up. Plead with them to restart the drip.

Don't. Don't go yet. Not yet.

His eyes darted to the monitor above the bed; the nurse had silenced it before she turned the drip off, but he could see the long green line, adorned with miniature spikes—tiny hills that crested with every beat of his heart.

Getting further and further apart.

"Come on, Bry. Fight," he choked out, dropping his head so that his forehead rested on Bryan's arm.

And then he heard her voice.

Gram was singing to him in her soft, ethereal way—the familiar words he'd heard hundreds of times in his life, whenever he or Bryan was restless, or hurt, or sick.

Or drifting off to sleep.

He's my treasure, he's my joy
He's my pleasure, he's my boy.
If he ever went away, lonesome I would be
'Cause he's my angel, my baby.

Those words had soothed him so many times, but today they rolled off him like drops of rain down the window—fleeting and futile.

Danny squeezed his eyes shut as a barrage of images assaulted him. Bryan's life, flashing before his eyes—he wasn't the one dying, but he could *feel* it happening. He could see it all unfold, as if Bryan were sharing the last few moments of his life with him.

Danny under the deck with a broken leg as Bryan held his hand, reciting batting averages with him to help keep his mind off the pain.

Bryan hanging over the fence of the dugout, shouting and cheering as Danny scored the tying run in their high school's championship game.

Danny helping Bryan sneak out of his bedroom window to go meet up with his girlfriend on Valentine's night.

Bryan and Danny sitting on his bedroom floor, laughing hysterically.

Hanging out in the garage, talking into the night under the hood of car.

Trick-or-treating in their matching Batman costumes, because neither one of them wanted to be Robin.

Sharing their first beer in the alley behind the grocery store the summer before eighth grade.

Standing in the middle of the vacant building they'd just purchased, toasting with embarrassingly cheap champagne to the shop they envisioned within its walls.

And then, two little boys. One sitting on the steps outside his house and the other stopped on the sidewalk.

"Hey," he said curiously. "Why are you sitting outside by yourself?"

The one on the steps shrugged. "'Cause my mom's not home."

"Oh. Well, when will she come home?"

The boy scratched his knee. "Dunno."

After a few seconds of silence, the other said, "Well…you wanna come to my house? I have a new video game, but it needs two players. My gram doesn't know how to play it."

The boy on the steps looked up. "Um... okay."

"Cool. I'm Bryan."

"Danny."

"Do you have any video games?" he asked as Danny approached.

"Not a lot."

"That's okay. You can bring what you have next time. We can play every day."

And for the first time since he woke up that morning, Danny smiled. "Okay."

"You saved me," he whispered into the sheet, his forehead still pressed against Bryan's arm. "You saved me, and I didn't save you."

I'm sorry.

I'm sorry I'm sorry I'm sorry I'm sorry.

He gritted his teeth until he felt pain in his jaw, chanting the words like an incantation, until they lost all meaning and form and sounded odd in his ears, like indecipherable words from some foreign language.

"Time of death, one nineteen p.m."

Danny whipped his head up; the monitor was still, the long green line smooth and placid.

Final.

Amanda was hugging Gram, rubbing her back gently as she said something in her ear, and Danny felt a hand on his shoulder.

"I'm so sorry for your loss," Dr. Racine said. "Please, take as much time as you need."

Danny didn't move as the doctor and the nurse left the room. He didn't move as Gram tucked the blanket around Bryan, as if she really had just sung him to sleep. He didn't move as she leaned over and kissed his forehead before brushing his hair out of his eyes.

"My angel boy," she said gently. "You always had my heart, and you have it still. It's how I'll find you when it's time for us to meet again."

She turned then and gathered her things before walking carefully toward the door. As she passed Danny, she placed her hand on his arm, giving him a feeble squeeze before she continued out into the hall.

And still, he didn't move.

He couldn't. Not before he memorized all of Bryan's facial expressions. Not before he committed the images to memory. Not before he was sure he could preserve the exactitude of each and every one. He couldn't let them fade away this time.

Because now, there'd be no way to get them back.

Leah held on to Catherine's arm as they walked her through the side yard toward her house with Danny supporting her on the other side. She had cried silently on the drive home, the tears trickling discreetly down her face. Every so often she would lift her hand to dab at them with a tissue, but otherwise she didn't move.

Leah had checked the rearview mirror frequently throughout the drive, but this time Danny wasn't looking for her. He wasn't looking for anything. He sat with his forehead on the window—his glassy, bloodshot eyes staring without seeing at whatever was passing by.

As soon as they parked in Catherine's driveway though, he seemed to snap out of it. His expression was guarded, his voice detached, but he was moving and functioning as he took care of Catherine, helping her out of the car while whispering reassuring words to her.

They helped her into the house, and Danny put on a pot of tea as Leah helped her change out of her clothes. The doctor had prescribed her a small script of sleeping pills for the next few days, and as soon as they all sat down with their mugs, she was asking for one.

Leah could remember that desperate desire for sleep, the need to disappear into a world that offered some type of reprieve from reality, or better yet, a world where—if you were lucky—you would have the good fortune of seeing the person you missed more than anything. She used to dream of her mother often when she was younger, to the point that sometimes she'd have her pajamas on before dinner was even on the table, anticipating the moment she could close her eyes and find her.

Danny spent a few minutes reading the label of the pills, checking the warnings and the drug interactions. Leah could see he wasn't thrilled with the idea of giving them to her, but she also knew that he'd move a mountain with his bare hands right now if she asked him to.

He wasn't going to deny her, no matter how much he disapproved.

They sat with her after she had taken the pill, and when she started to fade, Danny lifted her up like a child, carrying her to her bedroom and tucking her in.

When he came out of her room a minute later, Leah looked up from where she was rinsing their teacups in the sink. His eyes found hers, holding them.

She turned off the water before drying her hands on the towel. "Hey," she said softly.

He slid his hands in his pockets, leaning against the doorjamb of Catherine's room. "Hey."

Leah tossed the towel over the drain board. "Is she sleeping?"

He nodded.

She stepped out of the tiny kitchen, stopping just inside the living room, and the way he was looking at her made her feel like someone had punched a hole in her chest.

God, she remembered that hurt.

She remembered the feeling of being so lost, she thought she'd never find her way again. The feeling that things were always going to be this bad.

That she was going to spend the rest of her life trying to be whole again.

She wanted to tell him it wasn't true. That eventually, the hurt lessens. That one day he'd be able to think of Bryan and smile instead of curling up in a ball to ward off the ache. That while he'd never get this piece of himself back again, he'd find other pieces to counteract the pain and make it manageable.

But she knew the words would mean nothing to him now. They meant nothing to her when people said them countless times in those early weeks. They were empty promises, meant to appease, and nothing more.

Instead, she asked him the one question no one had ever thought to ask her in the weeks that followed her mother's death.

"What do you need?"

Danny took a breath before lifting his eyes to hers. "I need to go home," he said. His voice was soft but resolute, and Leah nodded before she turned to grab her purse from the couch.

He was quiet again once they got in the car, and when Leah reached over and placed her hand on his leg, he covered it with his own, prolonging the contact as he held her there.

As they drove back to his apartment, Leah couldn't help but think of how many times she'd wished she had the chance to say good-bye to her mother. It had always been one of the things that hurt her the most about the situation—the fact that she was suddenly gone, with no notice or warning. Leah had managed to convince herself that if she had just gotten the chance to see her, speak to her, say something to her before she passed, it wouldn't have hurt as much.

But watching Danny today, she wasn't so sure anymore. Having to say good-bye to someone you love carried its own caliber of pain, and she couldn't be sure which was worse anymore.

His hand was still on hers when they pulled up to the curb in front of his building, and Leah turned to look at him.

"Do you want to be alone?" she asked.

Danny turned to her, his eyes meeting hers before he shook his head.

"Okay," she said gently, and he released her hand as she put the car in park and cut the engine.

They rode the elevator up to his apartment in silence; Danny's eyes were trained on the floor as he chewed the inside of his lip, and Leah rested her head on his shoulder until they arrived at his floor.

He seemed distracted as he opened the door to his apartment, and Leah followed him inside, putting her purse on the entryway table.

"Do you want me to make you something to eat?" she asked.

"No," he said softly. "Thank you."

He was standing in the living room with his back to her, and she walked over to him, placing her hands on the sides of his waist as she rested her forehead against the back of his shoulder. After a few seconds, he turned to face her, and Leah lifted her head, looking up at him.

He stared down at her for a moment before he dropped his eyes, watching his hand as he hooked two fingers in the front pocket of her jeans. She saw him wet his lips, and then he gave a gentle tug, pulling her a step closer as his other hand came to the hem of her shirt, taking it between his thumb and forefinger.

Danny's eyes were trained on his fingers as he toyed with the soft fabric, and then his knuckle grazed her belly button as he started pulling it up slowly. When her stomach quivered in response, he glanced up, his eyes meeting hers before they dropped again.

And then he slid it up a bit higher.

She lifted her arms out of reflex, and suddenly, her shirt was off. He tossed it somewhere behind her before he hooked his fingers in the front of her jeans and gave her another tug.

"I'm sorry," he whispered, pressing his lips to the top of her shoulder as his fingers came to the button of her jeans. She felt it pop open as he exhaled against her skin. "I'm sorry. I just..."

Leah closed her eyes as she brought her hand to the back of his head. "It's okay," she whispered. "Take what you need."

He made a small sound in the back of his throat as he dropped his forehead to her shoulder. "God, how do you do that?" he asked, easing her zipper down.

"Do what?" she asked softly, running her fingers through the back of his hair.

"You make it stop hurting," he said against her skin. "Every time."

Leah exhaled as she brought her hand to his chin, lifting his head before she brought her mouth to his.

He kissed her hard as he pushed her jeans and underwear down over her hips, and she shimmied her legs before stepping out of them. Danny's hands came to the clasp of her bra, and Leah slipped her hand into his back pocket, pulling out his wallet and opening it as she continued to kiss him.

When she found was she was looking for, she dropped his wallet on the floor and started opening the package, and Danny released her momentarily as his hands came to the buckle of his belt, undoing it quickly. His mouth never left hers as she put it on him, and then he wrapped his arms around her waist and spun them so her back was up against the wall before he reached down and gripped the back of her knee.

He hitched her leg up and entered her in one smooth movement, and Leah gasped as she wrapped her arms around his neck, using his shoulders as leverage as she held herself up and hooked her other leg around his waist.

His hands came to the back of her thighs, holding her weight as he pressed her into the wall and rocked into her.

"Leah," he groaned, but there was contrition in his voice.

"It's okay," she said softly before kissing his mouth. "It's okay."

He cursed under his breath as he moved against her again, and Leah held on tight as her head fell forward, her cheek rubbing against the scruff on his jaw.

She was prepared for him to be rough, like the night after the fight at Paddy's, but after his first few thrusts, the movement of his hips slowed, and his lips on her neck grew gentle. The sudden change in pace caused goose bumps to erupt over her body, and she made a tiny noise of approval before she could stop herself.

She didn't want this to be about her. She didn't want him to be concerned with making her feel good. She wanted him to get lost in her and forget that he was hurting for as long as he could.

Leah rolled her hips against him, showing him it was okay to take her the way he wanted, but he shook his head, the movement of his hips now torturously slow.

"Like this," he said against her mouth. "I need you like this."

Her eyes rolled back slightly as she tried to stifle a moan, but the hum of her approval escaped anyway, and he leaned forward, taking her bottom lip between his own as he pulled almost completely out of her. He held himself there for several seconds before he pushed back in, and her head fell back to the wall with a thud as she tightened her legs around his hips.

Danny pressed his lips to the base of her throat. "Sweet girl," he whispered against her skin, and then he released one of her thighs as he wrapped his arm around her lower back and turned them from the wall.

He walked them the few steps over to the couch before he let go of her other leg, using his hand to support them as he lowered her back onto the cushions. She made a tiny sound of protest when their bodies disconnected, and Danny reached up quickly, pulling his shirt over his head before he lowered himself onto her.

He slid his arms between her back and the cushions, holding her against his body as he starting moving again, his strokes long and unhurried.

"I love you," he said against her neck. "I didn't know it was possible to love someone this much."

"Danny," she breathed, tightening her hold on him.

The scruff of his jaw scratched her collarbone as he kissed along her throat and the top of her shoulder. "I don't want you to ever leave me."

"Never," she said, tilting her head back.

"I need you," he said hoarsely. "I need you, Leah."

"I'm yours," she promised. "Always."

He lifted his head and brought his mouth to hers, and her hands came to his hair, twining her fingers in it as she kissed him, pouring her promise into it, wanting him to feel the weight of her words, the sincerity of her vow.

He loved her slowly for as long as he could, but as the sounds began falling from her lips at regular intervals, he lost himself to his desire, gripping the arm of the couch behind her head as he sent her over the edge before he quickly followed.

And as he lay on top of her with his forehead on her shoulder and his breath hot and fast against her skin, Leah closed her eyes and trailed her fingertips along the vale of his spine.

"Always," she said again, because in that moment, she knew she would spend the rest of her life loving him.

No matter where he was.

Chapter Nineteen

"Stop staring at me. You're making me nervous."

Jake and Tommy laughed as Danny tried to stifle a smile. "There's nothing to be nervous about. It's just an oil change, and it's one of our beater cars. You can't screw it up."

"Yes she can," Jake said. "If she strips the drain plug, that shit's gonna be leaking everywhere."

"See?" Leah said, gesturing at Jake.

"Ignore him," Danny said, coming up next to her and making sure the hood prop was secure. "If you strip the plug, I'll just make him replace the oil pan."

"What the fuck?" Jake said. "If she strips the plug, I'll just get a new plug. Why the hell would I have to replace the entire pan?"

"Because you're a dick, and I said so," Danny responded as he tucked a strand of Leah's hair behind her ear.

She pressed her lips together, fighting a smile as Danny said, "You won't screw it up. I'm right here."

Leah exhaled heavily before she turned to face the open hood. "Let's do it."

Danny smirked as he came up behind her, resting his hands on her hips and his chin on her shoulder. "Okay, so you have your supplies. What do you do first?"

Leah chewed the corner of her lip, and Danny found himself wanting to spin her around and soothe it with his tongue before he slammed the hood of the car down and laid her across it.

And if it hadn't been for Tommy and Jake, he would have.

She scrunched her nose before she asked, "Remove the oil filter cap?"

Danny smiled and nodded his approval. "Good," he said, gesturing to it, and Leah reached in and removed it easily, handing it off to him.

"Okay," Jake said, leaning on the other side of the hood with his hands. "The easy part's over. Time to get on your back."

Before Danny could even intervene, Leah turned to him. "Yeah, well, I would assume any woman you told to 'get on her back' should be prepared to suffer."

Tommy did a spit-take before he started choking on his soda as Danny burst out laughing behind her. Jake's initial look of shock quickly transitioned into one of pride.

"The force is strong with this one," he said to Danny before he nudged the creeper over to them with his foot.

Danny stopped it with his own before he grinned down at her. "Ready?"

"As I'll ever be," she said, turning to sit on the creeper.

He leaned down and handed her a pair of latex gloves, and she took them from him and put them on before snapping them at her wrist. "I feel very official," she said, holding out her hand. "Socket wrench."

"Socket wrench," Tommy said with a salute before handing it off to her, and she lay back on the creeper and used her feet to propel herself underneath the car.

"You got the pan set up where I showed you?" Danny asked, crouching beside the car.

"Yep. So I just remove this plug, right?"

"Right. Once you get it off, it's gonna come out fast, so move quick or you'll get it all over you."

"That's what she said," Jake said from the other side of the car, and Danny heard Leah laugh beneath it.

"Come on, Danny, you made that *way* too easy for him," she said through a grunt, and he could hear the sounds of her trying to remove the drain plug.

After a minute he heard a muffled shriek, followed by the sound of oil hitting the pan.

"Oh my God, so gross," she whimpered, and Danny laughed. "Nice job! You did it."

Her oil-covered hand came out from underneath the side of the car. "I need the rag to clean the plug."

Tommy reached down and handed it to her before he lifted his eyes to Danny's. "With all due respect, man? This is kind of hot."

"Agreed," Jake said.

He would have told them both to shut the fuck up—if he hadn't been thinking the exact same thing.

Danny stood and leaned back against the car next to the one Leah was working on, watching her legs shift with her movements as Tommy walked her through how to remove the oil filter.

She was the only reason he was okay. The only thing in the past three weeks that could make him smile.

That could make him forget.

The week after Bryan's death had been unbearable. Danny had promised himself he would spend the last few weeks leading up to his sentencing making the most out of the time he had left, trying to soak up and appreciate every second of his freedom.

But enjoying himself in any capacity right after losing Bryan felt wrong. It felt callous and cold and disrespectful of his memory.

So he spent the week existing in a self-imposed vacuum; he got up, went to work, ate meals, and carried on conversations as if he were programmed to do it.

It was rote, and robotic, and forced, and empty.

The entire time, Leah was there—giving him space when he wanted it and support when he required it. He didn't even have to vocalize what he wanted; it was like she could read his needs before he could, like she was always two steps ahead of him.

Danny knew she must have been remembering her own suffering, that she was using what she knew of the feeling to make everything easier for him.

He hated that she had to experience everything alongside him, but he didn't know how to move on. He was stuck in some horrible catch twenty-two, torn between his veneration for his best friend and his promise to the woman he loved.

The weekend after they took Bryan off life support, he and Leah had been lying in bed, and out of nowhere she asked him to tell her something he'd always wanted to do. They spent the next hour talking about it, running through their lists, and at some point Leah had gotten up and grabbed a pen and pad; she divided the paper in half and labeled the left side "One Day"—Leah had always wanted to go to Santorini, and Danny wanted to learn how to fly a plane—and the right side was labeled "Right Now"—Danny wanted to have dinner at Per Se in Manhattan, and Leah wanted to spend an entire day at a spa.

They talked until Leah had filled both columns to the bottom of the page, and after she had placed the pad on the nightstand and lay back down beside him, she told him she wanted to accomplish as many of her "Right Now" items as she could in the next few weeks.

And then she asked if he would help her do it.

He knew what she was doing; if he was helping her, it was an excuse to exist in the world again, to enjoy his time with her without feeling guilty.

She was absolving him of any culpability for moving on.

She had one of the most beautiful souls of anyone he'd ever known, and Danny wondered if he'd ever stop being amazed by her compassion.

The following weekend Danny went with Leah to Zen Day Spa, and just as he had committed himself to sitting in the waiting area with his phone and a magazine for a few hours, the receptionist called both of their names. They spent the next hour getting a couple's massage, and after that, Danny was sent to the sauna while Leah got a pedicure. By the time he came out, he felt heavy and sedated, and beautifully unwound for the first time in weeks.

And then they went to the reflexology room.

Danny had no idea that pressure points in a person's feet could affect the function of their internal organs, and even their mood. In fact, he wouldn't have believed it if he hadn't experienced it himself, but as the woman began the massage, he could feel his headache disappear for the first time in days, the slight but constant nausea he'd been feeling slowly melt away.

Before they left the spa, Danny purchased a book on massage and reflexology from the front desk, and he and Leah spent the rest of the weekend reading it and practicing different techniques on each other.

He could think of worse ways to spend his weekend than with his hands all over Leah.

After that, Danny started spending every night at her apartment. His own place was gradually becoming unlivable as he began breaking it down and putting his things in storage, but in reality, he could have made staying there work. It was just that she had managed to wake him from his fog, and in resurfacing he found himself needing her like air.

He didn't want to be away from her any more than he had to.

The following weekend, Leah surprised him by taking him to Per Se. They ordered a ridiculously expensive dinner and drank quality wine and spent the night making love on her living-room floor with Leah's Ray LaMontagne CD playing on repeat in the background.

And now, Danny had arranged for Leah to cross another "Right Now" off her list—she told him she wanted to learn how to do something on a car that most girls didn't know how to do. Something useful, like changing a tire.

So he explained to her how to do an oil change, and when she passed his "verbal quiz," he decided she was ready to come down to the shop and put her new knowledge to use. She was hesitant at first, but now, as he watched her stick her head out from under the car and reach for the new filter Jake held, he could see that her confidence had won over her anxiety.

He couldn't believe how quickly the days were disappearing. Time was a relative concept—Danny had always been aware of that. What he couldn't understand was why the relativity never seemed to work in a person's favor. For a specialist working to disarm a bomb, a minute is a mere blink of an eye—a fleeting breath. But for a mother waiting to hear her baby's cry for the first time, a minute can be a lifetime, an endless stretch of anxious silence.

In a little over two weeks, he'd be standing in a courtroom, waiting for the decision that would dictate the next several years of his life. Just two more weeks. It might as well have been tomorrow, considering how quickly the past three and a half weeks had gone by.

And yet somehow he was sure time wouldn't grant him the kindness of speed once he was locked away.

He watched Leah slide out from under the car, an oil-soaked rag in her hand as she ran the back of her forearm over her forehead, leaving a smudge of oil as she swiped the hair out of her eyes.

"Alright," she said as she stood. "Now what? Oil, and then I'm done, right?"

Danny smiled as he noticed the second smudge on the side of her chin.

"Did you retighten the drain plug?"

"Yep."

"Lube the O-ring on the new filter?"

"Lubed and ready," she said before holding her hand out to where Jake stood a few feet away, giving him the floor.

"That's what she said," he said casually as he searched through one of the toolboxes, and Leah nodded, turning her attention back to Danny.

He laughed as he pushed off the car and walked toward her. "Good job. Oil and then you're done," he said, leaning close to her ear when he reached her. "And then I'm taking you somewhere we can be alone," he whispered.

Danny saw the corner of her mouth lift before she turned her head slightly, looking over her shoulder at him.

"You're liking this, huh?" she whispered.

He nodded once. "A lot."

Her smile grew more pronounced as she turned a bit further, her lips almost touching his. "In that case, can the guys do the rest?"

Danny didn't say a word as he grabbed her hand and turned, towing her behind him as he made his way toward the door. "Finish the job," he called over his shoulder, and just before the door swung shut behind them, he heard Jake call back, "*That's what she said!*"

Spring break.

Traditionally, it was a time of year teachers prayed for, counting down the days until it became a reality. By the time spring break rolled around, the year was wearing out its welcome—the students all had spring fever, a precursor to summertime laxity. Everyone was desperate for a little reprieve.

But for the first time since she'd started teaching, Leah found herself wishing it would never come.

Because once it was over, he'd be leaving.

He'd been spending the night at her apartment for the past few weeks, but now that Leah wasn't working, they spent their days together too—if they weren't down at Catherine's or at the shop, they were back at his apartment cleaning. It was nearly empty now, with all his things in storage or with Catherine or the guys. With each passing day, Leah felt like she was being gutted along with the rooms. Scrubbing and washing and vacuuming and dusting what was left provided her with something to do other than stare at the barren space while trying to keep her heart from shredding into nothing.

By Thursday of that week, Danny's entire apartment was immaculate—from his ceiling fans to his appliances to his floorboards and everything in between. They had worked until the sun went down, and by that time, they were filthy and starving and far too tired to even think about going out for food. There were no table or chairs left at his place, but they ordered Chinese and ate it straight out of the cartons, sitting on the floor in the middle of his stark living room.

Leah looked around the empty space as she chewed a bite of her eggroll. She'd spent the better part of the week pretending she was just helping him move, but even something that simple came with a sense of sadness.

An essence of finality.

"Are you sad about leaving this place?" she asked, and Danny looked up at her before he smirked.

"You're cute."

"Why is that cute? I'm being serious."

"I know. That's why it's cute. And no, I'm not sad about leaving this place. It's just an apartment," he said, taking a bite of his eggroll.

"Yeah, but...it's been your home for six years."

He shook his head. "It's been where I've lived for six years. I wouldn't call it *home*. There's a difference to me."

Leah nodded as she looked down, twirling her fork in her hand; he didn't need to explain any further—she knew exactly what he meant.

"So, since you were down for a picnic dinner, is it safe to assume you're down for a living-room camp-out?"

"A living-room camp-out? What are we, six?"

Danny smiled. "Seriously, though, I'm fucking beat. Do you really feel like making the drive back to your place right now?"

Leah sighed. "No, not really."

He got up on his knees and began collecting some of the empty containers. "That settles it then. Living-room camp-out." Danny winked before he stood, taking the garbage into the kitchen.

Leah laughed as she grabbed the rest of the trash and followed him. "Okay, well, in that case, I'm gonna take a shower. You let me know when the campsite is ready."

He chuckled as she leaned in and kissed his cheek before she made her way toward the bathroom, turning on the shower and setting the water as hot as it could go. The sharp sting of it burned and then soothed, taking the tension out of her muscles as it washed away the grime of the day, and she found herself wanting to stand there under the stream until it washed away the constant ache in her chest as well.

When she finally turned off the water, the air was thick with steam, and as Leah stepped out from behind the curtain, she could just make out one of his shirts, folded on the edge of his sink and waiting for her.

She pulled it over her head, opting to wear nothing underneath so that the soft, worn cotton that smelled like detergent and Danny could touch her skin unobstructed.

After running her fingers through her wet hair to remove the tangles, Leah walked out to the living room, fighting a smile when she saw him.

He was crouched on the floor, setting up two sleeping bags. One was maroon.

And the other was Batman.

"Rock Paper Scissors for the Batman sleeping bag," she said, and he glanced up at her, his expression serious.

"Fuck that. Batman's mine."

Leah laughed, holding her hands up in defeat. "Okay, okay. But only because the camp-out was your idea."

He stood as she walked into the living room, and Leah watched his eyes travel over her body.

"You look good in my shirt."

She smiled. "You say that every time I wear one of them."

"Do I?" he asked, taking a step toward her.

She took a quick step back, holding up her hand and jerking a thumb over her shoulder. "I don't think so, buddy. Hit the showers first."

The shock on his face was comical, and Leah tried not to laugh when his dimples appeared.

"You know, you're lucky you're cute," he said, leaning forward and brushing his lips against hers before he made his way past her toward the bathroom. A few seconds later, she heard the shower turn on, and Leah smiled as she climbed into the maroon sleeping bag and lay back, blinking up at the ceiling.

And then she instantly regretted making him take a shower.

It was too easy for her thoughts to run rampant in this desolate room. Keeping busy, making sure she never had an idle moment, making sure she was never by herself for long periods of time, it was her method of survival for the past month. She wouldn't have survived it any other way.

Keep yourself busy. Keep your body moving. Keep your mind distracted.

But now there was nothing but silence, and time, and her.

When she was with Danny, it was so easy to pretend everything was normal. It was when she was alone that the reality of their situation reared its ugly head, because it was then that she started to imagine what it was going to be like without him.

Leah closed her eyes and started reciting passages and quotes from *To Kill a Mockingbird* in an attempt to occupy her mind.

Thankfully he showered quickly, and it wasn't long before he reappeared in the living room, clad in only his boxers. Danny came to the floor next to her and slid into the Batman sleeping bag, and Leah immediately turned onto her side to face him.

"Comfortable?" he asked, shifting onto his side and propping his head up on his hand.

"Very. My sleeping bag is actually surprisingly cushy. I think you chose poorly," she said, nodding toward his.

"Please. Try to keep your jealousy in check."

Leah smirked, and he grinned at her before he lifted the side of the sleeping bag, holding it open.

"What are you doing? Flashing me?"

He burst out laughing. "Get your mind out of the gutter. I'm inviting you in. You need to experience the wonder that is Batman to fully appreciate what a piece of shit your sleeping bag is."

"We're not gonna fit," she said with a laugh, and he shrugged.

"Let's try."

She smiled as she sat up and wiggled out of her sleeping bag before crawling over to him. As soon as she was inside, he draped the sleeping bag over their bodies and reached behind her, struggling with the zipper.

After a minute she said, "I told you it wouldn't work."

No sooner than the words left her mouth, she felt the sleeping bag grow a bit tighter around them as he zipped it closed. He smiled triumphantly as he lay back, pulling her partially on top of him.

"Damn you." She sighed, laying her head on his chest. "Batman *does* kick maroon's ass."

"Told you," he said, trailing his fingertips over her lower back.

"I'm ruined now. How can I ever go back there?"

"You're not going anywhere," he said into her hair, and she smiled.

"Aren't you uncomfortable with me lying on you like this?"

"I've never been more comfortable."

She laughed softly as she tightened her arms around him, and for a minute they just lay there in contented silence.

"So," she heard him say, and his serious tone caused her to lift her head. "Did you do what I asked?"

Leah reached up and brushed the hair away from his forehead. "I did."

It was quiet for a few seconds before he took a breath and asked, "And are you okay?"

A tiny smile curved her lips. "I am."

He stared up at her, and Leah could see that he was gauging her honesty.

Danny had become a permanent fixture in Leah's family. He had been at every Sunday dinner since that first one in January, and everyone adored him. And it was for that reason Danny had asked her a few weeks ago to tell them the truth about what was going on with him.

"It feels like lying," he had said to her. "They've all been good to me, and I don't like being dishonest with them. They need to know."

And while she knew he was right, Leah kept avoiding it at every turn. She just didn't want things to change; enough change was coming her way to last a lifetime, and she didn't think she could handle any more. She had no way of knowing if learning the truth would ruin their opinion of him, but she just couldn't bring herself to chance it.

Plus, if she were being honest with herself, she didn't want to discuss it with anyone. Discussing it made it real, and she was enjoying the fantasy world she and Danny had created for themselves—one where there was no looming future, just them in the present, crossing things off their wish lists and enjoying each other.

At first Danny had been lenient with her when she'd come up with excuses as to why she didn't get around to telling them, but last weekend he finally put his foot down.

"I know it's not a conversation you're looking forward to," he had said to her. "But it needs to be done. And it needs to be done before I go to court. I don't want them finding out after the fact; that's fucking spineless, and they deserve more respect than that. So if you can't do it, then I'm going to. But it needs to happen before this week is over. We've put it off long enough."

So that morning, before she headed down to Danny's apartment to finish cleaning, she took her family out to breakfast, and she told them. Surprisingly, she didn't cry. She was so nervous that she was incapable of doing anything except reciting the words she had practiced a million times the night before.

She should have known how they would react. If there was one thing her family was good at, it was pulling together and supporting one another in a crisis.

Rather than being horrified or disgusted or angry, they were sad—for her and for Danny.

"Don't hate him," she had quietly implored them. "The Danny you know…that's the real him. He's not a bad person. He didn't intend for any of this to happen."

And Leah's father had taken her hand and said, "You don't have to defend him, Leah. You don't think I understand the feeling of being ferociously protective of your family? He's a good kid who made a big mistake. And now he's going to pay for it. It's going to be hard. For both of you. But if he's what you want, princess, then I'll do whatever I can to make this a little easier for you. All I've ever wanted is for you to be happy."

Danny ran his hand through Leah's hair, pulling her from her musings, and she looked down in time to see his throat bob as he swallowed nervously.

"So what did your dad say?" he asked.

She shifted so that she was lying fully on top of him, and his hands slipped under her shirt, holding her waist gently as he looked up at her.

"He asked if you would bring some cannoli from Giovanni's to Easter dinner this Sunday."

Danny stared up at her for a second, and when his dimples began to appear, Leah laughed softly, slipping her hand behind his neck and pulling him up for a kiss.

The hurt will be temporary, she reminded herself as his lips moved against hers.

This is the forever.

Chapter Twenty

L eah sat in the driver's seat, her heart sinking as the call went to voice mail.

It was already four thirty; she'd been forced to spend the entire day without him, and it induced a level of anxiety in her she didn't know existed. The showing at the ASH program that afternoon had been one of the largest of the school year, what with finals on the horizon, so canceling would have been in poor form. Plus, Leah had already taken off the following day to be at court with Danny, and the day after that as well, just in case things didn't go well. Bailing on the program had been out of the question.

But sitting in a room full of students for two and a half extra hours on the last day before Danny went to court was nothing short of torture.

When the program ended, she'd raced out of the building, calling him as she made her way to her car. He was spending the day finalizing some things at the shop and told her to let him know when she was leaving so he could meet her at her apartment.

Leah chewed her lip as she listened to Danny's voice, asking her to leave a message, and when it beeped, she told him she was done for the day and to come up whenever he was finished. She ended the call and tossed her phone into her purse with a frustrated sigh. If he was in the garage, more likely than not, he hadn't heard her call. It was always so noisy in there, with people talking and tools and machines running nonstop—unless he had his phone set to vibrate in his pocket, he probably wouldn't even see she had called until he was already leaving.

She sent up a silent prayer that it would be soon.

But by the time she pulled into the parking space in front of her apartment, a gnawing impatience was beginning to mix with the anxiety already swirling in her gut.

He still hadn't returned her call.

Leah put the car in park and gathered her things quickly, as if her rushing could somehow make him do the same.

She hoisted her bags onto her shoulder as she approached the front door, promising herself that if she didn't hear back from him in the next ten minutes, she would call the shop and have him paged. The idea of wasting any more time without him tonight was making her want to crawl out of her skin.

Leah fumbled with her keys for a moment before she opened the door to her apartment, immediately stopping in her tracks.

It was dark inside, save for the faint flickering of candlelight.

After a stunned second, she walked in, closing the door softly behind her. There were candles on her kitchen table, along with wine glasses and place settings and a vase of red roses.

"Danny?" she called, her eyes roving the scene before her.

A second later he came out from the kitchen with a bottle of wine in his hand.

"Welcome home," he said.

Leah blinked at him before she put her bags down by the door. "What are you doing?" she asked, walking toward the table. "What is this?"

"An early birthday celebration."

She stopped short. "You remembered?"

"Of course I did," he said matter-of-factly, placing the bottle on the table as he began to uncork it.

Leah stared at him, completely floored. With everything he had going on the next day, celebrating her birthday should have been the last thing on his mind.

"I even bought you a birthday cake that I'm going to pretend I made. And you're going to pretend to believe it, just like you promised."

She looked up at him with a tiny laugh as she watched him pour her a glass of wine, and then he smiled as he held it out for her. "I hope you're hungry," he said. "I got us something from Il Bardona."

Leah's mouth dropped. Il Bardona was one of her favorite restau-rants, but it certainly wasn't an establishment that dealt in takeout.

She reached for the glass he handed her. "That's not the type of place that makes food to go."

"I know," he said. "I called in a favor."

She stared at him for a moment before shaking her head. "Danny..."

"Leah," he said, mimicking her tone as he poured himself a glass of wine.

She tried to stifle a smile as he placed his glass on the table, and then he pulled her chair out and gestured for her to sit down. "Your meal will be out shortly, miss," he said with a bow.

As he disappeared into the kitchen, Leah turned to look at the table.

He'd remembered her birthday. He'd gone out of his way for her tonight. Sneaking up to her place while she was stuck at work, mak-ing arrangements with her favorite restaurant, setting the table with stemware and flowers, getting her a birthday cake so she could make her wish.

What was she ever going to do when they took this all away from her?

Her vision clouded as her eyes welled with tears just as Danny turned the corner and placed several serving plates down on the table. He situated everything before he sat across from her, his expression turning serious when his eyes met her glassy ones.

"Leah," he said gently. "I realize what tonight is, but I don't want this to be about saying good-bye, okay?"

The sting behind her eyes doubled at his words, and she blinked quickly, trying to keep her tears at bay. When he saw her struggling, he reached across the table, taking her hand in his and playing with her fingers.

"It's not good-bye, sweet girl. It's only temporary. You're the one who told me that, remember?"

Leah forced a smile as she nodded.

"I want tonight to be about us," he said. "Just you and me. Nothing else. Can we do that?"

She nodded again. "That sounds perfect," she said softly.

"Good," he said, bringing her hand to his lips and kissing it before letting it go. He picked up his glass and raised it to her. "Happy birthday, Leah."

She tapped her glass to his before taking a sip, and she hummed, swirling the glass gently. "What is this?"

Danny reached across the table and spun the bottle toward himself. "Shafer Relentless Napa Valley, 2008."

"It's really good."

"It was the top-rated wine last year."

Leah lifted her brow. "Is that so? Since when are you a wine connoisseur?"

"Since I asked the guy at the liquor store to give me his best bottle, and he gave me this and said it was the top-rated wine last year."

She smiled at him before shaking her head, and he winked, picking up his knife and fork.

They talked and laughed throughout the meal, but every so often, Leah's mind would wander where it wasn't supposed to go—she'd find herself wondering where he'd be this time tomorrow, what he'd be doing, how she was going to get through knowing he was out of her reach and suffering. But when the lump rose in her throat, or when she felt her eyes burn with the threat of tears, she would distract herself by concentrating on him, memorizing his every detail: his light-blue eyes refracting delicate candlelight, the curve of his lips, the inky black hair that felt so soft between her fingers, the lines of his jaw, the dimples in his cheeks when he smiled her favorite smile, the sound of his laugh, the way he held his fork.

Despite the reality that was looming over them, it was surprisingly easy to get lost in those things.

When they'd finished eating, Leah and Danny left their dirty dishes on the table and moved into the living room with their wine. Leah curled into his side as they sat on the couch, and his arm immediately came around her, holding her against his body as he rested his chin on her head.

She couldn't believe she had ever existed without this. Being with him, touching him, laughing with him—there was nothing more satisfying, nothing capable of making her feel more content and gratified and beautiful and *whole*.

And as much as she was dreading the struggle that would be coming her way, the thought of never having met him rivaled the pain of losing him.

She often thought about how many facets of the universe had been at work the day their paths crossed. If that guy hadn't been tailgating her on the street, she would never have parked in front of Catherine's house and gotten out of the car. If Catherine didn't happen to be looking out the window when Leah stopped there, she wouldn't have invited her in. If her bracelet hadn't fallen off in the guest room, she wouldn't have left her number.

Leah slid her arm around Danny's waist as she pressed her cheek against his chest and inhaled his scent.

Those little wonders in life, the tiny miracles, they never ceased to amaze her. They were everywhere, overlooked too often because people were preoccupied with the minutiae of everyday life, or because the miracles themselves were too discreet to be recognized. But to see them at work was one of the most humbling things Leah had ever experienced.

Because there wasn't a doubt in her mind that the day she met Danny, the stars had aligned just for her.

"Do you believe in fate?" she asked softly.

Danny took a slow sip of wine. "I don't know. To an extent, maybe. Why, do you?"

"I never really did before, but now…I don't know. It's kind of hard not to."

"What do you mean?" he asked, tilting his head to look down at her.

Leah dropped her eyes, watching the light glint off her bracelet as she spun it around her wrist. "I've had this bracelet for almost fifteen years," she said, looking up at him. "And never once has the clasp failed. And I've had it back for over four months now, and it hasn't happened since."

He held her eyes for a moment before he smiled, looking down as he ran the tip of his finger over the bracelet, and then he pulled her into his side and pressed his lips to the top of her head.

"Can I give you your birthday present now?" he asked into her hair.

Leah smiled. "Did you get me a Slap Chop?"

He burst out laughing before he released her and stood from the couch. "You already have one."

"I know," she said, "but you can never have too many of those."

Danny grinned. "Maybe for Christmas, then," he said with a laugh as he turned and walked toward Leah's bedroom, and her smile fell.

Because he wouldn't be there for Christmas.

She wasn't even sure how many Christmases she'd have to endure without him, and the thought made her throat feel like someone had clamped their fist around it.

Stop it, she warned herself. *Stop it right now. Not tonight.*

Danny walked back into the living room then, and she could see that he held a small rectangular box in his hand as he sat back on the couch beside her.

"Happy birthday," he said, holding it out for her.

Her breath hitched as she looked down at the box. She had thought he'd gotten her something silly—a little trinket they would laugh about—but it was clear to her that there was jewelry inside that box.

"Danny," she said, her shoulders dropping, "you shouldn't have—"

"I wanted to," he said, cutting her off.

Her eyes met his before she took a tiny breath, and then she reached for the box. She lifted the lid hesitantly, the hinge creaking slightly as it opened.

Lying on the black satin inside was a necklace; the chain was white gold and glittered with every movement of Leah's trembling hand, but her eye was immediately drawn to the pendant hanging from it. It was a large, clear stone, perfectly round. She lifted her finger and cautiously touched the end of it, the tiny movement causing a prism of sparkles to flicker within the stone.

"Is this..." She trailed off as she looked up at him.

"Is this what?"

"A diamond?" she asked, looking back down at the shimmering pendant.

"Yes."

Her hand came up to cup her mouth. "Oh my God," she whispered, shaking her head. "Danny."

"Do you like it?"

She opened and closed her mouth, trying to find her voice. "It's... incredible," she stammered.

He smiled at her, and she reached down and touched the pendant again. "It's too much," she said, and he shook his head.

"It's perfect."

She lifted her eyes to his, and his dimples started to appear. "Can I see it on you?"

Leah held the box out to him, still beyond words, and Danny leaned forward and removed the necklace before undoing the clasp, holding an end in each hand as he wrapped it around her neck. Her hand came to the pendant, holding it against her skin as he fastened the clasp behind her.

He leaned back and looked at the necklace on her, his smile broadening as he took her hand and pulled her off the couch. Danny walked her over to the mirror on the opposite wall and turned her so that she was facing it. The diamond glittered against her skin, the bright stone a sharp contrast to her deep-blue V-neck sweater.

"See?" he said from behind her. "Perfect."

He stepped forward, closing the distance between them, and Leah leaned back into his embrace, closing her eyes as one of his arms snaked around her waist. A few seconds later, she felt his other hand come up to the necklace, taking the pendant between his fingers.

Danny brought his lips to her ear. "When this is over, I'm going to put one of these on your finger."

Her eyes flipped open, finding his in the mirror.

"We'll get through this, Leah," he said, his eyes on hers. "And then I'll spend the rest of my life making it up to you. I promise."

Leah turned slowly in his arms, placing her hands on his chest as she stared up at him. Danny's arms tightened around her waist, holding her against him as his eyes searched hers.

Her heart was thundering in her chest, and her body felt too small to contain the emotions reeling through it at breakneck speed.

"I am so completely and utterly in love with you," she whispered, her voice measured, wanting him to feel the magnitude behind the simple, inadequate words.

He smiled down at her. "Then you know exactly how I feel."

Her eyes fell closed as she dropped her forehead to his chest and slid her arms around his back, and Leah felt him press his lips against the crown of her head.

"Are you ready to go to bed?" he asked, and she nodded gently.

Danny ran his hand over the back of her hair before he released her, and Leah turned to the coffee table, grabbing their empty wine glasses. Danny took them from her, and a few seconds later, she heard the sounds of him putting them in the dishwasher as she made her way back over to the table, blowing out the candles and collecting their dirty dishes. She brought them into the kitchen and rinsed them before loading them in behind the wine glasses, and by the time she made her way back to her bedroom, Danny was already there, lighting the last of several candles he had lined up along her bedside tables.

Leah leaned against the doorframe. "You thought of everything."

He looked over his shoulder and smiled. "I tried," he said before he blew out the match, and Leah pushed off the door as she walked toward him.

Danny turned, his expression growing serious as she closed the distance between them. As soon as she reached him, she slid her arms around his neck and pulled his mouth down to hers.

Their lips parted and met over and over in soft, worshipful kisses, and he splayed his hands over her back, pulling her with him as he backed them toward the bed.

Danny broke the kiss as he sat down on the mattress, and Leah immediately crawled onto his lap and straddled his thighs, cradling the back of his head as she leaned down to kiss him. Danny groaned softly as his hands slid under her sweater, running them up the length of her back.

She reached down and grabbed the hem of his shirt, and he removed his mouth from hers just long enough to allow her to pull it up and over his head. And then her hands were everywhere, memorizing the contours of his body. His skin was warm and smooth, the hard muscles flexing and contracting as he moved, and her hands slid along the tops of his shoulders and down over his biceps. They bulged beneath her touch as he gripped the hem of her sweater and started tugging it upward.

As soon as it was off, he brought one hand to the back of her head and wrapped his other arm securely around her lower back, twisting his body and laying her down on the bed before positioning himself above her.

And then he ground his hips into hers, and Leah gasped as she dug her nails into his back. All at once their hands grew frantic, undoing buttons and zippers and clasps as they pulled clothes from each other's bodies. The movement of Danny's hips became more urgent with every inch of skin they exposed, fueling the fire growing between them and working Leah into a frenzy.

"I need you," Leah murmured against his lips, and he pulled his mouth from hers with a grunt, holding his weight up in one arm as he reached for her nightstand.

She took his chin in her hand and turned his face toward her. "No," she said through heavy breaths.

"No?" he asked, his brow furrowed.

She slid her hands behind his shoulders and pulled him back down so that his chest was flush with hers.

"Just you and me, remember?"

Danny looked down at her, a little crease between his brow.

"Nothing between us," she whispered.

He stared at her for a second before understanding swept over his face, and she watched his throat bob as he swallowed hard.

"Just you and me," she repeated softly.

There were several emotions flitting over his face, and Leah watched and absorbed and memorized every single one until finally he dropped his weight to his elbows, cradling her face in his hands as he positioned himself between her legs.

It took him a few moments to move, and when she felt him pushing into her, she forced her eyes to remain open, watching him as he joined their bodies inch by inch. As soon as he was fully inside her, a pleasant chill ran through her body, prickling her skin with goose bumps.

She was completely overwhelmed with the gravity of the moment: the feel of him inside her, the weight of his body on hers, the candlelight flickering on his face, his eyes looking down at her with adoration. And when her chin began to quiver, Leah let her eyes fall closed.

Danny lowered his head, bringing his lips to hers. "I know, baby. I know," he said against her mouth before kissing her softly.

She ran her fingertips up and down his back, and the tears building behind her eyes transitioned into tears of elation as he began moving, setting a perfect, unhurried pace.

His breaths were heavy against Leah's lips, and after a while, she could feel the muscles in his back trembling beneath her hands. She slid them around to the front of his shoulders as she shifted beneath him, pushing him onto his back and swinging her leg over his hips. His hands came to her waist, holding her as she lowered herself onto him, and he sat up immediately, burying his face in the side of her neck.

His grip on her waist tightened, and she remained perfectly still until she felt his hands begin to relax; they slipped down the sides of her hips and over the tops of her thighs before settling on her calves.

Danny unfolded her legs and guided them around his hips so that she was sitting on his lap with her legs wrapped around his waist.

The shift in her weight caused their connection to deepen, and she sucked in a sharp breath, wrapping her arms around him. His face was still pressed against the side of her neck, and he began kissing it softly, causing her to rock her hips imperceptibly against him. Danny splayed one hand across the small of her back as the other came up to the nape of her neck, holding her against his body.

She began to move against him with more insistence, and he lifted his head then, kissing her deeply. Leah could feel his arm muscles flex around her as he pulled her against his body.

"God, it's like I can't get close enough," he breathed against her lips, and she moaned softly, tightening her legs around him.

They continued moving together, their pace steady and passionate and more intimate than anything Leah had ever experienced. When her body began to tremble, she closed her eyes.

"Open your eyes, Leah," he whispered.

She did as he asked, bringing her hands to the sides of his face as she dropped her forehead to his. Their lips were parted and centimeters away from touching, but rather than close that distance, they stayed that way, their lips ghosting over each other's with each movement.

Danny's hand on her lower back pressed her more firmly against him, and with one last roll of her hips, the tension in Leah's belly shattered as a sated cry fell from her lips. Seconds later she felt his fingertips digging into the flesh of her back, and then he was groaning as he followed her over.

She had never been with anyone else this way before—and the fact that she could feel his release only amplified her own. Leah clutched at him, trying to keep herself grounded as her body broke apart over and over before it slowly pieced itself back together. They continued to sigh and pant into each other's mouths until both of their movements wound down and eventually stopped.

Leah felt him start to lie back, and she unhooked her legs from behind him, bringing her knees to rest on either side of his waist as he pulled her down onto his chest. Her body rose and fell with his labored breath, and his hand came to her hair, holding her against his heart.

After a minute he rolled them gently so they were lying on their sides, and Leah reached down and found his hand, intertwining their fingers. Danny brought their joined hands to his mouth, kissing hers before he brought them back to the bed and began playing with her fingers.

"Do I get birthday cake in bed now?" she asked, and he laughed softly.

"As soon as I can move."

Leah smiled before she snuggled closer. "Don't move yet."

Danny hummed contentedly. "As you wish," he murmured, and she grinned before closing her eyes with a gratified sigh.

They stayed that way for hours, alternating making love with talking quietly as Danny gently trailed his fingertips over her skin. She wanted to stay awake as long as she could, wanted every last minute with him that she was entitled to. But as the night crept on, her traitor eyelids grew heavy until finally, she couldn't keep them open anymore.

She had no idea how much time had passed before her eyes flew open in the darkness, and she turned quickly in a panic, clutching air until she felt his arms wrap around her.

"Shh," he whispered into her hair. "Shh, I'm right here."

She turned her face into him, nuzzling his chest as she tried to slow her breathing and her racing heart. "Danny," she murmured.

"I'm right here," he repeated against the crown of her head, his voice a strained whisper.

"Okay," she said sleepily, and it wasn't long before the rhythmic beating of his heart and the familiar scent of his skin lulled her back to sleep.

Seconds or minutes or hours later, she gasped loudly as she threw her arms out in search of him, relaxing with a small whimper as her body came in contact with his.

His arms tightened around her. "Baby," he crooned softly. "I'm here."

This time she was lucid enough to hear how broken his voice sounded, and she exhaled softly. "I'm sorry," she whispered.

"Don't be sorry," he said gently, running his fingers through her hair. "Try to sleep."

"You're not sleeping," she pointed out, moving closer to him.

He said nothing as he continued to stroke her hair gently. Leah fought with all her might to remain awake after that, but as soon as he realized what she was doing, he began to sing softly. His low, throaty voice filled the room, his chest vibrating gently against her cheek, and she teetered on the edge of consciousness, hearing bits and pieces of the song.

The last thing she remembered was the feel of his fingers slowly working their way through her hair as he sang, *"You'll look at me, with eyes that see, and we'll melt into each other's arms..."*

Morning.

She knew it before she even opened her eyes, and Leah felt her heart drop into her stomach.

She could feel Danny pressed up against her back, his arm draped over her waist and his breath fluttering her hair. She opened her eyes slowly, and it took a second for them to focus on the clock.

It was five after seven. The alarm was set for eight, but she knew there was no way she'd be able to go back to sleep now.

Leah rolled slowly under his arm, careful not to jostle him as she turned to face him. He always looked so beautiful when he slept—so peaceful—and she found herself fighting the urge to touch his face, his lips, his jaw.

And then suddenly, an image of Danny sleeping on a tiny cot in a cell flashed in her mind, and she squeezed her eyes shut, trying desperately to rid the image from her head.

But the floodgates had opened.

Image after image of Danny in prison flashed before her eyes: Danny wearing some type of prison jumpsuit, walking through a corridor in handcuffs. Danny at a table in some sort of cafeteria, eating what looked like a pathetic school lunch off a plastic tray. Danny sitting in a bare room with a bed, a toilet, and zero privacy.

She opened her eyes quickly, not wanting to see any more, and she was greeted with his beautiful face, innocent and untroubled in sleep.

She felt her composure slipping rapidly, and Leah struggled to get out of bed as quickly as possible without disturbing him. She pressed her lips together as her vision blurred, and just as she slunk out from beneath his arm, she felt the first round of tears spill over.

Leah padded over to the bathroom quickly, shutting the door softly behind her before she ran to turn the water on in the shower. As soon as the sound of rushing water filled the room, she slumped to the floor, burying her mouth against the crook of her elbow as she burst into tears.

Violent sobs racked her body, and she curled in on herself, gasping for air as she tried with all her might to keep the sounds muffled against her arm. She couldn't let him hear this. She had told him she was strong enough to take care of herself, that he didn't need to worry about her.

She wanted so badly for that to be true.

When Leah gained some semblance of control—when the ferocious sobbing subsided into pathetic little hiccups and sighs, she stood up and climbed into the shower, standing under the stream with her eyes closed as she replayed every beautiful moment from the night before in an effort to calm herself down. Every word, every touch, every smile. And then she remembered waking frantically several times throughout the night, reaching out for him in a panic, and her heart sank.

It killed him, seeing her suffer because of him. She knew it did. She'd heard it in his voice. And she couldn't allow him to see that level of weakness again. She would not let him carry that burden.

And just like that, Leah felt her resolve click into place.

She opened her eyes, allowing the last of her tears to run down her face with the water, and then she tilted her head back, letting the warm stream wash the remnants of salt from her cheeks.

She would not cry again. Not today.

Today she would be strong for him. He needed to see that she was okay. He needed to leave knowing everything back home would be fine.

Leah finished her shower, stepping out onto the bath mat and wrapping herself in a towel before she walked to the mirror and swiped her hand across it, erasing the fog.

"Shit," she whispered as her face was revealed in the glass. Her eyes were bloodshot and extremely swollen; there was no way this would go unnoticed.

She ran the cold water full blast, grabbing a washcloth and tossing it into the sink. Once it was saturated, she tilted her head back and laid the freezing cloth over her eyes.

After a few minutes, she tossed the rag back into the sink and sifted through her makeup case until she found some eye drops, blinking quickly as they stung her tender eyes.

Once her vision had cleared, she leaned close to the mirror, checking her reflection again.

Better, but still not great.

"Leah?"

Danny's voice came through the door and she jumped slightly.

"Yeah?"

"You okay?"

She cleared her throat gently. "Yep, just drying off," she said, keeping her voice as smooth as possible. "I'll be out in a second."

Leah grabbed her brush and ran it through her wet hair before securing the towel around her body and taking one last look in the mirror.

It was as good as it was going to get.

She took a deep breath before she turned and opened the door, walking back toward the bedroom.

He was sitting on the edge of the bed with his head down, and when he heard her come into the room, he lifted his head and smiled.

"I didn't expect you to be up," he said as he stood and walked toward her. Leah watched his smile fade as he got closer, finally noticing her eyes.

"I know, I look like hell," she said, forcing a tiny laugh as she rolled her eyes and gestured toward herself. "This is what happens when I don't get a full night's sleep."

"Leah," he said, and she unraveled her towel, bringing it to her hair as she squeezed it dry.

It was a cheap move, and she knew it, but she was desperate.

His expression smoothed as his eyes dropped to take in her now naked body, and Leah turned and walked toward her dresser, sifting though one of her drawers for a bra and underwear.

"Do you want me to make you banana pancakes for breakfast?" she asked, turning to look back over her shoulder.

"Hmm?" he asked, peeling his eyes from her body and bringing them to her face.

She smiled softly. "I said, do you want me to make you banana pancakes for breakfast?"

"I can just grab something easy. You don't have to cook."

Leah fastened her bra behind her back as she walked over to him. "I want to," she said, going up on her toes and kissing his mouth before she said, "Go take a shower. They'll be ready by the time you're done."

Leah turned from the room then, and as soon as she made it into the kitchen, she gripped the edge of the counter and bowed her head, exhaling a trembling breath.

After a few seconds, she took a deep breath and straightened, gathering the things she'd need to make him breakfast. By the time Danny came into the kitchen, she was setting a plate full of pancakes on the table.

"It smells amazing in here," he said, kissing her cheek before he took a seat at the table. "Oh, and Leah?"

"Yeah?" she asked as she sat across from him.

"I won't ask you about this morning. You can get dressed now."

Her eyes flashed to his, and the corner of his mouth lifted in a smile. "Very well played, though. I can't deny you that."

Leah stared at him, and as his dimples grew more defined, she felt the corners of her own mouth turn up.

They ate breakfast slowly and in relative silence, both of them seemingly lost in their own thoughts, and after cleaning up, they went back to Leah's bedroom to get dressed.

Leah zipped up the black pencil skirt she had paired with a green capped-sleeve silk blouse. Just as she was checking herself in the mirror, Danny stepped out of the bathroom wearing his suit. He stood next to her, looking in the mirror as he adjusted his tie, and she couldn't take her eyes off him.

It was the first time she'd seen him dressed up like that, and it killed her that it was under these circumstances. He looked so incredibly handsome, and she wanted to be celebrating something with him—holding him and laughing with him and posing for pictures.

Not fighting tears as the nausea rolled through her.

"It really does look beautiful," he said, adjusting the knot of his tie.

"What does?" she asked softly.

"The necklace."

She brought her hand up to it as he added, "And I meant what I said last night."

Leah's eyes found his in the mirror as her lips curved into a delicate smile. "I know you did."

His eyes held hers for a moment before he returned her smile, and then he took a deep breath. "Okay then. Ready?"

Of course she wasn't. She wasn't anything close to resembling ready. But she nodded up at him, and he ran the backs of his fingers down her cheek before he reached to grab his wallet from the dresser. He turned back to her then, handing her his keys.

"You want me to drive your car?" she asked, glancing down at them.

"No, I'm giving these to you to hold on to. Jake will be by at some point tomorrow to get my car."

Leah froze. Jake would be coming to get his car. Because after today...

"Okay," she managed softly, taking the keys and turning from him quickly as she walked to the jewelry box on the other side of the room, depositing them there as she tried to compose herself.

"Is there enough gas in your car to get down there today?"

"Mm-hm," she said with her back to him, pretending to look for something in her jewelry box.

It was quiet for a beat before he spoke softly. "Alright," he said, and then she felt his hand on her back for a second before he continued past her and out of the bedroom.

Leah exhaled heavily and closed her eyes; it took several minutes and quite a few deep breaths before she was sure she was in control of herself, and then she opened her eyes and grabbed her purse before following him out of the room.

The ride to the courthouse was spent in pensive silence. There was nothing left to say—nothing they didn't already know about each other's feelings—and so they both remained quiet, preparing themselves for what lay ahead.

Leah kept her hand on the armrest, gripping it tightly. Because if she released it, she knew she would lose her grip on everything—she would be dragged into the whirlpool swirling around her, and it would suck away her composure and her sense of direction and her breath and her sanity.

Danny parked the car and they walked to the courthouse hand in hand; externally, Leah was poised and composed, but inside she could feel herself falling to pieces with every step toward that building.

The place where he was going to be taken away from her.

Unconsciously, she tightened her grip on his hand, and when he felt it, he turned his head to look at her. She kept her eyes forward, afraid of what her expression might reveal if she looked at him now.

As they neared the steps, Danny stopped abruptly, tugging on her hand so that she was forced to turn and face him. She knew her eyes were glassy as she looked up at him, but this time she couldn't turn her gaze away.

"Before we go in there," he said, his voice low and somewhat rough, "I just want to tell you that I love you. And I'm so, so sorry."

"Danny," she started, and he shook his head, silencing her as he brought his mouth to hers.

Somewhere in the back of her mind, Leah knew this was their last kiss.

She melted into him, allowing herself to feel everything: his lips, his breath, his body against hers, his hands on her waist.

And then, too soon, he was pulling away from her.

"Okay," she heard him say to himself as he took her hand again, and then he inhaled deeply as he turned to walk up the stairs.

The second they walked through the double doors into the vast lobby, it felt as though her mind detached from her body. She knew she was physically there, seeing things and hearing things, but none of it registered. None of it felt real.

It was like she was watching the entire scene from outside herself.

She recognized Danny's lawyer in the vestibule as he approached them, reaching out to shake Danny's hand. He said a brief hello to Leah, and she couldn't even be sure if she responded.

"We need to meet for a minute before we go inside," Danny said, his voice muted through the rush of blood in her ears.

She nodded weakly, and Danny's lawyer directed her toward the courtroom where she could wait for them. Leah approached the doors in a daze, and for a moment, she just stood there, frozen and completely overwhelmed.

And then she saw her. The lifeline she so desperately needed.

Catherine.

She was sitting in the front row behind the tiny wall that separated the rest of the room from the judge's bench, and it was as if she sensed Leah's desperate need to feel grounded. As soon as Leah noticed her, Catherine turned, making eye contact with her as she stood in the doorway.

And then she smiled sadly, reaching her hand out to Leah.

She practically ran to her, clutching her hand as she sat beside her, and when Leah felt Catherine rest her head against her shoulder, she closed her eyes and pressed her lips together as her chin quivered.

"We're gonna be strong for him today," Catherine whispered. "He doesn't need to worry about us."

Before Leah could even process her words, she sensed movement in front of them, and she opened her eyes. Jake was crouched in front of Catherine, with Tommy standing behind him.

"How you doing, Gram?" Jake asked gently, and Catherine shrugged, a weak smile trembling on her lips.

Jake leaned forward and kissed her cheek before he stood, turning toward Leah. She was vaguely aware of Tommy whispering something to Catherine as Jake leaned down to hug her. "No matter what happens today, everything's gonna be okay," he said against her ear before he straightened, smiling sadly at her before he turned and walked into the row of seats behind them.

A few minutes later, Leah heard the sound of the doors opening again, and she turned to see her father, brother, and sister taking their seats in the back. Her father made eye contact with her, a comforting look in his eyes as he blew her a kiss, and she smiled softly before turning back around.

Danny's mother and sister were also there, sitting in the middle row. Leah had met them briefly at Danny's apartment during one of the days they'd spent cleaning it. They had come by to pick up some things they were going to store for him, and although they seemed nice enough, she could see there was definitely a distance between them and Danny. She had known he wasn't close to his family, but it was still such a strange thing for her to witness.

He had a family, she reminded herself. It just wasn't his own. Wasn't that what he'd told her?

A few minutes later, there was a murmuring and shuffling in the back of the room, and Leah turned to see Danny walking up the aisle with his lawyer beside him. His face was stoic and serene, and while that should have reassured her, it only served to make her feel sick.

They walked past the small wall and up to the table in front of the judge's bench, taking their seats. Immediately, his lawyer leaned over and began speaking to Danny in hushed tones, and every so often, he would nod slightly in response.

Catherine's grip on Leah's hand tightened suddenly, and Leah glanced up to see the judge walking out from a doorway along the far wall. Everyone was asked to rise, and the judge—a middle-aged man with glasses and dark, thinning hair—approached the bench and took his seat, prompting the rest of them to follow.

From outside herself, Leah watched as he opened folders and shuffled papers, and after what seemed like an eternity, he lifted his head and spoke.

"The state of New York versus Daniel DeLuca, docket number 11D-773492. At this time I will ask Mr. DeLuca to please rise."

Leah's heart thudded in her chest as Danny stood.

"Mr. DeLuca, it is the court's understanding that rather than have a trial in this case, you are submitting a plea of no contest to one count of aggravated assault, and one count of voluntary manslaughter, both felony charges. Is this correct?"

"Yes, sir."

"Do you understand the charges that are being brought against you?"

"Yes, sir."

The judge shuffled a few more papers before he lifted one, adjusting his glasses. "Mr. DeLuca, the court is satisfied that intent to kill was not present in this case. Based on information given by the officers on the scene, as well as witness statements and your own testimony, there is sufficient evidence that provocation was a factor. My condolences for the loss of your friend."

Leah felt Catherine's shoulder shake against hers, and she knew she was stifling her tears. She gave Catherine's hand a squeeze, keeping her eyes on the judge as she tried to read his expression.

His eyes were completely impassive, giving away nothing of his thoughts.

"Taking into consideration the facts of the case and the plea agreement that was reached, at this time the court declares the defendant guilty on both counts of aggravated assault and voluntary manslaughter."

Leah's throat was constricting, making it difficult to take a full breath, and she swallowed hard, staring at the judge as he shuffled a few more papers.

"Mr. DeLuca, you have taken responsibility for your actions and shown remorse for your crime. The court recognizes that you reached out to the victim's family and paid the hospital bills and funeral costs of your own accord."

Her eyes flashed to the back of Danny's head, immediately flooding with tears. He'd never told her that.

"The court also recognizes that you have had no prior convictions or arrests, and that you're in good standing in your community. Taking into consideration all factors, and in accordance with the terms of the plea agreement, I'm sentencing you to twenty-one months in the Federal Correctional Institution at Fort Dix…"

Leah's ears started ringing, a strange humming sound that blended with the droning voice of the judge until there was nothing but white noise in her head. She vaguely registered him saying something about a fine and anger management classes before the buzzing in her ears took over.

Leah felt a hand come to rest on her shoulder from behind, either Jake or Tommy, as an officer approached Danny, bringing his hands behind his back and cuffing them.

Her vision blurred and she felt as if she were going to pass out.

And then he was being led away from them, and Leah lurched forward in her seat, gripping the divider in front of her.

WAIT.

The word was thrashing around wildly in her head, but she couldn't make her mouth say it. She needed to do something—to say something to him—to touch him one more time.

Just before Danny walked through the doors, he turned and looked in their direction. It was a split second, but in that moment, his eyes conveyed everything.

Love. Remorse. Reassurance. Bravery.

And then he turned, walking through the doorway with a cop on either side of him. The door swung closed behind them, and the sharp click resounded through the room, erasing all the other sounds swirling in her ears and leaving an unsettling silence behind it.

Catherine clutched at her, and Leah turned and wrapped her arms around the woman who had raised Danny.

As her frail, trembling hands gripped the sides of Leah's blouse, a desperate, broken wail cut through the silence, and Leah couldn't be sure if it was Catherine's or hers.

Chapter Twenty-One

It wasn't supposed to be like this.

Somewhere in the back of his mind, Danny knew he should be overcome with excitement right now. He should be envisioning what it was going to be like to have Leah in front of him again. Leah wrapped in his arms, laughing as he buried his face in her hair. The lilting sound of her voice as she assured him she was okay. That everyone was okay.

That *he* was going to be okay.

But so much had happened since he'd last seen her in that courtroom, and he just couldn't reconcile that fantasy with his reality anymore. That sort of daydream didn't belong here. It seemed too far-fetched, too unrealistic.

And idealism was a childish indulgence in this place.

For the first ten days after his arrival, Danny hadn't been able to speak to anyone on the outside. Upon entering the facility, he had been told he wouldn't have access to the phone lines or computers until his inmate account was set up; they said it would be activated shortly, and he had believed them.

He should have realized then how disgustingly naïve he was.

Apparently, a ten-day wait was something to be grateful for; there were guys who claimed to have waited twice that long for their accounts to be activated. But hearing that information didn't provide Danny with any consolation. It only made him angrier.

Ten fucking days.

Ten days to program someone's name into a computer. Ten days of knowing the people he loved were panicking over not having heard from him. Ten days of the walls closing in by the hour.

An interminable wait, simply to prove he was at their mercy. That he was just a number now. That his suffering meant nothing to anyone in charge.

On the fifth day, his cellmate Troy had offered to call Danny's family to let them know he was waiting on his account to be set up.

Danny hadn't been allowed to go inside the call room, and the knowledge that Troy was a few feet away with Leah's voice in his ear was almost more unbearable than the first five days put together. When Troy returned, he told Danny she had appreciated the call and promised she'd pass the message along.

He wanted to ask how she had sounded. If she'd been crying. If she'd asked any questions about him. If she'd seemed relieved, or sad, or angry. He wanted to ask Troy to repeat every single thing she had said to him verbatim so Danny could memorize it.

But instead he had nodded and went back to his cell.

Troy's call home should have provided him with some level of relief, but the next five days were somehow more excruciating than the first. The need to connect with someone from home had become a living thing, twisting and churning and clawing at his insides until it could be sated.

The first time Danny had been allowed to call Leah, his rush to explain the visiting instructions had overshadowed the brief respite brought on by her voice. Danny had been required to provide the Bureau of Prisons with a list of potential visitors, and in turn, each person would receive a packet in the mail. As soon as the forms were completed and sent back, the BOP would conduct a background check and either approve or deny the applicants. Danny would receive word when the process was complete, and then anyone who had received clearance would be permitted to visit.

He had also explained that his phone use was restricted to fifteen minutes a day with a cap of three hundred minutes per month, and that within those restrictions, he would have to divide his time between Gram, Jake, Tommy, and his family. Leah had told him not to worry, that she understood they wouldn't be able to speak every day.

And then their conversation was cut off.

Fifteen minutes up. No warning. No countdown. Just a click, and then nothing.

He'd spent the rest of that day feeling completely unnerved instead of gratified.

He tried to be more aware of the time after that, but it was surprisingly easy to get lost within the confines of fifteen minutes. It happened almost every phone call—the abrupt disconnection when his time was up—and each time was just as unsettling as the first.

The ability to end a phone call with "good-bye" was a suddenly a luxury, something he hadn't even anticipated losing because it was such a basic fundamental of life, he'd never even given it a second thought.

So many simple, every day privileges—gone.

He shouldn't have been as shaken by this place as he was. Danny's life had been far from easy, but he had always taken pride in his resiliency; never once had he succumbed to adversity. Never once did he give in to the struggle.

But in his life before this, there had always been something to throw his energy into. Some distraction. Some way for him to expend his suffering.

Here, there was nothing.

He had enrolled himself in classes, but they only occupied ninety minutes of his day. He checked books out of the library, but he couldn't digest any of the words. Maybe it was because his thoughts were the only thing they couldn't put restrictions on, but Danny found himself perpetually lost in his own mind.

He had no idea it could be such an ugly place.

Thoughts would creep in uninvited, wafting in as sinuously as smoke and choking him just as quickly: Jake making a poor decision that would cause the business to go under; Leah growing bitter and resentful—seeking solace in another man's arms; Gram getting sick and dying before he was released.

Various horrors would flash through his mind like a slide show, over and over until he couldn't reason through them anymore. He couldn't determine what was real and what was fabricated, what was speculative and what was a guarantee.

Three weeks. Eighty-eight more to go.

He had no idea if this was part of the transition or if it would always be this way. Maybe his mind would eventually run out of nightmares. Maybe he'd just grow numb to them.

Or maybe his thoughts would wear him down until he couldn't remember who he was before this.

His lawyer had told him this place would be tolerable. Since the judge hadn't deemed Danny a danger to society, part of the plea agreement stated he could serve his sentence in a minimum-security prison, and Danny had lost count of how many times his lawyer assured him minimum-security prisons were more like dormitories than correctional facilities.

He wished he'd never heard that goddamn comparison—or at least that he hadn't been foolish enough to believe it.

There was nothing tolerable about this place. Nothing uplifting. Nothing redeeming. Nothing but the torturously unhurried passing of time.

He didn't give a shit if there were no barbed-wire fences surrounding the property. It didn't change the fact that he was living his life away from everything and everyone who mattered to him. That he didn't even feel like his own person anymore. That every move he made had to be approved. Every decision, every step he took had to be sanctioned by authority.

His lawyer had failed to mention that the lack of perimeter fences wouldn't compensate for how incredibly degrading it felt to be treated like a child twenty-four hours a day. The absence of sharp shooters in towers couldn't make up for the constant misery of not being trusted.

Danny couldn't resign himself to the fact that most of the people in charge had no reason to view him as trustworthy or honorable or decent. Most of them viewed him as a fuck-up. A criminal who raised suspicion, someone who had to be watched and questioned at every turn.

There were a couple of exceptions—those guards who managed to make him feel somewhat human even while doing something like frisking him for contraband—but most of them spoke to the inmates like they were shit on their shoes.

At first, Danny tried to rationalize their behavior with the fact that these men spent their lives surrounded by people who had broken the law—some worse than others and many more than once. He reasoned that after years and years of witnessing a revolving door of crooks and felons and delinquents, their tolerance must have worn pretty thin.

Still, it didn't make him feel any less shitty—or any less angry—when he was on the receiving end of that intolerance. Eventually he gave up trying to justify their behavior and accepted the fact that everyone had a role to play; they were the judgmental pricks on a power trip and he was a piece of shit criminal, and that was that.

Three weeks, and they had already managed to get inside his head.

Maybe he was never as strong as he thought.

Danny lifted his head off the pillow and looked at the clock on the wall. Any minute now, she'd be here. They were going to call his name, and he would make his first trip to the visitor's center, and Leah would be standing before him.

And it wasn't supposed to be like this.

Because instead of excitement, there was dread. Instead of eagerness, there was panic. And instead of relief, there was shame.

He was so afraid she'd be able to see it—that he was already different. That they'd both given him too much credit.

He didn't want to let her down. He didn't want her to wonder what would be left of him after another nineteen months if three weeks had already affected him.

It was all so fucking humiliating.

He didn't know how to keep the darkness of his thoughts from her, and if she saw it, what would she think? Would she pity him? Be just as disappointed in him as he was in himself? Begin distancing herself from him?

The thought alone was enough to incapacitate him, because he realized she would probably be better off leaving him at this point. He would be destroyed, completely and utterly gutted, but that seemed to be the path he was on anyway.

Leah didn't have to be subjected to this.

Danny rolled his head to the side as Troy walked into their cell dressed in his grays, one of two authorized outfits inmates were permitted to wear. A gray sweat suit was the required attire for the rec area or the gym; for everything else, there was a khaki jumpsuit.

"You working out?" Danny asked.

"Nah, just got back," Troy said, sifting through the small locker in the corner of the room. He pulled out a pack of tortillas, some dried pepperoni, and a little bag of shredded cheese, and Danny knew Troy was about to make what he called a "bootleg stromboli." He'd taught Danny how to make them during his first week at Fort Dix, after he'd already grown tired of the shit down at the mess hall.

Troy knew a bunch of resourceful tricks like that. He'd been down for thirteen months for possession of drugs while on probation, and he still had another three years to serve. But with good time, he could be out in just over two.

"They post the call sheet for tomorrow yet?" Danny asked.

"No, but I better be on it for the damn doctor. My knee is killing me."

Danny lay back on his bed, blinking up at the ceiling. He hadn't been down as long as Troy, but still, he knew there was no way Troy would be on the call sheet for the doctor tomorrow. Unless someone was bleeding or dying, he was basically forced to tough out whatever was ailing him. It had been one of the first things Danny had learned about this place.

Troy rolled up the stromboli and shook his head. "Wish I had some fucking soda," he said, pressing it together with his thumbs to make it stick.

"When's your commissary day again?"

"Thursdays," he said.

"I'm on Monday. I'm good with most of my shit for now, so I can get some when I go."

"Thanks, man," Troy said, licking his finger before pressing the tortilla down again. "I'll owe you."

Danny nodded.

Troy sealed the bag of cheese before he walked back to the locker. "Isn't your girl coming today?"

Danny wet his lips. "Yeah."

Troy shoved the bags of food in his locker before bumping it closed with his elbow. "If Shaw or Brighton are on duty, watch your ass."

"What do you mean?"

Troy walked back to his plate and pressed down on the tortilla again. "They're real dicks about everything. Touching and shit."

Danny sat up on his bed. "I can't touch her?"

Troy shook his head as he tucked in the ends of the stromboli. "You can hug her when she comes in, but that's it. And keep that shit respectable. If you get flagged, they'll take her off the list. And if you keep getting flagged, you lose visitation all together."

Danny ran his hand down his face.

"Shaw and Brighton, they're fucking hawks, man. Anything that looks like you might be passing shit back and forth and you're done. If Hanover's on duty, you'll get a little more leeway."

And just like that, his earlier fantasy splintered into a million pieces before it disintegrated like powder; in its wake was the image of Leah sitting across him, her hands folded obediently in her lap as the guards monitored the three feet of insurmountable space between them.

He wished he'd known this beforehand so he could have given her some type of warning. Now, he'd be faced with the task of pushing her away. It didn't matter that he could immediately follow it up with an explanation of the rules; he was still going to have to endure the initial look of shock and hurt on her face as he denied her affection.

"Did your girl know all this before she came the first time?" Danny asked.

"I don't remember."

Danny lay back on his bed, pressing the heels of his hands into his eyes. "This is so fucked up. I've been waiting for this." He dropped his hands and looked at Troy. "But this is gonna suck, isn't it?"

Troy sighed as he lifted his plate. "It is what it is, brother. You get over it."

And with that, he walked out of the room.

Danny stared after him before turning his gaze to Troy's side of the cell. There were four pictures taped to the wall above his bed: one of Troy with a woman who appeared to be his mother, and the other three were of him and his girlfriend. In one of the pictures she was sitting on his lap. In another, they were kissing.

Danny stared at the images, desperate to find a flaw in their relationship, needing to discover even an inkling of discontent—anything that would explain Troy's indifference just now when he talked about his visits with her. But the people in that picture were unmistakably happy, their affection for each other evident in their eyes.

Maybe Troy's apathy was just a front, just something he used to keep his true feelings at bay.

Or maybe thirteen months of this shit had managed to turn the people in that photograph into fictional characters—individuals who existed on paper but nowhere else.

Is that how he and Leah were destined to end up? Danny refused to believe he'd ever be capable of indifference when it came to her.

But then again, every last one of his expectations had been refuted since he'd come here, so what the hell did he know anymore?

"The following people have been requested at the visitor's center," a voice crackled over the loudspeaker. "Charles Velasquez, Darrel Simpson, Daniel DeLuca, Ray Brenner, Benjamin King, and Sean Foley."

Danny's heart came alive in his chest as his stomach churned.

Some small, unquenchable piece of his heart desperately needed to see her. He could feel it trying to fight its way to the surface, like someone submerged under water for far too long, striving for a restorative breath. But the more tenable part of him was terrified beyond belief.

He had no idea what he was going to do once they were in the same room together. What he would say. How he would behave. There were rules now. People were watching. Who were they supposed to be under these new circumstances?

As he approached the door leading to the visitor's center, he tried to convince himself that once he saw her, everything would make sense. He wouldn't have to think. This was *Leah*. Everything with her had always been so effortless, even when he was trying to fight it in the beginning.

This day was going to change everything for him. He just needed to have faith and let it happen.

Danny recited that mantra as he approached the inmates' entrance to the center. The guard at the door was someone he didn't recognize, but as he got closer, he could read the name *Layne* on his ID tag.

He gave Danny a quick once over before he opened the door and gestured for him to enter first.

On the other side of the door was a small room with an exit that led into the visiting area, and as Danny stepped in, Layne came in behind him.

"Arms out," he ordered.

Danny lifted his arms, staring straight ahead as Layne patted him down.

Contraband checks were so commonplace around here that Danny often wondered if there was an inmate black market he hadn't yet become privy to. But they were always conducted before a visit, and once the visit was over, they would check him again, making sure he hadn't been passed something from the outside that he could bring back into the facility.

"Shoes off," Layne said as he came to stand in front of Danny.

He dropped his arms to his sides. "You want my shoes off?"

"That's what I said, isn't it? Is English your second language?"

Danny felt his jaw flex before he reached down to untie his boots.

He'd never had to remove his shoes during a contraband check before. It would be virtually impossible for him to retrieve something from his shoe during a visit without being caught by the guards, which meant Layne was just trying to make this difficult.

As soon as Danny's boots were off, Layne grabbed them and turned them upside down, giving them a little shake before he inspected the soles.

And then he tossed them on the floor in front of Danny.

"Pick those up."

Danny inhaled slowly before he squatted down to grab his discarded boots. He slipped them back on and stood, keeping his eyes on the small window of the door in front of him as he waited for Layne to give him clearance.

And then he saw her.

She was standing near the civilian entrance to the visitor's center, looking beautiful and pristine and perfect, and all at once some dormant part of him resurfaced, making him want to rip the door off the hinges and run to her.

The sight of her did something strange to his body, like the shot of Demerol he'd gotten as a child just before the surgery on his broken leg. He could sense something warm rush through his veins, making him feel heavy and sedated, but oddly enough, it didn't do a thing to ease his pain; the hurt was still there—he could *feel* it—but it had temporarily lost its power over him.

Danny watched as two guards asked her to empty the clear plastic bag she carried in place of her purse, since opaque bags weren't allowed inside the facility. She did as she was told, taking a step back and spinning her mother's bracelet between her fingers. It was a nervous habit of hers that Danny had always found endearing, but today it made him feel like his chest was being crushed.

He watched her chew on her lower lip as she glanced back and forth between them. He watched her run her hands down the sides of her jeans as she inhaled a deep breath. He watched her standing in a windowless room full of felons as two strangers searched through her things.

And he knew she didn't belong there.

"You're clear," Layne said, his eyes on his clipboard as he wrote something. "Keep your hands to yourself or your ass will be thrown back through these doors so fast you won't even get a chance to say, 'I'm innocent.' Is that clear?"

Danny swallowed before he nodded.

"I said, *is that clear?*"

Danny closed his eyes. "Yes."

Layne dismissed him with a flick of his head.

As Danny reached for the door, he realized his hand was trembling, and he couldn't be sure if it was nerves or stifled rage that was responsible. With one tiny breath to strengthen his resolve, he pulled the door open.

She was still standing by the entrance with the guards as they placed items back in her bag, and Danny made his way over to one of the smaller tables and sat down. He watched her take her bag back from the guard and nod with a tiny smile before she turned to enter the room.

Her eyes landed on him instantly, and her face broke into a wide grin as she took two quick steps in his direction before she stopped and composed herself. Danny stood, drinking her in as she continued toward him, and when only a few feet of space remained between them, he reached his arms out for her.

She ran the last few steps to him and threw her arms around his neck, and Danny exhaled heavily as he circled his arms around her waist, pulling her against his body.

The smell of her hair enveloped him, making him feel like he was being ripped apart and reconstructed all at once.

She let go of him almost immediately, giving him a quick peck on the mouth before taking two steps backward.

"They told me the rules," she said, taking another reluctant step away from him, and it felt like his insides were spilling out onto the floor.

He hated every eye in the room that watched them right now. Every guard who sat glued to their interactions like they were watching an episode of reality TV. He hated every motherfucker who refused to let him have this one moment with her.

"Should we..." she asked, gesturing toward the seats, and Danny cleared his throat.

"Yeah," he managed softly.

They both sat across from each other, and Leah shifted in her seat before she smiled tentatively at him.

God, she was so beautiful.

"So...how are you?" she asked.

Such a simple question.

But as the seconds ticked by, he couldn't even begin to formulate a response. What was he supposed to say? That he was completely miserable? That he spent the first night here heaving over the toilet after eating the slop at the dining hall? That every day the guards spoke to him with vitriol, and he was expected to take it or suffer the consequences? That he used the bathroom in a room with six toilets separated by plastic dividers without doors, so even his most basic human privacies had been stripped from him? That on his sixth night in this place, he saw another inmate cry and couldn't decide if he wanted to console him or tell him his weakness was disgusting, because it mirrored his own?

He watched Leah waiting for his answer, and when her smile began to falter, she dropped her eyes and took a small breath. When she looked back up, her face was once again composed.

"How are your classes?" she asked, trying her luck with a different question.

"They're good," Danny said. "Keep me occupied in the mornings."

Her smile broadened now that he seemed to be responding. "I would have taken you for more of a night class kind of guy."

Danny smiled softly. "No classes offered at night because of all-call."

"What's all-call?"

"When we line up so they can make sure we're all behaving and accounted for, and that no one made a run for it."

Something flashed behind her eyes before a contrived smile curved her lips, and then she looked down at her lap. After a few seconds, she lifted the sandwich bag that held her ID and her money.

"I'm gonna go get a snack. You want anything?"

Danny shook his head. "I'm okay."

"Okay," she said softly as she stood and made her way over to the vending machine on the far wall. Danny watched as she stopped just before it and lowered her head, taking a slow breath before she looked up and began putting money in the machine.

She obviously needed a minute or she wouldn't have gotten up so soon. In hindsight, he could see how the idea of an all-call might upset her. The thought of him having to line up and be scrutinized was a reminder of his status as a criminal—but there was nothing he could tell her about his life in there that wouldn't generate the same type of reaction.

The absolute last thing he wanted to do was make her worry about him. He needed to be more thoughtful about what he said. This visit was supposed to be a little pocket of perfect inside a mess of shit, and it would never be that if he wasted their time together by upsetting her.

He needed to be the one asking the questions, and she needed to be the one talking. Stories from home would be safe topics of conversation. Funny stories. *Normal* stories.

Leah walked back to her chair with a bottle of water and a bag of M&M's. "Want some?" she asked, holding it out.

"Can't," Danny said, nodding toward the wall where two guards stood watching.

"Oh, right," she mumbled, glancing over her shoulder. "Sorry."

"So, how's Gram doing?" he asked, and Leah focused all her attention on opening her bag of candy.

"She's good. Keeping busy, you know."

Danny stared at her as she avoided eye contact, sifting through the bag before popping a few in her mouth.

Apparently, he wasn't the only one trying to censor the conversation.

An awkward silence fell over them, and Leah twisted the bag between her fingertips.

"Tell me a story," he said. "Something good."

She lifted her eyes. "Something good?"

Danny nodded.

"Um…let's see. I met Tommy's new girlfriend the other day."

"Oh yeah?"

"Mm-hm."

"What's she like?" Danny asked.

This was safe. Pleasant.

"She's adorable," Leah said with a smile. "Really nice. And *so* smart. She's going to school for forensic science. Like one of those CSI people."

"No shit?"

Leah nodded. "It was so cool talking to her. She's definitely a keeper. Gram loves her too."

Something flickered in Danny's chest. "Gram met her?"

"Yeah. Tommy brought her by one afternoon while I was visiting. We all ended up staying for dinner."

Danny nodded slowly as he pressed his palms into the tops of his thighs.

The thought of them all sitting at Gram's together should have made him smile, but the flickering in his chest tightened further until there was no mistaking what it was.

Jealousy.

What the fuck was wrong with him? He had no idea he was capable of such repulsiveness. How selfish was it to resent the people he cared about for living their lives? What would he have preferred to hear? That they were all sitting alone in their living rooms with the curtains drawn, crying into a box of tissues?

"Are you okay?"

No. He wasn't okay. He was the furthest thing from okay. He was spiraling into something ugly and he didn't know how to stop, because hearing about home was supposed to be the one thing that helped him.

"Danny?"

He leaned forward, resting his elbows on his knees as he dropped his forehead to his clasped hands.

Tell her, he thought. *Tell her you just realized you're so far gone that other people's happiness makes you angry.*

"Danny...it's okay," she said. "Whatever it is, you can talk to me."

But he didn't know what he was supposed to say anymore.

He didn't know how to be this version of himself with her. Trying to figure out the right words to use, what information to leave out of stories. Struggling to hide his reactions to things. She was one of the few people he could always be himself with, and having his guard up around her felt awkward and unnatural and *wrong.*

He couldn't do this.

"This isn't working, Leah," he said, his forehead still resting on his fists.

"What isn't working?"

"This," he said finally, lifting his head. "Us."

Leah blinked at him like he had just said something in a foreign language. "What are you talking about?"

The words were all there, just waiting to be said: that he couldn't be around her until he figured out how to be himself again. That he didn't want what they had to be dragged through shit in the process. That he needed to end their relationship now, because it was the only way to preserve it. And they could both remember it the way it had truly been—powerful and unblemished and real, not bruised and broken and so sullied it was impossible to remember it was ever beautiful in the first place.

Yes, the words were all there. But instead, he said, "I've been wrong about a lot of things, Leah. I'm realizing that now. And thinking we could make this work was one of them."

"Danny," she said, a hint of dread in her tone. The confusion on her face was slowly giving way to realization.

"It just doesn't make sense anymore," he continued. "For either one of us."

She shook her head. "Stop. Don't do this."

"No, *you* don't do this," he said. "Don't make this hard, Leah. I'm trying to tell you what I want."

She stared at him for several seconds before she spoke. "And you're saying you don't want this?" Her expression was smooth, but her voice quavered slightly, betraying her. "You don't want us?"

It took every ounce of strength in his body to keep the emotion out of his next words—the most despicable lie to ever leave his lips. "Not anymore."

Leah kept her eyes on him, and he could see the rise and fall of her chest gradually increase in speed. "Why are you doing this?" she whispered.

He needed to end this conversation. Her suffering would be the last straw—the thing that demolished him and caused his illusion of strength to burst apart and scatter to the floor like the house of cards it was.

"It's what's best for both of us, Leah. I promise you that. I know you don't think so right now, but eventually you will. And then you'll be relieved we put a stop to this when we did."

She opened her mouth to speak and he stood, cutting her off. Leah lifted her chin, looking up at him with eyes so full of vulnerability he knew he'd never recover from the weight of it.

"I just want you to know," he said. He cleared his throat and took a step backward. "I just want you to know that every time I told you I loved you...I meant it."

Leah shook her head. "Don't say that," she said, her voice hardening slightly. "You don't get to say those words to me right now."

Danny looked down and nodded. "Take care of yourself, Leah," he said, and then he turned and walked back toward the inmates' exit. He held his thumb against the buzzer that would alert the guard, and as the seconds ticked by, he kept his eyes on the door, refusing to look back.

Whatever he would find there—whether she was sobbing, or infuriated, or struck dumb, or relieved—none of it would provide him with any solace. No good could come of looking back. He had to keep moving forward.

The door opened and Danny stepped inside the small room, immediately putting his arms out to his sides, and as the guard patted him down, he heard the door click shut behind him.

He'd been right about one thing—this day had been a turning point for him. For the first time since he'd walked through the doors of Fort Dix, he felt something that resembled relief.

Because no matter how far he spiraled down now, he wouldn't be dragging her along with him.

Chapter Twenty-Two

"Rise and shine, gorgeous."

Leah flinched as a flash of brightness penetrated the room, assaulting her eyes even though they were still closed.

She pulled her brow together and rolled over, burying her face in the pillow and away from the offensive light as she curled her comforter into her chest.

"Nuh-uh," Holly said, grabbing her blanket and giving it a firm yank, forcing Leah onto her back again. "Come on. Up you go."

"Holly, what the hell?" Leah rasped, her voice gravelly with sleep and disuse. She sat up slowly, rubbing her eyes with the heels of her hands.

"It's almost noon, Leah. Time to get up."

"How did you even get in here?" Leah snapped, and Holly laughed.

"I have a key, remember?"

"Yeah, for emergencies."

"This *is* an emergency," Holly said, sitting on the edge of her bed. "I need to go shopping, and Robyn's babysitting her nieces today, so I have no reinforcements."

Leah's hands dropped from her eyes as she turned her head, staring blankly at her friend. "We clearly have conflicting definitions of that word."

Holly smiled. "Up you go, lovely," she said, grabbing Leah's hands and jerking her forcefully from the bed.

"Jesus!" Leah complained as she stumbled with the blanket tangled around her foot. "Take it easy!"

"Get in the shower," Holly said, completely unfazed. "How long has it been since you've done that, by the way?" she added, making a face.

"Holly, I'm tired," Leah said listlessly. "I just want to go back to bed."

"And you can. As soon as we get back."

Leah's shoulders dropped as Holly said, "You're making this a bigger deal than it needs to be. Shower, shop, home. So come on," she said with a sharp clap of her hands. "Let's get moving."

Leah would have protested again if she thought it would do any good, but she'd known Holly too long. It was either do what she asked or spend the next few hours dealing with her nonsense.

"I hate you," Leah grumbled, and Holly grabbed her wrist, pulling her toward the bathroom.

"That's okay," she said. "I still love you, and I'm very difficult to get rid of." She leaned into the shower and turned on the water.

Leah folded her arms. "Are you gonna take my clothes off and wash me too, or can I handle it from here?"

"There was a time I may have taken you up on that offer, but mama's let herself go lately," she said, gesturing at Leah. "Clean yourself up and ask me again later."

Leah didn't want to smile, but she couldn't help it.

Holly laughed before she walked past her. "I'll be waiting in your room," she said before she walked out of the bathroom and closed the door.

Leah sighed heavily as she began to strip off her clothes. Every movement felt like a chore, like she was fighting against the resistance of invisible rubber bands holding every one of her limbs in place.

She stepped into the shower, turning the knob so that the water would heat up. She welcomed the burn, forced herself to stay and deal with the sting.

She knew exactly what this little day-trip was about. Subtlety had never been Holly's strong suit.

It had been just over two weeks since her visit with Danny, and Leah hadn't left her house for anything outside of going to work. She would come home in the afternoon and crawl into bed, sometimes immediately falling asleep and not waking until the following morning.

Those were the merciful days.

There were other times she would lie there for hours on end, staring aimlessly at the ceiling or the TV or whatever else was in front of her, unable to sink into the benevolent refuge of unconsciousness.

She forgot meals entirely. She barely bathed.

Her colleagues at work knew she was sick. At least, that's what she'd told them to account for her bedraggled appearance, the bags under her eyes, her hair pulled sloppily into a ponytail rather than blown straight and shiny. Every day they'd ask how she was feeling, offering her their sympathies and their diagnoses and their home remedies.

But there was only one cure for what ailed her. And it was unattainable.

A constant ache resided in her chest—a crushing pain that had her wondering if it were actually possible for a heart to break. If it were feasible for an organ to shatter, sending jagged shards throughout her body that pierced her with every movement.

Sharp reminders of her misery.

She had never endured this type of suffering before. When Leah had lost her mother, it had been impossible to be with her. She was gone—no longer in existence. When she had lost Scott, there was no desire to be near him ever again.

But with Danny, she needed him so desperately it consumed her. And he was out there. Living and breathing and existing. And completely out of her reach.

It was the cruelest type of torment.

He hadn't contacted her at all since she'd gone to see him, which meant she couldn't even fight for him. It wasn't like she could call him. She couldn't text. She couldn't show up at his apartment begging to be heard. And even if she could, what would be the point? He'd made it clear what he wanted.

No, it was easier to just sit back and let the desolation have her. She didn't have the energy to fight against it this time.

Leah got out of the shower and brushed her wet hair, tying it back into a low ponytail without blow-drying it. And then she walked out of the bathroom, bypassing her makeup case yet again.

"I picked out an outfit for you," Holly said, holding up a pair of skinny jeans and a cute flowered tank.

"No," Leah said, walking toward her dresser and opening the bottom drawer where she kept her yoga pants and sweats.

She heard Holly sigh heavily. "Fine," she said, tossing the clothes on Leah's bed. "You're agreeing to come, so I'll give you this one concession. You can look like a complete dirtbag if it will make you feel better."

"It will," Leah said flatly as she pulled on a pair of charcoal yoga pants.

As they drove to the mall, Holly kept up a steady stream of small talk, filling Leah in on the everyday occurrences and little tidbits of life she'd missed out on over the past two weeks. Apparently, the shopping trip was for a party Evan had been invited to the following weekend. His ex-girlfriend was going to be there, so Holly needed to look "devastatingly sexy," as she put it.

Leah followed her through the mall, nodding when she was supposed to, smiling when she was supposed to, answering when she was required to, all the while counting down the minutes until she could crawl back into her bed.

They walked through the department store, and Holly pulled dress after dress off the rack, holding it out and examining it before tossing it over her arm or hanging it back up with a shake of her head.

"I think you've got enough," Leah said, gesturing toward the mountain of fabric piled over her friend's arm.

Holly shrugged. "I don't know that any of these are devastating, but I'll try them on. We can always go to a different store after this."

Please, Leah thought, *please let one of them be devastating.*

They walked into one of the fitting rooms, and Holly dropped the heap of dresses on the bench in the corner. "You have to be honest," she said, pulling her shirt over her head. "Don't yes me to death because you want to go home. If you send me to a party with Evan's ex looking like a heifer, I'll spend the rest of my life torturing you."

"How will that be different from what you already do?"

Holly smiled. "There she is! Oh, how I've missed bitchy Leah."

Leah smiled half-heartedly as Holly reached over and grabbed a dress off the top of the pile, handing it to Leah. "Here, put this on," she said, taking the next one for herself.

"What? Why?"

"I don't know. Because it's fun to try on dresses. Humor me," she said, pulling a dark green cocktail dress over her head.

Humor her. The quicker she's happy, the quicker you can get out of here.

Leah stripped her clothes off and stepped into the dress, pulling it up over her torso, and Holly came behind her, zipping it up.

It was a beautiful dress—simple, but elegant, chocolate-colored and strapless, fitting snugly around her middle and flowing out softly from her hips in a billowy skirt that hit just above her knee.

"Your body looks *sick* in this," Holly said.

Leah stared at her reflection: the slumped shoulders, the purplish rings under her eyes, the pallid skin, her hair flat and un-styled, her vacant stare.

She saw herself standing alone, without him at her side, and because of that, there was nothing beautiful about what she was looking at, no matter what she was wearing.

"Seriously, this is gorgeous on you," Holly said.

"Yeah, it's pretty," Leah agreed, turning so Holly could unzip her. "And not that one," she added, referencing the dress Holly was wearing. "It makes you look boxy."

Holly's eyes met hers in the mirror and she smiled. "That was a test, and you passed with flying colors, my darling."

Leah shook her head and laughed softly, stepping out of the brown dress and putting it back on the hanger.

About an hour later, they were hanging Holly's unwanted dresses on the rack outside the fitting rooms. She had chosen a red sheath dress that emphasized her incredible legs, and the color was guaranteed to turn every head in whatever room she walked into. Leah had assured her if she paired it with some platform heels and red lipstick, against the dark tone of her hair, she would most certainly be devastating.

When she picked up the brown dress, Holly turned to Leah. "You need to buy this. It looked amazing on you."

Leah shook her head. "I have nowhere to wear a dress like this," she said, taking it from her and hanging it on the rack.

"Maybe not right now, but you will one day. This dress needs to be on reserve in your closet. It's too perfect on you. I'm not taking no for an answer," she said, taking the dress off the rack and hanging it over her arm with the red one before walking to the register.

"Not taking no for an answer?" Leah mumbled to herself. "Shocking."

"I heard that," Holly called over her shoulder.

They paid for their dresses, and as they were walking out of the department store, Holly pressed a hand to her stomach.

"I'm starving. Can we stop and get something quick?"

Leah shrugged. "If you want."

"I'm dying for one of those Greek salads from that place in the food court. You want one?"

"I'm not really that hungry," Leah said.

"Get one. You can pick at it, and if you don't finish it, you can take it home."

Leah sighed, resigning herself to the fact that Holly was going to get her way in every aspect of today's outing.

A few minutes later, they were sitting at a small table in the corner of the food court with their salads on plastic trays, and Holly smiled.

"Thanks for being a trouper today."

Leah smiled softly, reaching to open her bottle of water.

"So, since I forced you out of your comfort zone and you were such a good sport about it," Holly said as she sifted through her salad, "you can call the shots now. Do you want to talk about him, or not talk about him?"

Leah lifted her eyes to see Holly watching her as she took a bite of her salad.

The shards in her chest came to life, twisting and piercing and slicing.

God, she wanted to. She wanted to say his name. She wanted to hear his name. She wanted to talk about him every minute of every day of every week until she could make sense of everything that had happened.

Until she could figure out a way back into his heart.

But whenever she thought about him, it hurt so badly she could hardly breathe through it.

She couldn't stand not being part of his life anymore—couldn't stand the thought of him alone in that place. She hated picturing him in a cell, wondering if he was sad, or scared, or angry. Wondering if he was lonely. Wondering if he thought of her even a fraction of the times she thought about him.

"I feel like I can't breathe without him," she said, her chin trembling as the words left her mouth. "I miss him."

"Of course you do," Holly said. "Let yourself miss him. Don't fight that."

Leah nodded as two tears slipped over her lashes, and she swiped at them quickly.

"But what you've been doing these past few weeks? That's not missing him. That's *mourning* him. There's a difference."

Leah raised her eyes to Holly's.

"And I'm sorry, but I won't let you do that. It's not over for you guys. So there's nothing to mourn."

"Holly—"

"Remember when we were in seventh grade," Holly said, cutting her off, "and N'SYNC was going to be on TRL? And we camped out in Times Square for two days so we could see them when they arrived?"

Leah pulled her brow together as she swiped at another tear. "Yeah."

"And you had your whole plan. Do you remember?"

The corner of Leah's mouth lifted in a half-hearted smile. "Yeah. I was going to sing for Justin Timberlake so he would take me on tour with the band."

Holly laughed as she took another bite of her salad. "And what happened when he finally walked by you?"

"You shoved me, and I face-planted in front of everyone."

"Hold on," Holly said, holding up her hand, "what happened *before* that?"

"What do you mean?"

"I mean, what happened before I pushed you?"

Leah shrugged. "Nothing."

"Exactly," she said. "Nothing. And why not? You had a plan. You practiced for weeks trying to make your voice sound a little less like a cat getting a root canal."

Leah threw her napkin at Holly and she batted it away easily. "You were ready," she said, not missing a beat. "So why didn't you go through with it?"

"I don't know," Leah said, sifting through her salad. "I panicked."

"Right. You freaked, and you bailed. So...I shoved you."

"And I landed flat on my face in front of him with my skirt practically over my head!"

Holly pointed at Leah with her fork. "That wasn't my fault. Who wears a skirt in the middle of January?"

A breathy laugh fell from Leah's lips as she looked down at her salad.

"But you remember what happened after I shoved you, don't you?"

Leah sighed. "He helped me up and asked if I was okay."

"And?"

"And he helped me back behind the barricade."

"And?"

Leah smiled softly. "And he signed my CD, and I got a picture with him."

"Exactly. You're welcome, by the way."

Leah laughed to herself as she twirled her fork between her fingers.

After a few seconds of silence, Holly sighed in exasperation. "You still don't get it, do you?"

"Get what?"

She gave Leah a patronizing look. "You had a plan. You thought you were prepared. But when it was go-time, you panicked. You got scared, and you bailed."

Leah blinked at her. "Okay?"

"Jesus, Leah! You still don't see it?"

"See *what?*"

"That Danny's just panicking!" she shouted. "He thought he was prepared, and he wasn't, and it scared the shit out of him, so he backed out! It's the same damn scenario!"

Leah stared at her friend, trying to swallow the lump in her throat. After a stunned second, she shook her head. "I don't think—"

"He loves you," Holly interrupted, her voice softening significantly. "You know he does, Leah. I can see it in your face, even now. He's just scared. That's all this is."

Leah swiped at a fresh round of tears with shaking hands.

"He just needs someone to shove him. Hard."

Leah laughed through a sob as she wiped her nose with her napkin, and Holly smiled as she picked her fork back up.

"So," she said, looking pointedly at Leah. "Are you gonna shove him?"

Leah inhaled deeply as she picked apart her napkin. "I don't know," she said softly. "I don't know if I can. If he even wants me to. I don't know anything anymore."

"Alright then, here's the deal, *chica*," Holly said, her expression turning serious. "I'm going to give you as much time as you need. I'm going to let you miss him. I'm going to let you cry rivers upon rivers if you feel like you need to, and you can talk about him as much as you want, until his name sounds like nails on a chalkboard if it makes you feel better. But I will *not* let you keep doing what you've been doing these past few weeks. If this is gonna get fixed, then one of you has to keep it together. And I don't think it's fair to expect it to be him."

Leah swallowed before she nodded slowly.

"Okay then," Holly said with a nod. "Now let's finish these salads so we can go get some shoes."

They spent the next hour at the mall, looking for shoes to go with their new dresses, and the entire time, Leah kept replaying Holly's words over in her mind.

They swam through her, collecting the little splinters in her chest so that each subsequent breath seemed a little easier to take.

If this is gonna get fixed, then one of you has to keep it together.

She wanted to fix it—more than she'd ever wanted anything in her life—but she felt the same way Holly looked the day she tried to put together Evan's entertainment center: the instructions were in front of her, all the tools right there at her disposal, and yet she didn't know where to begin.

When Holly dropped Leah off a little while later, she gave her a hug and told her she would call her the next day, and Leah walked up the path and through the front door to the utter paradox that was her apartment. It was the only place she felt at peace, yet at the same time, it was an endless source of torture.

The fact that Danny had spent every night and practically every day at her apartment for a month before he left made his absence that much more jarring.

His memory was all around her, in every single room.

Leah walked back to her closet and hung up the bag that held her dress before she kicked off her shoes and climbed into her bed, pulling the comforter up to her chin.

And then she closed her eyes, drifting off to sleep as Holly's words continued to course through her, gradually collecting little pieces of her fragmented heart.

Chapter Twenty-Three

"The following people have been requested at the visitor's center: Benjamin King, Daniel DeLuca, Michael Moroney, Steven Logan, Kevin Driscoll, and Duane Tanner."

Danny stood from his chair, putting his playing cards on the table. "You just got lucky," he said, revealing his hand.

Theo lifted his brow at Danny's straight flush. "Well, shit. Thank your visitor for me."

Danny smiled as he turned to exit the rec room. If Jake had shown up just five minutes later, Danny would have undoubtedly won the pot.

Thirty-seven postage stamps.

It was their only real form of currency, and something most prisoners took very seriously. Rory, the inmate-turned-barber, charged five stamps per haircut. Terrence, the guy who ironed prisoners' jumpsuits on visitation days, charged three stamps for his services. Any favor asked, any bet made, typically involved an exchange of stamps. After two months in this place, Danny still felt like a kid playing with Monopoly money.

He approached the inmates' entrance to the center, noticing that Marco was the guard outside today. He nodded a hello to Danny before he opened the door and gestured for Danny to enter.

"Arms out, please," he said, and Danny lifted his arms.

"You catch that game last night?" Marco asked as he patted Danny down.

Danny gave a short laugh. "Yeah. I wish I didn't."

"Unbelievable," Marco said. "Highest payroll in the MLB. Sure as shit didn't look like it yesterday."

"A lot of those guys haven't been hungry for a long time," Danny said, turning so Marco could pat down his other leg. "These owners throw money at their best guys, forgetting that money makes some people complacent."

Marco lifted his brow before he inclined his head in acknowledgement. "Very well-said." He straightened, and Danny dropped his arms. "Alright, who you got today?"

"A buddy of mine," Danny said.

Marco nodded as he checked his watch and then recorded the start time of the visit on his clipboard.

"Alright then, Mr. DeLuca," he said, reaching forward and opening the door for him. "Enjoy your time."

"Thanks," Danny replied as he stepped around him and through the door.

He walked into the visitor's center and turned toward the table and chairs set up near the vending machine where Jake typically preferred to sit, only to find an older couple seated there, waiting for an inmate.

Danny smirked as he realized Jake would have to walk a full fifteen feet to get his Skittles now. He typically went through four or five bags per visit, as if they were a luxury he could only get there and not something he could pick up in twenty different places on the way home.

Danny turned, scanning the other side of the room for him.

And then he froze.

She was sitting at the far table against the window, her eyes on him as she rolled her mother's bracelet between her fingers.

It had been over a month since he'd seen her—over a month since he'd had any contact with her whatsoever—but the sight of her hadn't even come close to losing its potency.

He couldn't afford this kind of test today. His daydreams of her, when they were furtive enough to creep in uninvited, were bad enough.

Ironically, his worst days in this place were the days he found it the easiest to be without her. At his lowest points, Danny managed to find solace and comfort in being alone—in knowing that the only person he stood to hurt was himself. The days he felt demeaned to the point of detachment, the days his thoughts ran rampant through dark corners and bleak paths for hours at a time, unable to resurface, the days he struggled to even remember a life outside these walls—those were the days he was so grateful she was out of his life. In a way it was pacifying, knowing he could spin as far out of control as he wanted with absolutely no consequences for her.

But then there were other days.

Days that Danny somehow made it to "lights out" feeling somewhat like himself. Days he was able to keep a rein on his thoughts, steering them out of sinister waters. Days when he could see an end in sight—no matter how far off it might seem—and all at once there was something to strive for.

Those were the days his heart felt like it was being shredded.

Because when things were good, he thought about her constantly. Wondering if he'd made the wrong decision. How she was holding up. Whether or not she was angry with him.

Wondering if there was even the slightest chance she might take him back when this was all over.

He wasn't sure it would even be possible to earn back her trust after everything he'd done, but on his good days, Danny promised himself he'd exhaust every avenue and deplete every resource trying.

And today had been decent for him, which meant it was a horrible day to attempt a conversation with her.

He couldn't allow this temporary sense of well-being to sway him, because tomorrow, it could be gone, and there would be no way to guarantee if or when it would come back.

Danny watched her shoulders rise as she took a deep breath, but her expression remained impassive as she watched him standing there, rooted to the ground.

He tried to summon the resistance he'd relied on so many times when the need for her pulled at him relentlessly. The same power that prevented him from dialing her number, despite the amount of times he'd gone into the call room to do exactly that. The same resistance that prevented him from sending her emails, despite the fact that he'd drafted several, only to delete them before logging out of the system.

Danny knew it wouldn't be fair to allow the good days to give either of them false hope. He couldn't call her on a good day and then abandon her when he was pulled back under. He couldn't email her one day and then ask her to leave him alone the next.

And so he resisted every urge he had to reconnect with her.

But she was here. And he could feel the unmistakable tug in his body, his heart galloping in his chest.

He wanted so desperately to know what she was thinking in that moment. Why she had come. But he had absolutely no idea what the past month had looked like for her.

The one time Danny had given into an impulse and asked Jake about Leah, Jake's response had been a lengthy tirade focusing on what a complete asshole Danny was being.

He vowed then and there never to bring her up with Jake again.

And he knew better than to ask Gram about her. She wouldn't be as blunt as Jake, but her quiet disappointment in Danny's decision would be even more cutting in its own way.

Danny didn't need a lecture from anyone. He knew he was doing the right thing by letting her go, no matter what anyone else thought. No one else was in there with him. No one else was living his every day. So how could they even pretend to know what was best?

As he stood there, watching her watch him, there was a split second where he contemplated turning around. No good could come of this visit with her—he knew that—but the thought of walking away from her made his gut wrench. It was excruciating enough when he'd done it the first time, and he hadn't prepared himself for the task of doing it again.

She wasn't supposed to come back here.

He felt himself take a step in her direction before he'd even made a conscious decision to move, and then she stood, releasing her mother's bracelet as her hands fell to her sides. He watched her curl and uncurl them into fists a few times before he lifted his eyes back to hers.

Now that he was closer, he could see the emotions fighting for control on her face: a knotty combination of sadness, fear, and determination.

Danny reached for the chair across from her and pulled it out. He could hear his heart beating in his ears as he sat before her, and Leah lowered herself into the chair, pulling her lower lip between her teeth.

For a few seconds, they sat there in silence.

Danny cleared his throat softly. "Jake?" he asked.

"Knows I'm here," she responded softly, and Danny looked down and nodded slowly.

Silence.

"He said I could have his visit if I promised to bring him back some Skittles."

Danny laughed before he could stop himself, and he glanced up to see her smiling uneasily. She reached up and tucked her hair behind her ear, and then her smile dropped at the same time her eyes did.

Leah took a deep breath, her eyes on her lap as she said, "A long time ago, I asked you to stop playing games. And you promised me that you'd never lie to me." She looked up and met his gaze. "I came here because I need to know the truth about something."

Danny nodded once. "Okay."

She wet her lips, the determination temporarily winning out in her expression. "Why did you break up with me?"

Danny closed his eyes before he exhaled. *Goddamn it.* He'd been prepared to answer any question but that one.

"Leah," he said weakly, rubbing the back of his neck. "I don't know what you want me to say."

"I want you to tell me the truth."

The seconds ticked by, hollow and unforgiving.

"Is it because you really don't want me anymore?" she asked.

Danny rubbed his hand over his eyes. "Don't do this, Leah."

"It's a simple question," she said, completely undeterred by his plea. "All I'm asking for is honesty."

Danny looked down at his hands. There was no answer he could come up with that wouldn't send him down a path he refused to travel down with her.

"Are you afraid the truth will hurt me?" she asked. "Don't be. Nothing you can say now will hurt me more than the words you said last time."

Danny's head snapped up; her eyes were on him, her expression unapologetic.

Her words hung in the air between them, acrid and insufferable, and Danny had to look away. He could feel little pinpricks in his chest, shame and self-loathing battling for control in his body.

"Do you still love me?" she asked.

He took a breath before he looked across the table at her. This time, there was nothing behind her eyes but vulnerability, and he knew if she deserved an honest answer to any question, it was this one.

"Yes," he said gently.

"And do you still want to be with me?"

"Leah—"

"No," she said, shaking her head. "Enough of the run-around. I want an answer, Danny. Because all of *this*," she said, gesturing around them, "is only temporary. Don't lose sight of that. And when this is over, what do you want? Do you want to start a new life with me? Do you want to come home to me every day? Do you want to have dinners with me, and go grocery shopping with me, and watch crappy TV together, and make love to me while we listen to our song? Do you want to get Christmas trees together, and go on vacations, and have babies? Do you want to take bubble baths with me, and teach me things in the garage, and hold me every night while we fall asleep?"

Danny's chest constricted, squeezing and compressing with vice-like intensity until it sent his heart up into his throat. What she had described was so agonizingly beautiful, it felt like there wasn't enough room in his body to accommodate it.

It had been so long since he'd allowed himself a fantasy of that caliber. Dreams like that cost too much to entertain inside these walls.

But her words were warm and palliative in his veins, and for a moment, envisioning what she described didn't feel torturous. It wasn't a cruel act of masochism. It wasn't a hopeless pipedream.

Because Leah was sitting in front of him, momentarily turning that fantasy into a promise.

He should have been used to it by now; from the moment she came into his life, she started reviving him—making him *feel* again, making him appreciate things, helping him learn how to forgive himself, making him think he was someone worthy of love. And here she was, offering to save him all over again.

He wanted to let her. God, he wanted everything she had described and more. He wanted to give her things she'd never even thought to ask for.

And for a split second, with her looking at him the way she was, he believed he could have it all with her.

"Do you want that life with me?" she asked, her voice trembling slightly.

Two answers bubbled up into his throat simultaneously—the sincere one and the safe one—and Danny felt like he was choking on their scuffle.

Leah's gentle eyes implored him for a response, but he couldn't open his mouth, too afraid that the wrong answer would escape.

Instead, he nodded.

The tension in her shoulders melted instantly as her eyes pooled with tears.

"But Leah," he said quickly, "I can't make you promises like that. I don't know who's gonna be coming home to you."

Danny ran his hands up through his hair; he could feel the words backing up in his throat, clogging like a traffic jam of candid statements desperately seeking an outlet.

And all at once, he lost the will to inhibit them anymore.

"This place, Leah," he said, shaking his head. "I feel myself bending to it. Every day, I bend a little more. I'm doing my best. I'm learning how to manage my thoughts, and I'm trying so hard to keep myself... *me.*" He looked up at her. "But some days, no matter what I do...it's just not enough. And I just don't know how many times I can bend before I break."

"But it's okay if you bend," she said earnestly. "It's okay if you break. I'm not going anywhere."

"I don't want that," he said with a firm shake of his head.

"Don't want what?"

"I don't want you to see it. Or to wait for me only to learn at the end of all this that I've become someone you can't see yourself with anymore. It's so much harder than I thought to be away from you all. And sometimes I just…I go to a dark place, and I'm not even *me* anymore. I don't want you to have to deal with it. I'm not going to ask you to wait this out when I can't guarantee you'll be happy when it's over. This is an ugly clusterfuck of a ride, Leah. And I don't want you to be a passenger."

Danny could feel his heart thrumming as he looked across the table at her. He had thought it would be humiliating to admit how he felt, but there was an odd sort of comfort in confessing his fears—like the weight of the burden had somehow lessened simply because he had allowed it outside of his body.

"Why did you sit in the room with Bryan when he died?"

Danny felt a tingle run down his spine. "What?" he asked, startled.

"Why did you go in when they turned everything off and let him go?" she asked. "Better yet, why did you go visit him, day after day, with all of those horrible tubes and machines attached to his body? When all the doctors said there was no hope. That he couldn't even hear you. Why did you do it?"

A heaviness settled in his stomach, quickly transitioning into a wrenching pain.

"Because he…because I…" Danny shook his head and trailed off, pressing the heels of his hands into his eyes.

"I know exactly why," she said gently, reaching over and pulling one of his hands away from his face. He dropped the other to the table as she intertwined their fingers, running her thumb over the side of his hand. "It's the same reason I sat with my father every night for two weeks, praying by his bedside. It's the same reason Holly and Robyn have been taking turns coming to my apartment every day for the past month, despite the fact that I've been miserable and wretched and depressing to be around."

She gave his hand a tiny squeeze. "Because when you love someone, you don't bail when it gets hard. That's when you stay the most."

It felt like his throat was closing.

"And it's not always easy," she said, running her thumb over his hand again. "It's hard to watch someone you care about suffer. But when you love someone, you do it. You do it without question or reservation. You do it because there's no other option—because the thought of being without them is a hundred times more excruciating than bearing their burden." She leaned over and brought his hand to her mouth, kissing the back of it before she said, "And I love you, Danny. You made it so easy to fall in love with you. You're funny, and loyal, and patient, and selfless." Her eyes welled with tears. "And you're considerate, and honest, and intelligent, and compassionate. And you were able to become all of those things—to *maintain* all of those things—in the face of all the shit life handed you." She smiled a watery smile. "And I know that's who you're still going to be when you come back to me."

She released his hand to swipe at the tears on her cheeks. "So that's *me*, being honest with *you*," she said with a sniffle. "There's no doubt we're both going to suffer through this. I've always known that. Some days will be bearable and some will be completely miserable. But I've made my decision. I know what I'm up against, and I know what I want. I want you. And I want us. I want our life together."

It felt like his heart might come out of his chest; like a strange current was running through his body, making his breath erratic and his muscles feel like they were humming.

"My father once told me that if something seems too hard, before you give up, you should always ask yourself if the reward will be worth the suffering." She took a deep breath. "So I guess what it comes down to... what I need to know...is whether or not I'm worth the suffering to you."

Danny rested his elbows on the table and dropped his forehead to his clasped hands. He could feel his chin trembling, and he inhaled slowly, trying to pull himself back together.

The magnificence and purity of her love for him—the all-consuming force of it—could break him and heal him simultaneously. It could destroy him and piece him back together, better than he was before.

And it could restore his faith faster than this place could take it.

Danny remembered wondering once how anyone could keep his head above water here. And suddenly he realized—*this* was how. When you have something to hold on to. A reason to fight every day. A beautiful lifeline pulling you through to the other side.

The guys who don't have it—or the ones who are foolish enough to let go—those are the guys that go under.

He thought he could save her by letting her go, but he'd had it all backward.

She wasn't the one who needed saving this time.

"Leah," he said, his voice rough with emotion. "I could suffer through anything if you were my reward."

A smile curved her lips before she cupped her hand over her mouth and burst into tears.

Danny was out of his seat in an instant, walking around to her side of the table, and she stood, throwing her arms around his neck as he lifted her off the floor and buried his face in her hair.

"My sweet girl," he whispered.

Her sob was muffled against the side of his neck, and he reached up and ran his hand over the back of her hair, glancing over at the guard standing by the door. He was watching them before his eyes found Danny's.

For a moment, they just looked at each other.

And then the guard gave him a knowing look, followed by a quick nod. He shifted his body, focusing his attention on the other side of the room.

So Danny got to hold her for a few more seconds than was permitted.

The most enriching and restorative seconds of his entire life.

Chapter Twenty-Four

"Thank you," Leah said as she reached for the glass of Pinot Grigio the waiter handed her, immediately bringing it to her lips.

"Another for you, miss?" he asked, looking at Alexis.

She eyed Leah before she smiled up at him sweetly. "No, thank you, I'm fine."

"Okay then. Your food will be right out," he said before he turned and left the table.

Alexis turned, her eyes landing on Leah's half empty second glass of wine.

"Don't judge me," Leah said, placing the glass on the table. "I had a rough week. My classes are out of control."

"Well, you're off now. You should just relax. Don't even grade anything if you don't have to."

"I have to finish one more class of essays, but after that I'm not doing a damn thing. I swear, the person who created February break did so to save lives." Leah twirled the stem of her wine glass as she fought the urge to finish it off.

Alexis laughed as she glanced down at her cell phone, trying to be discreet but failing miserably.

Leah smirked. "I'm sure he's fine."

She blushed, realizing she was caught. "I know," she said, slipping her phone into her purse. "I'm sure he's fine. You're right. I just…you know…you think he'd text me if he had a question, right?"

"Yes, I do," Leah said, trying to stifle a laugh. "He's fine. They're fine. Don't worry."

Alexis nodded and exhaled heavily as she brought her glass to her lips, perking up as the waiter approached the table with their food.

Leah found it hysterical, the mini panic attacks Alexis had whenever she left the baby with Christopher. In her defense, something always seemed to go wrong while he was watching her, but in her brother's defense, they were always inconsequential—and hilarious—things. The first time he watched her, he somehow managed to put her diaper on backward. Another time, after the baby had gotten food on the outfit she was wearing, he had changed her clothes, and Alexis came home from the hair salon to find Savanna wearing her very beautiful—and very expensive—christening dress while crawling around outside.

"So," Leah said, "tell me what you need me to do for the party."

"I think we're all set," she said. "You're making your spinach artichoke dip, right?"

Leah nodded, and Alexis looked up at the ceiling, running through some invisible list in her mind. "Yeah, so I think we're good. If you could come a little bit early to help me set up, that would be awesome," she said, twirling her fork in her pasta. She froze with the bite halfway to her mouth. "Is it supposed to be this crazy planning a one-year-old's birthday party? I don't even want to think about her sweet sixteen."

"Or her wedding," Leah added with a smile, and Alexis laughed.

"Don't go there. If we even joke about her dating, Christopher gets all bent out of shape."

"He's such a tool," Leah said, and Alexis laughed around her sip of wine. "I can't believe she's a year old already."

"I know." Alexis sighed.

The night Savanna had been born was the same night Danny found out he had a sentencing date.

An entire year ago.

It seemed like another lifetime, but at the same time, she could remember it like it was yesterday. In the nine months since Danny had been gone, her sense of time had been stuck in a sort of limbo; sometimes things felt rushed and blurry, and other times they dragged on painfully. Sometimes it seemed like both things were occurring at once.

"Danny can't get over how much she looks like you," Leah said, and Alexis smiled.

"How's he doing, by the way?"

Leah took a tiny breath. "He's as okay as he can be." She shrugged, pushing the food around on her plate.

"When do you get to see him again?"

"Saturday," Leah said.

"Do you like…get quality time with him when you go?" she asked tentatively, as if she were unsure whether to continue on with this line of conversation or change the subject.

"We don't get conjugal visits, if that's what you're asking," Leah said, trying to lighten the mood. She had gotten good at putting on a mask, displaying the proverbial stiff upper lip. She hated when people worried about her over this, treating her with kid gloves and tiptoeing around topics of conversation. Leah knew they were doing it out of concern, but it only served to make her feel weak, like deep down they knew she couldn't handle it.

That her fortitude was all just a charade.

She hated it, because sometimes it was true, and she didn't need the reminder.

"No, that's not what I meant," Alexis said with a tiny laugh, the curiosity overpowering the hesitancy in her eyes. "I meant, can you really talk? Can you touch him? Or is it…"

She trailed off, and at that moment, Leah wanted to jump across the table and hug her sister-in-law. While it still wasn't the easiest thing for her to talk about, it was the first time in a long time anyone had really broached the subject with her, inviting her to talk about it rather than trying to distract her from it.

All at once she felt like she might cry from gratitude.

Leah sat up a bit straighter. "Um…we can hug and kiss when I get there, and when I leave," she said, thinking of how much she looked forward to those simple, chaste actions. "And if the guard on watch is nice, we can hold hands above the table."

She nodded. "Is that weird for you? Not being able to touch him the way you want to?"

Leah inhaled deeply. "Not really. I mean, I'm kind of used to it now."

"And you guys are…still okay?" she asked, growing more comfortable with her questions as Leah continued to answer with no signs of breaking down.

Leah nodded. "We're getting by. It's just that…" She trailed off, lifting her wine glass quickly and taking a sip to swallow the lump in her throat.

"Do you want to stop talking about this?" Alexis asked gently, and Leah shook her head.

"Actually, no, I don't," she said through a tearful smile. "This is good. I know it doesn't look that way," she added through a laugh, gesturing at herself as she blinked back tears, "but it's good."

Alexis smiled as she reached across the table and squeezed Leah's hand, and Leah took a breath before she continued.

"I'm always scared, I guess. I'm afraid that I'll lose him again. That he'll have a bad day, or a bad week, and decide we're better off apart. Every visit, every time he calls, every letter—I'm always so excited, but at the same time, a little part of me is terrified of what he might say," she said, wiping under her eyes with her thumbs. "It just sucks being afraid all the time," she added before she lifted her glass and finished the wine.

Alexis lifted her hand and gestured for the waiter to bring her another.

"You're turning into quite the enabler," Leah said, and Alexis laughed softly.

"But…you don't feel like he's pulling away again, do you?"

Leah shook her head. "No. We've been doing really well. We've got our routine now. And he's getting really good about talking through his bad days instead of shutting down. It's just that…until he's home, a little part of me will always be waiting for the other shoe to drop."

Alexis nodded. "That's understandable. But you're almost halfway there now, right?"

"Well, we're hoping he's going to be eligible for good time served. If he is, that means we've already passed the halfway mark."

"Wait, what do you mean? What's good time served?"

"Basically it's a sentence reduction for good behavior. He has to serve a minimum of eighty percent of his sentence, but if he reaches that without incident, they can decide to let him out."

"So then he'd be getting out in..." Alexis pursed her lips, trying to do the math.

"Seven more months."

"Oh my God, Leah, that's great!"

Leah nodded. "I'm trying not to get my hopes up. We'll see."

Alexis smiled up at the waiter as he brought Leah's third glass of wine to the table. "So you get to see him every other Saturday?"

"Usually. I switch off with Catherine and Jake, but sometimes I have to go every third Saturday if his mother and sister want to rotate in."

"Okay, because I've been meaning to ask you, I have a few things for him. Some books and magazines. Can I give those to you to bring, or should I send them?"

"Send them," she said. "They have to pass inspection before he can have them. I'm not allowed to bring anything into the facility when I go."

"Inspection?" Alexis asked, taking a bite of her pasta. "What, like someone could hide a shiv in a magazine?"

Leah laughed. "No, it's more for content. They can't have anything R-rated or pornographic."

"Oh," Alexis said with a nod of her head. "Bummer." Leah smirked as she added, "No porn, though. It's some stuff your brother picked out. A bunch of automotive magazines. I have no idea if they're the ones he reads or not."

"If it's car stuff, he'll love it," Leah said. "Honestly, he'll pretty much read anything now. My dad sent him some book on US history a few weeks ago and he read it cover to cover. I keep telling him it's a pity he had to be incarcerated in order to become a good English student."

Alexis laughed loudly, cupping her hand over her mouth when the people at the next table looked in her direction, and Leah laughed too, feeling momentarily carefree.

"Thank you," Leah said suddenly, and Alexis's expression softened as she looked across the table at her.

"You're welcome."

They finished their meal, and as they hugged their good-byes in the parking lot of the restaurant, Leah had never felt closer to her.

As soon as she was inside her car, she rummaged through her purse and pulled out her phone before hitting the speed dial for Catherine.

After a few rings, her soft, raspy voice came through the phone.

"Hello?"

"Hi, it's me," Leah said as she started the car.

"Hi, sweetheart. How are you doing today?"

"I'm good. About a six today. You?"

"Hmm," she hummed. "Maybe a five."

"You should have a few glasses of wine," Leah suggested. "That's always good to add a point or two."

Catherine chuckled.

They spoke on the phone two or three times a week, and early on they'd come up with the number system to let each other know what kind of day they were having. Ten meant they were feeling great, and one was total meltdown.

"What time will you be here on Saturday?" Catherine asked.

"Probably around four or five? Depends on if they're running things on time over there," she said, pulling out of her parking space. It had become an unspoken tradition that after visiting Danny on her Saturdays, Leah would stop off at Catherine's on the way home and have dinner with her.

"Okay. How does eggplant rollantini sound for dinner?"

"Delicious," she said, "but you know you don't have to cook for me."

"Leah, old Italian ladies live to feed people. Don't take that away from me."

She laughed as she merged onto the highway. "Okay, you win."

"Alright sweetheart. I don't want you to get a ticket for being on the phone with me while you're driving. Thank you for checking in, and I'll see you Saturday."

"Okay. Call me before then if you drop below a five."

"I will. Bye now."

"Bye," Leah said before she cleared the screen, tossing the phone onto her passenger seat.

And then she reached to turn the radio off, allowing the silence to fill the car.

For whatever reason she just felt like thinking today.

She spent so much of her time avoiding it; her life had become heavily rooted in routine over the last few months, and she rarely allowed herself a reprieve from that. Consistency was comforting these days; she needed it like she needed air.

But even the routines that she took solace in were carried out with an air of detachment. It was like when she used to run on the treadmill for conditioning during field hockey season; whenever Leah would look down at the display and realize she still had a ways to go, she would try to separate her mind from her body, pretending it wasn't her feeling the pain in her legs, the ache in her side, the burning in her throat. And that's what most of her days were like now: disengaging herself from really feeling anything until the clock on the display ticked down to zero.

Until he was next to her again.

One thing she had going for her was her profession. There was no way she could mope or succumb to any kind of sadness when she had one hundred different personalities in and out of her room all day, with a hundred different questions and a hundred different needs. She had always loved her job, but now she let teaching absolutely consume her. She had to.

Robyn and Holly had been wonderful, of course. Always finding a way to check in or include her, always acting like everything was normal around her, just like she'd asked them to.

But despite all that, Leah knew she was just going through the motions. That every smile and every laugh came with some level of fraudulence. There were little blips of happiness for her, but she knew she wouldn't feel wholly content with anything in her life until he was home.

And every night, without fail, she cried.

It wasn't even a conscious thing anymore, and she barely felt anything when she did. Like everything else, it had just become routine for her, like breathing or blinking. She would lie in bed, and as if on cue, the tears would come, trickling down her cheeks without warning, without permission, without feeling, as if she were literally leaking the sadness away.

The sound of her phone ringing on the passenger seat pulled her from her thoughts, and she sighed in relief, deciding she'd had enough thinking for one day. Leah reached to turn the radio back on before she swiped her phone off the passenger seat and brought it to her ear.

"Hello?"

"What the hell did you do to your car this time?"

Leah smiled. "Hey, Jake. And I didn't do anything, I swear. It just started doing it on its own."

"Well, I'm in your neck of the woods. You want me to swing by and check it out?"

"Yeah, if you don't mind. I'm not home right now, but I'll be there in like ten minutes."

"Alright. Is it doing it right now?"

"Not really. It only does it at high speeds. It's like this wobbly-shake thing."

"Wobbly-shake," he repeated. "Thanks. Your technical terminology will make this much easier for me to figure out."

"You're an idiot."

He laughed loudly before he said, "See you in a few."

"Bye," Leah said with a laugh before she ended the call.

By the time she pulled into her development, Jake was parked in the space next to hers, leaning against his bumper with his arms crossed over his chest.

"Hey," Leah said as she got out of the car, and he walked over to her, giving her a hug and a kiss on the cheek.

"Alright, let's take it for a spin and see what the hell is going on."

"Okay," she said, handing him her keys before she walked around to the passenger door.

Jake started the car and pulled out of the parking space, immediately accelerating through the lot, and her eyes grew wide as she grabbed the handle on the door.

"Jake! Jesus!"

"What?" he said innocently. "You said at high speeds."

"Yeah, when you're *legally permitted* to drive at high speeds!" she scolded, and he laughed just as the car began to shimmy.

"See? That!" she said pointing to the dashboard. "Feel the wobbly-shake?"

"I do," he said, "although we usually refer to that as having unbalanced tires."

"I like wobbly-shake better. Can you fix it?"

"Yeah," he said, slowing down as he made the turn to bring them back to Leah's. "But not here. You gotta bring it down to the shop. And sooner rather than later. You really shouldn't be driving around like this."

"Okay. When do you have openings this week?"

Jake blew a raspberry with his lips. "Are you kidding me? Bring it down whenever you want. We'll take care of you."

"Thanks," she said softly as he pulled into her parking space and cut the engine.

"So..." His expression turned serious as he shifted to face her. "How are you doing?"

Leah shrugged. "I'm okay."

Jake nodded, looking out the windshield. "And no one's been bothering you?"

She smiled slowly. "Very smooth, Jake. Like greased ice."

He turned to look at her. "*Greased ice?*" he asked, fighting a smile.

Leah lifted one shoulder, laughing to herself.

"Seriously, though. Has he been around? Has he called?"

"No, he hasn't," she said. "And I told you I'd let you know if he did."

Jake nodded. "I know…I just…"

"No, I get it," she said. "Danny asked you to check in."

"Asked?" he said with his brow lifted. "No, Danny didn't ask. He *mandated.* Even back in the beginning, when he was being a complete douche-nozzle." He shook his head before his expression turned serious again. "I promised him I'd look out for you, Leah."

She swallowed, dropping her eyes to her lap. "I know," she said softly. "Sorry for giving you shit."

"I like when you give me shit," he said, reaching over and tugging lightly on the end of her hair. "It means the fire in you ain't out yet."

Leah smiled. "Isn't."

"Huh?"

"The fire in me *isn't* out yet."

"Yeah, okay. Save it for the classroom, toots."

Leah laughed, and he winked at her before he opened the door and got out of the car. She met him around the front, reaching to take the keys he offered her. "I'll talk to you soon, okay? Call me if you need anything, and bring this down to us as soon as you can," he said, patting the hood.

"I will," she said, kissing him on the cheek. "Thanks, Jake."

Leah stood there and watched Jake get into his car, waving to him as he pulled out of the parking space before she turned toward her mailbox. As soon as she opened the little door, it felt like her stomach turned inside out. She reached in and pulled out the stack of envelopes, completely disregarding the bills and credit card offers as she shuffled his envelope, the one she'd recognize anywhere, to the top.

Leah jogged up the path to her apartment, fumbling with her keys as she unlocked the door, trying to ignore the little ember of anxiety hidden just behind her eagerness. As soon as she was inside, she tossed the other envelopes on the table, sending a few skidding off the other side and onto the floor as she continued into the living room, opening his letter as she went.

Despite the fact that Danny had access to e-mail, he had told her early on that he preferred handwritten letters. Even though e-mail was much faster, he was only allowed to access the system once a day, whereas a letter was something he could keep with him, something he could read whenever he wanted, as many times as he wanted. In one of his letters to Leah, he had told her he'd reread his favorites so many times, he could practically recite them from memory.

She plopped onto the couch and unfolded the paper, smiling as she saw his familiar angled handwriting.

Leah,

It's two in the morning, and you're all I can think about. I wish I could talk to you right now, because I have so much to say, and I'd really rather do it in person, but I know I won't be able to wait until next week.

Me and Troy were talking today, and he told me what happened with him and his girl. Apparently after his fifth month here, she started missing visitation days left and right, claiming that the drive was too far and that she didn't have the gas money to come every week. But then a few weeks after that, she started missing his calls too. She'd say she got held up at work, or stuck in traffic, or was helping a friend and couldn't get to her phone. Troy said he wanted to believe her in the beginning, but I guess over the last sixth months, it's only gotten worse. He said every now and then he'll write to her and if he's lucky, she'll respond or he'll get her on the phone. But she's basically washed her hands of him. And I'm listening to this guy spill his guts, feeling like the biggest piece of shit on the planet, because all I could think about the entire time was how lucky I am. Because she gave up on him, and you never even entertained the idea of giving up on me. Not in the beginning, when my behavior was unpredictable and asinine, not when you found out I was going away, and not even when

I was stupid enough to push you away myself. You always fought for me—for us. Always.

I know this hasn't been easy for you, but no one looking at you would ever know that. You come here week after week with that beautiful smile on your face, walking through security and having your bag searched, sitting through chaperoned visits like it's the most natural thing in the world. You've taken a miserable situation, and you've managed to make it bearable somehow, for both of us.

Even in the beginning, when we were struggling to get it right, you never let me doubt anything. Not us, not your feelings for me, not myself. It used to be so hard for me, watching you walk away after a visit and coming back to this. All I'd want was to be with you again, to see you and hear your voice, and then I'd spend the rest of the day wondering if you were missing me as much as I missed you—if you were hurting as much as I was. And I'd hate myself, because it was me who put us in this situation. It's so easy to get caught up like that in here, to spiral down into the bullshit. But anytime I'd come close to sinking, I'd get your letters, or your pictures, or the books you'd send with the little notes you hide inside for me, and every doubt, every fear, would be gone.

I know it's not enough to say this, but thank you. Thank you for agreeing to have lunch with me that first day, and for not running from my ridiculous behavior after that. Thank you for allowing me to get to know you, even when I didn't deserve your patience or understanding. Thank you for trusting me—for giving me your heart and your body and changing me forever in the process. Thank you for dealing with all the trouble that comes with loving somebody like me. Thank you for being brave enough to fight for us when I was too afraid to do it. And above all, thank you for making me feel like myself again. For taking me, flaws and all, and loving me anyway. You have never once let me doubt your feelings for me, and I just want you to know that you are absolutely everything to me. And it's all I need, just to know that somehow, I managed to do something right in my life by finding you.

I love you more than I could ever express, in writing or in words.

Missing you always,

Danny

Leah read the letter three more times through the blurred vision of her tears before her eyes fell closed, and she folded it carefully and brought it to her lips. She could have sworn she smelled traces of him on the paper, and she inhaled deeply as a tear slipped over her lower lashes and down her cheek.

With a tiny sigh, she opened her eyes and pushed off the couch, making her way back toward her bedroom. She opened the box of his letters she kept next to her bed, placing the new one on top before grabbing the pen and pad off her nightstand.

Leah sat back against the headboard with the pad balanced on her thighs, beginning her letter to him the same way she'd started every one she had written for the past nine months:

Danny,

One day closer to the day you'll come back to me, and I love you more now than I did yesterday...

Epilogue

Leah had just turned off the water in the shower when she heard the muffled sound of her phone ringing in the other room, and she whipped the curtain open and hopped out, cursing as she caught her right foot on the edge of the tub in her haste.

She hobbled over to her towel and swung it around her body before she rushed out of the bathroom and over to her nightstand.

"Hello?" she said, attempting to secure the towel.

"Hey," Robyn said. "Why do you sound so out of breath?"

"Because I'm extremely out of shape, apparently," she said, walking back to the bathroom. "I just ran to get the phone."

"Well, sorry that I made you exercise," she laughed. "I just wanted to tell you that I'm definitely coming tonight. I'll bring a barf bag if I have to."

Leah grabbed another towel and used it to squeeze the excess water from her hair. "Not feeling any better, huh?"

"That would be a no," Robyn sighed.

"Did the lemonade help at all?" she asked, wiping the fog from the mirror and then opening the cabinet to remove her toner and moisturizer.

"Not really. I've had the most success with sour candies, but those only work while I'm sucking on them. I'd eat them all day if I could, but they're starting to shred the roof of my mouth."

Leah cringed. "This part doesn't last forever. Just keep telling yourself that."

"I know," she said. "And there are things I haven't tried yet. I read in one of my books that those sea sickness wristbands work for some people, so Rich just ran out to the drugstore to get me some. I'm sure they'll look sexy with my dress tonight."

Leah laughed softly, applying her face cream. "You know you don't have to come tonight. Honestly, everyone will understand."

"Are you kidding me? I wouldn't miss this for anything."

Leah smiled just as Robyn added, "Oh shit, I didn't realize how late it was. I need to get in the shower. I do *not* want to deal with your sister if I'm late."

"I think she'd go easy on you, preggers."

"Probably, but I'm not willing to chance it. See you in a little while."

"Bye," Leah said with a shake of her head before she put the phone on the sink and leaned toward the mirror, inspecting her skin as she tried to figure out how she wanted to do her makeup.

She glanced down, sifting through her makeup case until she pulled out a coppery eye shadow that would complement the brown dress beautifully. And then she smiled, remembering the day Holly had forced her to buy it.

She'd come so far since then.

Leah began singing softly to herself as she dusted some loose powder over her face to even out her complexion.

She had just finished putting on her eye makeup when a slight movement in her peripheral vision caught her attention, and she glanced at the reflection of the doorway in the mirror.

"Are you gonna hog the bathroom all night? I still have to shower, you know."

A smile tugged at the corners of her mouth as she turned, leaning back against the sink as she swept her arm dramatically in front of her. "By all means, go ahead. Don't let me stop you from getting naked."

He smirked, pushing off the doorframe as he walked toward her, and Leah straightened as his hands gripped her waist, lifting her with ease so that she was sitting on the edge of the sink. He stepped into the space between her legs, and she hooked them around his hips, her towel riding up with the movement.

"Do you want to hop in with me?" he asked, running the tip of his nose along her jaw and up to her ear, placing a soft kiss just below it.

"Mmm," she hummed. "Very tempting. But then I'd have to re-do my makeup, and Sarah will put a hit out on me if we're late."

He laughed, pulling back slightly to look in her eyes. "She's already sent me three texts, telling me to do whatever I need to do in order to move you along."

Leah smirked. "Well then, I'd say what you're doing right now is highly counterproductive."

He smiled a slow smile before he leaned forward and brushed his lips against hers, and she immediately wrapped her arms around his neck and pressed herself against him so abruptly that he stumbled back a step.

He laughed against her mouth but allowed her to take the lead, kissing her back with equal fervor.

It had been almost a month since Danny had come home, and yet she still responded that way every time he kissed her. She had no idea if it was a subconscious attempt at making up for lost time, or if it was more about trying to make the most of the time they had now, but either way, her reaction to him was as consistent as it was visceral.

Danny let her get away with it for a minute or two before she felt him ending the kiss, and she made a pouting noise against his lips.

He smiled his dimpled smile as he pulled back from her. "Sorry, sweet girl, but I promised your sister. She's going out of her way for me tonight."

"Alright, alright," she huffed, pushing him back slightly as she hopped down from the sink.

He laughed, kissing her forehead before he walked over to the shower and turned on the water.

"What time is it?" she asked, turning toward the mirror to put the finishing touches on her makeup.

"Almost six. We should leave in like a half hour. What are the chances of that actually happening?"

"Totally doable if you stop distracting me," she said, looking at him pointedly through the mirror.

He smiled as he held up his hands in surrender, turning away from her before he stripped off his clothes and stepped into the shower.

Leah quickly finished her makeup and grabbed the hair dryer, taking it into the next room. The steam from Danny's shower was clouding up the mirror, not to mention doing a number on her hair.

She took a little extra time, blow-drying it sleek and straight for the occasion. As much as she had protested the whole thing in the beginning, she couldn't help but feel a twinge of excitement over it now.

A few months back, when they had learned that Danny was being released for good time served, Sarah had instantly jumped on the opportunity to throw him a homecoming party. Leah was resistant to the idea at first, telling her they needed to let him get acclimated to normal life again before they bombarded him with parties and people.

Unbeknownst to them, Sarah had apparently declared one month to be the grace period for getting acclimated to normal life, because two weeks after Danny had gotten home, they received the invitation in the mail for his party tonight.

In retrospect, Leah realized that he probably would have been fine having the party that first weekend. She was the one who wasn't ready. She didn't want to have to share him so soon.

But even through her juvenile selfishness, she realized Sarah was right; he deserved this party. He deserved to be surrounded by all the people who loved him, celebrating his return, showing him how much they all missed him, how happy they were to have him back.

Leah walked back to her room, unraveling the towel as she went, and she could hear the sounds of Danny getting dressed in her walk-in closet. She had already laid her dress and shoes out by the bed, and she slipped into the dress quickly before stepping into her heels.

A smile curved her lips as she glanced at the clock.

"Five minutes to spare!" she called triumphantly. "And I'm ready before you!"

She heard him laugh as she walked back to the bathroom to get her necklace, the one he had given her the night before he left. She only ever took it off to shower, hanging it on the little hook behind the bathroom door and immediately putting it back on as soon as she was dressed.

Leah swung the door partially closed and froze, looking up at the empty hook.

She dropped her eyes as she moved the door out of the way, searching for it underfoot.

"Shit," she whispered as she spun quickly, her heart thudding in her chest as she swiped her hand over the vanity of the sink, feeling nothing but the smooth ceramic finish.

"Danny?" she called, trying to keep the panic out of her voice as she swung the door open and flew back out to the bedroom.

"Yeah?"

"Did you move my necklace?" she asked, frantically shaking out the balled-up towel from her shower.

"Yeah. I saw it on the hook and was afraid it was gonna get swept up with the towels. I put it in your jewelry box."

The towel dropped to the floor as Leah's hand fell limply to her side, and she pressed her other hand to her forehead.

"Can you tell me the next time you do that, please? I just almost had a heart attack." She crossed the room to where her jewelry box sat on her dresser.

"Sorry," he called sheepishly from the closet.

She approached the box and flipped it open with hands that were still shaking.

And then she froze.

The box was completely empty, save for one glittering diamond right in the center.

But it wasn't her necklace.

It took her a second to register what she was looking at, and when it finally clicked, she whirled around.

Her eyes landed on Danny, dressed in his suit, his expression tentative as he stood before her.

All at once her legs felt too feeble to support the weight of her body, and Leah reached behind her and gripped the edge of the dresser, trying to keep herself steady.

Danny wet his lips, glancing down for a moment before he lifted his eyes back to hers, and this time they were unwavering.

"I spent sixteen months away from you, Leah," he said, his voice rough with emotion. "And I don't ever want to be without you again."

Somewhere in the back of her mind, she knew she should be taking it all in, memorizing every last detail of what was happening: how gorgeous he looked in his suit, the way his tousled black hair adorned the blue of his eyes, the way his lip trembled ever so slightly with the effort to contain his nerves, or his emotion, or both.

There was a strange pressure building in her chest, making her feel like she was about to laugh hysterically or burst into tears.

Danny slowly lowered himself to the floor so that he was kneeling before her. "I love you," he said, his voice gentle but sure. "And I'm going to spend the rest of my life loving you. Marry me, Leah."

She dropped to her knees then. Not just because her legs had given up on supporting her, but because she needed to be as close to him as possible.

"Yes," she said through a tearful laugh. "Yes yes yes yes yes."

She took his face in her hands and pulled his mouth to hers, and his arms slipped around her waist, drawing her against his body.

"Yes," she kept whispering between kisses, and she felt his lips curve into a smile against hers.

He broke the kiss and reached up onto her dresser, pulling the ring from the box before he turned back toward her. Leah watched as he lifted her hand and slid it onto her finger.

She stared at the ring—*his* ring—on her hand, and a wide grin broke out over her face as she lifted her eyes to his. Danny smiled as he brushed the backs of his fingers over her cheek, and only then did she realize she was crying.

"Oh no," she breathed, her eyes growing wide as she patted the pads of her fingers beneath them. "How bad is it?"

Danny brushed the hair away from her face. "You look perfect," he said. "This party has a Gothic theme, right?"

She dropped her head with a huff, and Danny laughed as he gripped her hands and pulled her up to stand in front of him.

She could feel the diamond pressing into the skin of her pinky as he held her hand, and a smile lit her face again, ruined makeup be damned.

"Come on, Marilyn Manson," he said, lifting her left hand and placing a kiss just below the ring. "Let's get you cleaned up. We have an engagement party to go to."

A Note to My Readers:

First of all, I cannot thank you enough for the support and love you have shown me over the past fifteen months. When I published my first novel, *Back to You,* I had no idea it would reach as many people as it did or that I would make so many incredible friends as a result. Your kind words and encouragement have been invaluable to me, and I love and appreciate each and every one of you.

I hope you enjoyed reading Leah and Danny's story as much as I loved writing it. I have one little favor to ask: if you decide to write a review of this novel, please do not reveal Danny's secret in the process. The anticipation and discovery of that information is a crucial part of the story, and I want all my readers to have the same experience as they begin their journey with Leah and Danny.

I'm truly blessed to have some of the most loyal and enthusiastic fans. I've always been a writer, but you guys made me an author. Thank you all so much for helping to make one of my dreams a reality.

xo
Priscilla

Acknowledgments

To my husband: for your love, endless support, encouragement, and the many hours you've given me to write story after story. There's a little piece of you in every one of the heroes I write.

To my test readers: Beth, Joanne, Daniella, Therese, and Rachel. You guys are always my first line of defense, and I love you all for taking the time to help make these stories the best they can be.

To Sarah Hansen: cover designer extraordinaire. Your vision and talent surpass my expectations every single time. Thank you for always talking books with me and for being so incredibly awesome.

To Katja Millay: from the very beginning, you have been a source of friendship, guidance, and comic relief. You've talked me off the ledge countless times, and I hope you know I will always return the favor. You are one of the most talented people I know and your advice has been invaluable to me.

To Mollie Harper: for making sure my hospital scenes were medically accurate. Your tough love makes me a better writer and your quick wit makes me smile.

To Aestas: my banner girl in a pinch. You have a beautiful, genuine warmth in your personality that not a lot of people possess, and I'm so grateful to have met you. Thank you for your help, your talent, and your friendship.

To Madison Seidler: for somehow finding the time in your insane schedule to help me out when I needed it most. Thank you for your advice, your kindness, and your hilarious autocorrect fails.

And to all the readers, fans, and bloggers: I wish I could thank you all by name. Each one of you has played a role in my success, and I can't thank you enough. You keep me smiling, laughing, and most importantly, writing. Hugs and love to you all!

Other Books by Priscilla Glenn

Back to You

Emancipating Andie

8/5/16
1S

Made in the USA
Middletown, DE
03 August 2016